Shock Diamonds

E.R. Mason

E.R. Mason

Copyright 2014 by E.R. Mason
All rights reserved

All characters in this book are fictional
and any resemblance to persons living
or dead is purely coincidental

ISBN: 978-0-615-81218-2

EDITORS:

Joe Summars
FLUXFAZE Creative Enterprises, LLC
http://www.fluxfaze.com
contact info:
jcsummars@fluxfaze.com

Nancy Larson
contact info:
NLproof@aol.com

ISBN 978-0-9986637-2-2

Chapter 1

The impact was just above the Sabre Jet's nose, splattering half the bird over the front of the canopy, leaving the other half to be sucked into the intake. There were deathly thumping sounds and a sickening shudder, followed by a screaming whine as the turbine spun down. Suddenly, time seemed to have stopped.

I was thirty feet off the ground, directly over the runway, just at crowd center. We were in the three-V and from the corner of my eye I saw the other two hurry to peel upward and away. Having seen the hit, they knew my Sabre was probably now ballistic. They did not wish to share in the next maneuver.

Vanity is such a devious little rascal. It waits for you to be certain of your modesty and wisdom before stepping out. Your well-intentioned friends help it along. Flying this air show had been a setup from the beginning. They knew what a whore I was. You wave a fully restored Sabre Jet in front of my face and tunnel vision sets in. First, they just needed me to fill in a few practices while pilot number three was away with sick kin. After the orientation and training, it suddenly became possible pilot three wouldn't make the show. I could take the outside line and that would keep me out of trouble and be easy. After enough practices, they got happy with my rudder work and decided wouldn't it be great to announce the inside man was Commander Adrian Tarn of the spacecraft Griffin, the Commander whose ship and crew had rescued the Japanese expedition vessel Akuma.

Vanity took over from there, which was why I now found myself in a crippled Sabre Jet, thirty feet over a hardened runway with several thousand people sitting in bleachers a few dozen yards to my port.

In a stupid, panicky move, I jammed the thrust lever fully forward hoping to leave the crowd out of it. The grinding and howling of the jet's engine destroying itself remained unchanged. Adding to the finality of it, I suddenly rolled right and snapped inverted as if to say, "and you thought an exploding engine was bad." The white stripes on the runway strobed by overhead.

There is little sense in ejecting upside down that close to the ground. Some call it the pancake, though others have coined the phrase cow flop maneuver, which in many ways is more appropriate. Ejecting upside down over a hardened runway directly in front of an air show crowd would be the consummate version of that idiocy.

At that point, there was no sense in hoping to live, but there was the urgent desire not to take anyone along. Having established the thrust lever as quite a useless thing, that left me with only stick and pedals. For some reason, I remembered a dear friend long ago jokingly warning me to keep an eye on the airspeed indicator. I checked it and realized I still had enough energy, even inverted, to do something, one last and final choice in life to be made. I banged the stick to the left hoping to roll the aircraft back upright. It offered me halfway, leaving the cockpit sideways to the ground. Then, without warning, the ship suddenly nosed upward. I yanked back on the stick hoping that in a sideways attitude that would take me away from the crowd and allow an honorable flaming burrow into the ground. It worked. The hardened runway disappeared beneath me, replaced by the blur of centerfield grass. The aircraft continued to nose up sideways, bleeding off what remaining airspeed there was. The sound of the wind outside died with me as the nose approached the point where it would begin its death drop. I was now slightly better than sideways, the crowd somewhere behind me. For some reason, ejecting sideways away from the crowd seemed like a better way to go than in an exploding, compressing cockpit. I grabbed at the handle between my legs and yanked with all my might.

There are two kinds of fear at the top of the fear charts. The first could be labeled "stark terror." It is an alarm that switches off all cognizant reasoning and transfers all physical systems directly to the brainstem. It is an impetus that demands one run like hell in any direction available for as long as possible. It has served wild horses quite well throughout their evolution. The only fear rated higher is the end-of-life kind. Time is no longer a constant in those final seconds. The last two or three ticks suddenly become inconstant and can be divided and delegated in a variety of ways. Some people elect to relive their entire life in those moments, proof of just how long a second can last when reality is in transition. Others use the time to evaluate the horror of death, followed by a command for the mouth to open and scream. In some cases, "I love you" is transmitted to someone not present, who does indeed get the message on a level we don't yet understand.

Test pilots and stunt pilots are different. They are trained to keep thought and focus right through impact and bond with the object that is killing them. It is amazing how many of them have escaped death at the very last instant. Maybe some unknown time shift of material objects happens in those brief, horrid time strobes, instantaneous quantum changes that we don't know about, or instead maybe angels play a role.

The Sabre jet canopy was supposed to unlock .078 seconds after eject command. It felt like I had to wait for it. In that nauseating period between death and explosive departure, I had time to recount the entire day of briefing on the state-of-the-art ejection seats required for the Sabre before she was certified to perform air shows. Gyros were estimated to provide vertical correction for an ejection up to eighty degrees off vertical. I guessed I was still a bit beyond that. Still waiting, I realized my hands were positioned against my chest and my head bent down, acts initiated by my subconscious. Just as the first glimmer of fearful doubt began to rear its ugly head, there was a dull bang and the canopy snapped and slid back. I had the insane impulse to look up and see where everything was. I did not have the time.

The seat fired with a deafening "whomf." All visual was lost. Wind that felt like water ice struck me in the face and snapped my head deeper into the seat cushion. There were colors, green and blue, and white, but they were vibrating like a movie projector self-destructing. My chest had merged with my ass. There was no way to tell if I was heading for the blue or the green. The wind noise suddenly bled off and died. There seemed to be no blood left in my upper body. My stomach, which had been down around the rock hard seat cushion, suddenly catapulted into my throat. I was falling. The blur of green and blue quickly cleared to become ground and sky. Sideways. I was falling sideways. The wind noise was deafening again. A promising flutter from behind dared me to hope. The ground was too close. It filled my out-of-focus vision. There was a loud pop and I was jerked roughly upright, my chin forced down against my chest. I hit the ground hard. Tall grass. I lay there afraid to test body parts. Less than thirty seconds later, a face was staring down at me.

"Commander, how bad are you hurt?"

Vocalization did not seem to be available. Another terse voice was heard.

"Get out of the way, please. I'm the doctor."

It was a woman's voice. She appeared over me, long brown hair hanging down, bluish-gray eyes within a narrow stare. She began gently squeezing parts of my body, beginning

5

with the legs. When she was done with my head, she yelled at those with her.

"Help me roll him over, easy."

Now she was pressing all over my back and neck.

"My god, I'm not finding anything!" she said. She gently grabbed my shoulder and pulled me over onto my back.

"Can you move your arms and legs?"

I opened and closed my hands, silently rejoiced their obedience, and placed one hand on my chest. I bent both legs at the knee. They seemed to work okay.

"I don't believe this. I can't find a scratch on you." She lifted my left eyelid, then the other. "Not even dilation. Can you stand?"

She sat me up. I looked around. Nothing but high grass and helpers. She stood and pulled me up by my shoulder. The world came into view. In the distance, there was fire and a brown column of smoke from what remained of the Sabre. I turned to find a stone-silent crowd standing in the bleachers, staring in our direction. For some odd reason, I raised one hand and waved. A deafening cheer erupted. People began throwing things in the air. It went on and on. I turned and tried to focus on the doctor, then did something I have never done, something that will annoy me the rest of my life.

I fainted.

It must have been only for five or ten seconds. I awoke on my back in the high grass again. The same bossy woman was in my face, strands of her brown hair partly blocking my vision. Her skin tone was tanned. Her hovering stare seemed to penetrate and embrace me. I decided she had too much makeup on to really be a doctor. Cherry red lipstick that highlighted either a permanent smug smile or cynicism. She smelled like roses.

"I think I'm okay. Just let me get back up a second."

"Stay right where you are. I'm not convinced."

"No, really. I'm fine. Just let me back up."

"Not gonna happen."

"I'm alright, I tell you. Get the hell out of my face and let me up."

"Sorry, pal."

I tried to push myself up, intending to butt her out of the way. A tiny projectile popped off of something in her hand. Something sharp and pointed jabbed me in the arm. I looked and saw her pull out a syringe. I wondered where she had gotten it. I snarled at her.

"Oh, yeah. Big jet jockey thinks he's going to go lean against the nearest bar and tell tall tales of how he walked away from it, right?"

Shock Diamonds

"You're not the boss of me. You're not even really a doctor, are you?" I tried harder to push myself against her. I was suddenly much heavier. A strange warmth began to flow through my brain. To my surprise, she suddenly started to look good to me.

"Hold that thought," she said, and she pushed me back down with one finger on my shoulder.

"You can't stop me."

"Nighty-nite."

I opened my eyes, found clean white sheets, white hospital room curtains pulled open to a view of park in the distance, an IV hanging, someone in farmer's wear seated in a chair by the bed with coffee in one hand and a book held up to the face in the other. For some reason, I held up my right hand and inspected it. There was a tremor there, tingling like when some part of you is asleep. I could not shake it. I tucked it back under the sheets. The figure sitting by heard the rustle of sheets and lowered the book to look, but only stared and did not say a word. My partner in many an unorthodox scheme, R.J. Smith, gave a scolding grimace. He brought up his cup and sipped. We traded glances several times, both apparently unable to come up with something adequately absurd to mark the occasion. He looked as though he was daring me to say something snide. I decided not to give him the satisfaction. He sipped again, sat back, and in his most endearing tone said, "Anything to get attention, Tarn." He pretended to go back to the book.

"Where am I this time?"

"Jess Parrish Hospital, Titusville."

"Damned air show doctor gave me a shot."

"She noted on your chart that you were less than cooperative."

"She was trying to tell me what to do."

"Imagine that."

"Can I leave?"

"Only if you are comfortable with the Johnny. I believe she has withheld your other clothes."

"See?"

"I'd guess her to be no more than five-foot-eight. You could probably take her."

"I wouldn't count on it."

"Ah yes, to quote Shakespeare, 'and though she be but little, she is fierce.'"

"Five-foot-eight? When she was looking down at me, she seemed like a monster."

"Quite attractive and quick-witted, actually."

7

"Well, why's she got my clothes?"

"Seems there are test results to be evaluated, brain scans and such. Apparently your illustrious history provides a lot of previous data for comparison."

"Was anyone else hurt?"

"No."

"One less Sabre, damn it."

"It was heavily insured. The owner already has plans to recover another."

"Still..."

"Somewhere in here is where you mention you're glad to be alive."

"You said she hid my clothes. We are talking about the same damn doctor, right?"

"Oh, yes. Dr. Adara. I like her."

"Gestapo doctor."

"Actually, she's Australian by descent. No lineage to the Third Reich at all. In fact, she's not even affiliated with any particular hospital. She travels around on consignment for air shows, NASCAR, the AMA, the NFL, and a bunch of other extreme sports organizations. She specializes in acute trauma. She seems to have the same taste for peril that you have. Oddly enough, the two of you seem to have something in common!"

"R.J., sneak me some clothes so I can get out of here."

"And face her wrath? Not on your life. And your life is what this is all about, by the way."

"I suppose there will be publicity from all this?"

"No...ya think? You eject a few feet off the ground in front of thousands of people in a televised air show?" R.J. traded his book for a folded newspaper from the table beside him and opened it to the front page. There was a half-page blurry photo of an ejection seat emerging from a Sabre cockpit. The caption read "Pilot Survives Bird Strike At Tico."

"Oh...my...god."

"Some guys across the runway at the Zero-G hangar had the angle. The story picks up nicely on page 4. There's a half page spread of photos showing you all the way to the ground. But personally, I like the spectator videos the best. There are three different angles. You went viral 30 minutes after it happened. To be honest, it made me so damn glad I was not able to make the show that day. Makes me sick to watch the clips. I look away when they come on now."

"I'm sorry about that. It was a bird."

"Cathartes aura, turkey vulture, one of the most beneficial birds that Florida has. They are continuously at work cleaning up the place. They do it for free. It was probably flushed out of the brush bordering the airport perimeter by one of the many booms going on around the place. You could say it was nature showing up to contest technology. In the end, technology may have won the day, but nature's point was well made."

"Uh-oh, have I started you up?"

"No, no, just pointing out that the perpetrator was an innocent victim as well."

"Well, at least the safety systems worked."

"Oh yeah, it's okay that I have this 1950s General Electric jet engine stuck up my ass because I'm sitting on two gyro-guided solid rocket motors that will go off if anything fucks up. What could possibly go wrong?"

"Wow, I've never heard you this... profane?"

"I'm sorry. For millions the event was exciting. For me it was nauseating. Do you need water or anything?"

Before I could answer, two preoccupied figures came barging through the door. The first was a brunette in green scrubs, followed by Dr. Dictator herself in a white smock with a heavily laden clipboard. She was writing on it more than looking where she was going. I put on my indignant face.

"Dr. Adara, good morning!" declared R.J.

The aide went immediately to my left arm and began removing the IV. Adara stood at the corner of the foot of the bed, still writing, not looking up. After a few seconds, she finally scanned me. No acknowledgment deemed necessary; she went back to writing.

Her long golden brown hair was captured back behind her head. Her makeup was too precisely applied. She looked more like someone playing doctor on a soap opera than a real doctor. She had faint, very attractive age lines on her face that complemented her perfect skin tone. They made her look mature for her age. Golden brown eyes with big dilation.

She spoke without looking. "I'm releasing you, Mr. Tarn."

"Really? How wonderful. Will there be an ankle tracking bracelet?"

"We did not find any hidden fractures. No suggestion of spinal compression. I thought I might have seen an indication of post-traumatic stress disorder. You probably should consult a specialist."

R.J. came to my defense. "Oh, he doesn't get PTSD. He's like immune. He's wrecked himself much worse than this and never had any problems."

The Doctor looked at R.J. skeptically. "And you are?"

"R.J. Smith, at your service, Doctor. I'm in charge of picking up the pieces every time he does this sort of thing."

"Well, that's not the way it works with PTSD, Mr. Smith. No one is 'immune,' as you say. It all depends on the event, when and where it occurs, and the condition of the patient's psychology at the time."

R.J. raised his eyebrows and considered the Doctor's rebuttal.

Looking down at her tablet, she turned back to me and continued. "There was indication of a mild concussion. It's surprising you did not have a mean little headache."

"Just one...."

She looked up with a subtle sneer and continued. "Lack of sensitivity to left hemisphere head trauma is characteristic of a small number of humans and most primates."

R.J. choked back a laugh and then looked up at the ceiling, tongue in cheek. The aide wheeled my IV stand out the door. A second, in red scrubs, strolled in with my clothes and belongings. The doctor continued writing on her clipboard.

I swung out of bed, peeled off the stupid Johnny, and began getting dressed right in front of her, hoping to invoke some reaction of embarrassment. She glanced up, gave an expression of disinterest, and went back to writing.

"You'll need to see me in two weeks, Mr. Tarn. Your blood tests will all be in by then. We should be able to close this out."

"Two weeks. Sure thing. We'll call you."

Dr. Adara clipped her pen to the clipboard, turned, and headed for the door. She stopped and looked back. "It's your medical certificate, by the way. The FAA temporarily suspends them in these situations until the attending physician signs off the waiver."

I stopped dressing and turned to face her. "Medical certificate? My pilot's medical certificate?"

"Yes. Obviously they do not allow you to fly anything until a physician has verified 'no restrictions' from the accident. It's a single page document. It needs my signature in three places. You'll need to make your X mark on it also."

R.J. blurted out a high-pitched laugh but again cut it off abruptly and tried an insincere look of sympathy.

She finished with a flat, professional smile and disappeared around the corner. I stood holding the Broncos T-shirt R.J. had brought me, wondering how many points I had just lost on my man-card. I looked over at R.J. He raised his eyebrow, wondering if he was in trouble.

"I need a half gallon of coffee and maybe steak and eggs, something manly enough to mentally put her in her place."

"Lagoons on US 1. Johnny and Sue have the strongest coffee, and the servers will make you feel like a man."

And there we went, bruised pride and all.

Chapter 2

Back home in my section of hex-plex, I pulled the cold beer from the fridge, handed one to R.J., and plopped down on the couch. R.J. chomped on his unlit pipe. He sat back in my puffy, overstuffed recliner, his beat-up brown work shoes proudly pointed upward, his baggy jeans slightly soiled with grease from his restored Corvair, his blue collared work shirt buttoned to the top. He patted at his short reddish-brown beard, then tilted his Ben Franklin spectacles down to give me that Einstein look as I popped the top on my bottle and watched it fly across the room.

"You know you have a certain obligation that requires flying coming due soon, right?"

"I am aware of the gravity of the situation."

"Very funny. Would you please remind me again how you came to own the fastest little starship on Earth? So fast in fact, the geniuses in Washington are still struggling to understand the stellar drives?"

"We lost Erin Duan to those engines, by the way. She's now the lead scientist on that retro-tech chaos. We won't get her flying again."

"Well, I am sorry to hear that. She was something to look at. But, as I said, I still can't understand how that spacecraft came into your possession."

"What are you talking about? You were there. Seems to me I remember you spilling your coffee when poor Bernard Porre handed me the keys."

"Yes, I saw it happen. I still just don't believe it."

"It's easy. The Nasebian race is too advanced for us to understand. We did the Nadir mission for them. It made them happy. They transferred the ship to me. Other questions?"

"Doesn't it seem like a little bit of an overpayment to you? Wouldn't it be logical to think they might have something up their sleeves?"

"They wear those long glittery gowns with big drooping sleeves. You can't hide anything up those kinds of sleeves."

"Yet another skillful quip? The good doctor must really have gotten to you. All kidding aside..."

"Why question a good thing? The Nasebians said I didn't have to do anything I didn't want to."

"But you did promise to take that ship to the HAT system's planet Enuro to have artificial gravity installed. Next month is the deadline."

"Looking forward to it. Full designation is HAT-P-11, by the way. In the Cygnus constellation."

"You'll need another pilot. You got one?"

"Are you kidding? Danica Donoro would hunt me down and torch me if I didn't invite her along."

"How about Shelly Savoie?"

"Oh yeah, would you believe she's in the Air Force One starship group, flying diplomats to intersystem research junkets? She stepped off the Griffin and the White House reps dragged her away almost immediately. Fame has its perks."

"So you, and doll-faced kick boxer Danica, and I on a two-week float to Enuro?"

"A mere 120 light-year cruise or 700 trillion miles give or take a few. Add Mr. Wilson Mirtos to the flight crew, though."

"I thought he was fully engaged?"

"Apparently he needs a pressing obligation to cool that off."

"Has he agreed then to never, ever use the phrase, 'Now I don't want any trouble,' ever again?"

"No, he has not."

"In that case, I shall pack my mouth guard for this trip."

"You have a mouth guard?"

"I'll purchase one."

"I'm not expecting any trouble on Enuro."

"Custer wasn't really expecting any either."

"Touché."

"So the four of us float to Enuro next month, and then ride home in gravity, except for one thing."

"What?"

"You must first ask Dr. Catherine Adara to sign you off for flight status."

"Arrrrrgh!"

On Tuesday, Dr. A-damn-her's service informed me that she would be in attendance at the Jess Parrish outpatient clinic all morning. I consoled myself with the thought that the least I could do was show up without an appointment. In the auditorium-sized waiting area at Jess Parrish, I sat and poked at a tablet, developing my flight plan to Enuro. Nearby, a gracious older lady in a light pink ballroom gown played a beautiful golden harp strategically positioned next to a flowing fountain. It was a pleasant forty-five-minute wait. The bothersome tremor persisted in my right hand. In the treatment room, I tucked both hands in my jean pockets when the bad Doctor entered.

"Your scans and blood work came back negative. I can sign you off, for good."

"Ole'."

"The sign-off goes into the system immediately. You are cleared to fly as soon as you walk out that door."

"Then I will depart in haste and not look back."

"Did you pull up in that black Corvette?"

"Fully restored, '95. ZR-1 package."

"You have a thing for fast cars?"

"Since they mandated the bio-fuel conversion, it will snap your head off. Why?"

"We seem to have a healthy dislike for one another. In certain cases, that can be fun."

"I can't imagine."

"I'm on staff to NASCAR as one of their emergency surgeons."

"So I've heard. The drivers must really fear injury these days."

"Ever heard of the NASCAR Racing Experience?"

"You get to do a few laps with a certified driver."

"My family owns a team. They claim floaters will never be any good for pro track racing. Too wild in the restarts. They say there will always be wheels on the ground, and the two-hundred-mile-per-hour restriction will always be the limit."

"Yeah, so?"

"All things being what they are, and because their lives sometimes depend on me, the NASCAR crowd allows me a lot of special privileges. I can grab a NASCAR Racing Experience car whenever the track's not being used. They just throw me the keys, you might say. Only requirement is, I pay for any damage to the cars and a usage rate on the tires."

"Did you say cars, as in more than one?"

"I can bring someone along if I care to."

"Where exactly are you going with this?"

"I get you on the track; I can embarrass the hell out of you."

"Don't count on it."

"They give amateurs these little glass-blown trophies to mark the experience. I'd treasure ours forevermore."

"Bring it on. Expect disappointment."

"I can meet you in Daytona tomorrow morning."

"Count on it."

E.R. Mason

    Men tend to forget all good sense when certain opportunities present themselves. I made Daytona early the next morning in time for breakfast. I sat in Friendly's, trying to stop the concentric circles from forming in my coffee from the tremor in my right hand, staring across the street at the Speedway, plotting my moves against the queen-of-mean. There was no doubt she had something up her sleeve and intended to set me up. The offer was designed to be something most men could just not resist, which it was. That was the trap. Somehow, just showing up would spring it.

    I do not walk into traps very easily. Too many scars here and there have left me and my 6-foot-2-inch frame with heightened self-preservation instincts, especially where women are concerned. She had something up the sleeve of her lab coat. Maybe she would just be a no-show and laugh it off at that. Maybe a professional substitute driver would be there to take her place. Maybe it was something else.

    I have not survived this long without breaking a few rules and storing away tricks of my own. What Doctor Gestapo did not know was that I had a history with racing, a sincere love for the sport so great that had it not been for an equally primeval instinct for flight, racing would have been my chosen career. A close friend used to run short-track, and by helping sponsor him, I was able to cash in on some track time. In fact, back then, anytime I found myself ground-bound for one reason or another, I was in his garage or on the track.

    Along with the sloppy scratching of map she had given me, there was a Speedway badge. I found Williamson Boulevard without any trouble, and the entrance to Gate 40 was hard to miss. It was an off day, but to my surprise, quite a few cars were lined up in the parking lot. A guard in the center island started to step out as I approached, but the badge put him at ease. After a few wrong parking lot turns, the road to the tunnel came into view. There was a second guard waiting under canopy-covered street dividers, but he too retreated at the sight of my badge. It began to bother me that Dr. Pain had so casually been able to give me a badge that seemed enchanted with power. The dive into the tunnel brought me out to a maze of roadways confusing enough that I ended up driving half the length of Lake Lloyd before I found a left-hand turn toward the garage area. Creeping along like a typical male unwilling to ask for directions, I finally spotted two mechanic types in heavily endorsed coveralls, sipping coffee from paper cups and talking as they crossed the parking lot. One of them noticed me and stopped in recognition. He said something to his associate and came over to the car.

    "Commander Tarn, it's an honor to meet someone who travels faster than we do."

Shock Diamonds

"Thanks. There's almost no place I'd rather be."

"You're here to take on the iron maiden, I hear."

"Iron maiden?"

"Yeah, Catherine the Great. I guess I should warn you; it's attracting a bit of a crowd."

"You're kidding."

"If you pull over there by that side entrance, we'll take you into the garage area. She's already been on the track, by the way."

I swung around and parked, grabbed my gear bag, and locked the Vette. As I climbed out, the mechanic introduced himself as Matt Bean. He gestured toward his associate, "This is my best friend off the track, and my worst enemy on it, Bret Marks."

I nodded respectfully.

"That's a nice ZR you got there, man," said Marks.

"Fully restored from the ground up."

"Looks it. What'd you bring in the travel bag?"

"Fire suit, boots, gloves."

"You got your own fire suit, Commander?"

"Yeah, I've done some short track."

"Nice. You'll need to get it approved by the NRE rep, but it shouldn't be a problem. The crew chief is gonna be real glad to hear you've got some track time."

They led me to a side entrance in the network of garage space and down a cold, shadowy cement corridor lined with colorful racing posters. The air had the permanent smell of racing tires and oil.

"So, will Adara really show up?" I asked with appropriate sarcasm.

"Are you kidding us?"

"Why? What did I say?"

"You know her family owns half this business, right?"

"So you're saying she really is going to drive?"

The two men stopped in the hallway and turned to me. Bean spoke. "Listen, I never said any of this, okay? I was really glad when you said you had some driving experience. Most guys she brings here, she usually laps them by lap six. I've seen grown men leave here wanting their mommy when she's through with them. I've seen 'em pull in after ten laps and claim there was somethin' wrong with the car when there wasn't. I'm just telling you this 'cause if there's any chance you could put her in her place just once, you'd be doin' the rest of us a big favor."

It shut me up. In my mind, I quickly began erasing all the trick gimmicks I thought might be a part of her game. The

15

walk down this historic hallway of racing suddenly became the green mile of manhood lost. Suddenly there was a feeling that maybe this corridor led to the Roman Coliseum where a lion awaited fresh Christian meat. For the first time, I had concern. Self-confidence had become self-doubt. There was a crowd forming, he had said. This was to be a public execution. The great Commander Adrian Tarn, slayer of dragons, rescuer of shapely women, able to leap tall buildings with a single aircraft, now scheduled for humiliation by a merciless, 5-foot-8-inch ball of female fire, and I had walked right into it.

Where had I gone wrong? It is the question most men ask themselves on the way to the gallows. It was the vanity, the same answer most men finally admit on the way there. I had just assumed that Dr. Gestapo was not a real driver. Clearly, it was beginning to appear that was not the case. What a wonderful setup. She probably knew I would not find out in time. And, she had been completely honest. If she could get me on the track, she could embarrass the hell out of me, as she put it.

Oh, boy.

A heavy steel door pushed open to the garage. The bay doors were open, but the air inside was blowing cool. A dozen brightly painted race cars were backed up against the far wall. A red, white, and blue one sat in the center of the garage. A mechanic was leaning in the driver's window, with another man standing behind him watching. Bean stopped next to me, waved to them, and pointed at me. The man watching the work came over and held out a hand.

"A pleasure, Commander Tarn," he said as we shook. "Are you sure you really want to do this?"

"I may have underestimated my opponent."

"I can guarantee that."

Bean leaned over and coaxed my bag from my hand and held it out to him. "Fire suit, gloves, boots, Max."

Max raised an eyebrow, took the bag and smiled. "Well, that's a good sign. I'm Max Manning, Mr. Tarn. So you've driven some, then?"

"Short track. A fair amount."

Max turned to his associate still working on the car. "Paul, would you run these upstairs to the office?"

His associate quickly finished with a cable in the car, came and took the bag, and disappeared out the door.

"He'll be right back. The NRE rep has to sign off on your gear. You'll need to use one of our helmets. Radio and air are set up for them. The boys will take your car out to pit row, and we'll suit you up, then cart you out there. The iron maiden is already out there running warm-up laps."

They dressed me up like a sacrifice to a Gorgon, then we loaded into a golf cart and drove out to pit row. The mood was so somber I was surprised there was not a priest with holy water standing by. Even though I had been warned, it surprised me to look up at the stands and see twenty or thirty people pressed against the fence and another half dozen in seats above and behind them. There were two race cars parked on pit row, and only two. His and hers. She was already strapped, in waiting, helmet on, fiery eyes staring. They wasted no time ushering me in through the driver's window. Once I was comfortable and helmeted, Max plugged me in and spoke with the cool constraint of the professional he was. "Show me the gears, Commander."

I pushed the gear shift through its pattern.

"Okay when you start, hold it at two thousand. When you pull out, keep it at two thousand until you're on the track. I don't have to tell you about the red lines on your gauges. We usually have a lead car in front of you that you are not allowed to pass, but you-know-who won't allow that, so you're on your own. All I can say is be careful to keep it off the wall, and you probably know it'll want to dive left coming out of the turns. Catherine is on your intercom along with a spotter and some other interested observers so watch what you say. Gentleman, you may start your engine."

At the first roar from under my hood, Dr. Gestapo came on the radio. "Good morning, Mr. Tarn. Welcome to my world."

I chose not to answer.

"Mr. Tarn, did I mention to you that my stepfather was Dave Rand?"

"The Dave Rand, I suppose, Doctor."

"I'm not your doctor here, Commander. I am your intimidator, your very own Earnhart. Yes, that Dave Rand. NASCAR points leader three years in a row. I'll give you a few warm-up laps. I don't need any. Try not to hit me when you come around to the flag stand."

Max had an earpiece and microphone and had heard it all. He nodded to me and gave the go-signal. I dropped it into first and with that familiar, lovely roar pulled around the iron maiden, down pit road, and onto the track.

The Gs a driver pulls in the turns are of no consequence to me. They are such a smooth, comfortable, positive down-force they don't hold a candle to the wild positive-negative swings you get in a stunt plane, and the car's rotation in the steep bank is actually identical to the banking of an aircraft. You would think all that carefully designed down-force would give you enough weight in the turn that unlimited speed would be possible, but instead, ghost force tries to push you up into the wall. That, combined with the sudden unresponsive steering, pumps in new adrenaline and makes your right foot back off the pedal. You could call it Newton's revenge.

Though I had never driven Daytona, after the first warm-up lap it was like home. My chest pumped up a bit in response to the feeling of fresh masculinity. This was a car any driver could love. Although I had fully expected it, banking into turn one woke me up. It brought all that racing history in my blood to full alert. A second later, I was in euphoria. I hit 150 going into turn three and stayed well clear of the wall. A surge of joyful ambition made me bottom out the pedal, but thankfully good sense stepped in and backed me off. Going into turn one again, the max speed indicator had locked up on 158; the wall came up more quickly, but the car was set up nice and held. By the third lap I was holding 160 and, having found the right line, knew I had a good deal more beyond that. As I came down the front side on lap three, Dr. Exterminator's car was stopped a few hundreds yards short of the flag stand, waiting.

Her voice squelched in over the radio. "That all you got, Tarn? How many more laps you going to need?"

I went around once more, then pulled up next to her. She looked over, visor down. "Twenty-five laps, hot shot, if you're up to that many. No pit stops unless you get scared or rub a tire." She was pumping the throttle just enough to be annoying. She started to creep slowly forward. I matched her speed.

If memory serves me, drivers are limited to 55 mph under yellow or when behind the pace car. We did not have a pace car, but the track lights were yellow. The flag stand was still several hundred yards ahead of us. Without warning, the good doctor dropped the pedal and jumped half a dozen car lengths ahead and went past the flag stand wide open just as the lights turned green. I marked the event with the appropriate curse under my breath and stomped down after her. The jump put her halfway through the first turn as I was just entering.

The vibrating roar of the engine made the car shudder to life. It was the best kind of music anywhere. The strange, indescribable smell of a thousand races, persisting at the edge of time, permeated the air. In the back straight, there was the impulse to leave the pedal down too long to get back some of those lost car lengths. If you do that, once you're in the turn, it is too late to fix it. You either spin or leave tire on the wall. I reined myself in and watched as the back of the doctor's car made tiny zigs and zags trying to hold the corner. There would be no settling-in time for this contest. The doctor was already playing the edge.

Two more laps left me still half a dozen car lengths behind her, but somehow I had the feeling that bothered her. Though I was not gaining, I had room to spare in the turns. She began drifting higher, looking for a faster line. I decided to hold back a while longer, let the tires wear in, maybe frustrate the competition a bit more. My red, white, and blue number 3 was beginning to feel just a touch tight, but still any driver's dream, and I could tell she was starting to look loose.

On lap eight, she dropped down on the back stretch in search of a low line. I patiently followed and closed in a car length coming out of the next turn. It was beginning to be apparent to all involved there would be no lapping of the visitor in this race. Onlookers in the stands were quickly leaving their seats for the fence.

On lap twelve I used the first turn to get back to the high line while she persisted trying to make it work down low. It quickly gave me back the four or five remaining car lengths, so that I ended up cruising just behind and above her. But she was paying attention. She sideslipped up in front of me by inches and blocked any chance of passing.

Throughout the intensity of our high-speed mind game, the intercom had remained completely silent, no words even from the spotter. I began to wonder if it was broken. I floated behind her with only inches to spare. In the straights I could have pushed. The pressure must have been weighing on her, or maybe she misinterpreted some of the looseness a touch, because on the fifteenth lap going into turn three, she ever so lightly kissed the wall with her back end, got just a bit squirrelly, and had to work it back straight. Left paint on the wall.

It was too good a break not to cash in. I dove down low and past her, then came right back up a few feet in front. For the first time the intercom squelched on, just for an instant, just long enough for an unintended four-letter word suggesting dissatisfaction.

The lead change seemed to jack up her willingness to take risks. It made me begin to wonder if things were getting out of hand. She was on my butt up until lap twenty, the point we both knew made position imperative. Our speeds were approaching those of a packed track NASCAR race. The crowd at the fence had grown larger than anyone could have expected.

She seemed to be getting reckless, constantly breaking loose and catching it just in time. For whatever reason, my ride was sticking well. She may have been the better driver, but clearly I had the better car. I wondered if it was a gift from the garage guys. We came around on the backstretch and she had dropped to the low line as though attempting a pass. I knew the energy wasn't there so I relaxed and held my line. As expected, she slid quickly up behind me, but then, with the nose of her Chevy just alongside my quarter panel, the bitch tapped me! It

19

wasn't much, just enough to make the back end all squirrelly so that I had to get off the gas to get straight. It left me with a pretty good adrenaline rush as she darted past underneath and I heard the com squelch on just enough to pick her up laughing under her breath.

There are some indignities the male ego will just not accept. There must be some kind of master override built into the brainstem of most men. It triggers when a humiliation too great to live with vetoes all reason and logic. Brainstem authority then prevails. At that point, almost no consequence is of any concern. Remedial retribution is all that matters. Men who have undergone this transformation cannot be reasoned with. Brute force seldom can contain them. It is the same mind-set invoked by a bull elephant defending his colony. Under those circumstances, were you to run an EEG scan on the brains of both man and elephant, it is likely the readouts would be identical.

I was back on her ass going into the last lap, close enough that I could have given her a push. Instead I held it there, dragging along in the draft. Going into the final turn I dove down as low as I could go, stomped the pedal, unsure I could get back in line coming out, then slid sideways up in front of her so close she had to back off just a touch or get nosed into the wall. This time it was a curse that slipped in over the com.

But in that final straightaway, she had one more trick I did not expect, a death-wish kind of unwillingness to lose, an absolute resignation to never forfeit. As we stabilized into the straight, heading for the finish line, she was caught behind me, between my rear bumper and the wall. She had no chance of overcoming the drag to get by, even if the energy was there.

Halfway to the finish line, my victory now all but assured, she jerked the nose of her car into my back end. There was a chorus of grinding, bending metal along with a flush of tire smoke. From that point on, all I could do was keep my hands off the steering wheel to avoid broken wrists. The crash turned me into the wall so that I skidded along it with her front end buried into my crumpled passenger compartment. Her motor was whining so loud it hurt my ears even through the helmet. Hot water from her front end sprayed into the back of my car. Together we skidded almost to the finish line, paint marks, black tire, and grooves in the wall marking our progress. Our two cars, now one, sat in a heap, smoking and making loud ticking sounds of displeasure.

Still in brainstem mode, I unstrapped, pulled down the net, and cut my left wrist a good one on the net fastener getting out. I looked over at her as she struggled to disconnect her helmet. Our private audience was pressed against the fence overhead, silent. A piece of my rear bumper had skidded ahead just over the finish line. I trotted over to it, turned, and raised my fists high.

The crowd went wild.

She was sitting in the driver's window still trying to get out. She looked over, popped her visor up, and yelled, "No way! No way! We're under yellow. There's still one more lap!"

I glanced up at the crowd, looked back at her, then down at the piece of my bumper next to my foot, pointed to it, and again raised my fists high.

The crowd went wild.

Chapter 3

"No way, Tarn! No way!" Dr. Pain-in-the-butt climbed from her car and, hands on her hips, began a determined march toward me.

A drip of blood from my raised arm fell on my face. I looked up to see a considerable red stream running down my sleeve.

"Oh...my...god! Can't you do anything without having an accident? What are you, a human wrecking machine?" She came up, causing me to cower back, but instead of taking the expected swing, she grabbed my bleeding arm and pulled it down. After a quick inspection of the wound, she gave me a stolid look. "I don't believe it. I'm going to have to glue that, you know. It's too deep."

"Will I need to sign a living will?"

"Come on, you idiot. Here, hold your own pressure on the damn thing. Let's get over to the medical center. It's closed but I have a key."

"My god, is there anything you don't have a key to?" I obediently followed along. As she passed by the flag stand, Max was headed in the opposite direction toward the cars.

She snarled at him, "What was with the loose, Max?"

"Oh no. You ran the warm-up laps, Catherine. We set it up just like you asked." The two passed without stopping or even looking at each other.

"Yeah, yeah, yeah," she called back. I followed along holding my wrist, and as the adrenaline began dying down, I again began wondering how I had come to be there.

"You gotta pay for those cars, right? You caused the wreck...Catherine."

"Nobody said you could use my first name, Tarn. And don't get your panties all in a bunch. Those two cars were scheduled to be replaced by upgrades next week. They were to be torn down and used for parts."

"There are a few you won't be getting, I think."

She stopped to unlock and open a green metal door to a brick building set apart from the garage complex. The environment inside was dark and sterile. She switched on soft overhead lighting and went right to an aluminum refrigerator and began fumbling around inside it. There was a waiting area off to the left with an uninviting, worn-cushion green couch along with equally unflattering chairs. I took a seat on the couch and tried to look innocent.

"Come here," she commanded. Only the name Rover was left out.

I shrugged and obeyed.

"Drop the fire suit, idiot. Just to the waist. I don't want to see any more than I have to."

I pulled my arms out of the suit and let it hang around my waist, exposing my black T-shirt complete with NASCAR emblem on the pocket. For a moment, the size of the cut on my wrist startled me, but male vanity quickly kicked in.

"Don't worry. The blood will wash out of the fire suit. At least there's no damage to anything valuable." As she disinfected the wound, her own fire suit kept getting in the way. She paused, unzipped, and dropped hers down to the waist. To my surprise, she was wearing a sheer, formal, light-green silk blouse. Beyond it was the unmistakable silhouette of black lace capturing a very full, quite perfectly sculpted female upper anatomy. The fabric of both materials was so sheer that by using male x-ray vision developed over centuries of leering, it was possible to make out most, if not all, details concealed therein. I had to turn my head to the side to avoid the primal urge to do so, which left me with the same demeanor as someone trying to avoid smelling salts. I sensed a haughty pleasure in her from that.

"Hold pressure on there again while I set up the Epigun." She handed me a wad of gauze, then turned and removed what looked like a small laser pistol from a drawer nearby. It looked like one of those things doctors use that might hurt. I tensed up but tried to hide it.

"No, it won't hurt, and afterward you can have candy." She held my arm and drew a bead that any skilled artist would have been proud of. I was disappointed that it did not hurt at all, thus robbing me of a chance to reaffirm what a man I really was. When she was done, she bandaged the area up to the elbow and taped it off, but with the very last piece of tape, she pinched something and made me jump. With a look of annoyance, she pushed me in the chest and declared, "Big baby."

So I pushed her back.

She pushed again, harder.

I pushed back harder.

E.R. Mason

A look of sincere anger came over her. She reached out, grabbed the NASCAR emblem on the pocket of my T-shirt and tore it down and right off.

Indignant, I chose to respond in kind. I grabbed the front pocket of her silk blouse, only to my dismay, the entire blouse tore off in my hand, leaving her in only the widely laced black bra, which I was already more familiar with than I should have been.

This time her expression became rage. With both hands and all her body weight behind them, she shoved me backward as hard as she could. Still stunned by the sheer blouse in my right hand, I tripped on a footstool and went over backward, flailing wildly, trying to catch anything that might be in reach.

Let it never be said that God does not have a sense of humor. As I flailed in the beginnings of my death dive, there was only one thing within reach. My wildly groping left hand found the front of the widely laced black bra. It snapped off but provided just enough leverage for me to regain my upright stance. There stood Dr. Exterminator in all her glory, back arched proudly, completely exposed, a look of fury on her face that would have frightened Genghis Khan.

She came at me with both fists raised and hammering. Drove me back to the waiting area where I went backward over the armrest of the worn-out couch, the momentum of it bringing her and her amply exposed figure along with me. We crashed onto the cushions. She continued to hammer all the way down until, at the climax of the fall, I smacked my head a real good one on the opposite armrest. It made a loud enough thud that she had to pause for a moment to see if I was unconscious. With the half-naked doctor on top of me, I winced at the pain, and as it subsided, realized her face was only inches away from mine. She kept the narrow, warlike stare for a moment, but as realization set in that I was okay, her head jutted upward and she broke into hysterical laughter. I stared back like a puppy wondering if I was going to be punished for something I did not understand.

The laughter suddenly stopped. The stare continued. I braced. My next conscious memory was of her mouth clamped over mine. Jets of hot air from her flaring nostrils were streaming down my neck. The wrestling match quickly resumed, but this time the objectives were different. Clothing was blindly cast into the air. There was absolutely no script and no code of ethics to it. One thing quickly led to the next. Since nothing was taboo, no silent negotiations were necessary. The only constraint was the occasional necessity to breathe, usually done in gasps. It went on and on as though all unknowns had to be tested, all challenges met. It was the closest I had ever been to having my mind placed in complete standby.

At the end of it, she was back atop me, in a shallow sleep, one arm hanging off the side, the other tucked in alongside. The silent, dreamlike state of it was as good as the passion had been. I do not know how long we stayed that way, only that light from the small clinic windows became orange and then faded away completely. When she finally slid away, it left me so exposed I had to force myself up.

She was pulling on her fire suit with nothing underneath. She gathered the rest of her things as I stepped into mine. At the door, she looked back hesitantly. "This doesn't change anything, you know."

I stood up straight and tried to sound nonchalant. "Well, that goes without saying."

"You're still an idiot who kills innocent birds, wrecks vintage aircraft, and hurts himself getting out of a car."

"Well, I'm so lucky you were there to save the day, Ms. Fender Bender."

She zipped up the front of her fire suit, popped the door open, and looked back at me with exaggerated disdain. "Call me if you need some pain medication...or if you get scared..."

She stepped out and banged the door shut before I could think of anything.

On I95, with the full moon guiding my way, I set the Vette's cruise control, sat back, and tried to figure out if I had won or lost...at anything.

The next day was devoted to brooding. A month-long trip to the planet Enuro was closing in. In deference to everything that had happened, what a pleasant distraction it was. I picked up things at random and threw them on the bed, utilities for the trip. After each throw, I would pause to consider the victories of the previous day, taking time to inspect the bandage on my right arm. As soon as confusion began to invade, the search for items resumed. Later, I plotted a rough course through known space but did not submit it for approval. By evening, the brooding had not subsided. The bandage was beginning to itch. There was no choice but to call the doctor. Really.

"I took the dressing off. Is it supposed to be this red?"

"What the hell? You removed the dressing? You idiot! I used the Epi-ray gun on that. It's a special bandage. Those new stems will curl up and die. You sit right there. I'm coming over to rewrap that. I'm not having any dingbat lawsuits on my hands."

She was there thirty minutes later with fresh bandaging materials. She needed a sink and alcohol. We used the bathroom in my bedroom. I sat on the bed as she rewrapped it. On the last piece of tape, she pinched me again.

The same wrestling match immediately broke out once more, but this time there was no tearing of clothes.

The next morning, life had changed. I had grown to be ready with a block for any unexpected incoming slaps or fists. I lay in bed, ready, staring at the ceiling, replaying some of the more dynamic events of the evening past. She was curled up next to me, almost in a fetal position. She rolled over to face me. Her long shiny brown hair was draped over her face so that she had to part it with the free hand. Her makeup was smeared a bit, just enough to prod the animal instinct in me.

"I don't get you," she said softly.

"Why's that?"

"There's a line from a classic movie that I love dearly. The man says to the woman, 'You're still here. Why are you still here?'"

"It has been said that I attract trouble and seem to emerge relatively unscathed from it."

"Well, that would explain me. I am trouble."

"My favorite movie line: 'Have fun stormin' the castle.'"

"But why hasn't a healthy sap like you been harnessed and tamed by some attention-seeking woman in search of wealth and fame?"

"Who's a sap?"

"It happens all the time to both sexes. I watched my father's best-friend driver being drained by one of those when I was growing up. One day at breakfast she finally decided she had squeezed everything out of the poor guy she could and she boldly announced to him, 'Why am I hangin' out with you when I'm sittin' on a gold mine?'"

"I may have known her."

"So you got the scars then?"

"You sure don't sound like a doctor."

"Really? I'll ask it again, why haven't you been roped and tied?"

"Watch yourself, that's bordering on a compliment."

"Really, I'd like to know."

"If you must know, there was recently a kind of exchange of ideas with someone."

"I'm listening."

"It's personal."

"Certainly you can tell your doctor." She rose up on one elbow, her chin resting in the palm of her hand.

I became distracted by the irresistible glow of one ample breast but managed to hide it. I resorted to talk to help mask the impulse. "She was a science officer on one of my missions. We were on an EVA. There was an accident. Her suit got a bad tear. I had to plug her into my air. It was dicey for a while but we made it back to the ship. Later, she showed up in my stateroom insisting she had unfinished business. It went on from there. It seemed like neither of us were looking for a serious hookup, but it just kept happening. Then I got pulled into a twelve-month mission that I couldn't refuse. She was tied up here on Earth as head of a project. When I dropped her at the airport that last day, we both seemed to know the bonding had happened and there was no escaping it. That's what we thought. Months later, when I got back, I should have known something was up. She wasn't there to meet me. It's a long time to be away for the significant other not to meet you. She came down a few days later with the story. Her ex-husband, a diplomat, contracted some sort of exotic illness during a conference. His chances of survival were minimal. He needed twenty-four-hour care to have any chance at all. He did not have any family. She felt she had no choice but to help him. She had to move in with him to maintain the care. By the time I got back, the situation was so involved there was no way she could be with both of us. I had to gracefully bow out. I hate to admit it, but that little war we had on the race track yesterday really seemed to help. It got something out of my system somehow. God, I hope that doesn't go to your head."

"My head? I'm surprised yours fits in the helmet!"

"Oh no, I've set you off now."

She looked around the room. "I could sure use a cigarette."

"You have got to be kidding."

"Just one occasionally doesn't hurt. You breathe more than that in a month, especially at the race track."

"Are you really a doctor, or are you putting me on?"

"Got a proposition for you."

"You are going to proposition me?"

"You've made it through the gates of Gibraltar. It annoys the hell out of me, but there it is. I need a couple weeks with you."

"What?"

"Yeah, when somebody makes it as far as you have, there's a chance, be it a slim one, that I might actually have a thing for them. If I don't do something about it, it can nag forever. But there's an easy way to get rid of it. We spend two weeks together alone and then go our separate ways. After a month or so of reflection, we both decide it was nice, but no thanks, don't want no more of that. Nobody's feelings get hurt. Nobody gets dumped. It's a wonderful way of getting each other out of something that would have been a terrible mistake. What are you doing for the next two weeks?"

"You're something else. You know that?"

"But what are you doing for the next two weeks?"

"I've got a four-week mission to Enuro coming up next month. Otherwise, I'm pretty much open. But you think I'm going to spend two weeks alone with you? I might not survive it!"

"My father has a cabin in the mountains in Tennessee. It's right on a lake. Got a houseboat in the boathouse there. Sometimes I spend a few nights exploring the lake. Got the fiber composite scuba backpacks. Four dirt bikes. A bunch of other items that would amuse someone like you."

"Just how many men do you lure away to your hidden lair?"

"How many do you think survive what you have?"

"You got fishing poles?"

"Duh? Are you kidding? "

"Two weeks, you say?"

"I sense I'm winning my case."

And she did. It was an offer I just could not bring myself to refuse. We agreed to meet there in 48 hours. She gave me a hand-drawn map which required a certain amount of decoding. The place was deep in the woods, accessible only by a rutted rock-filled road bearing evidence of recent washouts in more than one spot. It was rough enough that it made me glad I had taken the insurance on the rental. She was not there when I finally pulled in. A PAV, personal air vehicle, was parked next to the cabin, making me wonder how she had possibly lowered it down through the forest canopy.

The place was breathtaking. The greenery threatened to hide the weathered cabin and porch completely. The ground was a bed of brown leaves. There was the smell of forest and kerosene. Except for the distant murmur of a mourning dove, the woodland was still, as the wary residents appraised the new arrival. The cabin was built on a steep hillside, wooden stanchions supporting the weathered porch. Firewood was stacked high beneath it. Makeshift stone and wooden steps wound down through the trees to the lake, a very large body of water that disappeared into the distance between cliff sides of forested mountains. A long dock and boathouse met the shore. The lake was glassy and inviting. I grabbed my things from the car, climbed the porch, and peered past the open planked door. No one was home. There was electricity here. The lights were on. It was a comfortable living room, a huge stone fireplace commanding. Colorful braided rugs on the wooden floor. A fat brown couch, bordered by recliners. One bedroom. As I entered and

Shock Diamonds

dropped my pack, she appeared in the doorway in tan shorts, a beige wraparound blouse, with an alien-looking camera hanging from her neck. She had on high, brown lace-up boots. One knee was dirty. We eyed each other with veiled distrust.

There remained a touch of awkwardness that first day, remedied by very little sleep that night. It may have been the only time in my life I did not contemplate boredom. Not with her around. She remained an unpredictable foe, capable of striking at any time for no apparent reason. I was never able to drop my guard. We took a day to settle in, but then the serenity of the lake was just too compelling. I was ordered to prep the houseboat and back it out of storage. She acted as though I should already know how to do that, so I pretended I did and faked it well enough. Beneath the silent distrust, an electric attraction began to replace the uneasiness. It was always there, underlining everything we did. We found reasons to get in each other's face, reasons for excused physical contact. Finally, at the apex of it, while handing off stores to each other aboard the boat, we suddenly ended up naked and spent within the scatter of our clothing.

But she never let me drop my guard. On the second day of our lake exploration, we dove sixty feet to the wreck of a large island ferry. I was hovering over an open hatch trying to see down into the engine compartment when she came up behind me and shut off my pack air, emergency feed and all. With the first suck on a dead mouthpiece, I knew exactly what had happened. You can make a free ascent from sixty feet, but it's not as easy as you might think. You hold in too much breath on the way up and you feel your chest begin to expand from the pressure change. It scares the hell out of you at the thought that the agony of the bends might be waiting on the surface. But, if you blow out too much on the way up, you can find yourself out of air too soon with too much water still overhead. I turned with a concerned, angry stare through the glass of my mask only to find her holding out her mouthpiece and coughing bubbles as she tried to contain her laughter. We did a slow buddy-breathe to the surface, where I tore off my mask to yell at her but was cut off by her mouth clamped over mine. From there it became an erotic water ballet. Later, I realized I had completely forgotten to scold her at all.

Her second outburst did more than startle me. It actually frightened me. Racing dirt bikes through the trails quickly became a competition. In several spots there were naturally formed jumps that put you a good ten feet in the air depending on how much speed you could muster setting up for them. She was a bike length behind. We cornered into a jump

29

E.R. Mason

and she cranked that wick wide open and came alongside as we went airborne. At the peak of the jump, something I would never have expected, the bitch stuck out one boot and kicked the side of my bike. It was a foolhardy thing to do. I missed the landing point off to the left. She tipped herself sideways and dove out of sight down a hill through the trees on the other side. I got scratched up landing in a large pile of cut brush. I stood, tore off my helmet, and yelled an appropriate curse. There was no reply. I scrambled up the hill and looked over the other side. Her bike was against a tree, rear wheel up, motor dead. She was on her back in a burrow of leaves, helmet still on, eyes closed. There was a pang of fear as I fell, crawled, and tromped my way down to her. There did not seem to be any blood anywhere. No arms or legs were bent in unnatural positions. I carefully lifted her head and said her name. Her eyes fluttered open. She looked around, wondering where she was. She stared up at me and blurted out a laugh. I opened my mouth to yell at her and she pulled me down on top of her, and it began again. Afterward, it occurred to me my life was completely out of control.

The very last day became ceremonial. It was as though some rite of passage had been achieved. That evening we set up a candlelight dinner outside the cabin. We sat at either end of a long folding table. A large barbecue grill was set up close enough to be within reach. She had an expensive wine carefully chilled, served in crystal wine glasses. A spoiled squirrel darted across the table. We devoured the food in silence. There just was nothing to say. She was scheduled as lead physician for the American Motorcycle Association racing circuit for the next month. I would be seven hundred trillion miles away on the planet Enuro.

I awoke the next morning alone. There was a vague, dreamlike memory of the sound of PAV thrusters gently disrupting the air. Where her PAV had been, there was a bare crop circle of scattered leaves. There was a short, disconcerting note on the kitchen table.

Darling,
How's the PTSD tremor in the right hand?
Love, Christine.

I held up my right hand. It was steady as a rock. There was a flush of anger, the realization that she had known all along, even though I had been so careful to conceal it. Next I tried to remember exactly when it had left me. Was it after the

Shock Diamonds

race, or after this place? No way to know. I packed up, locked up, and spent the trip home wondering what had just transpired. I had to mentally test my hopes and desires to see how much life had changed. To my dismay, it seemed as though something had.

Chapter 4

Space flight will never be routine. It is said that the ocean, if it can, will embrace you, then try to bring you down and keep you forever. Deep space has a completely different take on things. When you place your hand on a spacecraft bulkhead, you can feel the nothingness just a few inches beyond it. It is everywhere, and it goes on in every direction as far as your mind can imagine. To it, your spacecraft is an aberration that needs to be filled with vacuum, and unless you resist it every second, it will do so at its earliest convenience. Space then vacuums up the remaining debris field using its nearest gravity well, no haste required.

The unavoidable, ever-surprising laws of physics are perhaps not the most dangerous aspect of space flight. That peculiarity goes to the myriad of arcane life forms heavily populating each galaxy. Some are friendly. Some are not. Some do not even know what friendly is. When the long-held secret that our galaxy was busy with life finally became known, the unimaginably complex universe suddenly became infinitely more profound. That disclosure had been a consequence of the first scheduled manned test flights beyond the boundaries of our solar system. No longer could secret government contacts with aliens among us be kept hidden. Our ability to travel outside our solar system suddenly made us a liability to the galaxy and ourselves, and it brought us an unexpected delegation from the planet Nasebia, unearthly individuals requesting a conference with World Space Systems representatives.

While most Earth governments had already quietly made contact with several off-world species, the Nasebians had not been among them. This new close encounter was with a species so advanced their superiority was instantly apparent. The Nasebian delegation set the tone by making it clear the time for disclosure of the truth was at hand. Although six delegates had been provided, only one was actually a Nasebian. The others were Enuro representatives trained to negotiate. The lone Nasebian visitor remained out of sight on-orbit, in a spacecraft that looked like it was constructed of light. It did not take long to realize Earth was dealing with a species so advanced, and so evolved, understanding them was simply an unattainable goal.

The very first statement translated to Earth representatives by the Nasebian delegation was, "There are things you need to know." As the talks proceeded, Earth representatives found themselves listening carefully and rarely speaking. Questions were answered before they could be asked. New questions that Earth representatives had not even thought of were brought up by the Nasebian delegates and then answered immediately thereafter. By the time the meeting broke up, the message was clear. If Earth governments planned to begin travel beyond their solar system at their current level of knowledge, they should expect most of their missions to never return. The message had been delivered not as a threat or ultimatum. It had been offered in the spirit of caring, and along with it came a remedial suggestion. The Nasebians would provide an emissary to accompany each extra-system mission to provide the knowledge necessary to avoid interstellar threats or violations of territorial boundaries claimed by other species. Given the alternatives, the suggestion was heartily accepted, and a plan was quickly developed for each Earth ship to secretly have special accommodations for a Nasebian emissary. The knowledge that a Nasebian emissary was on board would be known only to the Captain and first officer, after they had undergone special training to learn how to communicate with their celestial guest.

As for me, I would have been considered the last person on Earth fit to interact with a Nasebian Ambassador. Adrian Tarn, breaker of rules, town crier of the obvious even when inappropriate, a discomfort to the aristocracy at gala events, frequent participant in two-day poker binges unbefitting an officer, women seen leaving his stateroom when they should not be, 84.6 percent more trouble reports than the average officer, known to sometimes smuggle bourbon aboard ship, listens carefully to orders then often disregards them.

Every "needs improvement" item ever listed on my annual appraisals has always been true, and it sometimes amazes me the things they deliberately leave out. The irony of it all is that when trouble crops up they come running like a Cavalry patrol being chased by bandits. And, when crew selection time comes around, if my name is on the list, I'm one of the first to go. It will always amaze me how quickly fear pushes aside all forms of prejudice.

I have always believed that the chemistry of fate includes a strong measure of irony. I once took on a routine star charting mission just to revive my dwindling credit account. It was supposed to be a dull and boring affair, a three-hour tour, you might say. By the time that hellacious trip was over, I had learned of the emissary and interacted with her on a level no human had ever before realized. As a token of the unlikely friendship, she had left me a walnut-sized crystal, an item as far beyond comprehension as my benefactor. Not long after, I was unexpectedly recruited by her to retrieve something from a distant solar system, and in return for having somehow achieved that Herculean quest, the Nasebians had bequeathed me the starship Griffin, along with a good deal of influence with Earth's Space Central. All that remained to consummate that arrangement was an easy trip to Enuro to have artificial gravity installed in the ship. Because this flight was along charted space, no emissary was necessary. It would be a simple, private flight to a planet few, if any, humans had ever visited. It was a trip I was looking forward to.

I filed our flight plan for 10:00, Tuesday morning. Orbital Traffic Control will accept flight plans 24 hours a day, but if your departure falls around shift change they can get grumpy. Late morning on Monday, R.J and I headed to the Space Center for the day-minus-1 spacecraft inspection. The ship had already been fueled and loaded with stores. As we passed though the main gate, R.J. switched into copilot mode.

"Have you been through the SIDs stuff yet?"

"SIDs?"

"Social Intercourse Directives, and believe me, that title is more appropriate than you might think."

"Oh, yeah. No, I haven't. Tell me, if nobody's been to Enuro, how do they come up with resident species profiling?"

"It says some info comes from the Nasebians' reps and other stuff is from contacts with off-worlders who have been there. There's a hair-raising warning in the preface that suggests one not bet one's life on the information contained therein. But you are going to review this stuff, right?"

"I have the feeling you're going to impress upon me that I should."

"Are you kidding? There's several dozen different species on Enuro. A few of them are pretty exotic. You could say the wrong thing quite easily, oh great master of the foot in mouth. There are other undesirable traps, as well."

"Like what?"

"It's quite amazing. They color code the profiles of each species. If a species is passive and no threat, the description is in green. If the species is extremely dangerous, the entire profile is in red. Other intermediate colors denote varying degrees of danger. I went right through the red ones. Apparently there is a female-dominant species called the Busharee. There is a dire warning that these women are nearly irresistible, but if you make the mistake of mating with them, they suck the life out of you."

"I've known women like that."

"No, you don't understand. It says that a single lovemaking session usually results in approximately twenty years of aging."

"Say that again?"

"In terms you can understand, you screw one of these women, then look in the mirror the next day, and you are twenty years older, and you stay that way."

"Man, I've heard of marriage doing that to you, but not sex..."

"Of all the red-print profiles, sex seems to be the most frequent problem area. There's another species, the Sirenians, that turn your skin color blue if carnal knowledge is pursued."

"Brother, that would be hard to hide from the wife."

"At least that one fades away within 24 hours."

"Honey, I'm unexpectedly going to be on travel the rest of the day."

"Very funny. There's another group that turns your eye color to match theirs. Two others believe they are automatically married to you after sex."

"Now I have been with a couple of those."

"Okay, okay, this is all a joke to you, of course, my leap-without-looking friend..."

"What's with all the metaphors this morning?"

"The point is, there are some profiles which are a bit more, shall we say, mortally dangerous?"

"I'm listening."

"For example, there is one warrior-class people, the Kantarians, who apparently have some primeval trait built into their brain and if you happen to make a particular group of phonetic sounds, it switches their brain into mortal combat mode and they kill you immediately."

"Wow! That could really spoil a party."

"It's no joke, Adrian. The tablet gives you the audio sequence so you can learn it and thus be sure to never, ever use it."

"I can see it now, everyone's singing Auld Lang Syne, and at the end, these guys finish up by wiping out all the guests."

"There's also a group called Sentians, who it is said can see through and even pass through solid walls or any material that is lower on the periodic chart than lead."

"I can't imagine the dressing rooms on that planet."

"You're just not going to take this stuff serious, are you? Well, how about this one? The favorite drink of the Tagon race is blood. If you offer to shake their hand when you meet them, you are offering to let them sample your blood."

"Oh, now that's just disgusting."

"I take it I have your attention."

"I will not be shaking any hands on Enuro."

"Then there are the women of Valturia. After lovemaking, they urinate on you to mark you so that other women will know you are taken. The smell is not easy to get rid of."

"How the hell many species are there on Enuro?"

"An ever-changing number. It's because Enuro is protected by the Nasebians. Other cultures feel safe doing business there, even some that don't get along. So by providing services to the Nasebians, Enuro gets protection and subsequently a healthy and very diverse commerce."

"I don't want to hear any more, R.J."

"You'll read through the profiles?"

"I'll read through the profiles but not until after a hearty lunch."

"After inspection, a hearty lunch at Heidi's, then?"

"I don't believe so. It may behoove us to avoid running into Jeannie. There would be awkward questions about Wilson."

"Oh. Yeah."

We drove past the Headquarters building and turned down VAB Lane. Not far from the Kennedy Space Center Vehicle Assembly Building lies the OPF, Orbiter Processing Facility. That's the real name. After the original shuttle was retired, the official name changed to On-orbit Processing Facility, intended to reference spacecraft capable of attaining Earth orbit or destinations beyond. By that same uncanny luck that delivered the Griffin to me, I was also endowed with custom hangar space within the OPF.

I parked the Vette on the north side, and R.J. and I headed for the Griffin, electronic badges in hand. There is strong sentiment attached to each Griffin visit. It is so strong it feels one step away from choirs of angels singing. There is a flush of adrenaline and pride, so much so that it must be concealed. It peaks when I first step in the hangar and see the light reflecting off her white, baked-on, heat-resistant coating, and the frosty windshields waiting to be cleared. On this occasion, the big bay lights were already on, the pristine hangar glowing from the beams.

She is stored with the wings swept back, just as they are in space, although they are exercised during routine maintenance cycles. Except for the pointy nose and high tail, she is a cigar-shaped UFO sitting on short stubby landing gears. To date, I have never needed to deploy those wings for atmospheric flight, her gravity-repulse drives providing all the lift ever called for. She was designed for a crew of eight, but the scrubbers could deliver O2 for up to sixteen. There would only be four of us on this easy cruise. We would have a spacious spacecraft, occupied by the best of friends. I found myself more than anxious to light up that flight deck.

As R.J. and I stood inside the hangar door soaking in the beauty of the Griffin, movement from behind the port landing gear strut suddenly caught my eye. A moment later, a familiar form sidestepped into view. She did not see us. She was bent over with her head tilted up, staring up into the gear well. Danica Donoro, the only person possibly as enamored with the Griffin as I, was dressed in gray sweat pants and a half unzipped matching sweat jacket with hood. The glimmering, rich brown hair was longer than last seen, a bit past the shoulder. The tiny, delicate nose had a spot of red from too much sun. The green eyes and intent stare still had that entrancing quality that usually induces a swell of lust in most men. Too many experience lines for a thirty-two-year-old face.

Danica actually has two faces. One is soft, warm, and bordering on glamorous. But when she slips into a pilot seat, suddenly the aura of warmth evaporates, replaced by cold steel, exactly what every passenger wants to see in their pilot. And it is no act. The woman has embarrassed many a male pilot and done a fair amount of damage to my own man-card on occasion. There is not a soul on Earth I would trust more with a spacecraft than Danica Donoro.

I called to her. "Have you kicked the tires?"

She snapped around to look at us, nearly bumped her head on a linkage, and broke into a big grin. "Well, shiver me timbers, if it isn't the Thunderbirds, Jeff Tracy, and Brains. Here to rescue some damsel in distress?"

R.J. blurted out a laugh. "Hey, watch it. That makes you Lady Penelope. God, I love her."

We met beneath the glimmering nose of the Griffin. R.J. made an awkward bow and kissed the back of her hand, after which she put a bear hug on me that almost forced the wind out of my lungs.

"When'd you get here?" I asked.

"Couple hours ago. Exterior pre-flight complete, Commander. You gonna unlock her?"

I looked over the Griffin. Ground power cables were hooked up, feeding the freezer units and other accessories to preserve battery power. "They were supposed to stock her for six months yesterday. Looks like they've been here. When'd you arrive in Brevard, Danica?"

"Late last night. Couldn't wait."

"You should have called us. Where you staying?"

"Nowhere. Why check in when you're getting ready to check out?"

"You got a rental? How'd you get to the Center?"

"I took a cab to the gate. Security was happy to give me a ride the rest of the way. I just couldn't wait."

"Well, you come back with me and R.J. and stay at my place tonight. We'll come in early tomorrow for the preflight."

"I'd justa' soon load up and stay on the Griffin tonight if you wouldn't mind."

"But where's your stuff?"

She motioned behind me. Against the hangar wall, three travel bags were stacked on the floor.

"That's everything I need. You assign me a sleeper cell and I'll be in seventh heaven staying on the Griffin again."

"You just love spacecraft that much?" mused R.J.

Danica smiled. "You know it."

We pushed the air stairs over to the Griffin's front airlock door. I whipped out my cell, linked to the ship, screwed up the password the first two times, then finally the door popped inward and slid open to the side. The inside courtesy lights cascaded on. As we climbed aboard, I could feel the flush of excitement in the other two. I struggled to conceal it in myself. In the forward airlock, the flight deck was cold and dark except for a single monitor at each pilot position and each engineering station displaying battery, ground power, and environmental status. My rush of excitement was quickly overtaken by pure love.

They had left the air conditioning on. The air smelled sterile, almost like a hospital waiting room. The forward airlock where we entered was cool silver metallic. Four ghostly-looking Bell Standard spacesuits were embedded in the walls in their docking stations. I passed through into the main habitat area. The lounge tables and chairs were retracted into the floors and walls, leaving a wide open, white cushioned chamber dotted with circular, closed viewing ports. The white photosynthetic carpet lining the floor, walls, and ceiling brought back an assortment of memories from the last trip, most good, a few not so. Being able to have the interior of a spacecraft project imagery can be a tremendous boost during long spaceflight, but if things happen to get out of control, it can also sometimes conjure up hell.

The twin kitchens at the rear of the habitat compartment were shiny chrome, clean as a whistle. Beyond them, the first four sleeper cells were closed, waiting for occupancy. It was fortunate the designers had made these horizontal cells. Now that gravity was to be installed, they would still serve us well.

I passed the two bathrooms, then the aft four sleeper cells, and emerged into the exercise area. It would probably be just as important, even with gravity. Beyond the gym, the science lab looked clean and well stowed. The three of us met in the aft airlock.

R.J. was fiddling with a space suit glove not quite tucked in. "It looks very ready, Adrian."

"What do you think, Danica?" I asked.

"Let's go right now."

I laughed. "Weather is projected to be perfect in the morning. OTC will probably turn us loose right on schedule. You sure you don't want to stay at my place tonight?"

"I'm going to stow my gear and enjoy the solitude before spending a few weeks locked up with you two. Okay?"

"I think I see her point, R.J."

"Yeah, but Danica, when we leave here, we're heading for The Italian Fisherman. It's making my mouth water just thinking about it. Why don't you come along and then if you..."

"No, thanks. I've got jet lag. You guys go on. I need some rest."

So we left her to her spacecraft solitude, but in the Vette, the gears in R.J.'s head were spinning, which can be a scary thing. "You see what's going on here, don't you?"

"Oh god, your famous catch-phrase. Every time I hear that I know I'm in for trouble I was not expecting."

"As if you don't find enough of your own."

"Agreed."

"Well, do you want to know, or not?"

"Shields up. Go ahead."

"She's got something going."

"Why do you say that?"

"Doesn't tell anyone she's here. No rental car. Taxi to the gate. Gets security to ride her in."

"So?"

"What if security wouldn't give her a ride?"

"Are you kidding? Danica Donoro? Hottest woman pilot in the world? Beautiful to boot? If she stuck her thumb out, she could stop a parade."

"Okay, okay, but doesn't want to come off the base with us?"

"We are sometimes questionable company. If you had a daughter, would you trust her with us?"

"Point taken. But that's not why she's hanging back. With her martial arts skills she could probably whip us both. Me for sure. You just might take a little longer."

"So what do you think she's up to?"

"I don't know. All I know is she's got a secret, and she's using the Space Center to hide out from it."

"You could be wrong about this. It could be things are just as they appear, Sherlock."

E.R. Mason

"I am seldom wrong about these things, dear Watson. You know that."

"Damn straight."

T-0 day was clear blue sky, a salty, gentle offshore breeze, but no Wilson Mirtos. Ground crews towed the Griffin out to Launch Apron Blue where we left the forward airlock open and the air stairs in place while Danica and I ran through the long power-up sequence. Before I could find a delicate way of declaring myself pilot-in-command, she had pleaded for the left seat, and like most men I could not refuse her. It put me in the right seat and gave me the challenge portion of the checklist, and her the response portion. I had to keep overriding the impulse to fold my arms in body-language discontent.

In a spacecraft, there really are no pilot and copilot. There are only pilots. But years of sitting in an aircraft's left seat, where the level of responsibility is at its highest, leaves an indelible imprint on the mind, and an ethereal completeness to the soul. It's like taking the training wheels off your bike or learning to water-ski slalom. You can never go back. Once you have experienced and come to terms with pilot-in-command, it is a disappointment to sit in any other seat.

There was a pause in the checks while Danica adjusted her headset and aligned her flight controls. The flight deck windows had already been powered up and switched to transparent. A flurry of activity by the hangar fence suddenly caught my eye. A second later, Wilson's hulky form came lumbering into view, dragging bags and briefcases along with him, more than most men could handle. Danica looked up, saw him, and broke out laughing. On closer inspection, he was wearing only a bathrobe and flip-flops, his bare, hairy, white legs escaping the terry cloth with each step. He hobbled along until the garbled sound of irritated cursing could be heard at the base of the air stairs as R.J. struggled to help him aboard. I turned in my seat and looked back in time to see Wilson appear in the airlock, casting a momentary look of annoyance in my direction before wrestling an overstuffed flight bag through the door to the habitat module.

"Auxiliary APUs are in standby," said Danica.

"What?"

"Auxiliary APUs are in standby," repeated Danica.

"Oh, sorry. Okay, departure sequencer initialized?"

"Sequencer initialized and online."

"L02 pressures in green?"

"L02 in green."

"Aerodynamic control surfaces in neutral?"

"Aerodynamics neutral."

"Execute Flight Management Computer programming."

"Did you upload it?"

"Transmitted it last night from home. And by the way, I reprogrammed my bio-keys to give you full administrator's privileges."

Danica tapped a few keys on the center console and our primary display screens came to life. "Execute complete. Flight plan accepted."

"Activate Flight Director."

"Flight Director activated and... it likes it."

R.J. popped his head in between us. I looked back at him. "You got Wilson safely aboard?"

"Yes, and I'm not sure, but he may have brought everything he owns along with him."

"Would you signal the ground guys we're ready for the stairs to be taken away, then close up?"

"Aye, aye, sir, or should I say ma'am?"

"Don't push your luck, Mister."

R.J. disappeared. A moment later the air stairs went by toward the hangar. There was the clunking sound of the airlock door being shut.

"Green light on the door," said Danica. "Pressurization coming on."

"So, you're in the left seat. That means you get Orbital Traffic Control."

"I'll use my womanly wiles on them."

"We're number one. There's nobody else on the schedule."

Danica readjusted her boom mike. "OTC, Griffin."

A male controller's cheery voice came back. "Go ahead, Griffin."

"OTC, Griffin ready for departure instructions," said Danica.

"Griffin, departure approved as filed. Contact departure control on 486.9 delta bravo."

"Switching to 486.9 delta bravo. Thank-you, sir. Departure control, this is the starship Griffin with you on LA Blue."

As we waited, R.J. returned, sat down at the engineering station behind me, and began strapping in.

"He's gonna get his butt up here, right?"

"Oh, yeah. He's coming. Apparently Jeannie held him up."

"He's not going to strap in wearing that robe, is he?"

"I hope to god not. The front of that robe doesn't close up all the way."

A moment later Wilson barreled onto the flight deck wearing khaki green flight pants and a gray sweatshirt. He squeezed into the engineering station behind Danica and began buckling up.

I looked back. "Glad you could make it."

He glanced up with a shoulder harness in his hands. "Oh, don't get me started."

The radio squelched on. "Griffin, Departure Control. Expect clearance at 10:25."

"Griffin copies."

R.J. said, "Hey, you guys didn't conduct the passenger briefing."

Danica looked at me with a smirk. I turned back to the two of them. "Passengers will remain seated and buckled in until everything in the cabin is floating. Okay?"

R.J. raised an eyebrow. Wilson looked at R.J. and began nodding. "Yeah, yeah, nothing could make me happier."

Danica transferred gravity repulse to active and brought the stellar drives up to idle. The familiar deep hum swelled in the cabin, accompanied by the dull vibration of an impatient spacecraft ready to fly, but still harnessed to the corral. We sat there within the cone of power, expecting a breathtaking ride into space, a lifting that is never routine and too starkly awesome to ever be less than exhilarating.

The radio squelched on. "Griffin, Departure control, you are cleared to the 50 and hover."

"Cleared to the 50 and hover, thank-you sir."

Danica eased the GR control forward and we left the ground with a sway and a slight turn. The walls of the hangar on our left scrolled downward as we gently lifted. More white and yellow line markings on the apron tarmac below came into view in the lower windows. By the fifty-foot mark, she had stabilized our orientation to north. I quietly ran down my checklist, then nodded to her. "It's all good."

"Departure Control, The Griffin is holding at 50. Ready ascent."

"Griffin, cleared for orbital insertion. Contact OTC on 543.7 alpha bravo."

"Cleared for OI, contact OTC, thank-you again. Griffin out."

Generally speaking, Danica is a hot shot. Anyone who does not know her well would think she is reckless. Her standard procedures are nearly always embellished with either style or aerodynamic decoration. She drops of out light speeds often too close to the objective. She keeps her speeds at the edge of the maximum allowed. She would probably make her ascents to orbit in the inverted except she would consider it gauche. Fortunately, those of us strapped into the flight deck knew what to expect.

Today it was the ground-facing ascent. She brought the stellar drives in too briskly. It kicked the back end of the spacecraft slightly higher than the nose giving all of us a diving view of the ground as the gravity repulse carried us upward. At the same time, the OMS engines compressed us in our seats in a maximum forward acceleration. Had there been passengers in the back, they would have likely believed we were crashing. Any one of us could have offered a disparaging remark, but we chose to remain silent, cloaked in male pride. Danica giggled over the intercom as we rose.

The brief sandy green terrain of the Space Center peninsula quickly fell behind, leaving ocean whitecaps to mark our increasing speed. At Danica's radical downward angle, the vision of sea grew larger and larger, yet farther and farther below, as though we were looking down at an ocean-covered world. When at last she nosed the spacecraft up, the Earth's horizon was in full view, Africa a mere few hundred miles ahead.

I keyed my mike. "OTC, Griffin leaving FL250."

"Griffin, cleared for insertion."

"Cleared for insertion, Griffin out."

We climbed toward the horizon line until the Earth became the big blue and white ball turning below us. The standard procedure is to park on orbit around 300 to 350 miles so that if problems are discovered you are close enough to reach the One-World Space Station for assistance. I put 317 in the flight plan, a much less-used corridor. Our nav certification was good for another twelve months and our panels were all green, so docking at the OWSS was an unlikely requirement.

Danica called in. "OTC, Griffin has achieved orbit."

"Griffin, please advise in advance of departure."

"Griffin copies."

R.J. unstrapped and floated forward between us. "Coffee, tea, cigarettes?"

I looked behind in time to see Wilson's butt gliding along through the air toward the habitat module. "If you're serious, I'll take a coffee, R.J. It's a long damn on-orbit checklist."

"And you, my good Captain?"

"Nothing for me, R.J.," replied Danica.

He pushed off and disappeared behind.

I pulled out the checklist tablet, called up "On-orbit," and we spent the next orbit meticulously going through all systems. Griffin was humming like a finely made watch. The final step on the checklist was a visual inspection of the aft service compartment. As I began to unbuckle, Danica said, "You want me to go back and do it?"

"He who occupies the left seat gets stuck strapped in."

"Looks like a typhoon forming down there south of Japan."

"One of a month's worth of events we'll be missing out on, milady."

"Wouldn't have it any other way, dear sir."

"I'll be quick and get back here so you can freshen up in the ladies' room."

"I haven't heard any gagging back there. Maybe the bathrooms will still be pristine."

"Wilson's got a cast iron stomach. R.J. seems to have learned zero-G. I think we're okay on this trip."

"I'm really looking forward to pointing the Griffin's nose away from Earth, Adrian."

"Something on Earth bothering you, Dan?"

The question seemed to catch her off guard. She looked away and then back, her normal steely-eyed stare slightly off. "Just the need for speed, that's all, my friend."

"Yeah, with you on that. I think we all are. Be right back." I pushed away and pulled myself past the engineering stations and through the forward airlock. R.J. and Wilson had deployed the conference table and lounge seats. They were wearing their mag-flight suits, seated at the table, craning their necks to look out the portals they'd opened. I paused to gaze out one of the side windows near them. An abundance of broken cloud cover obscured most of the ocean below.

Wilson sat with a smug look on his face. His big upper body made the magnetic seat look overstuffed. It made me laugh to myself at the thought that extra magnetic energy was probably being generated by the seat to keep him in it. His short brown hair was slightly receding but seemed to be holding out. Hazel-red eyes stared back at me ready to deploy or receive any form of humor available. Wilson is a well-loved character by all except jerks of the vain-strain. They tend to see his compassion as a way to demonstrate their command over individuals of greater stature than they. The problem is, Wilson transforms from teddy bear to grizzly bear too late for those particular idiots to be saved. When the confrontation is all but too engaged, Wilson generally tries to defuse the situation with the phrase, "Now I don't want any trouble." It is a diplomatic technique taught him by some altered-reality psychologist and serves only to alert Wilson's friends nearby that the situation has gone too far, and all hell is about to break loose.

Not surprisingly, all women love Wilson, be it the soft lines in the tanned face, or the deep, endearing looks when a woman gets too close. And, strangely enough, on those occasions in which the brawl transformation turns him into the green-faced, roaring Hulk, afterward they seem to love him even more.

Shock Diamonds

I left the two of them to their Earth-gazing. A strong pull on a kitchen cabinet allowed me to coast through the sleeper sections, gym, and science lab. In the aft airlock, I pulled myself upright and punched in my access code to the service crawlway pressure door. As it hissed open, I pulled in and glided along the removable grated floor panels, looking for any signs of trouble in the maze of conduits, black boxes, and cable runs that fill the very rear section of the Griffin. The accessway is barely large enough for my hulk to fit through and is even more of a challenge for Wilson. As I made my way to the back bulkhead, I thought there was a faint burn smell in the air, but after pausing a moment decided it was only staleness.

Back in the habitat section, R.J. and Wilson were still floating at the windows.

"You'd better get strapped in, ladies. Aft checks look good. We'll be breaking orbit as soon as we come around."

They looked back as I glided by. On the flight deck, I slid down into my seat and smiled at Danica.

"We're ready for high orbit and breakaway at your discretion, Ms. Donoro."

"Aye, aye, Commander. Stellar drives are balanced. There should be no surprise time maladies."

"God, don't even say that."

"Yeah, it's a bitch to return to Earth and find you're one hundred years in the future and can't go back."

Chapter 5

Traveling from one solar system to another is a mathematician's worst nightmare. It is an undertaking which cannot be done without the aid of computers. Charting space is not an exercise in simply documenting what objects are where. It is the recording of all objects, the direction and speed they are traveling in, smaller objects enslaved within their gravity field, and the composition and forecast of the condition of each solar body over time. It is not enough just to know if an object will fall within your flight path on any given trip, you must also know if that object is breaking up, susceptible to the influence of bodies around it, or gradually dividing itself into multiple dangers over time. Add to these complexities the gravity wells of everything along the way which affect the time and space you are traveling in, and dozens of various kinds of radiation bursts permeating that same space in your path.

So, for any given flight plan, you sit at home and log onto the agency's navigation and plotting system, and begin negotiating with it for the place you wish to go and the time period in which you wish to leave. Actually, it will give you a time and coordinates for a departure to anywhere, at any time. But if it is not such a good time to leave, or is a difficult place to go, the system might come back with one hundred stopping points for course changes. If you give the agency's system enough leeway, it will make a gazillion computations for you and come back with the best time and orbital position to make the jump in which the least number of flight interruptions will be needed. On this particular trip, we had a flight path straight through, with the condition that our ship's flight director computer did not detect any variations in debris from a large comet along the way. That monumental plotting task having been achieved, the last obstacle comes when you download your approved flight plan to the spacecraft. You sit back and wait, and hope that your navigation, autopilot, and flight director systems agree with the path prescribed. There is always a long sigh of relief when the data is accepted.

So when you bring the nose of the spacecraft around for the jump to light, everyone on board has been very, very careful to have all their eggs in a row to avoid any problems at the hard-fast jump schedule time. There are a long few moments of breath-holding when the jump command is turned over to the sequencer computer, the non-negotiating machine that checks each step and each piece of equipment, before allowing those stellar drive engines to pump out their special kind of light thrust. And when the moment hits, and you are pressed back into your jump seat as the inertia dampeners hurry to catch up, the first breath everyone usually takes is used to let out a cry of delight.

After our transition into beings of light, we settled into a very pleasant journey among friends, passing through curtains of space too profound to describe. We grew tired of calling each other to look and then being called back to look some more. Traveling as light creates a very strange viewing effect. You hang weightless looking out a portal for an hour and space outside does not change. You leave for a while, come back and look again, and the blanket of galaxy is suddenly completely different. It's as though stage hands snuck in while you were gone and dropped a new canvas, the next act for the puny audience in the little bubble of light in the ocean of darkness.

Danica and I agreed on six-hour shifts. Because this was charted space, it was acceptable for Wilson or R.J. to monitor in the right seat while the pilot on duty took short breaks. Five days into the flight, we all remained quite giddy about being underway. I sat, mag-locked in my seat at the conference table, sipping a beer and talking to Wilson while R.J. sat alongside, hammering away at a mini-laptop.

Wilson kept looking over at me with a touch of uneasiness. "What's goin' on, Wilson?"

"Adrian, since you asked, I need a favor."

"Name it, ol' buddy."

"Would you send a note back to Jeannie explaining how important it was that I come along on this flight and thanking her for sparing me for a few weeks?"

"Isn't it about time you filled us in on this need to be elsewhere, Wilson?"

"Adrian, I just needed some time away, that's all."

"Time away from what or who?"

"I suppose you're not gonna let this just rest."

"Hey, what are friends for?"

"Well, if you gotta know, it's not her, it's me."

R.J. looked up for a moment. "Oh, boy, how many times have I heard that one?"

"We know it's you, Wilson. After all, we're your buddies. Which part of you is the problem?"

"That's just it, Adrian. There ain't no problem. Every time I get this far with a woman, they always wind up handin' me the ring back. This one don't seem like she's gonna."

"So you think you love her?"

"Yep."

"So you asked her to marry you."

"Yep."

"She said yes."

"Yep."

"You gave her an engagement ring to make it official."

"Yep."

"Now you're patiently waiting for her to back out and give you the ring back."

"That's the way it's supposed to work, Adrian."

R.J. looked up once more. "Tsk, tsk."

"Actually, I think the way it's supposed to work now is that the two of you set a date and get married."

"Ya mean permanently?"

"Well, when exactly were you hoping she'd leave you?"

"Oh, I don't want that."

"You don't?"

"You're saying I want to be married to her, then?"

"May be."

"So you'll send the note?"

"Of course, along with my congratulations."

"Wow. I may not have thought this all the way through."

"Yeah, but even so, maybe you accidentally did the right thing."

Wilson pushed out of his seat and floated to the kitchen.

R.J. spoke without looking up. "The man is the consummate contradiction of logic."

"Well, look at you."

"Look at me what?"

"The president of people against technology spending hours tapping at a new mini-laptop. Don't you see the hypocrisy there?"

"Oh no you don't. I am forcibly effecting art into a representative symbol of technology. Just the opposite of succumbing to it."

"Effecting art? I don't get it."

"Look at this." R.J. pushed the mini to the edge of the magnetic table, tapped a key, and a life-sized image of Plato suddenly materialized in the middle of the room.

"It's a sculpting program. I can't bring a hunk of marble along on this trip, but I can sculpt all I want with this. I can create and enhance down to the pores of the skin, and it's 4-D so I can control the light within the image to alter its aura. In fact, I can program movement and speech into the image, and accu-

Shock Diamonds

rate phonetics is incorporated into the movements of the face. This one's just at the level one stage because I'm just getting started. It will have color and detail and personality when I'm done."

"That's one hell of a hologram emitter on that little machine."

"The latest quantum-laser array. When I finish with this particular image, I will link it to an A.I. program based on the Socratic Dialogues and other writings from the time, and sit and have conversations with Plato himself."

"Where did you find this thing, R.J.?"

"The science has been around for a while. Just recently it was compacted down to a real user package. I can also plug my finished product into any high-definition 4-D printer, and create a solid statue or replica of my designs."

"Boy, I can think of a dozen ways this will cause chaos in the average household."

"Like what?"

"Teen wants to sneak out of the house. Programs his image to be working at his desk, and whoosh, out the window he goes. Parents look in on him, happy to see him working away."

"Parental supervision required."

"It could provide an alibi for crooks or unfaithful spouses, or devious individuals like you or me, among others."

"I suppose."

As we sat staring at R.J.'s rotating image of Plato, a beeper sounded on one of the engineering stations, an alert for incoming message. We pushed out of our seats and floated over to the station.

Standby
Standby
Standby

Incoming Transmission

Office of the Global Space Initiative
Bernard Porre, Senior Advisor

Commander Tarn,

Your flight profile received and recorded. Profile ID# 1603 1700 7039. Destination Enuro service port approved. Ap # XX4792ZZ

49

E.R. Mason

    This transmission also confirms and authorizes all crew appointments as previously submitted by you. Crew Roster recorded at Z5099CC

    May I say Commander, it is quite a feather in your cap, so to speak, that those aboard are still willing to fly with you even after all the tilting at windmills on your last quest, a crusade so aptly supported by your trusted squire Mr. Smith, that somehow, against all odds, unexpectedly yielded satisfactory results.

    In keeping with the challenge of understanding our Nasebian benefactors, be advised the Nasebian representative has conveyed his government's sentiments that this trip is being made to their satisfaction and they have requested support be provided you in any way you deem necessary.

    Additionally, GSI Council members have requested you be cautioned to represent Earth in the most conservative manner possible as sensitive diplomatic negotiations are currently underway with representatives from the Enuro conglomerate. Any controversial missteps at this time could affect said negotiations in a very undesirable manner. I have advised the council that such a contemporary posture is typically not in your nature and for that reason they should keep expectations at or near the baseline. Please advise us as indiscretions occur so that we may intercept any ramifications as they arise.

    Office of the Global Space Initiative
    Bernard Porre, senior advisor
    End of Transmission

    R.J. looked up with a wrinkled brow. "The man simply worships the ground you walk on, doesn't he?"
    "He is an ogre in a Space Systems uniform."
    "Must've killed him having to approve all that."
    "He's a bit late, seeing as how we're halfway there, don't you agree?"
    "Yes, and I believe he was comparing you to Don Quixote, was he not?"
    "And you to Sancho Panza."

Shock Diamonds

"Well, on that note of confidence, I believe I'll return to my sculpture. Perhaps some day I should do one of Bernard in some less than flattering setting."

"Hear, hear."

As our Don Quixote quest continued, the Galaxy became new murals of stars and stellar matter all the way to Enuro. It was an astrophysicist's dream. The view out the forward flight deck windows was so profound our duty shifts became like movie tickets. Even the Christmas tree lighting of the flight deck just could not compete. Someone was almost always hanging out in the right seat when it was available.

The navigation computers had done their job well. Enuro was orbiting on our side of the solar system upon arrival. No big arcs around a strange sun were necessary. We had no idea what to expect of this new system. One sun, four times larger than ours, a host of colorful, sparsely documented planets, most of which appeared as diamonds in the sky. One happened to be particularly close to Enuro. It had a purple-blue surface aura. Its composition escaped us, even through the best telescope. We ran scans and stored the data for later analysis.

As we approached, my party crew finally became slightly nervous and very professional. No one had to be called to their station. Approach procedures were read out and performed without being called for. I could have sat back with my hands behind my head and let the Griffin park itself. Begrudgingly, Danica let me drop the Griffin into high orbit around our destination ball. It too was a strange and unfamiliar terraform. That label seemed appropriate since it did not appear that any part of Enuro was uncultivated. There were many forests, but all seemed manicured and designed. There were mountain ranges, but all were checker-boarded with architecture. Rivers seemed routed by design. Two oceans were barely large enough to be called that and formed shorelines that complemented civilization. Even the cloud cover seemed somehow controlled. The surface was awash with well-distributed bright color, and much of it appeared to be artificial light.

We sat back for one orbit to let the ship's navigation and collision avoidance system map Enuro's orbital corridors. About the time I began to wonder who to contact and how a strangely scripted machine message appeared on our com screens.

Welcome to the Earth ship Griffin and crew. Please enjoy a landing when you are excited at: 29*58'45.03"N, 31*08'03.69"E.

51

E.R. Mason

Wilson laughed out loud at the poorly translated message and keyed in over the intercom. "Well, I for one am excited."

"Nav has given us an OMS and gravity repulse descent to FL100," said Danica, ignoring his attempt at humor. "It's showing a .88 gravity."

"We will be Olympians here," said R.J.

"Atmosphere is O2 rich just as promised," added Wilson.

"Coming around, everyone." I replied. "Engaging descent profiles to the flight director. Here we go."

A moment of suspended pause was rewarded with the kick of OMS engines slowing us down, bringing the familiar sinking back in our seats as Griffin decelerated to the speed of falling. With gentle taps on the side stick, I coaxed her back around and we watched Enuro slowly rising up at us in the lower windows.

Danica spoke in her usually businesslike tone, "Gravity repulse has it. Descent grid onscreen. We are five-by-five."

As we monitored our descent, something unusual happened at FL100. Yellow warning lights flashed on our status indicators. Before I could ask, Danica explained. "It's a tractor from the surface. It's not overriding our thrusters, but it is making small corrections in our attitude. Did you expect a tractor beam assist in the landing, Adrian?"

"Nope. It must be an Enuronian amenity they just consider to be customary. I don't see any harm in the stress profiles. Just let it be and we'll keep a close eye on it."

"It's a new one on me," said Danica.

"They must not want any drunken sailors landing on top of somebody's roof," suggested R.J.

We descended in quiet awe at the sight of a never-before-visited planet rising up beneath us. The spacecraft's instrumentation clicked and whirred reassuringly.

At 10,000 feet, Danica remained her usual businesslike self. "The environmental controls and pressurization systems have finished sampling the outside atmosphere and they like it. Cabin pressure is adjusting and outside air is being introduced."

In response, we all suddenly became aware of the air we were breathing, concentrating to see if anything unpleasant was about to occur. Slowly there came a faint, cedar-like smell as our ears began to pop from the pressure adjustments.

"That's actually quite nice," remarked R.J.

"Coming down to four thousand," remarked Danica.

"Let's still hover at fifty and hope their tractor beam doesn't get upset."

"Tractor beam energy level is within the passive range, Adrian. It must be designed for backup."

"I see that."

We paused at fifty feet, took a good look at the colorful lights of the apron below, then stole a glance at the Enuro world around us. It made Las Vegas look like a watered-down imitation. Neon, or something similar, was everywhere. The colors were much deeper and seemed to invoke a pleasant sensation when looked at directly. It was possible some of the buildings were made purely of light. No entrances or windows deemed necessary. Pedestrians, many of unfamiliar heritage, passed directly through walls guided only by paths indicated by colored walkways. Vehicles traveled on elevated roadways of many different levels. At ground level, all traffic seemed to be pedestrian only, although some were using Segway-like devices in designated areas.

"Wow!" said Wilson. "What the hell is this place?"

"A city of the future, I dare say," replied R.J. "I am disappointed to see that nature seems to have been eliminated entirely, just as I have always feared."

"Gear down, Danica."

"Gear coming down," replied Danica. "Three green. Down and locked."

"Engaging touch down sequence."

The Griffin slowly lowered us down to ground level. We jerked about slightly as the wheels took the weight. Danica and I had to willfully ignore the busy city around us as we went through the shutdown checklist. R.J. and Wilson wasted no time in signing off their engineering stations and unbuckling to go aft and look out the portals.

At the end of the checklist, Danica looked over at me. "Flight deck power breakers to off."

I switched off the power and the cabin went cold and dark.

"What now?" she asked. "I have no idea what we're in for."

"Me either. Guess we may as well go find out."

From the pristine white carpeting of the habitat module, by the portal closest to the conference table, I could see three individuals standing outside waiting to greet us. Two of them were dressed in dark, skin-tight suits that looked like Spider-Man-wear. They were no more than four feet tall and had big round blue eyes similar to those frequently seen on Earth cartoon characters. Tiny noses, tiny mouths, and not a hair on their heads. Their skin tone was light, with a faint blue glow to it. Their expressions suggested that it was great just to be alive. The big eyes were scary. It was undeniable evidence that this was to be extensive, direct contact with aliens. A slight pang of fear forced me to wonder if I was up to it. Of the last two alien contacts I had made, I had become intense friends with one, and had killed the other.

Though the two big eyes seemed perfectly suited to the strangeness of this land, in contrast, the third individual was completely out of place. He was of comparable height, but there the similarity ended. He was dressed in something that made him look like a circus ringleader, complete with plaid tuxedo, black boots, and a glowing wand taking the place of a crop. He appeared to have slicked-back black hair under his derby cap. Squinty eyes, proportional nose, and red smiling lips over a double chin. The group waited patiently for us to open up.

"I don't know about this," said Wilson, and he looked at me as though he expected a change of mind.

"Phasers on stun, Captain," joked R.J.

"I'd better come with you," said Danica.

"Better we should invite them aboard, I think," I replied.

And that was what we did. As we opened the forward airlock door, to my surprise and before the ramp could deploy, escalator steps rose up out of the landing apron and aligned perfectly with the ship. The ringmaster rode up, bowed, and spoke, "Ne na na, ne ne na na na na ne ne ne, ne ne na ne."

I waved him on board. He saluted and marched in, seeming pleased to have been invited.

Once aboard, he looked around the ship with great interest, and having established me as the one in charge, came up and stood directly in front of me, staring up with a big smile, if that's really what it was. He held out one tiny hand, palm up, tapped it with his wand, and two small, intricately decorated plugs appeared in his hand. Though he did not appear to have ears of his own, he pointed to the plugs, and then to the spot where ears would have been on his head had he actually possessed them, then looked at me and waited.

I hesitated at the thought of plugging something into my head directly in line with my brain, but decided there was no real alternative. I took one, carefully inserted it in the left ear, jumped a tiny bit as I felt it worm its way into the proper position, then with great trepidation inserted the second one in the other.

"Greetings, Commander Tarn. On behalf of my staff and me, let me extend a warm welcome."

The effect was one of the oddest sensations I had ever felt. I was aware of the ne's and the na's faintly in the background, but I was hearing plain English as though it was actually being spoken. I rubbed my left ear for no reason at all. "Wow. These are amazing."

"The translators? Ah, yes. I have one other set so that we can communicate with someone at all times while the work is in progress."

"You are the one who will oversee the artificial gravity installation?"

"Yes. I am Lotho. It is a pleasure to make your acquaintance, Commander Tarn. My team also installed the stellar drives and other accessories during the Griffin's previous visit here. We know the ship quite well."

"Where will the work be done?"

"In this very spot, Commander. Why waste time bringing you in anywhere else?"

"Will we need to get off the ship while you work?"

"That will not be necessary, sir. Most work will be done in the underbelly. In some cases, when we require access to the floor panels, you and your crew will need to remain out of the way; otherwise you are free to stay aboard while the work is underway."

"Do you have a time estimate?"

"Five Enuro days. We will be working twenty-eight hours a day."

"What do you need us to do to get started?"

"Commander, panels are being removed around the landing gears, as we speak. We are already underway."

"Wow. Okay then. I'm sorry. It was Lotho, you said?"

"Yes, Commander. May I say, I feel a bit as though I already know you. I will remain your consul during this installation." He dug in a vest pocket and pulled out a gray button with a clip attached. "Simply press this tiny device if you need to speak to me. I will come to your aid shortly thereafter."

"Are we allowed to visit your city?"

"Commander, the city is available to you and your crew, as you wish."

"Is it safe for us to travel out there?"

"As safe as any city. Security is everywhere should you need them."

"What kind of currency is needed?"

"All currencies are accepted. Earth's is highly unusual, but that makes it somewhat more valuable, not less."

"So you have another set of translators. If I give those to one of my crew, they can also act as a translator for my people?"

"Certainly, Commander. Or you may procure additional sets if you have equitable resources to trade."

"What would be considered equitable resources?"

Lotho looked around, for the first time appearing slightly nervous. He grabbed my arm and pulled me away from the others, pausing momentarily to look at the flight deck as we stepped away from the airlock hatch. "Commander, this is a del-

55

E.R. Mason

icate subject, but your Nasebian benefactors might view it unkindly if I neglected to discuss it with you."

"I don't get it."

"Do you have music on board?"

Sensing this was some sort of delicate negotiation about to begin, I leaned down close and spoke in a low tone. "What kind of music do you mean?"

Lotho looked around nervously. "Any that has a beginning and stops at the end."

"You mean a complete song."

"Yes, a complete musical piece."

"Like country and western or rock and roll?"

"I do not know what those represent, but yes, as long as there is a beginning and an end."

"We do have some MP12 players onboard with songs on them."

Lotho continued to speak in low tones. "Do you have art on board?"

"What do you mean by art?"

"Original works done with paint or sculpture. Not video or photographs."

"Can it be digital storage?"

"Yes."

"Well then, we do have some of that sort of thing."

"You are a fortunate human, Commander. You come from one of the richest planets in this sector."

"I don't understand. Enuro is centuries ahead of Earth technologically. How can Earth be wealthier than your planet?"

"It is because we do not possess the attributes necessary to create music or art. The people of Enuro are the greatest anywhere when it comes to technology, but we were not graced with the kind of creativity and insight necessary to formulate music or art. We are unable to understand where to begin, what should follow, and when a work is complete, yet we are profoundly sensitive to music and art. There's no sense to the creation of it that we can detect, yet when it is complete it is a thing of inspiring beauty. Therefore, we are forced to obtain it from other species. And so many other species are obsessed with wealth, or power, or war, there are surprisingly few that take the time to create or appreciate art and music, even when they are capable of doing so."

"Can't you program computers to create art or music for you?"

"Certainly, but art or music is not what we get. We see the program in our minds even before it plays. There is nothing. All computer music or art is a progression of logic combined with random chance. To us, it is a simple string of mathematical progression. Real music possesses a creativity that cannot be anticipated. Therefore we are forced to obtain our art from those who are true artists."

"Well, what I'd really like to have is a dozen translators. How much music would you need for that?"

"How much can you spare?"

"How about one hundred songs, including four MP12 players?"

"Oh my! Done! And you will need to sign a certificate of authenticity that these items came from you. Otherwise we could be accused of stealing from someone. Fortunately, these do not fall under the prohibited technology exportation laws so no violations exist there."

"No problem."

"I will make the necessary acquisitions and meet you here later."

"By the way, how do I get them out?"

"They are thought-recognition devices. You simply tilt your head and concentrate and they will extricate themselves."

"How many languages do they translate?"

"All that we know of."

"How long do the power cells last?"

"Indefinitely."

"Do they need to be serviced periodically?"

"Never. They are constructed with a static superconductive coating that never actually touches the body's tissue. They also repel or dissolve any invasive particles. Most individuals never remove them unless they expect no further contact with other species."

"Well, thank-you again, Lotho. We appreciate your hospitality very much."

The little man gave a slight bow, looked around, and drew a cloth from his back pocket to wipe his brow, suggesting our negotiation had been so intense it had stressed him. He nodded to me as though the barter was our secret and stepped back to the airlock door. His voice returned to normal pitch.

"I will return within the hour, Commander. Once again, it is a pleasure to host you and your crew." He ducked out the door and was carried down the steps.

My three traveling companions stared at me blank-faced, not having understood a word of it. I motioned them to sit at the conference table and went over everything. When I was done, they all still had blank stares.

57

Chapter 6

Lotho returned a short time later with the promised contraband. From that point on, no one was willing to linger within the safety of the ship. They were inherently an adventurous bunch, the kind I always seemed to attract. Outside, there was a strange alien city with even stranger alien people. We were about as prepared as Christians exploring the arena. The reading of the social intercourse directives had only confirmed dangers from the unknown, but now we were all equipped with translators. Lotho suggested a place called The Black Cistern, nearby, reasonably safe.

One by one we emerged into Enuro's late afternoon sunlight and stepped down to the well-lighted landing apron. A sparkling silver, semitransparent electronic fence and dome had been raised around the ship. We were given special pins that allowed us and those with us to pass safely through the curtain. My first look around at the Griffin brought a flash of alarm at how many underside panels already had been removed. A dozen short little men in the same Spider-Man-style uniforms were busily charging to and fro, climbing up and in, down and out. They did not seem to speak, yet their efforts seemed fully coordinated.

We turned in place to see everything. Our view of the city wavered from the effects of the curtain, making the place seem even more surreal. Wilson charged on ahead.

Beyond the tingle effect of the curtain, we abruptly became aliens among aliens. There was foot traffic typical of New York City. We were of no interest whatsoever to anyone passing by. The majority were little people who looked just like those working on the ship, although they were adorned in attire of such wide variations it seemed there were no standards of style at all. Our bland gray flight suits were also of no particular note except that we were all wearing them.

Buildings of light surrounded us. The overhead roadways were busy with traffic that never seemed to stop or even slow. The street we were on looked like cobblestone with softly lit seams. Occasionally, passersby brushed against us, just as they would in a busy Earth city. The difference was, some of them were frighteningly alien. We all knew enough not to stare. Quick glances brought sightings of pedestrians with short elephant-like trunks in place of a nose. I was bumped at one point and looked up at a lizard face that ignored my flush of fear.

We stopped at a four-way intersection where each direction was illuminated by a different color.

"Just our luck. No scarecrow," mused R.J.

"I think he said something about the blueway," said Danica.

"Let's not ask someone," joked Wilson.

"I see it. Halfway down the blue light trail. That way." R.J. pointed.

"I wish I had used the restroom before we left," said Wilson.

Everyone laughed. Nervously.

The Black Cistern had the correct blue arched vestibule marking its entrance. We could not make out the obscure symbols on the sign overhead. We pushed in through the light into a busy, colorful serving area, and quickly spied a tiny glass table with four empty glass seats.

The place was packed, our entrance ignored. It was noisy as hell.

In any given jungle, there are certain species which respond negatively to eye contact: bears, gorillas, and lions, to name a few. To those particular predators, a moment of eye contact is an insult to their dominance. For whatever reason, this primitive trait has somehow survived the millennia and remains a primeval stimulus in some anthropoid males. The four of us were experienced enough to know about this frequently overlooked bit of wisdom, especially Wilson. So, as we took our seats, we evaluated our surroundings with cautious sideward glances. I had a table of cute little blue girls laughing and drinking nearest me. R.J. had a band of the Spider-Man-suited individuals. Danica's nearest neighbors were extraordinarily tall, green, hairless beings with long spidery fingers, wearing long shimmering gowns.

Unfortunately for us, Wilson happened to get the nearby counter with the six Norsican-looking individuals. The Norsicans were quite familiar to us, having been portrayed quite appropriately as a warlike species in a number of successful Earth movies. The Norsicans are a hearty bunch. They are spacemen Vikings, typically in excess of six feet, well-decorated with crude tattoos, long black hair with disgusting biological trophies woven into it, more hairy skin showing than oiled leather covering it. Their attire is decorated with weaponry. These were not true Norsicans. They were some other species, but close enough to be mistaken for Norsicans. That added a nasty little unknown to

E.R. Mason

the equation. Before Wilson had even begun to take his seat, the situation spiked a bit of fear in me. R.J., already seated, had seen the conundrum and was looking up at me worriedly. It was at that point I realized I was holding my breath.

I opened my mouth to whisper a caution to Wilson, but it was already too late.

"You lookin' at us?" The nearest Norsican's query was directed at Wilson.

As usual, Wilson tried his best. "No, no, sir. I wasn't lookin' at nothin'."

Another Norsican stood to face us. "You sayin' we're nothin', scab?"

"No, no. I'm sorry. I didn't mean anything."

The remaining Norsicans rose to their feet. R.J. slapped one hand against his forehead.

"You want a closer look? We'll give it to you," said another.

Having only half sat down, I froze in place, then slowly stood back up. Regretfully, Danica sprang to her feet. Rather than looking worried as I'd hoped, she looked excited and fully ready and made sure they knew it.

Wilson continued his best. "Please let's just all calm down. No problems, okay?"

The Norsicans began to push chairs out of the way from between us.

Wilson stood back up, held up one hand, and in his standard pre-holocaust booming voice said, "Now, I don't want any trouble."

R.J. raised both hands in exasperation, as though all hope was now lost.

"What'd you say?" demanded the first Norsican.

"I said, I don't want any trouble."

A strange silence came over them. They looked at each other for a moment, then back at Wilson. The Norsican who seemed to be the leader suddenly slammed his drink down on the counter and proclaimed, "Well, why didn't you say so? Drag your warrior's ass over here and tell us of your exploits. The swill is on us. Come on, then."

Wilson looked at me in disbelief and confusion. He gave a huge shrug, pushed his chair away, and plodded over to their table. Two of them slapped him on the shoulder, dragged chairs from neighboring customers without asking, and the motley bunch sat amid loud grunting and laughing. They began talking all at once too loudly in grated, belching gravelly voices, spilling ale as they poured it. In the oddest anticlimax of all, Wilson, with his back to us, looked like he fit right in.

I sat back down, fear quickly replaced by tension-relieving hysteria. The urge to burst out in uncontrollable laughter was so overwhelming I had to wince and bury my face in my hands. I dared not break out into laughter in front of them, but tears began to stream down my face, and tiny squeaks of suppressed guffaws kept leaking out. I tried to wipe my face with one hand, resting one elbow on the table, shaking from the effort to conceal the hilarity of it. I had to pause frequently to wipe away more tears.

Danica remained standing, looking at me with a disconcerting stare as though an opportunity had been lost.

When I was finally able to sit up and wipe the wetness from my eyes, R.J. looked at me with a pathetic and somber expression. "I do not believe it."

I spotted a queer-looking napkin dispenser, took one and continued to wipe, quietly bursting out gulps of laughter in between. "Maybe Wilson's shrink was a Norsican."

Danica remained standing, as though she had been robbed of Shangri-la.

"Danica, SIT DOWN, right now." I broke back into muted laughter.

With an annoyed stare, she obeyed.

The three of us sat back in silence to allow our pulse rates to drop back to John Young levels, finally taking a chance to look around again. Wilson and the Norsicans were the loudest bunch in the place. Beyond the packed disarray of tables, there were elevated circular platforms at the room's front. They were illuminated with white light, were no more than a couple feet off the ground, and were being used for some form of entertainment I did not understand. A dark-skinned individual with narrow red eyes, two dots for a nose, and lips that did not close all the way over spiked teeth was chanting something that sounded like duck calls. As annoying as the sound was, the Norsicans had distracted me so fully I had not noticed it until now. There was a smattering of applause for no apparent reason from one corner of the room, and to my relief, the spiked-teeth entertainer stepped down from his circle and disappeared into the crowd, shaking a few alien hands as he went. No sooner had he disappeared into the crowd than another even more bizarre performer mounted a different circle of light bearing something that looked like a lighted yo-yo. Immediately he began spinning it, creating circular light trails which brought a chorus of oohs and aahs from yet another section of the room.

There was a very long bar near the right side of the place. It was constructed of something that looked like a wooden telephone pole. Patrons of varying species sat at it but were unable to rest their food or drink upon it. Against the opposite wall, there were 3-D framed pictures of the city and its visitors.

They were the size of movie posters and periodically switched between video and still image.

    I glanced over at Danica and found her still eyeing the Norsicans' table as though she was considering paying them a visit. It was time for some fatherly intervention. I opened my mouth to ask her if she'd like a drink or something, but before the words could get out a server appeared next to us bearing a large seashell tray from which she drew three blue-colored drinks and placed them in front of us, then left without having said a thing.

    R.J. looked at me with his favorite comical expression. "This must be what we wanted," he said, and he raised his glass in a toast.

    Danica came back into focus, looked at him, and burst out laughing. She clicked her glass to his and took a drink. I obliged them by carefully sipping at my own and found the mixture a delightful cross between pineapple juice and strawberry. What I did not know was that there was some sort of delayed reaction, because as I lowered my glass I found my two companions sitting wide-eyed and red-faced. It hit me a second later.

    Tequila to a power of ten. I did my best to appear unfazed, but it was possible smoke was coming from my ears. As I struggled with it, R.J. suddenly spoke in a broken voice. "Oh my god, that is fabulous!"

    Danica agreed. "It is! It is! I've never had anything like this!"

    As the four-alarm fire in my head died down, I suddenly had the greatest feeling of well-being I had ever known, and along with it was the most pleasant taste in my mouth I could remember. And it sustained.

    R.J. gave me a smug look. "Adrian, I think I might actually like this place."

    Danica nodded enthusiastically.

    I suddenly realized this was a very pleasant atmosphere after all. It was completely relaxing. Everyone was friendly. Where else could you get this kind of escape?

    We sat in quiet satisfaction, smiling at everyone, trying to understand all the life forms around us. The yo-yo spinner had brought out a second yo-yo and was furiously spinning both, drawing circles of green neon in front of him. There were now extra trails I had not noticed before.

    R.J. stared down at the blue unknown in his glass and spoke in a voice raised just enough to be heard over the crowd. "So, Danica, what's a nice girl like you doing in a place like this?"

She made a curious face at him, then looked away. "Where else would a space-faring woman want to be?" she asked.

"Anywhere but on Earth?" replied R.J.

Suddenly a touch of discomfort returned to her manner. "What are you talking about?"

R.J. persisted. "We've come seven trillion miles from Earth together. If you can't trust us, who can you trust?"

R.J. has a special way about him, the ability to put people at ease, sometimes without their permission. He can listen with such devotion that you wind up feeling as though you are the most important person on the planet. Under R.J.'s compassionate stare, grown men have on occasion led themselves to weep, while many women have hurried home to call their fathers.

"Maybe later," answered Danica, and she turned away to watch the yo-yo guy recall his yo-yos and step down from his circle to a smattering of applause and extraterrestrial accolade.

R.J. broke the impasse. "Hey, look at the stuff hanging on the wall by the stage platforms."

We all looked. It was a mishmash assortment of articles I did not recognize, except for the item nearest us. One of the fanciest gold-inlaid banjos I had ever seen hung there on the wall.

R.J. took another shot from his drink, slapped the table a couple times, and rose to his feet.

I offered a happy word of caution, "R.J..."

He straightened up his flight suit, stood up straight, and headed for the banjo.

As before, our compatriots in celebration paid no mind to the short, bearded man in gray flight suit crossing over to the side of the room where the banjo hung by its shoulder strap. R.J. stood for a moment of close inspection, then looked around the room to see if he had attracted any of the wrong kind of stares. His watchful gaze was equally ignored.

But when he reached up to take the banjo down from the wall, the patrons nearest ceased talking and turned to look. R.J. rotated the instrument in his hands, carefully inspecting it, then looked again to see if any dissension was brewing. A few patrons continued to watch with great interest.

Satisfied he was not to be accosted for some unwritten establishment rule, he carefully slung the strap over his shoulder and hefted the banjo into place. A few more patrons stopped what they were doing and began to stare. As quietly as possible, he tested each string for tuning and twisted the appropriate tuning knob. He next fingered a chord and gave the instrument a gentle strum, but stiffened and looked around when the loudness of the instrument surprised him.

A slow wave of silence flowed over the place. There was not a soul in the establishment whose gaze was not locked on R.J. The atmosphere of anticipation was so thick you could have cut it with a knife. R.J., startled by the attention, froze for a moment, expecting the worst. To his surprise, the room remained as still as it was silent.

Not knowing what else to do, and without daring to look away from the crowd, R.J. fingered the first nine notes to the song, "Dueling Banjos." He paused and watched apprehensively as a few patrons across the room stood. When no assault seemed indicated, he continued looking out over the room and played the next nine notes and stopped once more. Several more individuals rose to their feet.

Confidence growing, he dared the next sequence of notes. Someone yelled out an unintelligible cry that sounded like a cowboy riding a bucking horse. Still more rose. A few more notes and more cries began to be heard and more admirers began to leave their seats. Finally convinced there would be no carnage, R.J. broke full into the song.

The place went wild.

People began jumping around and yelling, throwing things in the air, dancing, and clapping. A surge charged toward R.J., pushing past our table, knocking our seats out of place so that we had to cower down and protect our precious drinks until the onslaught had stabilized. We then sat with a multitude of strange and exotic faces towering in close above us, unfamiliar body parts pressed against us, all alien sensory modes captivated by R.J., an hysteria that the Beatles or Elvis himself would have envied.

With great diligence, Danica and I wormed our way out of the alien menagerie of bodies and found seats on the side of the room away from Enuro's new superstar.

Danica looked over at me shaking her head. "It could only happen with him."

"Bernard Porre wanted us to make a good first impression," I replied.

"Well, this should be a feather in your cap then, Commander." Danica toasted me with her glass.

"Or another windmill yet slain." I returned her toast.

"What?" she asked.

"Oh, nothing. It's a long story."

"I'm thinking one of us should get back and check on the Griffin, Adrian."

"I'll go with you," I said. "There's no way we can get through that crowd to pay, but I have a feeling these drinks are on the house."

Shock Diamonds

"I'd like to have a bottle of this stuff."

"Yeah, tomorrow I'll barter with Lotho for a case."

As we rose to leave, R.J. was being carried by the crowd over to one of the stage platforms. He was lovingly placed upon it, and quickly resumed his medley to the continued delight of his new alien groupies.

We made our way without incident back to the Griffin's worksite and found the place as busy as ever. Lotho was overseeing work near the aft entrance. He stopped when he saw us.

"Did you enjoy the Caldron, Commander?"

"What is that blue stuff, Lotho?"

"It is a common denominator among many, many species. That is why it is always available here on Enuro. It is used for many social occasions."

"Could we get some of it to go?" asked Danica.

"I'll have a case of fifty bottles brought over tomorrow, compliments of the Enuro high council."

"Lotho, why don't I ever hear your technicians speaking to one another even when they are working together?"

"Why they have the implants, of course."

"Implants?"

"In the frontal lobe. Communication and data implants. They can access all design criteria and discuss it as necessary with each other simply by thought transfer."

I glanced at Danica. "We are very impressed, Lotho. Thank-you for everything."

"It is my pleasure indeed, Commander Tarn. If you will excuse me, the tail-section team is uncertain about something." He smiled, gave the impression of a bow, and headed aft.

"You know what gets me the most about this place?" said Danica, as we rode the automatic stairs up.

"Gee, there's so many possibilities."

"Well, the majority out there on the street are the cute little Enuronians, but there's an awful lot of other visiting species, as well. But the atmosphere walking along the streets is pretty much identical as if you were walking along Times Square. People are intent on getting where they're going. They seem to be preoccupied with the problems of the day. If you block out the alien faces, and plug in New Yorker faces in their place, it's the same. And if you think about it, there are some pretty strange creatures walking the sidewalks of New York, or Chicago, or Los Angeles, anyway. So it's like no different. No matter how strange the different species look, there's a certain familiarity to it all."

"Wow! Am I speaking with Sigmund Freud?"

"No. Really, don't you agree?"

E.R. Mason

"Yes, except what we see out there are only the species capable of interacting in this kind of community. From what I saw in the SID documents, there are others not so socially adaptable."

"Yeah, but we have those on Earth, too." Danica paused for a moment in thought. She refocused on me and her expression became strained. "Now that you mention it..."

"What?"

"I guess I need to get this out in the open sooner or later. You and R.J. are already suspicious. Maybe now's a good time."

As we entered the habitat module, she suddenly paused, then went back to her sleeper cell. She lifted her bed and drew out a brown, imitation-leather satchel. Back at the conference table, she placed it on the floor, hesitated for a moment as though she might change her mind, and finally unzipped it and drew out something the size of a melon wrapped in ash-colored terry cloth. She placed it on the center of the table between us, sat back and stared with a look of disdain, then looked at me as though she was again having second thoughts.

I tried to sound reassuring. "If you back down now, I'll go insane."

She gave a big sigh, reached out with one hand and gently peeled the terry cloth away.

It was an exquisitely crafted crystal skull. The soft lighting from the ship illuminated it within. Hazy reflections of light beamed out from the eyes, giving it an aura of power. There were glows from within that seemed to fade and change. It was a stunning thing to behold.

"Holy crap, Danica."

She seemed to remain as mesmerized as me, and said, "There's nothing holy about how I got it, unfortunately."

"You're not known for your thievery."

"I am now."

"You're kidding!"

"It was the only thing I could think of."

"Who did you steal it from?"

"Ever hear the name, Dorian Blackwell?"

"Maybe, but I can't get a handle just now."

"He was the primary investor in the construction of the Griffin."

"I've got it now. He ended up in prison for something."

"Off-world smuggling. He was, or I should say is, incredibly wealthy and powerful. It surprised most people that they were able to convict him." Danica squirmed in her seat. "The government confiscated the Griffin at the same time they arrested him. We were still flight-testing it at Bonneville at the time. But that's another story."

Shock Diamonds

"So maybe you'd better tell me the whole thing from the beginning."

"After Charles Rutan finished his design concept, he had a lot of trouble getting financing for the prototype you and I are now sitting in. He used up every lead he had and struck out. The accepted story is that he called in favors to get the Griffin built, but the truth is he ended up going to Blackwell. Blackwell had a questionable reputation. Maybe that description is too kind. When Blackwell finally got busted, there were rumors he had messed with classified technology, or something like that, something that set the government off so that they stepped in and locked him up on some kind of Earth security violation. Nobody really knows what it was about. Anyway, he served a lot of time and was released just about a year ago. The word is, this skull was secretly delivered to his estate before he got out. He is still a rich bastard. Two of his companies were still operating and his portfolio was pretty much intact, being carefully watched over by his lieutenants, you might say. He contacted me personally a few months ago. At first I thought it was just some kind of catch-up call. I expected him to ask about the Griffin, but he didn't. After the usual trivialities, he said he was calling because he needed a test pilot. One of his companies had just pumped out a new style of personal air vehicle. They were concerned about a technology leak in the company. Blackwell wanted a test pilot from outside to do the initial parking tests on the two prototypes. As you know, that's where you take the vehicle up to twenty feet or so, put it in park, then do every roll and spin you can think of to prove somebody's crazy teen can't crash the thing. You do that every day for a month, and then get certed for cross-country testing. I was kind of bored at the time, and the credits offered were generous, so I took the job on the condition it was temporary. That seemed to make ex-con Blackwell very happy. For the first week, the testing went just as expected. Sitting in that transparent eggshell was a blast. Blackwell began wanting daily reports over drinks at his place. He has a way of keeping you off balance like he's figured things out one step ahead of you. At first, I was worried about some kind of come-on, but the aura wasn't there. Finally, one day the subject of the Griffin came up. He kept it real casual, then changed the subject pretty quickly. But as the days went by, there were more and more incidental Griffin questions. Where was the ship now? What had they done to it? Who had control? He knew you by reputation. Next he began to talk about an upcoming trip he had planned outside the solar system. He thought I'd be the perfect pilot in command. He began to give himself away, making the trip sound like a spacewoman's dream. I kept my cards close to my chest. I began to see that he had ulterior motives. Finally, one day when he thought he had me in the palm of his hand, he brought out this skull. He said it was part of a major deal he had been making before being interrupted by the government and sent to prison. He said it was his most treasured possession. It's not crystal, by the way. It's diamond."

"My god, you're kidding!"

"Well, that's what he said one evening when he'd had too much. Anyway, as the PAV flight testing got near completion, I had to start thinking of ways to extricate myself from the world of Dorian Blackwell. I had no intention of going anywhere with him, even though he was convinced he had sold me his bill of goods. I had never agreed to any of it, but I had been afraid to deny him outright. A few days before the final test flight, we had our usual briefing drinks and he seemed a little more distracted than usual. He rambled on about needing a final piece for the skull. That night, during our talk, I fucked up. I said something about wanting to tie up some things at home and he picked right up on it. From that moment on, his attitude changed. We both began to pretend things were moving along as planned, but he was distant and trying to conceal it. He had obviously told me too much. I soon came to understand I had become more of a liability to him than an asset. It scared the hell out of me. I had gone from trying to strategically withdraw from his world to realizing my life was probably in danger. It was too late to agree to his trip and plans. As far as he was concerned, I could no longer be trusted."

"And there was nothing to go to the police with, either, was there?"

"Not a thing. That last week it became clear to me that I was either going to have an accident or just disappear on an involuntary, off-world trip. And even if I made a successful escape before then, his network would find me. I'd never be able to stop looking over my shoulder. I could think of only one thing that might protect me from him. I had to steal the diamond skull, his most prized, important possession. As long as I was the only one that knew where it was, he could not have me killed. I could make arrangements that if he laid a hand on me, it would be automatically turned over to the authorities with an explanation of what was going on, and that's about where I'm at now."

"But how could you possibly have gotten access to it? It must have been Fort Knox there."

"Easier than you would think. He'd never let it out of his sight. He kept it in a safe, in a safe-room. State-of-the-art alarm systems. It was impossible to get near the thing, except when he was with it. That was the weak link in the chain. You ever hear of a Caton lamp?"

"Can't say I have."

"It used to be that some people who looked directly at red light for too long became catatonic, particularly people with epilepsy. Some scientist eventually derived those same effects and engineered a lamp that can do the same thing to anyone. During one of Blackwell's debriefings, I secretly photographed the skull in 3-D. I emailed the images to a friend using an outside computer line. This friend had a crystal duplicate of the skull made. Every day, I had to make a five-mile trip to the flight testing facility. My friend flew in with the fake skull and a Canton emitter and met me on the road to the plant."

"Must've been a really good friend, Danica."

"Yeah. That's a whole other story. She's an engineer with a taste for murder mystery novels. When the time was right, I packed a small travel bag with the fake skull hidden inside and went to my usual meeting with Blackwell. I explained that an urgent matter had come up and I needed to leave to take care of it and return in the morning. I knew he wouldn't allow it. He was sitting with his skull, staring at it even more distracted than usual. I sat on his couch across from him with the Caton emitter pinned to my jacket as jewelry. When he angrily looked up at me and began complaining, I flashed him good. He sat there staring right at me while I switched skulls. He came out of it just as I folded my hands in my lap. I apologized and said I could probably get a friend to handle the problem. Otherwise, I'd let him know. He never knew any of it had happened. He just went back to staring at the fake skull as I left."

"I will never turn my back on you ever again. But how did you manage to get out of there in one piece?"

"Yeah, on the final test flight, I pre-inspected the vehicle the night before to be sure it hadn't been tampered with. I didn't think they'd do it that way anyhow. They really did need the cert on their PAVs. I hid all the stuff I needed aboard and at the next morning's test flight I climbed in with only standard test pilot gear so they wouldn't be suspicious. Then after all the rolling and flipping was done, instead of lowering back down, I took off like a bat out of hell. I had an airplane prepped and waiting for me at a nearby airport. Dumped off their PAV right there, and headed for Cape Canaveral. Never did get paid."

"So what's the rest of the plan?"

Danica's face went blank. Finally she said, "To be determined."

"Well, at least we have seven trillion miles to figure it out."

"I'm not sure that's enough," she said uneasily.

"One thing I don't get."

"Which thing is that?"

"The Griffin questions Blackwell kept asking you. Were you thinking that the Griffin is somehow connected to this skull?"

"I don't know, but maybe. The skull was his main thing. I think I was brought there to answer questions about the Griffin, not because an outside test pilot was needed. Maybe he had plans for the Griffin, and he needed someone who knew how to fly it. I'm really sorry about getting you involved in this thing, Adrian. I didn't know where else to turn."

"Maybe you did me a favor. Maybe I'm getting a heads-up that bad guys will come calling."

"Blackwell seemed frustrated about that last piece he needed for the skull. That's got something to do with all of it, but that's all I know."

"To quote a famous prophet, 'These people sound like a wretched hive of scum and villainy. We must be cautious.'"

Danica gave a hesitant laugh. "We need to hide this thing real good."

"I have just the place."

Most aircraft and spacecraft use the space under the pilot's seat for storage. Being the shifty character I have come to be, I took the time to improve upon that in the Griffin. I left enough space beneath the seat to give the impression of a proper storage compartment but sectioned off the area that extended below the flight deck floor. I created a pressure cover with four real pressure bolts and twenty fake bolt heads. On the cover plates I engraved the words "DANGER GEAR HYDRAULIC PRESSURE WELL. NO ACCESS." In smaller print, I added instructions for removal of the cover, instructions that would take any normal man a good eight hours to comply with. In reality, the cover can be removed very quickly with just the four bolts, and it was there we hid what was undoubtedly the most valuable diamond known to man.

Chapter 7

By 03:00 hours, two of my crewmen had still not returned from the Cistern. I sat, a worried mother, slouched at the conference table sipping black coffee, my mouth still asking for the blue drink. I was having trouble deciding who to worry about the most, R.J. or Wilson.

The forward airlock door remained open. Just as I was deciding to go in search of them, there finally came the sound of a ruckus outside. I made it to the door in time to see Wilson and four or five Norsican buddies staggering through the security dome screen, some singing, some chanting, all holding on to each other for balance. Wilson was in the middle, a large heavily engraved mug held high in one hand, his other arm draped around the shoulder of a very merry Norsican companion. They sang their way to the stairs, and stopped and looked up at me, swaying silently together in unison. The biggest of the bunch gathered his gusto and called out in slurred overtones, still honestly translated by my earplugs. "Captain, we are returning this warrior for proper duty. He is worthy of honor guard and minstrel. We salute you, sir and the fine crew of the….." He looked at his companions, still swaying.

Wilson blurted out, "Griffffinnnn."

"Fine crew of the starship, Griffffin."

With that, the Norsican seemed to forget the context of what he'd been saying.

Wilson's teetering head looked up at me and then back at them and they all broke out in such laughter the whole bunch nearly fell in a heap. Only their obvious experience with such inebriation allowed two of them to support the others enough to prevent the collapse. Before I could respond to their salute, a flurry of backslapping and celebration broke out and the troop separated and wavered away in a resumed chorus of some Norsican victory chant, as Wilson teetered unsupported below, one hand on the rail, the other raising his mug to them as they disappeared through the security curtain.

To my surprise, he made it up the moving stairs. Onboard, he swayed, handed me his irreverently carved mug of very naked alien women, then fell forward toward the sleeper compartments. Once there, I turned him to face the correct cell and tapped the open button. He fell in, instantly asleep, butt sticking out so that I had to lift his legs inside to close the compartment.

That left R.J.

Ten minutes later, a new entourage arrived.

The three females that were holding him up were no more than four feet tall. They were blue-skinned and wore form-fitting violet suits that looked like wet suits except they were adorned with wonderful designs of luminous colors. They had Spock ears and tiny mouths below pert little noses. Their eyes were dark and inviting. In place of hair, they had such delightful indefinable patterns of dull color that I could not tell if it was a form of tattoo or natural markings. Overall, each of them was so cute, they were nearly irresistible. Their appearance made you want to hug one or all and take them home and keep them forever. They seemed to know every man felt that way about them.

To say R.J. was disheveled would have been an understatement. His hair was thoroughly messed up and rose upward in a shape that could have almost been described as the Eiffel tower. His facial expression was that of a drunken Stan Laurel. He did not seem certain of where he was. His flight suit was crumpled and wrinkled and looked like someone else had put it on him. The right side of his mouth seemed to be stuck in a half-smile.

None of the cute little women spoke. They gently rode up the stairs with him and patiently waited for me to take over. They paused for a very long smile, then one of them came forward and handed me a fancy flat black case the size of a tablet. I opened it to find a set of twelve perfectly-cut matching diamonds. I looked up at them, not understanding, and somehow without speaking they conveyed to me that it was payment for R.J.'s music. With a final set of seductive smiles, they turned and hurried away. I guided the non-communicative R.J. to his center sleeper cell and helped him in. His eyes were still open, staring at the ceiling, the half-smile still locked on his face as the compartment door slid closed.

The Enuro sun was rising in the south. Work on the underbelly of the Griffin had continued through the night with only occasional noise from below deck. With my wayfaring crew securely tucked in, I finally began to think about my own sleeper cell. Coffee had not seemed to diminish the lingering effects of the Enuro blue. As I looked in on the flight deck, the noise of someone stirring behind me interrupted my instrument checks. Danica, in pink silk pajamas, came forward rubbing her eyes.

"I don't know what was in the blue stuff, Adrian, but I slept like a log. How about you?"

"I'll let you know as soon as I sleep."

"What? Aren't the..."

"Just now, the last of them anyway."

"Dad stayed up all night worrying?"

"The Norsicans brought back one. Three little blue elves, the other."

"Geeez.... Were they...?"

"Just a bit."

"The work went on all night?"

"Enuronian technicians apparently never stop. With your approval, the ship is yours. I shall now acquiesce to the effects of the blue stuff."

"Sweet dreams."

I awoke that evening to find Danica busying herself running navigation checks on the flight deck while Wilson sat sheepishly looking at me from the conference table with his Norsican mug steaming with Earth-standard coffee. On the counter in the galley was a four-foot high case of Enuro blue. There was no sign of R.J.

"Is he still in his cell?" I asked Wilson, pointing over my shoulder with a thumb.

"Uh-huh."

"Have either of you checked on him?"

"Uh-uh."

I went to R.J.'s sleeper cell compartment and tapped gently on the door. At first there was no response. After the third try a muffled voice trying to whisper through the panel answered. "Yeah, what?"

"You okay? You need anything?"

"Just a little hung over, Adrian. Let me sleep it off, okay?"

"Okay, sorry to disturb you."

That was all I got. I went back and sat with Wilson, still sporting his boyishly guilty face. "He's okay, isn't he?"

"I think so. It's not like him, though."

"Well, everybody's got to turn loose sometime."

"What about you? Conquer and loot any villages last night?"

"Those guys were something else. They said they're from some place called Barbium Prime. They're a Chancellor's forward guard, on leave. We ended up at this combat sim place underground. By the way, the underground city is four times bigger than what you see up here. That's where the real action is. Can you believe I fought hand to hand with a hologram that

73

E.R. Mason

felt solid? We should have that on Earth to train our special ops guys."

"Sounds like you won us some allies, maybe?"

"I wouldn't want them as enemies. I'll tell you that."

Later that night, with everyone else sacked out, I began to be concerned about R.J. again, but was hesitant to knock on his cell. I paced around checking things, looking his way. At about 1:00 A.M. I heard a thump against his cell door, and finally couldn't stand it any longer. I winced and tapped. This time a voice answered right away.

"Wait, let me call up the habitat cam. Oh. Adrian, is anyone else with you?"

"Just me, who slept too long today and can't get back to sleep."

"Wait a minute." After a few moments, his sleeper cell door scrolled upward. There in all his glory was R.J., with a smoking pipe in his mouth, a tablet in one hand, wearing a standard issue tan flight suit. There was one other thing that was different. R.J. was as blue as a robin's egg.

"What the...!"

"Yeah, yeah. And I bugged you about reading the SIDs before we got here."

"You're quite a beautiful blue, R.J."

"See? That's why I can't come out. I'll get an endless amount of innuendos like that one."

"Is this...."

"No, of course it's not permanent. It should clear up tomorrow."

"But you were with three of them. You didn't..."

"Never mind that. It doesn't matter how many you're with. It just takes twenty-four to forty-eight hours to clear up."

"Why, you dog. I didn't know you had it in you."

"Don't speak of this to anyone. I'm just in here with a hangover. It's embarrassing enough as it is. I wouldn't have told you except I knew you'd be insisting."

"If it makes you feel any better, in case you don't remember, I was there when they delivered you. Those tiny women were extremely intoxicating."

"Try drinking that blue Culatta with them."

"You're not automatically married or anything, are you?"

"Oh, for god's sake, no."

"You can't blame me for asking."

"Well, if I were you, I'd keep a short rein on Wilson. If this can happen to someone like me, imagine how he'd end up."

"So when will you stick your head out of the gopher hole?"

"Tomorrow around noon."

Shock Diamonds

"I'll tell everyone I spoke with you tonight and you're fine."

"Anyway, I've been watching them work on the ship on some of the below-deck monitors. They are incredible."

"Agreed."

"Any problems with the ship?"

"Just that same radar interference in the tail. Otherwise, we should be leaving on schedule."

"Okay, I'm gonna close down now in case somebody suddenly gets up. I'll see you tomorrow."

"That sure is a nice shade of blue."

"Oh, shut up." R.J. banged the key and his sleeper cell door dropped down.

The next morning, the three of us foraged around finding space in stores for the fifty bottles of Culatta Blue. R.J. finally emerged from his hibernation. He milled around, casting wary glances at his crew mates, worried they might detect the faint remnants of his blue-man experience. Although most of the blue had subsided, there was a faint aura of it about him, though no one seemed to notice except him and me.

We held a short crew meeting in which it was agreed that from now on, all excursions into the world of Enuro would be made using the buddy system. No one offered any objections. Over the next few days, we took turns exploring the arcane, perplexing world around us, both on the surface and below. There were so many structures of such abstract architecture; it was impossible to get comfortable on any given tour, an awkwardness enhanced by the many individuals of equally absurd physiology that continually passed by.

By week's end, we had learned many things. Fortunately, there were no further instances of blue skin tone, changes in eye color, or spontaneous fights to the death. But by the end of it we were all ready to get back into space. When Lotho finally declared the project complete and handed me a memory module with all the pertinent artificial gravity system documentation, there was a great sentiment of relief throughout the ship. People busied themselves stowing gear, whether it was needed or not.

Enuro provided for an odd departure. There was no Orbital or Space Traffic Control System. Ascent was based solely on our ship's navigation and collision avoidance system. It kept the attention of all four of us strapped in on the flight deck. We went directly to high orbit, then jumped out after only a single loop around.

It took a full two days to acclimate to a Griffin with gravity. We still did some things required in zero G even though they were no longer needed. The magnetic playing cards were a nui-

75

sance and had to be exchanged for Wilson's regular ones. The magnetic seats in the habitat module had to be turned off because they were annoying. Galley facilities had to be switched to gravity mode. Our sleeper cells seemed slightly less comfortable. Standing at the portals to look out at the stars felt strange. The comment, "Man, this is weird," was repeated regularly. Some of us tended to grab onto things as we went, even though we did not need to.

On day three of the trip, I sat up front in the left seat, talking with Danica.

"So, what is your plan for when we get home?"

"I don't know," she replied.

"Well, what you gonna do?"

"I was hoping you'd have a suggestion."

"Are you absolutely sure the man has murder or something on his mind?"

"I'm sorry to get you involved in this."

"As I said, if he's asking questions about the Griffin, I was already involved and just didn't know it. Probably wouldn't have seen that coming. Besides, anyone threatening you, if you hadn't told me I'd have really been pissed off, girl."

"I've been worried this whole trip he'd show up in a spacecraft somehow."

"So I guess we better come up with something good. When do you think he'll figure out his skull is a fake?"

"There's no way to tell, Adrian. He meditates to the thing several hours a day like he's trying to get it to do something, but it never works. Maybe he won't even figure it out."

"Even so, he'll still be coming after you, right?"

"Of that I'm certain. His henchmen are either looking for me right now or waiting for me to return."

"Any chance it could all blow over?"

"I doubt it. The bastard is not that kind of person."

"How about if I had a word or two with him?"

"You'd never get that close, and you'd be added to the list."

"So how about we hide you real good, and then bring certain authorities into this?"

"Who you got in mind?"

"Some friends in the agency's security division. They've got connections."

"But the bastard hasn't done anything yet."

"Yeah, we'll have to play out line and get him to make a mistake."

"Or we could just take the Griffin away somewhere we couldn't be found."

"And start a new life?"

"Very funny. I meant just hide out for a while. Maybe the asshole will get busted and thrown back in jail. I wouldn't be surprised."

"How 'bout we make that plan B?"

"From outer space?"

"It's a classic."

"Where would I hang?"

"With me, in disguise."

"I heard you got a thing going on with a doctor. Won't that get too cozy?"

"I don't know if I've got a thing going on or not. She is a real wild card, that one."

"Don't tell me you've met your match?"

"Well, with this one, even if she does have a thing for a guy, she might just kill him."

"She's a doctor, right?"

"Yeah, that sometimes smokes, and sometimes wrecks your car at one hundred and seventy miles an hour."

"I believe I'm starting to like this woman."

"My god, now that I think about it, the two of you may be related."

"When can I meet this person?"

"No one on Earth ever really knows where she'll be at any given time, probably not even her. Anyway, in the meantime, we'll get you a good wig, sunglasses, and other adornments to turn you into my latest love interest. Then you will never go anywhere alone. Either R.J., Wilson, or I must be there. As soon as we get a lead, we'll turn it around and put my friends on them and they will be the prey instead of the predators."

"Well, that makes me feel a little better, even though I'll be a kept woman."

"Maybe we can do some digging and find something out about your diamond skull and that other thing Mr. Blackwell is trying to get his hands on."

"So we're going to need to bring the other guys in on this. You may want to break out the skull for that."

"R.J. is a genius on these kinds of problems. He comes up with the damnedest stuff. I'll be interested to hear what he thinks."

"Well, you guys are the best bet I've got. Let's do it. I sure hate this."

We switched primary control to the left pilot position, and under Danica's watchful eye I removed the wrapped diamond skull from under my seat. I walked it back to the conference table and set it there, motioning R.J. and Wilson to join me. They took seats with matching captivated stares.

I unwrapped the skull, set it on table center, and told the intriguing tale of how our crew mate's life seemed to be in imminent danger, and what I planned to do about it. R.J. could not resist. As I spoke, he took up the skull and began examining it, millimeter by millimeter.

"Holy crap, this isn't crystal, you know."

"Yeah it is, I've seen one of those in a Mayan artifact museum," said Wilson.

"I beg to differ, Compadre. This is diamond. One very large chunk of diamond. You won't find such a thing on Earth. This could only form on a giant body somewhere outside our system. This is not from Earth."

"No kidding?" said Wilson.

"Not only that, this is not representative of a human skull."

"Why do you say that?" I asked.

"The indentations on the temple and the parietal and occipital regions are too large. Also, beside the indentations, the frontal area is too pronounced."

"He's bullshitting us, Adrian. How can you possibly know this crap, R.J.?" demanded Wilson.

"Ah, yes, to study flight dynamics or battlefield strategy is such a natural undertaking, but if one chooses to consider something as basic and natural as human anatomy, oh look out. It's something more basic than any science, evolution created from the ground we walk on before time began, yet to delve into it is considered an anomaly to present day human nature..."

"Oh my god, we've lost him," said Wilson. "It's my fault. I'm sorry."

"Easy, R.J. It was a compliment, not a slam on Earth science."

"What? A compliment, you say? In that case let me add that this representation of a hominid cranium was not constructed by any means known to us."

"Why do you say that?" asked Wilson.

R.J. pushed himself up and drew a hand scanner from a drawer within his engineering station. He began scanning the skull in green-beam mode. "Yep, just as I thought, irregular atomic alignment and quantum..."

I jumped up and yelled, "R.J., your scanner is smoking!"

I was too late. The scanner erupted into small jets of flame and flew from his grasp as he shook it away. The device bounced off the table and slid on the galley floor, still on fire, emitting sparks, and leaving a trail of smoke. Wilson sprang into action, stomping the thing until the fire was beaten into crumpled ash. We stood there dumbfounded, looking at the electronic corpse and the diamond skull that had apparently destroyed it.

Danica called back from the flight deck. "What the hell is going on back there? You've set off a smoke indicator on my panel."

"It's okay, Danica. A scanner caught fire but it's out. There's no danger."

"What the hell are you guys doing?"

Wilson picked up the scanner remains by one charred wire, looked over at us for objections, and then dropped it in the galley disposal unit. We regrouped around the skull and took our seats where Danica could see and hear us on monitors.

"Well, that was unexpected," said R.J.

"If that's what it does to a hand scanner, what the hell would happen if you fired a sidearm at it?" asked Wilson as he eyed the thing warily.

It set R.J. off again. "Oh, yeah. There goes the military mind. A beautiful diamond artifact, an exquisitely sculptured idol perhaps millions of years old, and the first thing you guys start thinking about is what kind of weapon is needed to destroy it."

"Easy, R.J. Easy. It was just a joke," said Wilson.

"What were you starting to say before the scanner roasting?" I asked.

R. J. wiped his hands on the legs of his flight suit, looked at them, and wiped some more. "This skull is not a simple sculpture from diamond. The scanner confirmed that before it torched."

"Go on..." I begged.

"It is an artificial construct. From subatomic up."

"How do you artificially recreate something that takes millions of years under pressure to form?"

"You don't. You take something that has formed over millions of years, and you modify it."

"Modify how?"

"You redistribute the subatomic patterns within it."

"For what purpose?"

"In this case, I have no idea. All I know is that the subatomic structure is not linear. It is a maze of billions of patterns, rather than the nice orderly rows of molecules that are normal in this type of crystalline product."

"You're saying this skull does something but you don't know what?" asked Wilson.

"Well, it destroys scanners, for one thing."

"Can you theorize what it does, R.J.?" I asked.

"Let me have it for a while. I'll see what I can come up with."

E.R. Mason

"You think that's safe?" asked Wilson. "We don't wanna be floatin' home later."

"I'll use single pulse scans so I'll know if anything upsets it. That scanner problem may have just been from reflection or something."

I stood at the table and nodded to him. "Go slow, R.J. Real slow. And if you go data searching, keep it inside the ship. We don't want anyone picking up any data streams and finding out we're interested in that thing, you know?"

Back in my seat on the flight deck, Danica waited for me to begin the conversation. "So that thing is not simply art. Did you get a good enough look through the monitors at what happened?"

She looked at me with a wrinkled brow. "You really think the skull destroyed that scanner?"

"It sure looked like it. I have a hunch R.J.'s relentless brain will come up with a whole lot more about it. In the meantime, at least everybody's signed up for the Danica guardian angels plan."

"When they're not back there setting fire to stuff, you mean?"

"Hey, we're men. It's what we do."

The final day of our return trip brought new mumbling from Wilson about his situation with Jeannie and her seemingly non-returnable engagement ring. R.J. had spent every waking moment studying his newfound nemesis, the diamond skull. He was completely consumed by it, but would only confirm to us that it was designed to do something. He did not know what. He had found nothing in library records, which only made him all the more intrigued. I had to practically pull it from his grasp to return it to the designated hiding place before landing. At the Terran outer rim, we reported to Earth's Lunar Receiving Station and were cleared for a 218.44 Earth orbital insertion and parking. A dedication ceremony going on at the Space Center made air traffic unusually heavy.

The plan was, after landing, only three of us would disembark. Danica would remain on board. If unfriendly eyes were on us, we wanted to give the impression she had not been a part of the crew, or if she had, she did not return with us. Crew manifests are never made public without agency approval. Dorian Blackwell would have to pull some pretty long strings to get that kind of information out of the Flight Planning Group.

When we finally touched down late in the evening, we did so with Wilson in the left seat, just in case. Jeannie was waiting at the gate. We left Wilson to his dilemma, though the passionate exchange immediately following their reunion suggested there was no dilemma at all.

R.J. and I pulled the cover from the Vette, and before letting him off, I gave a stern second lecture about searching the net for diamond skulls. It was certain Blackwell would have triggers set up for such things. R.J. scoffed and complained that was obvious. I watched him trudge toward his apartment and resisted the urge to make any remarks about avoiding blue women.

As I pulled into my hex-plex, something shocking made me stop short. There was a familiar-looking PAV parked outside. I crept around back, cursed at finding the back door unlocked, and peered inside warily. There was no one. Stealthing through the kitchen, I looked into the living room and found the good Doctor Catherine Adara sitting on the couch, her feet up, drink in hand, watching cartoons on the main video screen.

With appropriate indignation, I stepped into the room and tried to sound displeased. "How did you get in here? Didn't I lock the back door?"

"I heard you sneaking around out there. I was afraid you'd get scared and leave. How'd I get in? Screw driver. Oh yeah, I broke a little piece of wood off the door. I'll get it fixed."

"My God!"

"Oh, don't get your panties all in a wad again. I polished off your bottle of bourbon, and left dirty towels on the floor by the shower, too. What're you going to do, spank me?"

"It's a thought."

"Women's college wrestling coach for three years. Take your best shot."

And with no further discussion I did, though no spankings were achieved.

The next morning, we sat staring at each other across the kitchen table, scarfing down the eggs and sausage she had demanded I make.

"I thought you weren't supposed to be back or something like that."

"Nobody was waiting again when you returned from this mission of yours. I thought this would be good remedial psychology."

"Like the PTSD treatment?"

"Worked, didn't it?"

"So all that stuff about you needing to just get me out of your system so you wouldn't have any doubts, that was all bullcrap."

"Nope. That was real."

"So now it's safe to be around me, 'cause you're comfortable that there's no real attraction going on?"

"How's the wrist? I couldn't get a look at it last night. You were banging around so. I see there's no bandage. It should be completely healed by now."

"Did you just avoid my question?"

"Did I? Or did I answer it?"

"What are you saying?"

"I need another month. It's highly unusual, just a technicality, actually."

"Is that because you were unsuccessful in killing me last time?"

"As I recall, I was successful in everything I did last time, except for one thing."

"Dismissing me?"

"Unfortunately, yes."

"Maybe that's your own special neurosis. If you can't convince yourself someone's unworthy of you, you kill them to take care of the uncertainty. You know, kind of like a black widow?"

"I like the comparison, but no."

"By the way, I need to go rescue a woman."

"To what kind of woman are you referring?"

"One who apparently already likes you, figure that."

"You've told your friends about me? How flattering."

"Yes. I've given them instructions in the event of my death."

"So where must we go to perform this rescue of a damsel in distress?"

"The KSC Visitor Complex. It's time to go, as a matter of fact."

"You have to go to the Kennedy Space Center Visitor Complex? Isn't that like an airline pilot touring an airport?"

"Can you be discreet when we get there? This is a clandestine operation."

"Let's take my PAV, then. It'll be slightly less conspicuous than a black '95 Corvette."

We dropped into the PAV parking area at 10:15, just in time to catch the first VIP bus tour. I wore standard tourist clothing of loud Hawaiian design, a Yankees ball cap backward, dark glasses above an unshaven face. It seemed an adequate deception. Christine wore the same beige silk blouse and light-blue stretch slacks that I had wrestled off of her the night before. She has the unusual talent of wearing makeup too heavy and making it look as though it needs to be smeared by some virulent male.

As the tour bus took us by the Spacecraft Processing Facility, a bit of uplift kicked in knowing the Griffin was in one of the center hangars. We blended in with the crowd for the foot tour inside the VAB, where they never fail to boast about how weather forming inside such a large structure requires special environmental control to prevent rain and even lightning.

As our group passed by the far end of the open hangar, Catherine and I hesitated by a hallway door marked "NO ADMITTANCE" until Danica, wearing street clothes, a large sun hat of R.J.'s, and dark glasses emerged to join us. We reboarded the bus and quietly enjoyed the rest of our tour.

In the good doctor's PAV, our disguises were quickly shed.

"My god, is that just one day's beard stubble?" asked Danica with a smirk.

Catherine tapped the side stick on the PAV, pointed us away from the Center, and responded, "It's great for facial micro abrasion, but it can irritate the more sensitive areas."

"Well, how do you avoid that then?" asked Danica.

"You just don't," said Catherine.

"I guess the rest of him is just as coarse anyway," said Danica.

"How did you know?"

"He doesn't realize it, but I saw him naked in the spacecraft shower once."

"Oh my God," I blurted out in protest.

"We should exchange impressions sometime," said Catherine.

"I'm Danica, by the way."

"Catherine Donoro, Danica. I understand you like me."

"I've heard that men often find you intimidating. I like that."

"We must go shopping, Danica."

"Oh, I need to badly. What little I have with me had to be left aboard the Griffin."

"It's settled then."

I sat silently with a look of helpless despair on my face, wondering how I would survive with these two women in my home.

Chapter 8

The return to my modest hex-plex brought a great deal more settling in than expected. There was even some unauthorized redecorating. Although I did not completely understand how it had occurred, I was suddenly living with two very independent women. After dropping us off, Catherine made a quick trip to the nearest Worldmart to "pick up a few things." She returned with what seemed like the average load limit for any four-seat PAV. The unloading of it brought a celebration of women dividing things up. I was ordered out back to revive the barbecue grill.

There is a strange social chemistry that occurs when a lone human male finds himself amid multiple associates of the opposite sex. Suddenly he is required to converse with far less frequency. In fact, in most cases he is cued as to when his input would be appropriate. Daring to make an offering to any particular subject matter without such cuing can be fraught with danger. Fortunately, when the male does throw caution to the wind and speaks, in most cases he receives a protective screen from the female nearest him, thereby avoiding any verbal transgressions that might otherwise upset the group.

So, having ensured we were all stuffed with the barbeque of choice, and additionally contented with drinks of an intoxicating nature, I sat on my couch, head moving back and forth like a spectator at a tennis match, trying to keep up with the exchange from these two women who had somehow inherited my home. After a respectable amount of restraint, I was eventually able to find a rare pause long enough to assert myself and bring the topic of Danica's problem to the floor. It sobered the mood, and when Danica had finished explaining it to Catherine, she gave the first expression of true concern I had ever seen from her. There was enough finality in the recounting that it actually caused an extended moment of silence between us followed by a lingering sense of fear within the group. Faced with my first chance to take control of the conversation, I abruptly realized I had nothing to add.

The doorbell rang, causing all of us to jump a few inches off our seats.

No one was expected.

I rose slowly, placed one finger against my lips, then went quickly to my bedroom and into the master bath. Long ago, I installed a false wall in the walk-in closet there, with a full-length mirror as the access point. I pushed in on the mirror, leaned in and grabbed three small sidearms from the nearest shelf and made my way back to the women, handing each one of them a weapon. I wondered only for a second about Catherine's ability to handle a gun. She took it with all the familiarity of a well-trained marksman, quickly dispelling any doubts.

I tucked mine in behind and looked out each window. There were no unidentified vehicles parked anywhere nearby, no one with an engine running.

At the front door, I stood to one side and called out. "Who is it?"

There was a dull thump against the door and no response.

Wrong answer.

"Who's there?"

A mumbled reply came through, incomprehensible.

"One more time, please. Who is it?"

This time the mumble had a drunken slur to it, still not coherent.

I opened the door a crack, still standing aside. Usually at that point they will crash the party, and open fire on everyone in sight.

Nothing happened.

I made a very quick check and backed away. A single person stood outside the door. He was not protecting himself. The flash glance suggested it was a homeless man looking for handouts.

"You just needing a few credits, buddy?"

"Pacshess, aa yur sersic."

He was too good a drunk to be an act. I slowly opened the door and shook my head at the sight of the dirty, unshaven, greasy-haired man braced with one hand against the door jamb, still swaying at the edge of the envelope. Finally, one of the knees gave way and he started down.

I caught him under the leading shoulder and winced at the thought of what I might be wiping on myself from the dirty tan scrub he was wearing. The thought that perhaps he was some medical assistant exposing me to unknown pathogens abruptly made me hurry and drag him inside. I sat him at the kitchen table. He slumped over, his head down against one dirty bare arm. I looked up to see both women peering around the door, wide-eyed, with their guns drawn. I blurted out a rude, hearty laugh. I couldn't help it.

Catherine responded with a "tsk" sound.

"I don't believe he's a threat, ladies, except for the possibility of germ warfare."

The two lowered their weapons and came into the kitchen.

"Did you relock the front door?" asked Danica.

"Of course."

"Sorry. I had to ask."

"I agree."

Catherine plunked her weapon down on a counter and went to the unconscious man. Suddenly she was no longer the irreverent, rebellious she-devil. In an instant, she had metamorphosed into a doctor. She gently lifted the man's dirty head, and with the touch of a surgeon pulled back one eyelid.

"This is no joke, Adrian. This is serious. This man's way past dehydrated. Alcohol poisoning to boot. We need to get him to an emergency room, right away."

Before I could offer, the man's eyelids fluttered. "Nooo! No ergency room. No damn doctors. I em a docker, for Christ's sake." His head rolled around in Catherine's grip. He managed to open his eyes wide enough to look me in mine. A spike of fear shot through me. I stepped back and stared in disbelief.

"No way!"

Catherine looked up at me in wonder. "What? What is it?"

"Patrick?"

His head continued to tilt to one side. "Adian?"

"Oh my god! What the hell?"

I hurried around the table and began lifting him. "Let's get him on the couch. Danica, would you get some stuff to clean him up a little. Cath, what can we do for him, right now, right here?"

"I have a kit in the PAV. I'll get it."

We worked on the patient as furiously as any triage team would have. The clothes were too dirty for the inside trash. I had to stealthily take them outside, watching the shadows for Danica assassins. Danica had the patient in a pair of my golf pajamas by the time I returned, while Dr. Donoro was performing miracles I wouldn't have thought possible. Somehow, she had fashioned an old-style intravenous tube and bag and was giving the last of several injections as I arrived beside her.

"How bad?" I asked.

"We'll need twenty or thirty minutes to know if this is life-threatening. You own a BP tester, don't you?"

"Yeah."

"Get it."

"Why didn't you ask for it sooner?"

"I can tell his BP with my fingers, dummy. But the tester's a lot easier."

"Oh, okay."

When the situation began to settle, we gathered around, staring down at the sleeping patient, my newest tenant.

"Okay, what's it all about?" asked Catherine.

"Ladies, let me introduce Doctor Patrick Pacell, chief medical officer from the Starship Electra. Most of the last few times I saw him, I was staring up at him, instead of down."

"So I take it he's a close friend, someone we can trust?" asked Danica.

"I'd have to say I owe my life to him several times over. R.J. can tell you."

"Adrian tends to have close relationships with his doctors," mused Catherine.

"From what I've seen, he probably has quite a few," replied Danica.

"Ladies, please! The patient! Cath, he didn't want a hospital. Are we going to be okay with this?"

"If he gets through the next hour or so, we'll only have to worry about the detox effects. I have stuff for that, but there's no way to know how long he's been alcoholic."

"Should I like make some black coffee or something?"

"Oh yeah, sure. Let's pour some acid into his stomach. That'll help."

"Sorry! I don't know about these things."

"It's alright, Darling. We know you're a professional patient, not a healer."

"You guys are cruel. I'm going and change my shirt."

On a previous mission, R.J. had worked with Dr. Pacell just as closely as I. When I phoned him and told him what was going on, the line went dead without a goodbye. Twenty minutes later, there was the sound of his trusty restored Corvair pulling into the driveway.

The four of us milled around the living room, speaking in quiet tones, watching over our unexpected and troubled friend. Catherine hovered over him at regular intervals, causing the rest of us to stop whatever we were doing and watch. Her expressions of concern softened with each check, giving us all a reason for hope.

Danica sat at the living room computer station, running a search engine. It worried me. I brought a stool over and sat beside her. "So back to your situation. When we last left our heroine, she had made Blackwell's last test flight, then stole the test vehicle and took off for a nearby airport. She ditched

Blackwell's vehicle there and made off in her own aircraft. Where'd she go from there, again?"

"I flew in to Merritt Island and hid out in a Denny's, where I read your email about the Enuro trip, which seemed like a blessing, the perfect way to hide. I got a taxi to Badge and ID, and you know the rest from there."

"Did you file a flight plan to Florida?"

"Of course not. Not with him on my ass."

"So he's probably filed charges against you for stealing his prototype, right? He'll get the authorities to help track you down."

"That's what I've been sitting here searching. I haven't found any police reports or criminal justice references associated with Blackwell or his company. It doesn't look like he's filed anything at all."

"Then he must not want to call attention to himself. Plus, if he did file charges, and then something bad suddenly happened to you..."

"All I know is if he figures out his skull is a fake, he'll go through the roof."

"What's our liability here? Who can Blackwell reach out and touch to get control of you? Can he get to your family?"

"Doubtful. My mother passed away several years ago. My father is in a full care facility for Alzheimer's. Not much they can do to me there."

"Close friends?"

"A few, but I'm in the air or space so much, I don't see any of them often. He could try to leverage one of them, but he'd know it would be a weak play at best. All he would get is a whole lot of that unwanted attention."

"So he wants to silence you, and really the only way is to come find you."

"No charges filed for running off with his prototype PAV. He must have something in the works."

Before we could continue, Patrick Pacell finally began to stir. It was almost midnight. At first there was only the head turning with blurry-eyed stares of confusion. That was followed by cracked-voice, incoherent questions to no one in particular about what was going on, and where he was this time.

I pulled a chair over to the couch and sat. Almost immediately, R.J. appeared next to me. Patrick squinted up at me. A shaky hand came up and wiped his unshaven face. "Adrian, I'm sorry."

"I'm not, Patrick. What the hell is going on?"

He tilted his head over and finally noticed R.J. "R.J., what are you doing here? Am I hallucinating again?"

"No, Kemosabe. It is I, R.J. Smith, your trusty errand boy from days in space past."

Pacell tried to push himself up, but his arm strength failed him. "Water?"

Catherine appeared next to me with a glass of cold water complete with straw. She handed it to him but held it as he drank. He wiped his mouth once more and this time managed to push himself up just a bit. "Where am I?"

"My place, Patrick. Looks to me like you just made it."

He looked at Catherine, and then the water, and gestured for more. When he had drunk, he asked, "Who are you?"

"Dr. Catherine Adara, at your service, Dr. Pacell."

"Thank-you, Doctor."

"I need to ask, how deep into the bottle are you?"

"No, no, just this week or so, I think. When I finally gave up all hope, I was looking for a way out. It worked...for a while."

"So the withdrawals can be managed then."

"How long have I been here?"

I pulled the cover back up to his neck. "A few hours. Do you feel well enough to tell me how the most eminent physician in the fleet ends up wrecked on my couch?"

"I'm sorry, Adrian. I shouldn't have come. There's nothing anyone can do. It's not fair to you."

"As I've said, Patrick, as far as I can tell, you are exactly where you need to be. Now at least give me a hint. What's going on?"

He looked around and noticed Danica facing us from the computer station seat.

"Do you need some privacy to talk about this? Should I clear the room of these other misfits?"

He looked up at Catherine and reached for the water once more. He spoke with hesitancy, his voice still broken and hoarse. "It's something the whole world should hear about. It's a new kind of hell."

"Why don't you start at the beginning?"

"My daughter, Adrian. I watched them take her and there wasn't a damn thing I could do about it."

"Who? Who took Emma?"

Pacell pushed himself up more and suddenly noticed the intravenous tube and bag. "Whoa, what the..., Doctor...what was it?"

"Adara, Catherine Adara. You're welcome."

He turned his attention back to me. "The Children of Caelestra. You think some of the Earth-based cults are bad? Imagine one from another world. Magic tricks you can't imagine. Strange and beautiful people surround you. Sales pitches designed to work on any species. Of course these individuals are all close to God. They're from outer space."

Patrick was interrupted by a raspy cough. He took more water and shook his head. "So you try to convince your daughter that it looks like a real bad deal all wrapped up in Christmas paper with ribbon and bows, but kids are so sure they know more than their outdated parents these days. Then the bastards pick one particularly compatible alien to begin the romance phase and the human target doesn't stand a chance. Add to it the off-world drugs, delivered in a variety of innocent ways, and what chance does a father have against it? God, if only she wasn't eighteen. I could have ordered her to come home for a reality check, but I didn't even have that."

The cough kicked back in. Patrick tilted his head forward in his hand. His face became flushed. Catherine interceded. "That's too much, too soon. By morning, he should be strong enough to talk. Right now I have his headache medicated away but it's still there and it's catching up. He's got to lie back and be quiet." She gently pushed him down into the pillows. She checked his pulse as he drifted back into unconsciousness. R.J. and I pulled back and stood a short distance away as she worked. When she was finished, the four of us stood in the center of the living room trying to sort it out.

"I'll check on him through the night and remove the IV as the situation improves."

"What are you going to do, Adrian?" asked R.J.

"I don't know. We need more information. We'll give him a day and try to figure it out tomorrow."

"And what about Danica? Is it safe here?" he asked.

"You know me. Mr. Neurotic. This place is wired. I have six video monitors built into my night stand. Anyone tries to come in any window or entrance, it wakes me up and shows me where. We're as safe here as we can be."

"In that case, does anyone care if I take the spare bedroom? I'm beat," said Danica.

"I'm going to sit up with Patrick," said R.J. "I'll sound the alarm if anything happens."

Everyone dispersed. I made my rounds, checked locks twice, looked out all the windows for things that should not be, and headed for the master bedroom. Catherine was already there, sitting at the foot of the bed.

"So you run a regular rescue center here in your spare time, don't you? Why didn't you tell me? It's a side of you I couldn't have imagined."

"Hey, I think I've got you figured out."

"Really?"

"Yeah. As long as there's other people around you're on your best behavior. It isn't until we're alone that you change from Dr. Adara to Mrs. Hyde."

She ignored the slight, quickly shed every stitch of clothing she had on, and climbed into the bed. "You're not going to sleep in those tourist clothes, are you?"

"How come we're together again?"

"We're trying to prove we really don't like each other."

"Oh. Okay. That's what I thought."

Chapter 9

I awoke late; a man lost in his own home. There was a flurry of activity outside my closed bedroom door, producing a drone of energetic voices. The person who had shared my bed was long gone. I pulled on jeans and had the blue Cammardy shirt half buttoned when the Doctor Adara persona jerked the door open and stuck a head in. "Are you getting up?"

I ran one hand over the beard bristle on my face and grumbled, "Uh-huh."

Her voice became musical. "There's coffee out here. R.J.'s making special pancakes."

"How is…"

"Much better than expected. Sitting up, waiting for food."

"I gotta shave."

"God knows." She backed out and shut the door.

They were a festive bunch. Keeping track of everything that was going on was too much for early morning eyes. Patrick looked like a different man. He had been allowed coffee and was guarding it against his bare chest as Catherine took his pulse at the neck. As warned, the place smelled like pancakes and coffee. It triggered the hunter-gatherer instinct in me. Danica was dashing back and forth between the kitchen and the living room, distributing paper plates, napkins, and plastic utensils.

We ate like ravenous wolves, interrupted only by occasional off-color jokes or commentary on the culinary discourtesies exhibited by some of us. Escape from the dark problems hanging over us lasted only as long as the food. Cleanup quickly brought sobriety. With the other three in the kitchen, I dragged my chair and coffee over to the patient and sat back with my feet up on a nearby armrest.

"I didn't expect you to look this good so quickly. You know, I've never ever seen you unshaven."

"Adara. That woman really knows her stuff. I have the feeling I feel a lot better than I am. It's stupid and embarrassing. I just lost it."

"This is what happens sometimes when the last road is a dead end."

"Well put, Adrian. Very well put."

"So obviously the problem has been repeatedly brought to the attention of the appropriate government agencies?"

"I was forcibly removed from the State Department main office on my last attempt. That was the dead end road you mentioned."

"And their position is?"

"She left voluntarily. They cannot send ships into space searching for people who do not want to be found."

"It's a valid argument."

"What you want to bet she wishes badly to be found by now?"

"How can you be so sure?"

"From the beginning, all the parental alarms were going off. The first thing that set me off were the costs."

"They were bleeding her dry?"

"Just the opposite. They were giving her credits. She wasn't being asked to pay for anything or even provide any kind of service. I tried to look into how they funded their extravagances, but it was a brick wall. That's when I really began to get scared. Nobody, even off-worlders, set up a religious retreat for the sole purpose of giving away wealth. Their sales pitch was that enlightenment leads to a life of abundance, a complete freedom from dependency on the material world. I'm pretty sure they introduced mild hallucinogens into the food or air, telling their members that the effects were from advancing spiritually by being there. They kept promoting my daughter to new meaningless titles of higher authority. I couldn't get anywhere investigating them. But one thing I finally learned really set alarms off. Nobody was coming to Earth to expand or join the colony. But people were leaving all the time. Periodically, groups of Earth students who had achieved a high enough spiritual level were awarded the chance to study at the advanced school on Excelsia, if there really is such a place. I could not find any evidence of any of them ever returning. A short time later, as you would expect, my daughter was awarded that same chance. She did not contact me before leaving. I was not allowed any information about her. You pretty much know the rest."

"That's an ugly little story, Patrick."

"It has happened on Earth so many times, you would think the government would be up in arms about it."

"And they just blew you off?"

"They gave hints that this particular off-world group was under investigation, but they would not provide any details. They did not want me interfering."

"How did you end up here?"

"Nira Prnca. I ran into her in one of the government offices. I gave her a quick rundown. She seemed to know something about the whole thing. She said I should talk to you, though I still don't know why. How can anyone do anything?"

"You saw Nira? How was she?"

"Busy. She looked like she was putting in too many hours."

"So is that it? Do you have anything else to go on?"

"There are a few bits and pieces I picked up. One of the investigators asked me if I had heard the name, Lugal Amar. Another time, I was asked if I had been approached by anyone claiming to be from the Mu Arae Tolkien Minor, whatever that is."

"Tell you what. I'm going to make a call, see if I can get a lead on what's going on with this. Why don't you hang on a bit longer before you throw yourself in front of the bus again, okay?"

"I don't see what you can do, Adrian, but thanks." He leaned back with a new expression of despair on his face. It was complete despair with some doubt added. It was a slight improvement.

I went to the kitchen door and stuck my head in. Three faces sitting at the kitchen table stopped talking and looked up at me.

"Don't anyone go anywhere, okay?"

They all stared back, awaiting an explanation. I ducked out.

With coffee cup in hand, I took refuge in my den; a spare bedroom converted into an office to preserve all of the paperwork items I had not completed and never would. I plunked down in the big simulated leather swivel seat, chosen especially for its conduciveness to sleeping, and placed my feet up on the only bare corner, space specifically designated for that purpose, all other surface area being covered by layers of ignored documents or rejected attempts to reply to them.

A glance at my watch told me it just happened to be the perfect time of morning for the call. I dug the phone out of my jeans and fumbled around in the desk drawers until I found the number. He answered on the third ring. There was no reciprocal image on my display.

"Stan-Lee, you dog."

"Adrian Tarn! What a damn surprise. I heard you augured one in. But of course, here you are without a scratch. How'd you do it?"

"Believe me, Stan. There are scratches."

"Yeah, I heard you became a pop-tart at the end of the toast cycle."

"Stop any bullets lately, Stan?"

"I try not to think about it, Adrian."

"We're two of a kind."

"You know I still owe you one for cheating me through that two-week survival course."

"Wow! That's way back. I forgot all about that. You shouldn't have mentioned it, but since you did..."

"I have never eaten snake again, by the way, but when you're starving and about to flunk out, it can taste pretty damn good, you know?"

"Not my favorite either."

"Yeah, so I can tell this isn't a social call. You got something going. What you got, Adrian?"

"How about two for the price of one? Think of it as interest on that very old debt you just mentioned."

"You'll be pushing your luck unless you got something useful to me."

"What's the deal with a guy by the name of Dorian Blackwell?"

Too long a silence followed. I began to worry.

"Whatcha mean, deal?"

"I've got a close friend who thinks she's marked by him. Know anything about that?"

Once again, too long a silence. This time it was a message.

"There's nothing I can help you with on that name, Adrian."

"Wow. It must be pretty big."

Silence.

"What else you got, Adrian?"

"Well, what can I do about my friend?"

"Don't let her out of your sight."

We both sat again in too long a silence.

"How about Patrick Pacell's Children of Caelestra problem? Got anything on that one for me?"

"As I've said, there's nothing I can help you with on that name."

"Nothing else at all you can give me?"

"Actually, I'm late for a meeting. I'll be gone on assignment for the next few weeks. We need to get together for drinks someday, though. I really want to hear that pop-tart story."

"Thanks, Stan. Take care."

"You too, Adrian."

It left me with such a queasy feeling in my stomach; I almost regretted making the call. Not one thing he had said was by mistake. Yes, there was some type of major investigation going on about Dorian Blackwell, sensitive enough that he couldn't talk about it. Most alarming of all was the warning to not let Danica out of my sight. That meant Blackwell's people were indeed looking for her, but Stan's agency was not in a position to go after them. The reference to going on assignment for a few weeks meant "Don't be comin' 'round here for more information." Whatever the agency was up to, they were trying to remain invisible to their prey. It left me in a terrible spot. I couldn't sit by and do nothing, but anything I did might be akin to a bull in a china shop.

One calamity at a time. What else had Pacell mentioned? The name Lugar Amar. A place called Excelsia. Someplace else named Mu Arae Tolkien Minor. That one rang a bell, though I couldn't quite put my finger on it. I tucked my phone in and spun my chair around to the computer station. Searching the web was dangerous, but I could do it from within the agency search engine, protected by the best firewall on Earth. I logged in and went to the broadest engine available. Mu Arae came back instantly with hundreds of hits. It was a G-type star within the constellation Ara. A mere six trillion miles away. Midway between Scorpius and Triangulum Australe. Five planets circling, numerous moons, one named Tolkien. I clicked around trying to get info on it and came up empty-handed. There was little or no interest in that particular body. Next, I tried Excelsia. Tons of hits, nothing relative, nothing meaningful. On to Lugal Amar. Nothing but some Latin and Indian references that didn't help.

On a whim, I went into flight plan filing requests and filled out a preliminary request for a trip to Mu Arae Tolkien Minor. Something unusual happened. Normally the "application pending" screen comes right up, but this time the screen went blank for a few seconds and came back with "processing." It scared me just a touch. There was no doubt I had triggered something. Too late to cancel. A few seconds passed and I finally got the "Your request has been submitted, expect a response within one hour." I wondered what kind of demons I had inadvertently conjured. I began to stand, expecting the answer to my make-believe flight request to take hours, but as I rose, the screen flipped once and a new message appeared.

Form 8216 B
Amplified Reasons For Request
Applicant; Flight Processing Center Management is requesting additional details for the destination you are requesting. Please elaborate in the space below and return at your earliest convenience.

A new spike of fear went through me. If I did not respond to this request, there would probably be new questions. If

I did respond, what to say? We want to search for someone's missing daughter because you guys won't? It was a fake request anyway. I sat and typed in "Mu Arae private exploration and charting."

I submitted the dummy reason and stood and stretched. My coffee was cold. I turned to head for the kitchen and once again my screen dinged with an incoming message.

Flight Plan Tentatively Approved.
Please submit your formal long-form when ready.

Spacecraft flight plan requests are never approved that quickly. You can't get approval for a trip to the moon that fast. Something was happening behind the scene. Either somebody wanted me to go to Mu Arae, or they were just helping, or both. I sat back down and nervously rubbed my chin with one hand. Stan-the-Man did not have any connections to Flight Plan Processing. He couldn't have pulled strings that quickly. The strangest feeling of all was that I was now sitting here with complete agency approval to take off for Mu Arae Tolkien Minor any time I pleased. And I had an almost complete crew, stuffed with pancakes, sitting in the next room.

Sometimes life has a way of telling you what you will be doing next.

I went in search of R.J. and ran into him outside my door on his way in.

"Can I go now, boss? I gotta get some sleep."

"R.J., want to go flying?"

"You bastard, don't toy with my emotions."

"A naturalist who's a whore for spaceflight. How does that work, R.J.?"

"Adrian, space is the nature that created the sun."

"Wow, that's too heavy for this early."

"When do we leave? I need to get a shower."

"Don't you even want to know where we're going?"

"Wherever it is, how long will we be gone?"

"That's open-ended. We're going to Mu Arae, a moon in that system called Tolkien Minor. I need you to find out everything you can about it."

"Okay, but what are you gonna do about you-know-who on the couch there. He's in no shape."

"I'm working on that. Get your shower and sleep. And watch yourself. Bad people are after Danica. I don't want them taking any friends hostage before we have time to get out of here."

"Switching to stealth mode in my mind. I'll check in regularly."

We went to Catherine as she stood doting over Patrick. R.J. said something reassuring to the patient, then headed for the door.

I called to Catherine, waved her over, and quietly asked, "How long before he can travel?"

"He's still feeling far better than he really is. As long as he's monitored regularly and the drugs adjusted, he's okay. Without me, I'd guess he could travel in a week or so. With me, he can travel now."

"A week? No sooner?"

"What've you got going? Tell me."

"I need to take him someplace far away to check on some leads about his daughter."

"How far would that be?"

"Six trillion miles."

"No problem. When do we leave?"

"You? Spaceflight? You ever done that?"

"What the hell? It's not rocket science."

"Actually, it is."

"You think I can knock your ass off the track at one-eighty and I can't sit in a spaceship?"

"You have a point. But you can't go. We don't know how long we'll be out there."

"I'll clear my schedule."

"We get out there, you won't be able to change your mind."

"Have I ever seemed uncertain about anything?"

"Just me."

"No, I'm certain about you. I don't trust you completely."

"But you're willing to fly with me."

"This little talk is getting annoying. I've already gone flying with you, Flash. I'll take my PAV and pick up some things for the trip, and get some extra medication for my patient. Once more, when do we leave?"

"So you've made my decision and that's it?"

"That's a good way of putting it. When do we leave?"

"As soon as the formal flight plan is approved. But some of us don't know they're going yet."

"Is that a problem?"

"Nope. It'd only be a problem if I told them they couldn't go."

"My kind of people. I'll break the news to the patient." She turned away and returned to Patrick.

I found Danica in the kitchen washing dishes. "We're leaving for the Mu Arae star system as soon as the formal flight plan is approved."
"Oh, thank God. Where is that?"

Chapter 10

Over the next twenty-four hours my place became a way station for satchels, luggage, and numerous decorative bags containing recent feminine purchases. Any normal person would have thought we were going on vacation. The mood, however, was quite the opposite.

I had fought with myself about calling Wilson. Need finally overcame guilt. To my surprise, he was good to go. Jeannie was taking some new-wave three-month sabbatical for modern women approaching marriage. Separation from the betrothed was prescribed. It all sounded like a dumb-ass idea. Wilson seemed too glad to be going.

The plan was to launch at dawn. Ship's stores and expendables were replenished and ready. Wilson and R.J. made several trips delivering the baggage. Danica was not allowed out of the hex-plex. No one slept, except Wilson.

At 04:00, R.J., Wilson, and a disguised Danica took Catherine's PAV and dropped into the VAB parking area. A very short dash across an open patch of lawn put them inside the SPF and into the Griffin hangar in less than a minute. Catherine and I walked Patrick to a rented floater limo and made the trip by land.

We silently loaded into Griffin while still in the hangar. At 05:00 a ground crew of three showed up with a tug. They opened the bay doors and pulled off the ground power cables. We sealed up while being towed out. They positioned the spacecraft on the apron, waved us ready through the flight deck windows, and drove away. Starlight was fading in the night sky, the predawn haze just beginning to distort the horizon.

After hatch checks, I returned forward and was pleasantly surprised to find Danica had allowed me the left seat. The power-up procedure had already been completed, filling the cabin with Christmas tree lights and busy display monitors. I found the right place on the checklist and joined in. Systems were all sound until we reached the very end and began switching on external telemetry. Almost immediately there was a master alarm and a red flashing symbol on the collision avoidance system monitor.

"Damn, it's that same interference with the aft-facing radar arrays, Adrian."

"Yeah, I wasn't expecting to use Griffin so soon. There wasn't time to even think about it." I twisted back to look at R.J. and Wilson. "You guys, can we climb to insertion and ride out just one orbit safely?"

Wilson responded. "We'll have ground coverage all the way, Adrian. There's no danger of being hit from behind by anything."

"We'll need to talk about it en route," added R.J. "I have the rundown on the Mu Arae system that you asked for. There are considerations."

I looked at Danica. "If memory serves, Orbital Traffic Control doesn't monitor this. They're not seeing our "no-go," are they?"

"Nope. All it takes is a manual one-step bypass command and the autopilot and flight director computer will be happy."

I gave a sigh and nodded to her. "Okay. Let's do it then. You want to type that in for me, Dan, and then let's call in and tell them we're ready."

R.J. cut in. "Oh no, I think I left a sprinkler running at your place, Adrian."

Danica shook her head. "R.J., that's not funny anymore."

As she typed in the override commands, I keyed my mike. "OTC, Griffin is ready for direct departure."

"Griffin, continue to hold, expect clearance momentarily."

"Griffin holding on the apron."

Danica said, "Override command accepted, Commander. All green to the sequencer."

"Let's skip the hold at twenty feet and turn right into ascent attitude. Catherine, are you paying attention back there?"

"Every now and then you ask really dumb questions, Adrian," came the reply.

"How is the patient?"

"Asleep in his bed, all strapped in."

"Liftoff in just a minute. Standby."

"Exactly what else would I do back here?"

Danica covered her boom mike with one hand and leaned over toward me. "She seems to get the better of you quite often."

"You don't know the half of it."

"Griffin, OTC. Cleared for launch at your discretion."

"Griffin cleared for launch. Thank-you."

E.R. Mason

With a quick look around the cabin, I tapped in the engage command and Griffin rose gently off the tarmac. At twenty feet, the gears clunked up into their wheel wells, and the OMS engines kicked in and sank us back in our seats as the spacecraft nosed upward. With terrain racing by below, I watched the spacecraft lock onto the flight plan departure line on the primary navigation computer, as the altitude readout scrambled digits trying to keep up.

"Passing through eight thousand, Adrian," said Danica. "Ship's pressurization has taken over. Hey! The new gravity system just switched on and is in self-checks. Oh, that's so cool."

"R.J., how's the CAS looking?"

"All rear-looking transducers continue to have interference or distortion intermittently, Adrian. There's no improvement, but it hasn't gotten any worse, either."

Danica glanced over. "Well, we expected that. Leaving FL100. OMS cutoff counting down."

The night sky returned in all its splendor, eclipsed by Earth's cloud-covered blue horizon arc. There seemed less coronal haze this time, allowing stars to be seen scattered along the barrier between Heaven and Earth. It is invariably a silent moment in the cabin of any spacecraft. There is nothing more mesmerizing than those first moments on top.

Satisfied we were in the proper orbit to hurtle ourselves in the direction of the constellation Ara, Danica and I went into parking checklists to be followed by break-orbit checklists. The guys behind us had it a lot easier.

"Engineering station A is complete, Adrian. Am I cleared to move freely about the cabin?" asked R.J.

"B-station also complete," added Wilson.

I twisted around to look back at them. "You guys better check on Catherine and Patrick."

Wilson had already unstrapped and stood. "Holy crap! There be gravity here. This is so weird!"

"Wow! I keep wanting to grab on to stuff," added R.J. and the two of them began guffawing and shoving each other.

"We had this all the way back from Enuro, but I still can't get used to it," joked Wilson, as the two of them disappeared back toward the airlock.

As we continued our checks, I looked over at Danica and found Catherine suddenly leaning over between us, staring out the front portals.

"You doin' okay, Cath?"

"I am speechless," she said. "For the first time in my life."

"My gosh! It must be the end of the world," I replied.

"You see so many pictures and videos of this, but they're nothing compared to the real thing. I have to keep pinching myself."

"You have about thirty minutes to enjoy what's below; then we'll be strapping in to leave."

"I can't wait." She smiled and left to try the habitat view ports.

Danica laughed at me. "You really know how to show a girl a good time."

We slung around Earth, and when the countdown timer hit zero the OMS fired once more, kicking us out of orbit, followed by a big boost from the stellar drives. We watched Earth quickly shrink away on our rear-facing cameras. There were oohs and aahs from Catherine, sentiments rarely heard. With final checklists complete, we went into single-pilot mode, with Danica opting for the first shift.

I took a moment to enjoy the blanket of stars so far ahead of us and then tried to sound casual. "So tell me, what are the chances of Mr. Blackwell getting access to a ship and coming after you?"

"Getting access to a ship? Chances are good. Remember, the man was an off-world importer-exporter. Finding out where I am? Not so good, I think. Catching up with us if he did? Nobody's as fast as the Griffin. It would take him a while. But there's one other thing."

"What's that?"

"The man has connections. It's always possible he might have a way of getting word out to the wrong people that there's a bounty on me."

"How does a maniac like that get out of prison?"

"Out early on good behavior. Remember, all of this could be in my head. I could just be neurotic or something."

"You ran off with a prototype PAV, and not a single report was made to the authorities. You're not imagining this stuff, believe me."

"I'm sorry I dragged you in, Adrian. Really."

"Like I said before, I want in. My contacts weren't any help except to tell me not to let you out of my sight, which means they know something's up but are not in a position to do anything about it. They've got something going on with Blackwell, but it must be very high-level stuff. In the meantime, we'll just keep our eyes open and stay locked and loaded. You going to be alright?"

"There's no place I'd rather be."

For only the second time after an orbital departure, I had to lift myself out of the seat, rather than float from it. As

E.R. Mason

Wilson had so aptly phrased, it felt weird. After an uneventful walk-around inspection, I joined my compatriots at the conference table. R.J. was hammering away at his little laptop. Wilson was throwing cashews in the air and catching them in his mouth. Catherine was twisted around in her seat by the bulkhead, still looking out.

"Ladies and Gentlemen, now that we're underway let's see if we can try to put things in perspective a bit." I reached over and tapped the intercom. "Danica, would you put the conference table on monitor and sit in with us?"

"I see you," was the reply.

R.J. looked up from his laptop. Wilson continued casting cashews into the air, paying attention in between catches.

I opened my mouth to speak but was interrupted by a beeping from one of the engineering stations.

"Incoming message," said Wilson.

"Hold that thought." At the A engineering station, a flight approval form scrolled across the screen. It validated crew members' certifications, all except Catherine's. She was listed as a civilian passenger. It also designated the trip as "NENR," Nasebian Emissary Not Required. It meant Nasebian representatives had reviewed the flight plan and again decreed oversight unnecessary. It surprised me and left mixed emotions.

Back at the conference table, I remained standing, opened my mouth to speak, and was again interrupted by a different form of beeping from an engineering station.

"Video communication," said Wilson as he tossed another nut in the air.

I tapped the controls on the conference table and brought the message up on the main habitat monitor. Immediately an extreme close-up of Bernard Porre appeared on the screen. There were moans and other guttural sounds.

"Commander Tarn, what a surprise to be in contact with you again so soon. Your flight plan took us all a bit by surprise this time. We are somewhat at a loss at how quickly your trip was processed and approved. I can only think those at the higher levels must find allayment in the thought of your being several trillion miles away. Oddly enough, the Nasebian high council has also decreed that a Nasebian emissary is not required for your little trip. One would think they would be the most concerned of all. But enough of these mundane courtesies."

"Given your excursion is classified as private, the agency would like to request your scans, imagery, and ship's logs as you are able to provide, if you have no ob-

jections. It is a standard request intended to enrich data compilation on file for the Mu Arae system. Any SID related information would also be very much appreciated."

"As you know, Mu Arae is quite a dynamic environment and is outside the boundaries of any governing body, marshaled only by local, non-recognized groups. We have very little information on the many mining operations and shipping conglomerates that operate there. Perhaps, if you do surmount the obstacles that lie ahead in this latest of your irregular quests, you may be able to fill in some blanks for us."

"We await your data expectantly. Porre out."

I cleared the screen and rubbed one side of my face in exasperation.

"The man is such a delight," said R.J.

"Yeah, nothing like a subspace message while en route to let everyone know where we're going," added Wilson.

"It's all encrypted, isn't it?" said Catherine.

"Yeah, but so was the enigma stuff in the big war, and they didn't have a galaxy of spies," complained Wilson.

"Being a bit melodramatic, aren't we?" said R.J.

I held up one hand. "R.J., let's give Porre's message the attention it deserves and go on to the important stuff. Can you give us your rundown on Mu Arae and Tolkien Minor?"

"Mu Arae, big star exactly 50.5 light years from Earth, or 15.51 parsecs. It has a parallax of 64.47, a radius 36% greater than our sun. It's helium enriched, giving it an even greater gravity ratio. Spectral type G31V-V. You could say it's a hotty." R.J. looked up from his laptop as though he expected laughter. There was none.

"Anyway, that particular sector is so rich with asteroids, planetoids, rogues, moons and other stuff, it's a haven for mining colonies and prospectors. There are so many various races involved, no one particular race has been able to lay claim to any of it for fear the others would band together and take action. For the most part, they leave each other alone. There is no military or police organization, just local marshal or constable types here and there, and they answer to no one in particular."

Catherine said, "Not a tourist haven, I think."

Wilson added, "It's the Old West in space."

R.J. continued, "So anyway, the place we're going, Tolkien Minor, a moon of Mu Arae-E, the outermost planet in the system, a gas giant by the way. It's a stopping-off point for anyone who dares. It's got a gravity of 1.1 of Earth's so we'll all be heavy. There's no atmosphere at all, but there's a little bit of hard-to-get subsurface water. The place had large gold deposits so huge that electronic dome installations were set up for mining. When the gold ran out, those outposts were abandoned, but because of its central location and with so much prospecting in the area, it became like a way station for everybody and anybody. The topography is mostly gray, rocky desert. There's not much other information. That's probably partly why Bernard Porre is interested. There's local law only, which is governed by anybody who can pay the most if you get my drift. Maybe Wilson's old west analogy is not such a bad comparison."

"Sounds like a pretty iffy place," said Wilson.

"But it does sound like a place one could get information about bad people," said Catherine.

"What about the landing, R.J.?" I asked.

"Strictly pick your own spot. The electronic domes are all public now. Don't expect any ground crew assistance. Do not leave the keys in your spacecraft."

"I'll hand out sidearms to everyone before we set down. Obviously there'll be no solo trips by anyone."

"There's one other item that we seriously need to consider, Adrian," said R.J.

"Okay. I'm listening."

"The problem with the rear-looking radars. We're going into a sector so busy with solids, we've got to have the rear-looking radar or we'll get something rammed up our..."

"I think we get the point, R.J."

"It has to be fixed."

"In space?"

"You should not enter the Mu Arae system without it."

"Can we even fix it on an EVA?"

"The most likely problem is that one of the transducers or emitters is loose inside the vertical stabilizer. It's moving around, reflecting off stuff, and interfering with all the other sending units. Most likely, you'll open the port center panel, find the thing out of place, reinstall it, and we'll be on our way."

"Boy, I hate stopping midway."

"You'll hate flying blind where we're going even worse."

I considered the dilemma. "If someone were following us, we probably wouldn't see them, would we?"

"Not like we are," replied R.J.

Wilson said, "It's an easy job, if that's what it is, Adrian. Anyway, it's my turn to go outside."

Danica keyed her intercom. "Adrian..."

"No. Danica. I want to go out with him myself."

The intercom turned a sulky silent.

It took us a day and a half to go through the ship's schematics and find all the tools called out in the procedures.

EVAs are best done after a sleep period, so we set up and left everything until the next morning. I had just a touch of trouble getting to sleep. EVAs are wonderful things to behold. At the same time, I knew Wilson was probably snoring away, without a care in the world, except maybe Jeannie.

As we were finishing breakfast, a sudden irresponsible whim came over me. I looked at Catherine and my mouth moved without my brain's consent. "Cath, you want to go outside with us?"

Wilson was in the aft airlock getting ready. R.J. was setting up the A-station for EVA monitoring. He heard me and bent over backward to peer through the forward airlock with concerns.

"Are you kidding? Where do I sign up?" she replied.

"Wilson's back there already. Ask him to fit a suit to you."

"I'm going before you change your mind."

As she hurried aft, R.J. came back and leaned against the table. "You sure you want to do that?"

"I doubt she'll ever get another chance."

"She doesn't have a single certification."

"Not a one."

"She's never even seen the inside of a spacesuit."

"Wilson or I will be within reach at all times. If she goes into the panicking-swimmer mode, we'll push her back into the airlock and lock her in the docking station, but she won't. I know her."

"Hyperventilation?"

"We can manage that with the mixture. It won't happen."

"Can she maneuver?"

"We'll bring out the backpack control arms for her. She's better with a joystick than anyone I know."

"Is that a carnal joke?"

"No. I mean a real joystick."

"You know this is against every statute in the books."

"I wasn't planning on entering it in any of the logs."

"Well, I guess it's been too long since you did something like this. Adrian Tarn, breaker of rules, rescuer of fair maidens in distress. You wouldn't want your reputation slipping."

"If you stay in her ear for me, it'll be just fine."

"You can bet I'll keep a close eye on the helmet cams and the suit readouts."

We waited patiently as Danica idled the stellar drives, reversed them, and bled off all that incredible speed to stop us and bring us to park in deep space. I was afraid she might not

107

be speaking to me, but bringing the spacecraft out of light forced her back into pilot mode.

We dressed Catherine in spaceman white, suited up each other, then stepped up into our docking stands. Wilson considered the Catherine indiscretion as fun, of course. With the airlock depressurized, the three of us hung in our suit docking stations waiting for green lights from the suit bio-acclimation readouts. Though the intercoms were active, everyone waited quietly. After fifteen minutes I could not resist a coded question to R.J. as he sat up front monitoring us.

"R.J., specs on red unit?"

There was a short scoff, then, "125 and 83. 78, normal aspiration."

Catherine's haughty voice broke in. "What'd you expect, Adrian?"

A flush of irritation annoyed me. Catherine was in the suit with red trim. R.J. was telling me her blood pressure was 125/83, pulse 78 bpm, and her breathing normal. Here she was about to journey outside a spacecraft for the first time, and her vital signs were less than if she was shopping at Macy's. There was just no way to get to this woman. There had to be ice water in her veins.

"Hey, Adrian, this is gonna be cool. Instead of floating to the door and out, we're gonna walk up to the door and fall out," said Wilson.

I looked around the silver environment of the airlock and realized that wasn't the only thing new. Usually the place was filled with floating cables, hoses, and cover flaps. This time, everything was hanging in place as though we were on the ground. It felt like something wasn't ready, or like this was a ground rehearsal. The air in our suits smelled slightly odd, just as it should, and as the suit automatically varied the mixture to our dropping pressures, the curious flavor of chemicals became even more apparent. As always, the inside temperature was almost uncomfortably cold as the suit environmental controls caught up.

With the airlock and suit indicators finally green, and a verbal blessing from R.J., we watched the oval hatch slide open to black nothingness. The well-lit airlock seemed to have a hole in it. Wilson and I stepped down from our docking stations. As Wilson turned to wrestle with the tool pouch, I rocked around to face Catherine and held out a fat, doughboy arm to steady her. She stepped down and we stared at each other for a few seconds through untinted visors. I expected the wide-eyed look. Instead, I got back an "I trust you" stare.

Wilson was the first to the door. He let out a muted "Yah-hoo," and stepped into a float. His control arms were immediately brought down and he jetted around to face us, then backed away to give us room.

Catherine looked at me with a furrowed brow. "This is really happening, isn't it?"

"Yes, Alice. You go through that door over there and you become very, very small."

She gave a half smile, took her first step, and quickly became serious about the spacesuit weight.

"Don't worry. Just a few steps and it will weigh nothing at all."

She rocked along quite adequately and stopped at the open hatch, with me holding her backpack from behind. She leaned partway out the opening and for the first time I heard Catherine-awe. "Oh my god. Oh my god."

"I heard someone else describe it that way once," I said.

"I'll fall forever down there."

"No, you won't fall at all."

"My mind is certain of it."

"Would I lie to you?"

"It feels funny."

"Yes, you're not only weightless out there, you're weightless inside your suit also, so you bump around a little bit. That's normal."

"Maybe just one step."

And she did. The momentum brought the rest of her out the door, one hand still clinging to the side of it like a skydiver changing his mind. Her feet came up behind her until she was horizontal to me, but she rotated sideways so she could still see me. I could hear R.J. thinking, "I knew this wasn't such a good idea."

"Let go, Alice. The Mad Hatter has you by the foot."

Wilson had jetted up behind her and was pushing her into an upright position. She let go and he turned her to face him. As I launched myself out, he pulled down her control arms and smiled reassuringly. "Just like I showed you, Cath. You twist or push the left-hand joystick to face a certain way, then the right-hand joystick will drive you forward, sideways, or back. I'm going to back away. You come forward and follow me."

A dance in emptiness ensued. With the first thrust from the right-hand joystick, Catherine instantly became a master. Something in her mind clicked. There was no learning curve. While following Wilson away from the ship, she turned herself 360 degrees without slowing her forward motion, like a ballerina in space. She stopped without bumping him and turned back to face the ship.

"My god, the ship is so beautiful. The light from the airlock is like the sun."

"Not too many people get to see this," remarked Wilson.

"I've got to take up space medicine."

"Uh-oh, another life ruined, Adrian," said Wilson.

"There are so many stars!"

"There's no ship window to interrupt your field of vision," replied Wilson.

I jetted over to the two of them. "Cath, you're going to want to roam. You can't do that. You must stay within arm's length of us. You're not trained in emergency procedures. You understand?"

"Okay."

"Let's head aft and remove cover plates."

We made a slow cruise back to the tail section and climbed to the port side of the vertical stabilizer. The access panel was a large, four-foot-high, two-foot-wide section of reinforced carbon-carbon composite. There were no good clip-on hooks so the suits had to be left in micro-station parking, leaving us to frequently correct for drift. It also made removal of the fasteners tedious, since there was no easy way to put pressure on the removal tool. Wilson and I braced each other and patiently worked on each fastener, while Catherine kept herself close by, as promised. Though she was very prudent about it, she could not resist rotating her attitude for different looks at the stars and the ship. At one point I heard Wilson blurt out a quick laugh when he looked back to find Catherine's upside down butt an inch from his visor.

As the panel gave free and floated out, we put her to work holding it, while the two of us beamed our headlamps into the transducer assembly mounting area in search of something amiss. The open panel was a very neat layout of chilled tubing and shielded cables. Starting at the top, there were transducers and emitters cascading down, one for each kind of radar or scanning system. We didn't see anything out of place. There was nothing hanging down or out of place.

"Jeez, Adrian. I don't see anything."

"Crap. Nothing's ever easy. There's got to be something in here."

"It could be something in one of the core crystals. Maybe one of them is cracked, and we can't see it and it's throwing radiation everywhere even though it looks fine."

"But we'd see one particular system consistently bad, wouldn't we? Catherine, stop bumping me, please."

"Sorry."

"Yeah, I can't imagine we wouldn't. I just don't see anything physically wrong in here like we expected."

"I'm gonna see if any of them are loose. Brace me."

"Be careful. You get one of them out of alignment and it'll be a real bitch trying to readjust it in space."

I began with the uppermost emitter head, carefully grabbing it with my right glove while holding on to the back of the vertical stabilizer. It felt solid as a rock. It was the same with the next three down. By the time I reached the second to the last transducer, I was starting to lose hope. Then, as I twisted the very bottom unit, something fearful happened. The entire softball-sized unit came right off in my hand.

"Oh, shit!" exclaimed Wilson.

"Oh, crap," I agreed.

R.J. cut in on the intercom. "Gentleman, something is very odd here."

"No kidding, Sherlock," replied Wilson. "We just broke a transducer right off the mount! Now we're really screwed."

R.J. ignored the sarcasm. "Adrian, that was the eighth transducer, correct?"

"Yeah, R.J."

"You are still looking at seven in the compartment, correct?"

"Wait... Yeah, the other seven are still fine."

"My circuit layout here says there's only supposed to be seven emitters and transducers."

We hung there in the silent cold of space, staring at the dark amber, dome-shaped lens in my gloved hand.

"Well, what the hell, then?" said Wilson.

"We got outdated drawings on the Griffin?" I asked.

Danica cut in from the pilot seat. "No, Adrian. Everything we have is from the final Rev date unless something was added afterward, that is. But that would have to be noted in the drawings database and there is no flag."

"It wasn't connected by anything, either. It was like a magnetic mount."

"Oh, that is so weird," said Wilson.

R.J. cut in. "You're going to have to close up that access panel and bring it in here, Adrian, so we can take a good look at it. Even if you have to go back out to replace it, there's no choice."

After trading Catherine the lens for the access panel, Wilson and I went about reinstalling the fasteners with the annoying thought we might be doing it all again in an hour or two. With the vertical stabilizer closed up, we jetted our merry way back to the airlock and stepped through the open hatch into gravity, changing from graceful seahorse people to bludgeoning heavy monsters in white.

111

E.R. Mason

We helped Catherine into her docking port, and after closing the outer door stepped up to ours. As soon as the airlock was pressurized, the inner door slid open and R.J. came scurrying in. We were expecting him to help us de-suit. Instead, he rifled through Wilson's pack, pulled out the mysterious transducer, and dashed away toward the science lab without saying a word.

Wilson looked across the airlock at me with a wry expression. "No tip for him."

"That's going on his permanent record," I added.

"Wow! The water from this drinking tube is nice and cold," said Catherine.

So when recomp time had passed, we helped each other out of our suits. I stood in front of Catherine, turned her helmet, and lifted it off. She smiled a bigger smile than I had ever seen.

"That's one for you, Tarn. I will never, ever forget. Nothing will ever top it."

"Don't think twice. I owed you for the Daytona experience."

"I really am going to look into space science."

"It's a lot of time away from home," I said, as I twisted off her gloves.

"Already do that. I'm qualified."

"Careful what you wish for."

We stripped naked out of our suit liners and pulled on flight coveralls without giving it a second thought, though Wilson couldn't help but steal a few quick glances at the good Doctor. We found R.J. in the science lab, looking like an Emmett "Doc" Brown as he hung over the errant transducer. He looked up at us, but it took a moment for his brain to switch into social mode.

"Adrian, we've got to open this thing up."

"Is that a bad thing?"

Wilson cut in. "It will decertify the thing! We won't be able to use it."

"That's a bad thing, R.J."

"I don't think we have been using it. It's like a placebo transducer."

Catherine joined in. "Why would you have fake equipment on a ship?"

R.J. became earnest. "It should not have been installed in the tail. It serves no useful purpose that I can find. In fact, I think the outer case is just a disguise to hide something. There are no manufacturer markings of any kind on it, but scanners show there is something inside. The material used on the fake lens cover won't allow a good interior scan. We need to open it."

"Is it pressurized?" asked Wilson.

R.J. sounded reluctant, as though that might ruin his chances. "Yes."

Wilson persisted. "What kind of gas was used to pressurize it?"

"Well, I can't tell."

"Well, you can't just open it without knowing what gasses you're releasing into the ship's atmosphere."

"I'll use the science lab's vacuum chamber."

"Still, it could be explosive."

"There's definitely something in there. Not much free space is left. There can't be much gas volume. There's too little to be dangerous. We need to know what's inside this thing."

The four of us stood in silent standoff.

Catherine broke the impasse. "Are there any other options besides opening it?"

R.J. was adamant. "No, I've tried everything."

"Could there be just as much danger if you do not open it?"

"Possibly," replied R.J.

"Not if we chuck it out into space," said Wilson.

I shook my head. "We can't do that. Somehow that thing was put in the tail. That's not an easy thing to do. We've got to know by who and why. Ditching the thing is not an option."

"Then since there is a possibility of danger whether you open it or not, your only option is to open it as safely as possible," said Catherine.

R.J. smiled. "You know, I like her."

I looked at Wilson. Neither he nor I could argue with the Doctor's logic.

"Crap. Okay, R.J. Open it."

Chapter 11

The three of us jockeyed for space as R.J. sealed the vacuum chamber and inserted his arms into the flex sleeves. Danica remained on the flight deck watching the proceedings on a monitor.

Wilson said, "I already know what it is."

We all stopped and looked at him.

"It's some kind of tracking device Blackwell's henchmen somehow planted on the Griffin to track Danica's movements. It's got to be. It's the only answer."

R.J. disagreed. "A long-range tracking device that does not require external power? It had to be something installed by the Enuro technicians to support the artificial gravity system. They're the only ones who were removing panels on the Griffin."

Wilson was not swayed. "We're not floating R.J. Gravity's still turned on. Couldn't have been anything to do with that. Plus, they would've told us about it. It's not on any of their diagrams."

R.J. turned back to the task at hand. "There is no way to disassemble it. Somehow the lens is bonded to the base. The only way in is to cut the lens around the base and lift it off."

"Destructive disassembly. We may be creating more problems than we're solving," said Wilson.

I offered responsibility. "Proceed, R.J. Delicately."

"I'll set the laser Dremel to a depth of 4 millimeters. If it's not enough, we'll cut again. We should expect rapid depressurization almost immediately. I have the chamber set to collect whatever comes out and store it. Here goes."

We had to squeeze together to see through the observation window. A tiny blue beam popped out of the tool in R.J.'s black rubber-gloved hand. He braced the strange amber dome with his free hand and began to cut around the base. One half-second later gray gas began escaping from the bead. The vapor trail lasted only two or three seconds. R.J. turned the dome as he continued. A strange glow seemed to be emanating from the new seam.

When the cut around the base was complete, we craned our necks to see as he put down the tool and slowly lifted the dome lens off of the base. Hiding beneath it was the strangest jewel I had ever seen. It was the size of an egg and was mounted upright on an intricately carved golden pedestal. It slowly pulsed silver light on one side and white light on the other. A narrow golden band ran down both sides of the egg shape from the top, dividing it in half.

"What in the hell is that?" asked Wilson.

With one hand still holding the base, R.J. looked back at him. "See what kind of gas we collected from it, will you?"

Wilson went to a spectrometer readout panel, dialed in a few commands, and called out, "Nitrogen. Pure nitrogen."

Catherine spoke. "Nothing exotic. Just standard storage techniques to preserve the metals inside."

R.J. looked at me. "I see no reason we can't bring it out."

I glanced at Wilson. He raised an eyebrow and shrugged.

"Okay. Pressurize the chamber and remove it. Let's get a closer look."

When the chamber had achieved neutral atmosphere, R.J. spun off the locking wings and opened the sample door. He carefully drew out the strange diamond on its base and held it up in front of us. Both sides of the stone continued to slowly glow, both so heavy with facets they could not be counted. Silver rays from one side, white rays from the other, extremely beautiful, like pin-sized beams from a laser scanner.

"I could just sit down and stare at it all day," said Catherine.

"I need to do a bunch of spectroscopics, Adrian. We need to know what kind of light this is."

"Wilson, could you take a look at our systems and see if we've cleared up the radar interface at all?"

Danica's voice came over the intercom. "I started that already, Adrian. The rear-facing scanning arrays are now looking clear, so far. There are no more master alarms."

"Well, I'll be. Oh, this is so weird," said Wilson.

I resisted the urge to take the thing from R.J. for a closer look. "We need to get underway. Everybody strap in. R.J., stow that thing, and once we're up to speed I'll give you thirty minutes with it. Then let's gather in the habitat and see if we can figure this out. Danica, you hear that?"

"I'm already waiting for the Nav computer and Flight Director to reconfirm course and give us a time, Adrian."

We hastily stowed our tools and gear, secured the airlock and lab, and when permission came from the ship we hurled ourselves back to light. R.J. was out of his seat and back in the lab before I could unbuckle. We hung out in the habitat module, drinking coffee and waiting. An unshaven, weary-looking Dr. Patrick Pacell stuck his head out of his sleeper cell, climbed precariously out, and made a trip so awkward to the nearest restroom that we all stopped and stared, ready to rush over and pick him up from the fall that never quite happened.

As the restroom door slid shut, R.J. appeared in the corridor carrying the crystal with the same care he would have given an explosive. He sat among us, continuing to stare in awe at his newest mystery.

I tried to bring him back to reality. "Well? Don't keep us in suspense. What have you got?"

He looked at me and shook his head. "It's something really, really special."

"But function, R.J. What the hell is it for?"

"I have no idea," he replied, and he seemed disturbed by the admission.

"There you go. I told you. It's some kind of deep-space tracking device to keep an eye on Dan," said Wilson.

"I don't think so," answered R.J.

"Based on what?" demanded Wilson.

"Watch this," replied R.J. and he drew the unit closer to him, picked it up with one hand, and gently removed the crystal from its mount. Holding the egg of light in one hand, he carefully separated it into two halves. The half emitting silver light became a heavily faceted stone with a flat back. Its counterpart was the same except for the gold band running around its edge. Both halves continued to pulse their radiance, both as spectacular individually as they had been together.

R.J. spoke as he stared at his treasures. "I have scanned both of these in every range there is. I've tried for every known wavelength of light. I was not able to measure or even detect the light you see emanating from either of them."

Danica keyed her intercom. "Are you certain they are crystals, R.J.?" she asked.

"Actually all rocks are crystals, Danica. Only the ones of a higher order possess transparency. There's no way these were formed naturally. They were artificially created to do just what they're doing, whatever that is."

"So couldn't Wilson still be right?" I asked. "These are something made to transmit through subspace or something?"

"Watch this," replied R.J., as though he had not even heard my question. He took the stone with the gold border around it and placed it in the palm of his left hand. With a quick glance around to be sure we were all paying attention, he turned his hand palm-over as though trying to drop it on the table. Instead, it seemed to stick to his hand. He glanced up once more, expecting us to be impressed. We were. Next, he took the stone from his palm and stuck it to his forearm, then moved it around in every possible way. It held as though it was glued in place.

"I don't get it," said Wilson. "Adhesive on the flat side?"

R.J. shook his head. "Nothing. Not a thing. It is attracted to skin on a molecular level. Put it where you will, and the only thing that can remove it is the touch of human skin. In the lab, I tried to pull it off with forceps. It would only have come off with some skin. I can slide it around my arm as long as I use my hand. Anything else, it won't budge."

"Really, really weird," said Wilson.

"Just how do you know these aren't harmful?" asked Catherine.

"I ran some tests with the med lab computer. Like everything else, the equipment doesn't seem to know these exist at all. They have been located in the tail of this ship for weeks, but none of us have exhibited any adverse symptoms. I'm open for any other tests you might suggest, Doctor."

"I don't suppose there's anything to suggest a point of origin for them?" I asked.

"Nothing that I've found," answered R.J., "I think we can assume these were not created on Earth, of course."

"So all we know is that these were deliberately installed in our tail section and were interfering with our radars?"

"That's all I've got," said R.J.

"When did we first begin having radar trouble?" I asked.

After a moment of silence, Wilson answered. "Enuro. It had to be after Enuro. The thing had to have been installed there. They had the perfect opportunity, or at least somebody did. The ship was torn apart for days. Guys were running around working on it continually. It would have been a piece of cake to install that thing."

We sat together in yet another moment of silence, wondering what it all meant. I looked at R.J. "You can't say for certain this is not some kind of tracking or monitoring device then, right?"

"I guess not. I just don't think so. Why would the thing separate into two pieces? Why is it designed to adhere to human skin? That just doesn't sound like a subspace transmitter."

"Well, I for one am lost," said Catherine.

"Is there any other analysis at all you can do on it, R.J.?"

"I'll have to think about it."

"Well, when you're through, please store it in the science lab vault. We're approaching Mu Arae. We need to start getting our act together."

117

"What exactly is the plan, Adrian?" asked Wilson.

"Because we know so little about the place, we'll put into high orbit around Tolkien Minor and run some scans as inconspicuously as possible. We'll see what kind of installations are down there, then make a decision to land or not. Everybody should get set up for a surface excursion in case it comes to that. In the meantime, Wilson, would you take a look at our rear-facing arrays now that the interference has been removed, then run scans as deeply as possible and see if there's any hint that we're being followed?"

"Will comp, Adrian."

As the group began to break up, a clean-shaven Dr. Patrick Pacell sheepishly emerged from the rest room dressed in fresh green flight coveralls. Greetings of surprise were exchanged as he came forward and took a seat at the table. He looked like a shaky scarecrow in a flight suit. Catherine and I looked him over like concerned parents.

"My god, Patrick, you look a damn sight better than you did," I said.

He gave us both quick glances as though embarrassed to look us in the eye. "Where exactly are we? I seem to have had a lost weekend."

"We are en route to a moon of Mu Arae-E in the Mu Arae system to see if there's any information about your daughter."

"Wow! That's one hell of an answer, Adrian. Whose ship is this?"

"Believe it or not, it's mine."

"Okay, I must still be in detox and this is another hallucination."

Catherine asked, "How's the dehydration, Doctor?"

"I can't tell. I'm so jumbled; I don't know what I feel. And, forgive me, you are?"

I interceded. "Doctor Patrick Pacell, let me introduce Doctor Catherine Adara. Your guardian angel."

"Doctor Adara, where did you learn that particular recovery program? I'm not familiar with the parts of it I can remember."

"It's not written down anywhere, Doctor. I have a lot of experience treating daredevils and fools. It's my home-brewed remedy and it varies with each individual and each condition. That's why I can't publish. The book would be the Never Ending Story."

Patrick wiped one hand down his face. His voice was still slightly gravelly. "How will I ever repay you, Doctor?"

"Start now by calling me Catherine, Patrick."

"Okay, Catherine, but that's not enough."

"Nice to finally meet the real you, Patrick. Time for solid food."

Shock Diamonds

      I pointed at the galley. "Anything you find out there is yours, buddy. You should stuff yourself, as necessary."
      "Or maybe start slow," said Catherine.
      "I'd better listen to my Doctor," said Patrick. "Adrian, why are we going to somebody's moon?"
      "You were mumbling that someone mentioned it when you were questioning people about your daughter. It's the only real lead we have. It may be a dead end."
      "I was? God, how many engrams have I destroyed?"
      "I'd start with soup and see if it stays down," said Catherine.
      I pushed myself up. "If you two will excuse me, I should say hi to the pilot. She's going to start feeling neglected."
      On the flight deck, Danica had the right seat partially reclined, her left leg squeezed in over the armrest, and her right arm hooked over the seat. As I entered and sat, she said, "You must like multitasking."
      "How do you mean?"
      "I can't tell which of us is the biggest pain in the ass, me or Doctor Pacell."
      "It's not like that. We know there's trouble out there looking for us. We just have to avoid it."
      "You? Stay out of trouble? That'll be the day."

Chapter 12

Solar systems are always too large to navigate in sub-light. If you try, it takes days, weeks, months, or longer just to get from one body to another. There is also a tiny bit of a problem in that you do not wish to make a series of jumps here and there going to light each time and then back out of it. So the prescribed method when traveling from system to system is to drop out of subspace within a sub-light speed day's journey of the celestial body you are trying to reach. But since everything in space is moving, that tends to be a somewhat inexact science. With Danica acting as pilot-in-command, however, overshoot or undershoot is never a problem. The woman tends to plot her dropouts to the doorstep of wherever she happens to be going. It scares the hell out of me every time she does it, but I have to act nonchalant so as to not lose any additional points on my man card. Someday she is going to drop out, find herself in the most cluttered orbital corridor of some populated planet, and get blasted by space debris on her way to burning up in the atmosphere. Chances are I'll be there and get in at least one sarcastic comment.

When the Griffin at last burst into normal space, Tolkien Minor was directly in front of us, too large to be seen in its entirety.

"Better back us out a touch for surface scanning."

She stared at me, wondering if the request was a compliment or a cut.

I began to hear oohs and aahs coming from the habitat module as we backed away from Tolkien. The solar system around it slowly came into view. The reason for the cries of awe quickly became apparent. Tolkien's parent planet Mu Arae-E began to appear, and there was even more to see beyond and around it. We are so used to a clean solar system view from Earth, planets neatly separated by nearly identical distances, all quite far apart, not much else but the sun and moon to clutter the view of those nearest bright bodies. But here in the Mu Arae system things could not be described as orderly in any sense of the word. The place was an astrophysicist's dream or an astrologer's nightmare. Too many contrasting bodies to plot in every direction. Not just bright planetary bodies that looked like big stars, but actual physical geological companions so close they could be made out with the naked eye. Some were tumbling in place, others making an excruciatingly slow transit through the black sky. It was no wonder this place was a miner's dream. Endless candidates for mineral rich asteroids or planetoids all around, going on as far as the scanners could read.

"Wow!" said Danica.

"Wow," I agreed.

Wilson stuck his head in between our seats. "Wow!"

"What's Tolkien's rotation?" I asked.

"I'm reading once every thirty-two hours. We're already seeing numerous installations down there on the surface scans. Most of them are equatorial for some reason."

"Let's map them all, then maybe we'll pick one to study more closely."

"You don't want to sit out here and wait the thirty-two hours, do you?" asked Danica.

"Nope. Set us up for a one-hour orbit. Wilson, you want to arrange the surface scans for that period? Make them high-res with imagery, of course."

"I'm on it."

I keyed the intercom. "Ladies and Gentleman, welcome to Tolkien Minor."

The moon's surface scans came back ominous. There were several small industrial complexes, mostly around the equator, two or three others at the poles. They were well spread out, and none looked hospitable. It wasn't even possible to tell what was being done at those locations. None seemed to support species familiar to us.

But there was one sinister-looking exception. Directly on the equator at the eighty-one-degree, four-minute longitude, a huge complex was built into the bottom of a massive, ancient crater. The corresponding imagery showed dozens of ships of varying design and markings. There was enough atmosphere inside the electronic dome that occasionally inhabitants could be seen traversing the place. Twenty or thirty makeshift buildings formed a main street of sorts, although there were very few vehicles present.

We sat around the conference table, staring up at the main display monitor. R.J. was the first to speak. "I don't like it. I don't like it at all."

Wilson countered with his usual irreverence. "Who you gonna call?"

R.J. looked at him with disdain. "Where did that worn-out cliché come from again?"

121

Wilson smiled back. "I have no idea, but it makes my point."

"Which is what?" R.J. persisted.

"Either we go down there, or this is the end of the trip."

"Maybe we could get somebody on a com line," countered R.J.

"Oh yeah, hey everybody, there's a ship in orbit wants to know about some kidnappers, anybody know anything? Yeah, that'll get us some attention."

"I withdraw my suggestion," said R.J.

"There's one main area for spacecraft," said R.J. "Or you could put down out of sight about a mile away behind some dunes and still be under the curtain."

"We don't want to sneak up on them, R.J. We don't want to make anyone suspicious. We want to look like good ole' boys, as casual as possible."

"Who goes?" asked Wilson.

"I'm thinking you, Danica, and me."

R.J. complained, "Adrian, I've faced aliens and biker gangs with you and you're leaving me behind? Plus, you'll be taking both pilots?"

"You are very good on the flight deck, R.J. One person who knows engineering and basic piloting needs to be here. I'll set up a program titled "home." If the worst happens, you call that up on the flight computer, engage the flight director, and the ship will plot a course and return directly to high Earth orbit. From there, you contact ground control and they'll bring you down. You can then request they come find us. But all of that is only the worst case scenario. I don't expect any of that."

"Well, it sure is an ugly little scenario," he replied.

Patrick stiffened. "Adrian, this is about my daughter. I have to go."

"Patrick, you're in no condition to go. We've got to be smart about this."

"But if she's down there somewhere you'll need me to help spot her."

"I pulled a photo of her, Patrick. It's in my pocket. I'll know her. Wilson and Danica will have copies of their own. But she's not down there. This is not a place where you get big money for slaves."

"But I should share in the risk. I should be there."

"Patrick, you will only add to the risk. We've got to be smart. We'll want to get in and out quickly. We're strangers here. We don't even know what's down there. We may encounter some resistance if you know what I mean. I'm taking people who are best at defending themselves."

Shock Diamonds

"What about me?" demanded Catherine. "I'm no pushover, and I'm bigger than Danica. You'd still have a pilot on board if I went."

"Cath, Danica has certain skills you don't know about. Listen, you guys, you've got to trust me on this. I know what I'm doing."

A disgruntled silence followed. I tried to sound conciliatory. "Do all you guys still have the translators in your ears?"

Wilson said, "You know, I forgot about those things. I went in a Chinese restaurant back in Cocoa Beach, and the servers were making insulting comments about me. I pounded my fist on the table and one of them spilled a tray."

"I'll pull a couple more sets out for Catherine and Patrick, just in case."

R.J. spoke. "May I suggest something more, Adrian?"

"What's that?"

" Why don't we use three of the bio-trackers?"

"Those we tag alien wildlife with to track them? The ones that are inserted under the skin?"

"That's the ones."

"You want to inject those things under our skin?"

"We have two eminent doctors aboard."

"I hate needles," said Wilson.

"He doesn't pass out, does he?" asked Catherine.

Wilson ignored the comment. "I'm thinking serious weapons, Adrian."

"Well, we can't go in there loaded for bear. We'll take the small stun guns that fit in your pocket."

"Nearly naked," complained Wilson. "I'm at least wearing a vest underneath."

I tapped the intercom. "Plot us for a descent to the large complex on the next orbit, Dan."

"Already programmed, Adrian. De-orbit in twenty-eight minutes."

"She doesn't believe in waiting around, does she?" said Patrick.

"She probably can't wait to go," said Wilson.

After rushing around to assemble everything needed, I managed to slide down into the right-hand pilot seat just as Danica was rotating the spacecraft for the de-orbit burn. When the turn was complete, she paused to rub her forearm where Catherine had injected the tracking device. I strapped in and a moment later the OMS engines gave a kick and the ship began to sink toward the surface.

So down and down we went. Black sky faded to gray. Through the lower windows, surface details began to come into

123

focus beyond the hazy, dirty-gray micro-atmosphere. Misgivings crept in. The terrain below looked less and less inviting. It was not a place to live. It was an untrustworthy way station for creatures far from home, there only because there was no better layover available.

Down we went, to a place where the inhabitants were less familiar and probably more dangerous than the unknown chunk of rock they inhabited. The space above Tolkien's corona was extremely clean, no satellites, no space junk, leaving our collision avoidance system display unmarked. Griffin's gravity repulse system had no problem adjusting to ground radar readings. Within the moon's corona haze there were varying layers both of temperature and pressure, but nothing extraordinary.

"Hold at one hundred?" asked Danica.

"Briefly. Let's look for a parking place that's not reserved, shall we?"

"How would we know?" she replied.

"Let's hope we don't get any tickets on our windshield. That open area just ahead is far enough out. It seems less popular. Try there."

There seemed to be more spacecraft on the ground than had been apparent in the surface imagery. Most were about half the size of the Griffin and looked like they belonged to a mother ship somewhere. Scattered among them, however, were a few considerably larger. None had a sterling, shipshape appearance. They were all beat-up, uncared-for work horses. It made the Griffin stand out more than I liked.

We bumped down onto hard ground, and as we ran through our shut-down procedures a portion of the complex was visible through the forward viewports. Dust was constantly blowing between buildings and vehicles. The only thing missing was tumbleweed. A few indistinguishable biped forms, ankle-length desert outerwear billowing out behind them, pushed through the wind, quickly disappearing indoors. One particularly unsettling, shape-changing life-form kept passing by on the street. We couldn't tell if it was one individual or several. One other resident was equally confounding. It was a brown spider-like thing, the size of a shopping cart, and had five thick spider legs with camel feet that pumped up and down like pistons. The oval body was a soft brown with no discernable markings, no eyes, and no mouth. It was impossible to tell if it was a pet, a predator, or a person.

Wilson, Danica, and I strapped on our utility belts and pulled on hooded jackets to shield us from the sand. Our colleagues stood by with worried stares. We popped open the door of the aft airlock, stood back from the first blast of air and dust, then deployed the ramp and hurried down so they could close up. Standing at the bottom, we were all asking ourselves what the hell we were doing, but none of us was willing to admit it. The air was chilled and smelled like ozone. There was a chorus of howling in the wind coming from different directions. The protective atmospheric dome twinkled overhead through the haze.

With a raised voice Wilson asked, "Where's the visitors' center do you think?"

Danica laughed nervously.

"There's an awful lot of landing craft around here. Remember, let's just try to be one of them." I replied.

"Okay, but if that spider thing starts coming my way..."

No sooner had he started to speak than one of the creatures appeared from behind the nearest vehicle on our left, passing close by in front of us. It was making a chirping sound like a cricket, and to our amazement, the translators in our ears converted the sound into a seafaring-styled song any longshoreman with enough whiskey in him would have been proud to sing.

As it disappeared from view, Wilson looked at me with a forced smile and shouted, "Well, that's not something you see every day!"

A fifty-yard hike through parked spacecraft brought us to the main dirt street. Periodically, we had to shield our faces with our arms from the blowing sand. Most of the vehicles we passed by bore paint and markings scarred from the effects.

Emerging onto the wind-blown street, we found a very crudely arranged township of metallic structures, most of which had been created from expended materials originally intended for other purposes. One structure on our right was a fuel storage tank with doors cut and welded. Next to it, a ten-foot tall round cement piping system had been closed in with metallic sheets, one of which was an entrance. Farther down, the fuselage of an old spacecraft was positioned sideways to the street, its view ports glazed over, a rear port door hatch banging in the wind. We watched a hooded figure cross over and enter what looked like a huge boxcar on the left. There seemed to be a trail in the sand more frequently traveled there. It was our best bet. I headed for it.

The entrance to the place was a hatch, adapted to the sidewall of the boxcar. I pulled hard to open the spring-loaded, makeshift door, and we all stepped inside, our hoods shielding our faces. The place was so well-lighted and packed it startled me. There were a few hard-to-identify forms, although most of the occupants were of the humanoid variety, features and extremities notwithstanding. The interior was bigger than expected. There were long and short tables scattered around the room. A variety of gaming was in progress. It was noisy and

125

alien-stuffy. Makeshift booths lined the right-hand wall, separated by panels of uneven cut metal supported by junk pieces of conduit. There was a counter at the far end of the place, backdropped by a wide variety of supplies. A creature with a vacuum cleaner mouth, no nose, and beady eyes manned the counter. He had reptilian skin for a scalp. Oddly enough, he looked friendly.

Most of the clientele looked us over as we entered. Most quickly returned to what they were doing. It looked like business transactions were taking place everywhere. In only a few moments, voices became raised again as negotiations resumed. There were bottles on some tables, along with discarded paper plates well cleaned of food products. A quick count gave me thirty-four individuals. To my surprise, ten of them looked perfectly human. There was an empty table with four chairs near the entrance where the wind was a nuisance every time the door opened. We moved over and sat.

Trophies decorated the walls. They were parts from spacecraft repairs, drilling rig components, duct work with shards from some sort of significant explosion, some beaten up paper with photos of creatures who did not appear to be heroes, various types of alien labeling printed by each image. Before I had a chance to say anything, a very short man with green-brown hair on the sides of his head came trotting up to us. His face was so wrinkled it was impossible to see where specific features began or ended. He wore a plaid vest over no shirt, baggy canvas trousers, and black boots. He seemed cheery. He pointed to a sign on the wall that was written in script that looked like Arabic. After questioning stares from all of us, he laughed and proclaimed, "If you must sit, you must drink."

Wilson slapped his hand on the table and declared, "Well, I think I like this place! What have you got, my friend?"

I interrupted. "We'll all have water, please."

The little man turned to me with an even bigger smile. "Water is the most expensive."

I dug in my flight suit pocket and pulled out a gold coin and handed it over. "Will that do?"

"One more will cover it and me," he answered hopefully.

I gave him another and he dashed off.

The faces nearest us were exotic. I couldn't tell if the two on our left were male or female or neither. They wore Mideastern-styled robes and black veils pulled across their faces. There seemed to be a permanent smile through the veil, though almost nothing else was visible. They were bald with deep-tanned skin, the eyes orange-yellow.

At the rectangular brown table beyond them, two individuals were shoving a tablet of some sort back and forth at each other. It was not possible to tell if it was a negotiation or a game. They remained expressionless the entire time. One had short green tubes for ears and golden scales for skin. The mouth protruded from the face; the eyes were sunk back in it. His companion was nearly the opposite. A brown, wooly shag covering allowed only the eyes, nose, and mouth to be seen. Four fat fingers with black fingernails, also covered by shag.

We had to look around with extreme care. We all knew the wrong eye contact could produce undesirable results. A moment later the short little man returned with our drinks. Yellowish-brown water in shot glasses. Danica tried to hide her revulsion. Wilson smelled his glass carefully. As I took my glass, I also took my first chance. I summoned our little waiter closer. "Lugal Amar."

I watched him closely for a reaction. The little man had the best poker face I had ever seen. There was not a glimmer of recognition or surprise. I held another gold coin out low. It surprised me when he snatched it up, leaned forward, and pointed to the man behind the counter at the other end of the room. He wiped our table quickly with an oily rag and dashed off.

Danica quietly proclaimed, "I'm not drinking this. There's someone's urine in it."

"What did he tell you?" asked Wilson.

I glanced quickly around. "Nothing, but he pointed to the guy behind the counter when I mentioned the name Lugal Amar."

"It can't be this easy," replied Wilson.

"That was the name Patrick was given. And this is the place he was asked about. It was either a false lead, or we're in the right place."

"So we should go talk to the man behind the counter, you think?"

"Not we. Me. I'll pick up some of whatever he's got over there, and do my best to make small talk."

"May still be a dead end."

"May be."

I slid my chair back, stood, pretended to take a sip of my urine, and swaggered nonchalantly toward the man at the sales counter. The only thing he was selling that I could recognize was a wooden box with cigars in it. He crossed over to meet me as I came to the counter. I gestured to the cigars and held out a gold coin. He removed two and handed them to me without speaking. I held out a second gold coin and softly said, "Lugal Amar."

He looked me over carefully and did not try to conceal his understanding. He nodded and pointed to a man sitting alone in a booth at the back of the place. There was no one else around that spot, so no question about who he was pointing to. I slid the coin across the counter to him, tucked my cigars inside my coat, and headed that way.

The man in the booth was human in every way. He did not look up as I approached. He seemed completely sure of himself. I stood a moment trying to get some clue from him. Big leather trench coat with a high collar. Black stovepipe boots. Rings on his fingers. Short dark hair, weathered skin on a rough-cut face. A scar under the left ear running down to the neckline. Finally he looked up, nodded, and gestured to the opposite seat.

We sat in silence for a moment. He glanced up occasionally as he pulled out a cigar, then dug in the breast pocket of his coat for a light. I reached into my jacket and drew out the photo of Patrick's daughter and slid it across the table in front of him. He dragged a big wooden match on the table's edge, let the flame rise up, then leaned forward and lit his cigar. After a good long healthy draw on the thing, he smiled and blew it in my face.

That was the last thing I remember.

Chapter 13

"Tell me something, are you fucking stupid, Tarn?"
 The place had more shadow than light. Crates stacked high overhead. Enough gravel on the floors you could not make out what kind of floor it was. One overhead light beneath a dish-shaped, silver shade that never stopped swinging. I was in a hard wooden chair. Hands well-tied behind. Ankles fastened just as securely. The man with the cigar sat backward in a similar wooden chair. There were others behind I could not see. He kept looking up at them and smiling. They did not speak.
 "Where are we? How do you know my name?"
 "That answers that." The man looked up at his cohorts behind me. "He is fucking stupid. Tarn, you show up here in a government-confiscated ship, you go waltzing into The Barter Zone asking for a name that is a code word for somebody snooping around who shouldn't be, and you don't even wear dark glasses. You think these people don't know who you are, dumb fuck?"
 "Look, there's no need for all this clandestine shit. I'm only trying to track down somebody's daughter."
 The room erupted into laughter. I estimated six of them. The smell suggested the others were a bit grungier than the one interviewing.
 "Well, good luck with that! You know how many daughters have passed through these doors, Tarn? Human females are especially valuable. They're in demand, you might say. They are popular meat, and best of all Earth's government doesn't bother to come looking for them. Once they leave the main auction, they can end up anywhere within a few trillion miles of here. How would you track a single one down, even if you were a free man, which you're not?"
 "How can you do this? Sell out your own species? Is that what you're saying?"
 "It's a simple import-export business, Tarn. It's just that people happen to be the commodity."
 "You steal their lives."

E.R. Mason

"You think? We take some overly attractive bitches who are so vain and spoiled they think they are royalty. Or sometimes some asshole executive pisses off the wrong person somewhere and we take the self-important idiot and show him how the other half lives. Sound like much of a crime, Tarn? World governments rip people off worse than that every day. Man, you are a naive bastard."

"Sorry, I just can't see it. There's better ways to make a living."

"Are you kidding? What would I be on Earth? A shipping clerk trying to work my way up to supervisor? Out here I am a Captain of a ship with a crew of thirty or more. I can go anywhere and do anything I want and get wealthy while I'm doing it. Does that answer your question?"

"It's going to catch up with you."

He leaned back and smiled. "But not today, Mr. Tarn. Today it has caught up with you."

"At least tell me one thing. How did I go so wrong, exactly?"

"Where didn't you go wrong is more like it. Don't you know who built that nice ship you're flying?"

"What's that got to do with anything? It was designed by a carrier pilot. I don't recall his name."

"I asked you who built the thing. Who paid for it? Don't you know?"

"Some conglomerate."

"No, it was financed by a man name Blackwell."

An idiot light suddenly went off in my head. I had missed something in the short conversation with Stan Lee. When I had asked him about Patrick's problem, he had repeated that he could not give me anything else on the name Dorian Blackwell. He had been telling me the two cases were connected, but I hadn't picked up on it. "What's Blackwell got to do with it?"

"I handled Blackwell's shipping requirements before the asshole got visions of world domination. How do you think an idiot like that got where he was? He was in the import-export business, just like me. His product was those precious sons and daughters you're so concerned about."

"Blackwell was set up with those off-world religious groups?"

"He was set up with anybody willing to pay the right price."

"So how does the Griffin fit in?"

"I got to spell it out for you? Your ship, a ship designed to fly like an airplane. You know how governments track us when we're moving illegal goods? Mostly they follow engine signatures or gravity repulse trails. Your ship was designed to glide into pickup points without leaving a trail. It was never put into service because idiot Blackwell got thrown in prison, but the point is, you're flying a ship that was built from money for slaves. Still feeling holier than thou, Mr. Tarn?"

"Look, I'm not after you. I just need to track down one person for a friend. That's not such a big deal, is it? Can't I make you a really sweet deal where we both come out ahead?"

"Tarn, you don't get it. You think we're gonna turn you loose so you can report back on all this stuff? You were headed for a new life the minute you walked through that door. You're lucky you got the body for physical labor. Otherwise you'd be six feet under, face down in gray sand right now. Your life's gonna be down in the mines where the radioactivity makes your skin feel prickly. We'll get a pretty penny for you."

"Come on; there must be some kind of deal we can make."

"That is the deal, Tarn."

"What about my crew? They don't know anything. Leave them out of it."

"Oh, yeah. I'll give you that much. Six of my guys were supposed to round those two up after you passed out. We knew that big guy was experienced. We were ready for that. But what's the deal with that freakin' bitch from hell you brought along? That bitch broke one of my guys' knees, gouged the eyes on another, and head-butted a third into dreamland before the marshal finally had to show up to stop the place from getting completely trashed. They're all in lockdown right now. I gotta go buy my guys out. Yours should be able to buy out okay. So you get a free pass for your crew. Too much attention on them to bother now. It wouldn't be cost-effective."

"About that deal. What if I had something you could use?"

"I got that, Tarn. You. Have a nice sleep."

Somebody stabbed me in the shoulder with a needle, and the world went black.

I was aboard a spacecraft traveling at light, in a dingy, tiny closet with a small illuminated panel near the floor. There were no windows, and barely enough light given off to see anything. The air was cold and smelled like oil. I was in a sitting position, chained to a bench originally intended for use as a shelf. There was a similar shelf inches above my head. It was a cell of dark metallic walls with conduit running floor to ceiling. What little vision was possible cycled in and out of focus. There were shackles on my ankles. Similar shackles were attached to

E.R. Mason

my wrists with the chain hooked around the overhead shelf support. My ears were ringing.

You do not need gauges or view ports to tell you when traveling at light speeds. Just as ancient sailors could always tell when their ship was underway, there are many similar sensations associated with a starship. The hum within the cold steel, the subtle waves of vibrations that come and go, the minute sensations of continuous motion all around you are all familiar indicators of travel through warped space. Finding yourself traveling at such speeds, against your will, on an unknown starship with an unknown crew, is particularly disturbing. Any incompetence in balancing those light-speed engines, any unexpected erroneous diversion from a plotted course, can take the ship and crew to the wrong time and place, leaving you in a universe centuries older than it should be, your life a tiny fragment left behind in human history. Although unproven, it is theorized that when this happens, the victims live only a few days thereafter.

Hours passed. My vision slowly returned to focus. No one came. The anger in me slowly simmered to new highs. Finally, there were indications we were dropping to normal space. I was jerked around against the walls of my compartment. The whine of sublight engines kicking in came from somewhere outside. Not long after, there was the squeal of the compartment door being unlatched and a seam of light so bright I had to shut my eyes.

Four of them in makeshift combat garb came in to take me. They clamped a new chain on my wrists before unlocking the other one. They were human, seemed to know their job quite well, and were not taking any chances. They dragged me out into the piercing light of a long corridor. They pushed and dragged me along for quite a distance, two in front, two behind. It was a big ship.

We came to a four-way corridor where others were waiting. They were not human. Lizard people with cattle prods. Little tails in back, sticky-looking three-fingered hands, lizard faces. Three of them. Some sort of monetary exchange took place. One lizard man grabbed the chain on my wrists. The other adjusted his cattle prod, and in one swift motion swung it up and stuck me. A loud bang went off in my head, my vision again blurred in and out, and they dragged me along into a different ship, a ship that seemed filled with all the amenities lizard people preferred.

I was guided to a small, wet, green room with shower nozzles and drains in the floor where other lizard men were waiting. My shackles were dropped to the floor under the watchful stare of six of them. The lead lizard man poked at my boots with his cattle prod. I had no choice but to kneel and remove them. He then poked at my flight suit, and when I resisted, pulled the trigger on his cattle prod and made blue arcs in front of my face. When all clothing items had been removed, I stood naked as the spray nozzles began showering me in yellow liquid. A lizard man pulled a fire hose out of a wall fixture and blasted me with even more high pressure. There was a strange yucking sound from them. Lizard laughter. When they were done, they threw my flight suit back at me and shoved my boots close. I was made to carry those things naked down their lizard corridor as they planted weak bursts of cattle prod on my buttocks. All along the corridors, yellow lights were pulsing on and off. It was easy to guess. Caution, preparing for jump to light speed.

 I was shoved into a gray lizard cell, much more plush than the one I had been in. There was a hard, formed bed built against one wall with a flimsy silver blanket piled on it. There was a waist-high water tap above a drain in the floor. A metal half-cup sat on its side near the drain. A knee-high bucket with a small seat atop it sat in one corner. I was kicked into the room with the intention of being thrown to the floor. I managed to drag along one wall and stay upright. The door slammed shut. No knobs, levers, or locks, only an oval-shaped viewing window not made to open.

 A change came over me. A frightening change. With the first blast from the high-pressure hose in the shower, a circuit breaker in my mind had blown. I had become pathological. Rational thinking was no longer required. No further consequences were of any concern at all. They call it right-brain in stallions. You confine a stallion and if something frightens him badly enough, he switches to a right-brain mentality. At that point, everything around him is kicked, crushed, slammed, or run into repeatedly. The assault continues until the barriers are broken and the horse is free or the horse dies.

 I would be leaving this place soon. I would wreak havoc upon this place and its occupants until the barriers were broken or I was dead. I pulled my flight suit back on, stomped my feet back into my boots and laced them, sat on the hard composite bed, and began. The flashing yellow glow of the ship's warning lights filtered through the viewing window and changed suddenly to red. A loud hum rose up from the gray walls and abruptly broke into a whine. I slid back along my new bed and was pressed up against the wall as we went to light. Quickly, the acceleration equalized, releasing me back to equilibrium. I stood and went to the door, peering out the window. Nothing but a portion of gray conduit-filled hallway could be seen. A green three-fingered hand suddenly slapped the window heavily. My lizard-faced guard stared from behind it, telling me to get back. I nodded thanks to him and backed away. He had given me my answer. There was only one. In a ship used for delivering slaves, no one slave is all that important.

Sitting on the bed again, leaning back against the hard, cold wall, I began my scan. The room was probably ten by ten. Bare walls. Low, bare ceiling. Nothing for a prisoner to use. Four twelve-inch rectangular opaque lamps built into the wall near the floor. One on each wall.

There was no need to wait. This was a good time, actually. The bridge crew would be busy checking systems. Engineering would be doing the same. Everyone else getting settled in.

I went to the footlight nearest me, took a front stance position and kicked the thing as hard as I could. The light cover was something akin to plastic. It shattered into four pieces. One of the pieces was perfect. It was triangular, ending in a point, and had a very nice twelve-inch jagged edge. I couldn't have shaped it better. I pulled off a boot and sock, cut off the top of the sock, fashioned it appropriately and wrapped it around the handle end of my new plastic knife. I put the rest of my sock back on, pulled the boot over it, and tucked my knife into the thigh side pocket of my flight suit.

If I lay on the bed moaning that I was sick, there was no way he would come. These people were seasoned killers. They didn't care if you were sick or in pain. This was not a meal and movie flight. But, there were two things people like this could not ignore.

Death and greed.

I gathered up the tin cup on the floor by the drain, then pulled out my plastic knife. The forearm just below the elbow was a good place. I sat on the floor in the lotus position and began working the tip of the knife into my forearm. If you rock it back and forth it doesn't hurt as much.

The red began to show. A fairly good flow was needed. As soon as the red stream began to run down my arm, I dropped the knife and positioned the cup beneath the flow. I had to work the cut to keep it open. Ever so slowly, the tin cup began to fill with blood. Three-quarters of the cup would be plenty.

When I had what I thought was enough, I used the sock end of my knife to stop the bleeding. It was more persistent than expected. I had to unwrap the knife and use the sock as a bandage. Guarding my cup of blood carefully, I pulled off the other boot and sock, cut a second piece, and rewrapped the knife handle. A powerful grip on the knife would be prudent.

With my boot still removed, I twisted open the heel and pulled out my Nasebian crystal. The colors within it were so brilliant, and swirling so rapidly, I had to quickly hide it in a pocket for fear of attracting attention. With sock and boot back on, I shimmied around to make it look as though I had fallen from the bed, then set my cup of blood nearby. I pulled up both flight suit sleeves so that the wrists were plainly visible. With great care, I used the knife to visibly scar up both wrists, but not so much as to draw blood. Laying back to test my position, I took the cup and poured just enough on each wrist, then spread the rest out to make it look like very large puddles.

With my knife tucked behind my waist where it could be drawn quickly, I drew the Nasebian crystal from my pocket and lay back in my puddles of blood, the crystal glowing brightly in one dead, open hand. I kept my eyes open just a slit in my best death stare.

It was much closer than I had expected. He must have seen crystal reflection on the window. I had expected to lie there twenty minutes or more as the blood dried around me. It only took about three minutes.

Had it been just the bloody death of a prisoner, he would have called in immediately. But, in this case, there was an unusual crystal involved, possibly one of great value. Calling in to headquarters would blow any chance of acquiring it. A quick inspection of the suicide would allow him to pocket the treasure and no one would be the wiser.

The cell door creaked open. The large puddles of blood could not have come from anywhere else. He tromped quickly to the body and immediately reached over for the stone. I swiped up the knife and drove it into his throat and up into his brain as deeply as it would go and twisted it in a final knee-jerk reaction.

His eyes glazed instantly and lizard man fell dead beside me.

Chapter 14

Busy, busy, busy. Up on the feet quickly, bloody knife withdrawn and stored in thigh pocket. Might need it some more. Crystal placed carefully back in heel compartment without getting bloodied. Drag the guard's body up onto the bed. There was a wide black belt with a nasty-looking hand weapon attached. The belt tore off at the front like Velcro. I strapped it on. A badge attached to a strip of cloth around the neck came off with a yank. I tucked it into my breast pocket, then covered the body with the silly little tin blanket. I did not bother about the blood on the floor.

The cell door was half open, waiting for the guard's quick exit. The hallway was clear in both directions. The crew alert lights were not lit. Cruise had been achieved.

Which way? The slide on my bed had told me which was forward and which was aft. Lots of crew forward. Not so many aft, and some real important stuff back there. Maybe escape modules along the way? Too soon to think about that. You can't just pop off a healthy ship, after all. Even if there was a way to, they'd just turn around and come back for you all pissed off. Besides, you should only bail out if there's someplace nearby to go. On the other hand, a slow death in an escape pod would be better than staying aboard this hell hole. Next thing on my list; it's pretty difficult to keep a ship running in top notch shape. It's not too hard at all to screw it up royally.

I stomped along the grated corridor like a bull elephant that had escaped the circus. I drew the hand weapon and studied it as I went.

Contrary to popular belief, there is no fundamental layout for starships. On any given craft, you may be required to climb decks three, four, and five to get to deck two. That's depending on how forward or aft you happen to be. Spacecraft are laid out solely based on the necessities of the systems they house. For that reason, a stranger on board a ship cannot possibly know how to get from point A to point B unless corridor maps have been provided, or a personal guide is proffered. In the case of someone wishing only to cause hatred and destruction, this navigational constraint is of no concern at all.

Shock Diamonds

The particular corridor I was traversing ended at a closed pressure door. I checked the blaster in my hand, found a small circular knob on one side which seemed like a power level control, and turned it to what looked like full. With the weapon in one hand, I listened for a moment against the heavy door, then cranked its handle down and watched the locking mechanism clank down and out of the way. It pulled open easily.

Weapon ready, I peered into the next chamber. It was a huge storage area with a high ceiling. Car-sized crates created alleys to get around. A gantry crane waited overhead. There did not seem to be anyone in attendance.

I wove my way aft, pausing at each crate intersection, glancing around corners for lizard men. At the back of the hold, there were three more pressure doors, one on either side of the room, one dead center. These were much more official looking. Signs above them in unreadable lizard left no doubt that you should not enter these doors for fear of whatever punishment is meted out to lizard crewmen. The center door looked like the most serious, so there I went.

With one hand on the door release latch, I paused to ask myself what was going on. Had I just killed someone without a second thought? Reality was seeping back into my inner rage. I looked around at the unfamiliar surroundings of a slave trade ship. The rage resumed.

It was important now not to become a simple nuisance to these people. I could take a position, strike them, and then retreat to a new vantage point and wait to strike again. With that tactic, I could raise hell on this ship probably for days or even weeks, but eventually they would run me down. That was not what was needed. I needed to cripple this ship, and cripple it badly enough that it could not get underway for a week or more, if ever. I needed to find my way to one of their critical systems. Main power, light speed propulsion, or even navigation and guidance would do nicely.

With a last look around, I carefully lowered the locking bar so that it would not clank. I opened the door and looked inside. It was an important place. Bays of computer consoles lined the room. The place was kept in pristine condition, another indicator of criticality. I stepped inside so as not to be visible in two areas at once. As carefully as possible, I sealed the door, keeping the weapon ready in my right hand.

Moving with stealth along the back row of consoles, I spotted two lizard men on the opposite side of the room. They were talking in lizard chatter, a heated exchange. I was too far away for the translators to translate. They wore green and brown uniforms that looked like Jujitsu outfits. The colors and

E.R. Mason

patterns complemented their skin tone. They had high black boots to cover the big lizard feet. They were arguing as though both wanted to be in charge. Finally, one turned and stomped away. A door swished open and closed. That left just the one.

A wide cutaway in the wall near lizard man opened to a control room for the towers of computer racks surrounding me. Lizard man turned and went into the control room to a console against the far wall. Cable conduits the size of Roman pillars were scattered around the area near him. This was a place of special importance, though I could not tell exactly what kind. There was emergency gear affixed to the walls, and too many unreadable signs bearing too many red warnings.

Keeping a close eye on him, I moved along the racks and stood just outside the control room, occasionally stealing glances around the corner. Too late I noticed the mirrors attached to the ceiling in each corner. I dared one more glance around, hoping to keep tabs on him, and instead met lizard man staring back at me from a foot away. He had a frozen, inquisitive stare on his scaled face.

All hell broke loose.

My quick draw was not quick enough. To make matters worse, I had set the blaster on full and it discharged all of its energy in less than a second off to the right. It made a hell of a boom, blew two-foot holes in two of the fat cable stanchions, knocked down one small console and exploded a hole the size of a beach ball in a larger one. The little blue charge light on the side of the gun immediately turned red and began to flash. Charging in progress.

Lizard man was furious. He opened that huge protruding mouth to reveal spiked teeth and let out a roar. He slapped a sticky three-fingered hand around my neck, forcing me to let go of the gun, both hands needed to save the tracheal tube. Despite his apparent evolution, he was also not above tearing his adversaries apart with those spiked teeth. He lunged repeatedly at my face, snapping jaws missing by millimeters, as I flailed wildly trying to gain some semblance of a defense. In the fury of battle, I managed to notice the small flapper holes on each side of his head, and on a wild gamble I gave up my grip on his upper arms and clapped those as hard as I could.

His roar turned high-pitched. He staggered wildly, still trying to keep the six-fingered grip on my neck. I brought up a boot and caught him squarely between the legs. It didn't faze him a bit, part of the difficulty of fighting unfamiliar species. I managed to get one hand around and over his forehead and began bending his head back as he continued to howl. He let go of my neck with one hand and began slapping at me. Apparently the lizard hands were too soft to make fist fighting effective, but the choke hold was working quite well, even with just one hand.

I began to fear loss of blood to the brain. We were clenched together, muscle against muscle. The problem was, he had a lot more of it than I did. He was quite a bit bigger, but had he not been, he would still have been far too strong. As we braced and continued the wrestler holds, the lizard lips began to slowly show in a sickly little lizard smile. He knew he was winning.

I was going to have to release my grip and try to twist out. The odds did not seem to favor me. But as I positioned for the move, something unexpected occurred. Lizard man and I began to drift upward off the floor. The contents of my stomach joined in as the feeling of weightlessness took over.

There was a great deal of smoke hanging near the ceiling. It was coming from the destroyed cable conduits and control consoles. Red lights on the wall had begun flashing. As we drifted up, an irate voice came over an intercom demanding to know what was going on down here.

It was then I saw the look in lizard man's eyes. He was sickened by the zero G.

I, on the other hand, was right at home in it.

Lizard man abandoned his grasp and frantically pedaled and swam around the empty air. His tail kept bumping against things and turning him the wrong way. Between choking back sickness, he would glance back at me in fear. I ripped off my gun belt, pushed off of the nearest console and caught him smartly around the neck. I wound it around tightly and Velcro'd it in place. He did an ugly little struggle, his soft lizard hands too weak to undo it, his lizard tongue protruding out the side of his mouth. Finally, as I held to a side wall gasping for breath, he closed his eyes and went to death.

My right-brain fury continued. It seemed like a good time to leave the artificial gravity control room. It was a good bet there were an awful lot of very upset lizard people floating around in zero-G. No doubt, they were hurrying this way hoping to replace a fuse or something. They would be even more pissed off when they discovered the carnage. I needed to find a more critical section of the ship as it was still my intention to bring this spacecraft out of light and get off. Perhaps I could eventually find a shuttle or escape pod and take my leave of this sadistic place. I reassured myself I would be leaving, one way or another. I would not be going to the mines. I pushed down and gathered up my gun floating under a low shelf against the wall.

The layer of smoke hanging around the ceiling was now billowing around in the air conditioning. It was becoming difficult to breathe. The lizard voice on the intercom continued to angrily demand answers. There were double sliding doors to the left of

E.R. Mason

the large console I had destroyed. I pulled against a conduit in the ceiling and flew over to it. It popped open automatically. Either it accepted human biology, or it liked the guard's badge I still had in my breast pocket.

The door led to a new, more industrial corridor. I stuck my head out and froze at the sight of yet another lizard man in a gunmetal guard uniform, hanging onto conduit, his feet floating higher than his body. He was engulfed in a cloud of green vomit and was about to make more when he saw me. He was only fifty feet away and for a moment I thought more combat was at hand, but instead, he began frantically swimming along the conduit in the other direction, vomiting as he went. It suggested to me that lizard man reinforcements lay in that direction, so I headed off in the other.

Crew alert lights were now flashing a persistent yellow all along the passageway. There were service hatches every few yards, some open, some closed. More and more conduit runs were entering the corridor from the floors and ceiling. The tubing was becoming larger in diameter, the accessway narrower. It meant I was probably nearing some type of propulsion area. I hurried along.

At the end of the corridor was a much larger, more sophisticated pressure door. It was colored ash-red to make it stand out from the gray metallic walls and equipment around it. There was a green light above. Behind me, the yellow crew alert lights were still flashing away. As quietly as possible, I pulled down, unlatched, and opened the big door. It swung aside to reveal a laboratory with transparent walls on both sides, a row of control consoles running along each. Behind the glass walls were junctions of large, frosty conduits. Gauges protruded from some of them, various colors denoting some relationship between each.

A single lizard man in a white lab jacket was floating by the right-hand row of control consoles, intently moving his head up and down to study the console below him and the critical systems beyond the glass wall. In between contractions of sickness, he seemed concerned about the weightlessness affecting his system flows. This had to be a fuel or coolant distribution point, a delightful place to cause severe damage to a spacecraft at light.

I pulled myself in and the movement caught his eye. A forked tongue darted nervously out of his mouth. From a nearby console, an audio com message suddenly began advising that repair crews were working on the gravity problem and there was no cause for alarm. But the message was lost on lizard man. He stared at me, pulled down closer to his control console, then grabbed with both hands at something. I jerked my blaster up but held my fire. Lizard man missed the grab, lost his grip on the console, and floated upward, twisting and swimming in place trying to gain a hold on anything. He kept worriedly glancing back over his shoulder at me. Keeping the weapon leveled, I pushed down to floor level and held to a switch on the wall.

The conduit runs beyond the glass on the right were much larger and had many more gauges and sensors attached than those behind the glass on the left. The "Don't panic" announcement from the address system was now in standard repeating mode. The yellow crew alert light near the top of the far wall had become a steady yellow. Lizard man struggled around helplessly in the center of the control area, staring fearfully at me, slowly drifting to the left. I moved toward him and his expression became even more alarmed. With a last look around, I pointed my weapon at the largest conduit behind the glass on the right and fired. I had forgotten the gun was still set to max and had now fully recharged.

It is customary aboard spacecraft to issue weapons that will produce the necessary amount of damage without setting off fuels or creating other sources of ignition. The weapon I had confiscated was apparently of that genre. With that tiny squeeze of the trigger, it shattered the glass wall into a million pieces, tore through half a dozen smaller conduits, and exploded a hole the size of a man in the waist-high horizontal pipe beyond. The concussion from the blast blew us back into the left-hand glass barrier, and it too shattered, raining glass down as we struggled to grab something. Lizard man let out a hair-raising scream as he spotted the damage done. The superstructure of the ship shuddered. I managed to grab a wall fixture and hang on as debris shot around in every direction, ricocheting off of everything in its path. As the debris settled down into a slow float, lizard man kicked himself off of the conduit, toward the center consoles, some of which were still lighted and flashing urgent alarms. He managed to make some headway through the rain of fragments, keeping his right arm against his chest as though it was broken. I had the impression he was hoping to call for help. I brought myself around to get my feet against the wall, intending to intercept him, when something on the opposite side of the room made me take pause.

Half a dozen conduits and pipes were fractured, including a very large one. Liquids were oozing out of some of the fractures. There was an aqua blue fluid that was separating into droplets as it drifted toward an air-conditioning intake, and nearby green ooze was holding itself together as it rose up from a junction box. Near the door at the opposite end of the room, another yellow chemical ooze the size and shape of a child's blanket was fluttering along toward lizard man as he moved to-

E.R. Mason

ward the room's center. He spotted it, and with a kick from one boot against the top of a console, managed to get out of the way just in time.

There was no doubt these chemical spills were caustic. But there was something else that held my attention. Within the large, ragged hole of the big conduit, there was a bluish inner sleeve. It too had been compromised. And from that odd-looking secondary containment wall, tiny sparks of light were being emitted, like little stars drifting from a star well. They looked just like the shock diamonds you see in the plume of a rocket engine running at more than 100 percent power. There was a sparkling static sound associated with them, and when lizard man spotted them, his look of desperation turned to one of complete horror. He froze with one sticky hand clamped against the far side wall and came to weightless attention. Seconds later a dark red glob emerged from the big hole, crackling and emitting light almost like a Fourth of July sparkler. It changed shape as it drifted along, reacting with the atmosphere in the room, the crackling growing into burning sounds, the surface of it covered in tiny white sparks. Behind it, another glob followed. It was then I noticed that the hole in the damaged conduit's inner sleeve was growing larger. An ominous, broad, grinding noise started up from outside the room. It sounded like pumps running dry.

Lizard man forgot all about the communications console and his broken arm. He pushed frantically away from the gyrating glob of twinkling, burning red, but somehow it seemed to have locked onto him. He slid back against the wall, turning his face away to avoid it, flattening his body. He might have made it except at that moment there was another great shudder from the ship, followed by a tremendous bang and buckling sound as she fell from light. Everything loose in the room plastered itself against lizard man's wall. I held with my back against the side of a console. The force of deceleration lasted only a few seconds, but it had to have been 9 Gs or more. It forced the air from my lungs and stretched the skin on my face to new limits. As weightlessness returned and the trash around me resumed floating, I struggled around fearing lizard man was trying to make a move.

Through the maze of debris I could still make him out plastered against the far wall. He seemed to have weathered it all quite well, although a console cover was floating in front of him, concealing his shoulders and face. I searched hurriedly for the gun. It was nowhere to be found. I braced for weightless combat and stared, waiting to make eye contact, but as the console cover drifted away, it revealed a new horror. Lizard man's head and most of his shoulders were missing. Behind him there was a new hole in the wall roughly the shape of the sparkling red blob. Through the hole, I could just make it out still rolling along, burning away everything in its path. As I watched, a second red blob passed by lizard man's remains and into the wall where it made a dull bang, many new tiny stars, and a second gaping opening. The large hole in the big conduit was now the size of a pickup truck, and the flow of sparkling red was continuous.

The crew alert light over the wall suddenly turned a rapidly flashing red. Loud horns began blaring. The stream of explosive red glob began eating everything in the room. I stared in disbelief. There was only one thing that could do that much damage that quickly.

Antimatter. Some form of docile antimatter, at least docile as antimatters went. Most antimatter instantly exploded upon contact with the real world. This stuff took its time.

Once again, I had worn out my welcome. I hurried back the way I had entered and found the corridor beyond the hatch completely redecorated. Rapidly flashing red lights were everywhere. Ear-piercing horns and bells were sounding continuously. Garbage was drifting in the air. And there was something else, even more significant.

Running lights in the floor. Arrows pointing crew to where they needed to go. At the instant I noticed them, a lizard voice came over the P.A.

"Abandon ship. Abandon ship."

No further invitation was needed.

The lighted arrows in the floor led me through a maze of equipment and storage rooms, places I would never have thought to go. The warning lights and repeating audio seemed to intensify with each passing minute. I pulled, pushed, and kicked my way along as quickly as possible, finally emerging into a new, very wide, long hallway where the floor lights became wider and even more insistent. As I pulled ahead, I spotted two lizard figures struggling badly. Somehow, I knew they were female, dressed in soft green one-piece suits covered with Velcro pockets. One lizard woman was trying to drag the other along in the direction of the arrows, but both were vomiting too frequently to keep going. They were caught, waving and kicking in a cloud of their own nausea. One noticed me approaching, paid no attention at first, but then looked back and became alarmed. They froze in place, still vomiting as I approached.

I did not slow. In zero-G, I was apparently the most adept person on this ship. I flew past them, being careful to

E.R. Mason

avoid getting puked, showing no concern whatsoever for their plight. They watched with perplexed stares as I glided away.

The arrows led through a last pressure door, already open. Beyond it were the objects of my desire. A row of maybe thirty escape pod doors on the right, status lights and control boards for each directly left. A few pods had already been deployed, their pressure doors sealed with a big X. Most, however, were open, green, and waiting for escapees.

The ship gave another great shudder, like an earthquake in space. I looked ahead and behind and suddenly spotted a lizard man in a guard's uniform heading in my direction. At the very first open, oval escape pod hatch, I pulled myself in.

Four seats. No manual controls. A repeating verbal message playing over and over. *"B4-6 is ready for immediate launch, B4-6 is ready for immediate launch."*

I pulled the hatch door shut and spun the handle to seal it, then strapped into a seat that seemed to have the best view out the two tiny circular windows on each side and the larger one in the pressure door. The verbal message changed. *"B4-6 is now armed and ready for deployment, B4-6 is now armed and ready for deployment."*

As I searched for a control, there was a sudden slap against the hatch window. A second later a lizard face came into view. It was a face with one blinded eye shut. It was the guard who had hosed me down in the showers. At that moment, I recalled his lizard laugh as he had done so. He was yelling something unpleasant, although I could not hear a word of it. He did not seem to want me to leave just then. By my left knee, there was a large button flashing red. With nothing to lose, I slapped it down. Lizard man's good eye opened wide. He spun around just as the inner door behind him slid shut. He turned back in horror and looked at me through the glass as though I should abort the pod ejection. I gave him my best lizard smile and waved.

The kick from the explosive bolts was extreme. It threw me forward against the seat harness to the point of pain. As the pod jetted away from the ship, lizard man, still wide-eyed, was sucked out with it. He flailed around for a few seconds until the frosty look of frozen death came over him. The one good eye was iced open and still had a stare of utter disbelief. He drifted away to the right, leaving me with the first view of the pirate ship that had been chartered to deliver me to the mines.

It looked like a blackbird aircraft without wings. Two large nacelle tubes ran along the aft section on either side. There was a terrible fire back there. It was flaming up over and over, billowing like an erupting volcano, and it was spreading. It was a hideous, sickening thing to see. A few more pods were

Shock Diamonds

popping off the side, very few. Not all of them made it. There was an ominous moment without eruption, followed by the most massive explosion I had ever seen. An orange-green fireball consumed half the superstructure. There is no sound in space, but I could feel it. I watched in dread as the largest fragment of bow went tumbling away with a ferocity that would have killed anyone left alive within.

They should never have brought me aboard.

The plume of debris headed my way, spreading out as it approached. It was unlikely my pod would survive the impacts. Time to pay the piper. No matter. I was off the ship. I had kicked my way out of the stall and was now running free. I had won. The Grim Reaper was of no consequence.

Little ticking sounds on the sides of the pod were the first of it. Quickly, larger bangs joined in. Then, frightening thuds shook the pod and knocked it around, causing jets to fire for stabilization.

Finally the big pieces arrived. The first was a glancing blow off the top that put me into a wild spin so intense it tried to pull the skin off my face with negative Gs. The world nearly disappeared into blackness, until a subsequent big bang drove the capsule in the other direction, making me wonder if the end was just moments away.

The last piece was so large it filled all three windows even before impact. It collided with such force I could see the superstructure flex inward and felt the pressure pop my ears. The push slammed me hard into the seatbelts and the world went black so fast I did not even have time to wonder if it was death.

Chapter 15

One of the bad things about right-brained violence is that often it leaves you during sleep. You wake up with all the guilt and none of the satisfaction the Neanderthal mind should have compensated you with.

The sound of chirping alarms and growling radar scanners lured me back to life. The first thought is always, am I alive? One hand instinctively goes to the chest to see if the body is still there. The sensory systems kick in and the feeling of cold saturates the body. Eyes flutter open and struggle to focus in hopes of asking the second most important question, where the hell am I?

When the eyes finally focused, my chin was down against my chest, my legs and boots front and center. I snapped my head up to find my world was a circular container filled with floating debris. There were flashing red lights here and there. On the left there was an incredibly huge dent pushed into the cabin. I sucked for air and found plenty of it available. Fingers and toes were responding to commands. No flowing bodily fluids seemed apparent.

I looked around my tiny, messy world and wondered how I had come to be there. Ugly memories began to surface. For a moment, I recalled the feeling of having won, the feeling that nothing much mattered beyond freedom. Then reality reared its ugly head. I was indeed beyond that. This was a tiny bubble of atmosphere in a remote area of space vacuum. As a friend of mine used to say, "Two choices, sit and wait for the end, or try to do something."

Generally speaking, there are two kinds of escape pods. There are the ones that pop off the wounded ship and just float around aimlessly hoping somebody will come along and pick you up. They usually carry food and water in enough quantity to give you time to think about your slow, impending death. The second kind, much less common, have a limited propulsion system designed to get you to the nearest heavenly body if there is one. They are generally reserved for ships that fly a repetitive flight plan where the neighboring star systems are well known, and where some class M planets, moons, or asteroids are known to

Shock Diamonds

exist along the route. These vehicles have reentry systems which are not for the faint of heart.

There was no choice but to face up to my dire situation and see if any hope existed at all. I unbuckled and quickly discovered I had either broken or bruised ribs, front and back. Probably bruised. It was hard to breathe, but the sharp pangs associated with cracks did not seem to be there. There was some burning on the right lower leg and a tear in the flight suit there where something had cut. It was already scabbed over. On my right forearm, I still had the top of my sock, painted red with dried blood. I pulled it up and peeked under. The self-inflicted cut was healing.

Was this the drifting coffin type of escape pod, or the fall-from-the-sky-in-a-flaming-ball kind? I began pushing away the floating garbage in front of me and something suddenly came to mind. It was the persistent grinding sound of radar scanning.

A panel in the floor had slid back to reveal a display screen, positioned so that passengers in all four seats could see it. I hooked a foot under my seat for stability and swept away more of the floating garbage. The display was packed with star-like objects, forcing me to wonder what the range of the thing was. Near the center of the display, all the tiny spots were painted in a wide variety of colors, some circled. Data I could not read was printed alongside each.

Alarm set in. The centermost object was bright green, enclosed by a flashing green circle, and had a green flight path leading directly to it. Within the extra data displayed alongside, there was some kind of numerical counter rapidly counting down.

I stiffened in weightlessness as realization set in. This was a heavily damaged escape pod, with a very basic reentry system, and it was planning on dropping me in on some unfamiliar rock somewhere. I could either try to figure out how to abort the programming or take a wild ride down. After careful consideration, I decided it was not a question of which option gave me the best chance of survival. It was a question of which option would be the least excruciating death.

There was no way to judge how long it would take this pod to reach its chosen destination. In space, without the equipment to measure them, size and distance remain absolute unknowns. Every answer in the pod was written in a language I did not understand. I would have to wait until the little blip on the radar screen had traveled enough distance along the little green flight path line so that I could estimate real time against it, and from that maybe judge how much time left before arrival

147

at my destination internment. There would probably be a computer voice warning to buckle up for impending death.

The silence behind the alarm chirps and radar growling reminded me how alone I was. I pushed over to one of the small, round portals and scanned the space outside, thinking maybe there would be another pod. There was not. Nor could any be seen from any of the other windows. I had killed almost everyone on that ship. How long would it take to put a thing like that aside? A lifetime maybe? Mine was that little green line on the pod tracking display.

They had been dealing in the slave labor of innocents, but maybe to a lizard culture that was a perfectly reputable thing to be doing. But the prisoner cells on their ship meant they knew it wasn't voluntary. Had I destroyed other innocent hostages? Or had I saved them from a slow death in radioactive mines? No matter. A fiery ride down in a bashed-up escape pod was sure to balance the scales.

Totally alone. Where was I? How far away had I been taken? Cigar man had put me aboard a ship. I was unconscious most of that time. He had delivered me to the lizard ship, collected his bounty, and left. The lizard ship hadn't been underway very long but they had been at light speeds. This area of space was still densely populated with stellar material. That meant this might still be a part of the Mu Arae sector, but that was a long-shot guess. Plus, it was hardly a consolation. The odds of someone finding me out here were nil unless it was a lizard people rescue ship following a pod beacon. Wouldn't they be glad to see me?

As distance along the little green flight line was covered, the view out the forward portal began to change. The twinkling light from the pod's destination planet began to dim into shape and detail. Surprisingly, it was a bluish green, even though it was shaped like a malformed potato, making it most likely an orbiting asteroid. I could just make out its sun by pressing my face against the forward window and looking up with one eye. My guess was, there would be no auto-orbit but rather a straight-in, ballistic dive with a roll-of-the-dice landing without regard to terrain. As the pod closed in, the entire ragged circumference of the destination planetoid was visible in the window. Then the voice warning system came on and suggested I buckle up. Peculiar attitude adjustments began to kick the pod around, making it difficult to fasten straps.

It was the braking system that bothered me the most. There just didn't seem to be any features outside the pod to adequately provide the speed braking necessary to mitigate a severe impact. A parachute system was out of the question. Every atmosphere is different, so even when there is an atmosphere, one chute system does not fit all.

When the braking finally began, I wished I had chosen a different seat. The engine firing was in front of me, which meant my body was trying to leave the seat, burying itself in the harness straps. It was a respectable amount of negative Gs. I had to squint for a few seconds to keep my eyes from popping out of the sockets. The determined little pod shuddered and roared as it hit the edge of the atmosphere. It arrived over the destination and slowed in anticipation of a gravity dive toward the surface.

Next, the main braking rocket died and a few moments later orange glow began to appear in the windows as air-braking took over. The impetus pushing me into my seat belts eased off, but a few seconds later there was an ominous change in direction. Suddenly I was being lifted out of my seat as the downward plunge began. Those impulsive, familiar thoughts of, "Wait a second, hold on a minute," reared their ugly head as the orange glow filled all windows. I was about to find out if this bent-up pod with its unexplained soft-landing system was, in reality, a crater-maker.

To my surprise, braking rockets did fire, making a throaty roar inside the cabin. It was a nice development, although clearly not enough for a soft landing. I was gently pressed down in my seat, expecting something more when the answer came.

Big "wumps" came from all around. All windows became obscured by dark gray material. It took me a moment to accept the idea of airbags. It was yet another reason to worry. Here's your best chance, buddy, as long as you don't roll off a cliff, land in a volcano, sink in quicksand, submerge into liquid mercury, impale yourself on a mountain peak, or any of the other countless epilogs available to air bag landers.

Before I could exclaim, "Oh, shit," the breaking of branches began. The pod was knocked harshly from side to side, front to back, followed by one big impact that knocked the wind out of me and compressed the already damaged rib cage. I was not able to take in a breath to scream.

The rolling began. I was the ball in a pinball machine. Having managed to take in some air, I was able to yell with each crashing blow, until the third or fourth finally turned my lights off.

Chapter 16

I do not know how long I lay crumpled up in a heap in that torn-up module. I am certain several days passed. Upon waking, bits of fragmented memory lingered at the fringe of awareness, refusing to organize. One was of a heavy rain imposing dampness within the capsule. Another fragment was of a large snout of some type trying to invade my domain.

The pod's round hatchway had blown open. My fingers and toes worked. One eye opened just fine. The other was swollen part way closed. I was lying sideways on the seat, still strapped in. The left leg was bent back against my thigh; my foot caught behind the backrest. My right leg was sticking straight up, tangled in torn cables.

There was a brooding indulgence to just lie there for a moment. Why be in a hurry to get bad news? Beyond the open hatch was a blur of green. Gentle, warm rushes of air were drifting in. I was breathing it. Without my consent, sensation began to turn on. There were too many telegraphs of pain and damage to handle at once. Perhaps, if I could free the left leg and straighten it out, I could resolve some of them. The right hand was behind me and wasn't busy. I wiggled the fingers again and used them to climb up my rump as a preflight test for the arm. The elbow made a cracking sound, but the arm came to life. It hurried down to the captured foot and helped it work free. The leg obeyed and straightened out, coming to rest in a pile of broken pod fare. The left arm was under me. I pushed up into a sitting position and rubbed the back of my neck. Things popped back into place.

There were sounds of life coming from outside, the buzzing of insects, punctuated by calls from other unfamiliar life. It meant I had been here for some time. My pod had become accepted as a non-predatory visitor.

Swamp. That was the smell. It was unmistakable. There was a charred smell along with it. A quick examination of torso, head, and limbs came up with too many bruises to count, a few abrasions, and no real lacerations other than the one I had made myself.

There was a meager first aid kit, probably put there by the people who designed the landing system. The only human-useful items: a small signaling mirror and a bar of magnesium with a striker in a small leather case. I went to tuck these things in my ragged flight suit pockets and came across the still-bloody plastic knife along with the dead guard's passkey badge. Inventory of my resources complete, I maneuvered around to look out the open hatch without exposing myself any more than necessary.

Primitive jungle. Leaves as huge as picture windows. Vines the size of fire hose. Tree canopy sixty feet up, patches of orange sky beyond. Rich black dirt heavily decorated with plants that looked like Jack-In-The-Pulpits except they were as tall as a man. Spots with clumps of grass covering nests of some sort. Fruit hung in places. A charred patch a short distance away where something hot from the pod had started a small fire. It had burned itself out.

The jungle became silent the moment my head emerged. My first instinct was to withdraw into the pod and cower there for a while. Instead, I withdrew the plastic knife, crawled out on my hands and knees, and cautiously stood, rechecking body parts as I went.

There was now a rough-hewn path back in the direction from where the pod had come. The torn and broken trail led up the side of an embankment and disappeared over a sharp rock overhang. There were pieces of airbag all along the way. As uninviting as it looked, I needed to get a vantage point for an overview of this place, and since all four limbs seemed to work reasonably well, up I went.

It was thirty minutes of slipping and sliding, and reclimbing lost ground. The overhang was forbidding. I had to work my way around, pausing after each section to let the rib cage reset. Hoisting up over the edge onto my stomach brought the clenching of teeth to keep from screaming, but the suffering from the climb was worth it. The view was spectacular.

Above the ledge behind me, a rock pile led several thousand feet up to the snow-covered peak of a dormant volcano. Looking out over the landscape, there lay a breathtaking world that went on forever. The horizon was oddly cut, a gradual climb on one side, a sharp drop on the other. This was not an egg-shaped world. The broad forest my pod had chosen to carve a path through went on for miles in both directions, drawing its life from mountain runoff. It led down to a vast open plain of innumerable hills and mounds covered by brown, waist-high grass. Beyond, a haze-covered line of mountains ran the entire width of the alien horizon. Far in the distance, a massive herd of something was moving slowly across a portion of the plain. I did not recognize their vague silhouettes. On my left and right, other mountain peaks in the distance rose up within the forest canopy. The sky was milky-orange with tall cumulonimbus clouds that did not seem to move.

Below me, I began to notice life moving within the forest. Small creatures darting above and below the canopy. Farther in the distance, vines and branches were being disrupted as leaves were harvested. Those creatures were not visible through the dense overhang, but some of the motion around the trees and overhang seemed to be from something of considerable size. As my concern arose, out of the corner of my eye I spotted something flying far off to my left. It was not an aircraft. It was something with a great wingspan. I began to be concerned about standing out in the open, and at that moment there came a roar from somewhere to the right that sounded like the aborted test firing of a rocket engine, except it was primeval. Suddenly, shelter became a priority. Perhaps the metallic pod wreckage was not such a bad place after all. Escape pods do not taste good and are hard to chew.

I skidded my way back down through the forest, knowing that a slip and roll on the busted-up chest and back would probably be fatal. I hung on to vines and earth and sledded down the broken pod path with an agility any professional X-game player would have been proud of. At the pod, I searched quickly for the hatch cover, did not find it, and climbed in, hurriedly stacking pieces of panels for a makeshift door. In the shadowy light, I parted the trash and lowered myself into a seat and sat considering just how much of an indiscretion standing out in the open had been. Almost in answer to the question, there began to be noises in the jungle nearby.

It was an occasional rustling of brush, a branch cracking here and there. Probably my imagination fulfilling my fear. These sounds had not been apparent in the silence before. Was it all in my battered head? I had so many bruises and abrasions it was hard to think straight. When had I last eaten anything? There had been so many periods of unconsciousness; I didn't even know that.

More cracking of branches. More rustling of brush. If there was to be a fight with a wild animal, I had no chance. I couldn't even take a deep breath. Tiny gulps of air brought an awareness of something else. An animal smell. I had indeed become prey. He was out there and was searching for me. There was nothing else to pile on the flimsy door covering. My plastic knife was all there was.

Suddenly there was a loud bang overhead on the pod wall. Then another on the side. Then three more followed quickly by more rustling, and again silence.

I could still only take shallow breaths but managed to push up into a squatting ready-stance, braced for a last stand.

Without warning, there was a crashing boom as a heavy tree branch came bashing through my makeshift door. It quickly withdrew. Sunlight again filled the cluttered cabin. An ominous silence followed.

Next something unexpected. A chorus of grunting and moaning. The shaft of the branch was thrust in the door again and poked around wildly. I had to step back and up to stay out of range. It withdrew again, and for a few more moments there was nothing. Then more crackling and crunching of leaves and branches, just outside the door.

Very slowly, something frightening blocked the light from the door as it crept cautiously in. I positioned myself with the knife and braced for attack. It was one of the strangest creatures I had ever seen, a rat's nest of brown hair that formed a moving mound. It looked like a giant, dirty tribble. I repositioned in the best possible way, hoping repeated stabbings would find a vulnerable spot. The thing jerked around, tilted up like an animal smelling for its prey, and, then abruptly turned sideways until something else finally came into view. Buried within the mound of hair was a face.

It looked up at me and jerked up in surprise, hitting its well-insulated skull on the top of the hatch. There was a loud, fearful growl as the head frantically backed out.

Much more trampling could be heard outside the pod, complemented by murmuring and animal sounds, followed by more silence. My mind was doing back flips. The face hadn't been quite human. Neanderthal was the closest I could come. There had only been a glimpse of it. The large protruding forehead stood out the most. Fat lips covering oversized teeth. I took in another shallow breath and tried to contain my fear. There was no place to run.

The big stick made another appearance. It banged around, this time more on my side. Occasionally it would pause and a guttural voice would yell, "Doga, doga, doga yam!" My translators weren't translating, but "doga" had to be, "Get out here." My best bet was that "yam" meant right now.

When I did not comply, greater exertion was used to rattle the big stick. It pummeled around banging against dead pod equipment, forcing me to move to one side or another. Finally it withdrew again.

I resigned myself that introductions were inevitable. If I held out so long that the invitation became confrontation, there was certain to be quite a lot of suffering involved, probably accompanied by additional injury. I tucked my plastic knife back in the leg pocket, winced at the pain from pushing out of the seat, and got down on all fours at the door. With the greatest of misgivings, I crawled out and holding the side of my injured chest, stood.

There were eleven, covered mostly in fur that hadn't been properly cured and beaten. Some had leather wrappings on their feet. The rest were barefoot. They all had the rat's nest hair, brown or black, down to their shoulders or longer. Above the accentuated brow was one long, fat eyebrow that ran full across the forehead. Human-like eyes and eye colors, except they all had a ring of yellow outlining the pupil. It made for a fearsome stare. Wide nose, too much hair on the sides of the face and temples, some of it quite long. They had tattoos, mostly of dark stain, a few ash-red. The designs were swirls and symbols I did not recognize. Some of them wore colorful feathers braided into their hair. They all had wooden spears shaved to a fine point.

We stood in silence, appraising each other. They had no idea what I was. Hoping to maybe have some control of the situation, I patted one hand on my chest and said, "Tarn."

They stood at the ready with spears well-aimed and looked at each other for answers, but found none. The largest, most elaborately decorated of the bunch had a long nasty set of scars down his left cheek that looked like claw marks. He stepped forward, twirled his spear so that the blunt end was facing me, then poked at my left shoulder, apparently to see if there would be any consequence from doing so. I moved with the jabs trying to minimize the pain, at the same time doing my best to hide it. Satisfied I was not some sort of god, he yelled, "Ga-don, ga-don!" at his cohorts and they spread out around me. I wondered if this was the end.

Scarface raised one hand and pointed toward a rough-hewn clearing in the forest. He shook his spear and yelled, "Doe, doe!" His friends became agitated and excited and backed him up with grunting. Given the alternative, I gimped along in the requested direction, trying to keep an eye on each spear tip. Five went ahead of me, the rest behind. When I slowed too much, I was tapped on the back with the blunt end of a spear. At least I was not hanging from a post like a trophy deer.

It was a trek of several miles over uneven ground through jungle so thick it was already retaking their trail. My injuries were killing me, the ribs being in a class all by themselves. Somehow, my captors were smart enough to know. I was close to passing out from lack of breath. Each time I staggered, the spear prodding was held back for a few moments in a gesture of patience that surprised me. It may have been that they did not want to carry me. On two occasions there was a growling from the forest that caused the entire caravan to pause and take a ready stance, but no predators ever appeared.

After a hike that took every bit of strength I had left, we emerged into an encampment clearing busy with many more Neanderthals. It was an elevated plateau in front of a huge, fifty-foot-high cave entrance. A quick count of the population was thirty or forty individuals working inside and outside the cave. There were waist-high stone platforms at various points around the place used as work stations. Empty wooden cages were stationed alongside the right side of the clearing. There were more men than women. I was encircled by my captors, and to my dismay, led toward one of the chest-high cages, but instead of being thrown in, I was forced to sit on a rock seat near them. Half a dozen spear holders stood guard. I waited, hunched over, too exhausted and in too much pain to complain.

A gathering of curious Neanderthals began to form. There was grunting, exclamations, and guttural sounds of disapproval. The wait was not long. To my right, an entourage emerged from the mouth of the cavern, headed my way, growing in size as it came. Leading the assemblage was the oldest of them, a man whose hair was just as much a bushy rat's nest with a primitive tangle of gray-brown.

He led his pack to me where Scarface greeted him, making the necessary grunts and exclamations with finger pointing. Gray-hair gave a one-grunt command and two subordinates approached me cautiously. They pulled on the fabric of my flight suit, rubbing it between huge thumb and forefinger, looking back at Gray-hair and shrugging as they rocked back and forth.

They did not understand my zippers. They did not understand the shiny metal or the mechanism itself. I obliged them by ever so slowly reaching up and unzipping the chest pocket. There were subdued oohs and aahs from the crowd. Neither subordinate seemed able to master the procedure. One at a time, I opened every pocket on my suit. They fished around in each, finding my plastic knife, still with dry blood. The stain did not faze them for even a moment. The plastic did. It was handed to Gray-hair, who flexed and turned it in every possible direction, inserted it in his leather string belt, then looked up with an expression of "What-else?"

Next came the bar of magnesium. They managed to unsnap the pouch and remove it, but quickly decided it was some kind of ceremonial rock and threw it back in my lap as though it was unimportant to a tribe of their advancement. I hurriedly placed it back in my chest pocket.

All pockets explored, Gray-hair took the spear from his nearest guard and pounded the blunt end once on the ground. "Tup!" he commanded. I did not need a translator to know what that meant. Wincing from pain, I slowly forced myself up.

155

"Dom," he continued, and I knew he wanted me to step forward.

We stood facing each other in silence. Perhaps I was expected to do something. I took a chance and pressed my hand on my chest several times and said, "Tarn....Tarn."

The reaction was swift. One spear handle caught me behind the knees, the other just below the throat. I went down over backward, broke the fall slightly with my right hand, and crashed to the ground against those badly abused ribs. I screamed in pain and rolled, trying to find a position less excruciating where I could breathe. Gray hair made several more grunting commands and turned away, heading back to the cave.

I was indelicately hoisted to my feet, a guard under each arm. I wondered what the current mode of execution was. They dragged me along through the dirt in the same direction Gray-hair had gone. I struggled to help them, hoping to take some weight off my rib cage. We passed into the shadow of the cave where the air immediately cooled and a smell of dampness pervaded the air. Hand prints and primitive drawings covered the walls. There were mini-encampments within the cave, marked by furs and stone constructions. They led me to one of them and set me down on a rock seat covered with animal hide and fur. They tugged at the main zipper on my flight suit and then grunted commands. They wanted me to open it. I was too beaten down to put up a fight. I unzipped it to the waist.

To my surprise, the two guards left. Two Neanderthal females carrying wooden bowls took seats beside me. They were dressed just as the men, but with more attention to detail. They had primitive makeup on their faces. Their huge heads of hair were better kept. Their footwear looked more like laced-up boots. They spoke in gentle tones, and without warning pulled my flight suit down to the waist. There were more oohs and aahs as they inspected the damage. The one on the right had a big bowl full of water and fur. She began washing me with special attention to the wounds. The other began scooping out a mixture of green goop from her bowl, gently pasting it onto the wounds. Nothing had ever felt that good. While they worked, a young Neanderthal wearing little more than a loincloth came up to us with a bag. It was filled with strange roots and what appeared to be alien fruit. He placed the bag at my feet and backed away. I grabbed a root from the top of the heap. It was gray-white and shaped like sausage and still had a little bit of black dirt on it. I tore into it like the starving man I was. My nurses giggled.

I awoke naked within a heavy layer of fur. My freshly cleaned flight suit was stretched out on a rock next to me. It was completely dry. My boots were within arm's reach, unlaced as though someone had tried them but didn't like them. The laces were spread out on the ground alongside. There was also a thick, brown fur vest beside the flight suit, a gift from my new benefactors.

There was no way to tell how long I had slept. Light from a rising sun was casting long shadows in the cave. Or was it a setting sun? The place was busy. Heavily cloaked Neanderthals were moving about. I pulled down my covering to find my chest and most of my naked body covered with dried green paste that had hardened and cracked. I suddenly realized my breathing had improved greatly. I tried for a deep breath and got it with only a bit of sharp sting at the end. Both shoulders were working much better. I pushed up on one elbow and a large chunk of green paste fell off. Further inspection revealed that indeed, almost every inch of my body had been coated with the green goo. I sat up, watched to see if anyone took notice, then began peeling off the rest of the green. When all of it was removed, I leaned over and recovered my flight suit and slid into it. Checking the heel compartment in my left boot, my Nasebian crystal was still there. I pulled the boots on and took the time to re-lace them all the way. When it was done, I dared to stand. Amazingly, no one paid me any attention.

It seemed I was free to move around the encampment. There was a good chance that meant I was not tonight's dinner, although guards stationed around the settlement looked as though they might not approve of my leaving, had I a place to go. I moved around with my hands in my pockets, trying to look less threatening. The morning's work was in full swing. Leather was being hammered and chewed. There was a stream on one side of the camp where washing was going on. Back by the empty wooden cages, spears were being sharpened, and men were grouping together in what looked like a hunting party. I took a seat on a stone near the cave and tried to look inconspicuous. It did not work.

Scarface showed up at the hunting party. There was a serious discussion. To my utter dismay, he looked over at me, pointed, and gave his men orders. Two of them grabbed their spears and headed my way.

I could have put up a good fight at that point and then tried to run like hell, but the thought occurred to me that I might need these people. There was a chance I would be spending the rest of my life here. They knew the dangers. I did not. They knew how to survive. I had a lot to learn.

The guards were more respectful this time. They came up to me and one took some red pigment from a shell and drew two lines down each side of my face. They pointed to their party and grunted, "Dom." I had already learned the word for "go." I

157

nodded and followed them back to the group where the others looked at me with Neanderthal smirks and utterances of idle ridicule. Not far away, a second hunting party was forming, but they did not seem connected to ours.

We moved out toward a well-worn trail at the far end of the clearing. Two Neanderthals seemed assigned to keep me in line. There was no doubt in my mind that given the opportunity, I could not outrun them. The others, busy around the encampment, paused to watch our departure as though it was something of significance. Every man in the group was well armed with spears and clubs. I, of course, had nothing, leaving me to wonder exactly what my role would be. It concerned me.

The trail was rough and uneven. Climbing was required in places. The place was mineral rich in every direction. I spotted beds of yellow sulfur against some of the cliff walls, glints of various metals along others. Walking a good half mile along a narrow running stream I was certain there was flint within the polished boulders that lined it. Animal sounds from the forest were frequent and unnerving.

When the column of fur-covered hunters suddenly came to a halt, the dense forest overhang made it impossible to see up ahead. No matter. I was immediately summoned and ushered along past the others to the head of the line, where Scarface waited.

We had arrived at a huge clearing filled by grass that towered a foot overhead. A trail was cut through the grass and disappeared around a corner forty or fifty feet ahead. Far in the distance, treetops could be seen where the clearing ended and more forest began. My captors stood silently staring at me. At first, I thought they wanted me to lead as bait for any danger that lay in wait. I was only half right. I held out my hand for a spear, but Scarface grunted a negative. I decided I could break into the grass and hide as well as any of them, so I took a few steps toward the high grass, but Scarface grabbed my arm and stopped me. He grunted more negatives and punched a fist into his open hand several times saying, "Da-bow, da-bow!"

The hair on the back of my neck stood up. He was telling me to run. I guessed the other forest edge to be a football field away. It did not take a genius to know I would be running for my life. I looked at Scarface. He knew I understood. He grunted, "Shoo, shoo." It was supposed to be encouragement. They were not trying to kill me, but there was a good chance something in the high grass would. I had no idea what was out there, but I was certain it was unpleasant. Looking back at the line of silent faces, it was the first time I had seen respect from all of them. I began to hyperventilate, ignoring the remaining rib pain. I ran in place and pumped myself up. Scarface grunted approval. They all understood.

With a last look, I took off in a sprint for the other side. There was no sense trying to take cover in the grass. It was there the predator dwelled, one that probably had a hunter's sense of smell. I quickly worked up to a full-out run, consciously regulating my injured breathing, using the arms to add thrust. The trail was a good ten feet wide with dirt-grass footing. There were no sharp corners, just gradual bends through the stalks of grass.

Three-quarters of the way through, I sucked air and started to think I had a chance. The treetops on the other side were getting nearer. Maybe I had been too quick for the predator.

Male ego rearing its ugly head.

The beast picked me up a second later. I heard its scream as it mashed through the grass somewhere behind. I dared a quick glance back, and that was enough to add speed to what I had thought was my maximum.

It broke into the trail about thirty feet behind. It was a type of flightless bird. It was as tall as a backhoe. Ostrich legs. Long neck with a dinosaur head. Long pointed teeth that formed a smile where there was not one. Eyes on either side. Long tail held high in anticipation of an upcoming meal. The ground shook with the stomp of each of those pile-driver feet.

I gasped for all the air I could get, rib cage pain no longer a concern. I twisted my head sideward stretching for even more power. The beast screamed at me to stop. The ground shook from the pounding of its feet. It was close enough that I could smell it.

I did not need to look back to know I was losing, but the forest edge was a mere twenty yards away. Would the drooling mouth clamp down on my shoulder and lift me away? If I made the forest, could I cut into the underbrush in time to run interference and maybe hide?

It is a strange sensation when your body starts to give out, even though it knows it will be killed. It feels almost like a promise broken by God. Death that comes while every inch of you is full bore trying to stay alive. It is a contrariety well-known by soldiers on the battlefield, emergency rescue personnel, and some accident victims. It was a mind-set I did not care for.

I pumped beyond what seemed possible and tore through the line between clearing and forest, the creature's breath on my neck. I dove for the nearest brush expecting a huge clawed foot to lock me down.

From out of nowhere, heavy vine snapped up, catching Big Bird square in the neck. With a loud snapping, cracking sound, he flipped over backward and was immediately besieged by a small army of Neanderthals hiding along the forest's edge, the second hunting party from the camp. There was a fierce session of spearing and clubbing and yelling. The predator had become the prey.

I struggled onto my hands and knees, gasping, while the celebration broke out around me.

Chapter 17

We marched back to camp victorious, large pieces of Big Bird hanging from shoulder-carried, freshly cut tree limbs. For me, something had changed. There were no more guards. All spear-prodding had ceased. I had the feeling I could have left anytime I cared to.

The encampment immediately became filled with whooping and hollering and jumping and rolling on the ground. As the hunting party dispersed into the celebration, I suddenly found myself a free man to do as I wished. That eventuality had not occurred to me, so I went to a rock platform by the cave and sat, hoping to sort out my new life.

Furious butchering of big bird parts was underway at various points around the camp. As I sat in a pose reminiscent of The Thinker, Scarface appeared carrying a healthy chunk of bright red meat. He plopped it down on the rock next to me, gave a prideful shake of his hairy head and left.

Very few Earthlings eat real meat these days. The substitute steaks and other products are so packed with protein and healthy ingredients, and taste so damn good, there's just no real reason to. I looked down at the thick red portion bequeathed me and wondered if I could. And would it be an insult not to? I gazed around the camp at my newly adopted family, most of them gobbling away, the hair on their faces stained red. A new realization suddenly hit me.

There was no fire here. I had seen a large fire circle of rock nearly covered by dirt in the center of the camp. There were similar smaller ones within the cave. There had been fire here once, but there was not now.

I stood and looked around to see if anyone was paying attention. They were too busy enjoying big bird. At the edge of the woodland behind me, I gathered up a huge armload of leaves and kindling and walked tentatively to the old fire circle at camp's center. I kneeled and quickly dug it out, then filled it with kindling. Some of the tribe took notice but kept eating as though it was entertaining but of no significance.

Back at the edge of the woods it was easy to find enough half rotten logs. I carried an armload back and stacked them accordingly. More of the camp began to watch as though this was the meal's entertainment.

I slipped the magnesium bar from my pocket as inconspicuously as possible and held it in my hand in a way it could not be seen. With a special pile of very fine tinder, I began my subtle striking of the magnesium. I had embers within thirty seconds, and with the proper amount of blowing, a small flame a minute later.

They did not notice at first. They seemed to think it was all some useless offering to the gods. Maybe I was going to pray for fire.

But when the smoke became apparent, things changed very quickly. Grunts of exclamation came from various points around the camp. A few onlookers rose to their feet. And as the first flame licked above the logs, all hell broke loose. Someone let out a scream so bloodcurdling it made me straighten up and look. A stampede broke out around the camp, a wave of Neanderthals heading at full gait toward me. I thought they would tackle me and beat me for violating some tribal taboo. Instead, those first to arrive fell to their knees and began wailing, "I-ah, i-ah." Others leapt and screamed, rolled on the ground, danced, and embraced each other. I stood in the midst of it, wondering what I had done.

Suddenly there was a disruption in the celebration. Scarface charged through the crowd, knocking worshippers out of his way as he went. He pummeled through the front line, came to the just-growing fire and began to stomp it out furiously. When sufficiently pounded down, he stopped and waved angrily at his companions and pointed off to the distance yelling, "Scabas, Scabas!" The crowd immediately became silent. He turned and looked at each of them with a scolding stare, then waved instructions to several closest to us. They quickly obeyed and gathered up all the wood from the fire and ran furiously toward the cave. Another used his bare hands to scoop up the glowing embers that remained. He cried out in joyous pain as he hustled off for the cave. The masses ran to follow.

Within the cave, an old fire circle was frantically dug out and the wood and kindling carefully stacked within it. The hero with the embers in his burned hands quickly bedded them and began blowing and moving in hopes of resurrecting the fire. Echoes within the cavern fell silent.

They were too late. The embers collapse into white ash. Moans and cries broke out, amplified by the hard cavern walls. Everyone stood in silence, almost in a funeral pyre moment. A path opened up and Chief Gray-hair came to the fire pit's edge.

He looked up at me, stepped forward and held me gently by the arm. He pointed at the fire pit and grunted, "I-ah. i-ah."

Something new startled me. The chief had clearly said "I-ah," but in my head I had heard "fire." My translator was beginning to work. The magnesium was still in my hand. I kneeled and, concealing it as best I could, began the necessary strikes until embers reappeared. The one with the burned hands took over from there. He slinked in and began the blowing process until smoke and flame broke out again. I backed away to escape the renewed screaming and dancing, and as I did, saw the trail of smoke from the fire being drawn deeper into the cavern. Scarface had not wanted the smoke trail to be seen ...by someone.

Within a matter of minutes, other fire circles within the cave were brought to life. People hurried to find sticks to cook their bird meat. A rotisserie was set up at one fire. The place gradually settled down to cooking, eating, and the frequent grunting of pleasure. I managed to find myself a stick and with my hunk of bird meat was allowed a VIP position at one of the central fire circles.

As the feast subsided and the camp quieted, the Chief approached me with Scarface and several others in tow. I rose to meet him. He looked around, grunted a few declarations to those around him, and held something out in front of me. It was a tooth from big bird, braided into a leather cord. He placed it over my head and around my neck, made a few more boisterous declarations, nodded to me, slapping me on my upper arms, then walked away making more Neanderthal exclamations as he went. The others stared for a moment and returned to their celebration.

My life as a Neanderthal had changed again. My unkempt beard made me blend in even more. I was no longer the malformed hostage-slave. I had passed the big bird initiation and even trumped that as the stranger who could summon fire. They now looked at me with more than respect. They were now even a little stand-offish.

The mood in the camp was very different. Conversations were more frequent. Laughter erupted more than usual. The people seemed hopeful. There was an unmistakable feeling of joy, the joy from fires burning. That evening, my nurses were waiting at my fur bed with more green goop. I slept as heavily as any successful Neanderthal could.

The rest of that week, universal harmony continued in the camp. The translators seemed to have found a foothold in the primitive grunting. More and more translated words were coming through. Scarface's real name was Oo-da. Chief Gray-hair was Dawn-a. The tribe called themselves the Tusani. I was Tonn. That was as close as they could come. R's and L's were not yet a part of their phonetics. I was beginning to have rudimentary conversations with them, and beginning to learn they were a much more complex society than my prejudice had allowed me to see.

Ooda had a mate named Bee-o. Beeo seemed to be secretly in love with another high-ranking soldier named Ah-boo. Both she and Ahboo seemed intent on disallowing the relationship to develop. There was a code of honor these people respected. I could not tell if Ooda was aware of the situation. Either he was not, or had chosen to ignore it.

Chief Dawna's mate had been killed quite some time ago. I did not know how or why. He could have easily taken a new mate, but for some reason chose not to.

There were small communities of friends that formed the smaller camps within the encampment. There was trading and interaction between them. Some were families. Others seemed to simply be friends or allies. I had also noticed that one particular female would sneak off alone at a specific time during the day, and return an hour or two later. My first impulse was to try to spot a male doing a similar disappearing act, but I could not. It was a mystery to be solved.

My formal title remained "Tonn the Fire Starter," though they no longer needed me for that purpose. Several fires within the cave were kept alive day and night, as though they feared I could not do it again. It made me wonder how they had lost their fire and made me decide to teach them how to make it themselves without the need of a magnesium strip. Long ago, Wilson, Stan Lee, and I had attended the agency's survival training together. One hard-fast requirement was that each candidate could produce fire with nothing but what a forest had to offer. It was there I quickly learned that the legend of rubbing two sticks together was a myth. The usefulness of a bow drill, on the other hand, was quite extraordinary.

I chose exactly the wrong morning to make my way down to the best streambed that had the greatest number of small waterfalls to gather parts needed for a bow drill. Granite outcroppings along some parts of those streambeds offered exactly the right sized round stone with a million-year-old, water-dripped perfect indentation for a handhold piece. Flexible wood for the bow was easy, along with shards of broken pieces fit for a platform. The forest also offered a certain vine that felt just like cloth but was as strong as carbon fiber. I proudly headed back with my kit, looking forward to the shock and awe my first fire instruction class would bring. I had no idea of the disaster that had taken place in my absence.

Shock Diamonds

The attack could not have lasted very long. It was exactly what Scarface-Ooda had feared. I do not think it was signs of fire that brought them. It was just bad luck. They were just finishing up when I reached the edge of the camp and became alerted by the unusual cries. From cover it was easy to spot the few enemies that remained. They were golden-gray apes, walking upright except when they ran. Fine gray hair covered their bodies. They had light-skinned ape faces, ape hands, and almost human feet. They were no taller than the Tusani, but their body mass was considerably more powerful. The Tusani had scattered, except for the three or four that lay dead around the camp in heaps of fur, blood, and body parts. In the distance, I caught sight of one Tusani female being dragged off by two ape-men. It was the most disheartening scene I had ever witnessed. For the first time, I realized my allegiance to the Tusani. Anger quickly followed. After the last of them had gone, a few Tusani began to filter back into the desolation.

The encampment had been systematically looted. Work stations were thrown about; platforms overturned, resources scattered or stolen. Inside the cavern, all fires were out and buried. Most furs were gone. The only things left of value were those not understood by the ape men. I turned to find Chief Dawna walking among the dead, waving a special stick and chanting a Tusani prayer over each. Ooda came alongside me, surveying the disaster.

I went to the Chief. "Why?"

He looked back with sorrowful, wise eyes you would not expect from an early man. "No why " he replied, and he continued shaking his ceremonial stick.

"How many?" I asked.

Ooda answered. He held up four fingers, "No more." He closed his fist and held up five fingers, "Taken."

"Taken why?"

Ooda answered, "Food or mate."

I did not know how to say, "What now?" in Tusani, so in a questioning voice I waved a hand over the camp and asked, "Tusani?"

Chief Dawna replied, "Tusani move far."

The flush of anger returned. I punched a fist into an open hand and exclaimed, "No, Tusani fight!"

The Chief lowered his head, "No, Tusani move far."

But Ooda looked interested. He did not contradict his chief, but he stared at me waiting for more.

I punched my fist into my open hand once more and said, "Tonn and Tusani fight!" I slapped my chest.

165

E.R. Mason

The Chief looked up at me through his sorrow, wondering if I had something to offer.

Other Tusani were slowly returning and gathering in the cave, most looking over their shoulders in fear that the ape-men would return. I needed time to make the Chief understand. I pointed upward and held up one finger. "One sun. Just give me one sun."

The Chief nodded dejectedly, as though he doubted anything could come of it. They probably needed that much time to regroup and pack anyway. Ooda looked on. I could feel restrained hope within him. He gave me his "ready" look. I did not waste time.

The women were my best bet. The males were a bit too brutal for the arts and crafts I had in mind. I gathered a crowd from the beaten-down masses as the Chief and Ooda looked on. Step by step, I showed them each piece of the bow drill fire starter and then assembled it into a bow and its other components. I was inept at first, not having done the process in years, but as the smoke began to rise from the spinning wood spindle, understanding quickly came over those who watched. And, as fire appeared within the bundle of tinder and dry grass, they began to forget about the day's massacre. Enough of them tried the process that we soon had all four fires in the cave burning again, with no embers needing to be borrowed.

Next, it was time to begin the war machine. They were already breaking flint and other hard rock to use the sharp edges for butchering and cutting. I gathered the best edge makers, and with Ooda's help translating, drew an arrowhead in the dirt. I had seen flint knapping done many times but had never attempted it myself. I sat in front of them and began trying glancing cuts at various rock pieces until the best type was found. From there, I swiped and swiped, trying to get a Clovis point. As I chipped, I would pause occasionally and point to the image drawn in the dirt. Something finally clicked in one of the women. She picked up a piece of stone and began hammering with me. Though she did not understand the purpose, she knew what the goal was. She began a verbal exchange with the others, and soon they were all attempting to fashion arrowheads out of stone. When it began to look promising, I motioned Ooda to follow and headed for the woods.

The surrounding forest had everything needed. The Tusani men were strong as oxen. A bow would need to be just as strong. I found the perfect piece of green limb and broke and cut it with a sharp rock. Ooda looked on without a clue. The vines so like cloth were available everywhere in varying gauge. I cut what I needed. Last but not least, there was no shortage of very straight wood sections that could be cut carefully to length and shaved clean. On the way back to the campsite, I found pasty sap flowing from a broken limb, and scooped some up to bring along.

The arrowhead manufacturing was already going well. The women even seemed enthralled with it. Ooda continued to watch with hope, as I sat and notched the ends of my would-be bow and carefully split the end of the first arrow, notching the back of it. The first moment of truth came as I stood and strung the bow. Chief Dawna joined in the watch. The bow took the tension nicely. The bowstring gave a gentle tone when snapped. Leather works had been done nearby. I found a strip and wound it around the center of the bow for a grip. A small crowd was beginning to form.

The best arrowhead so far was slightly lopsided but acceptable. I inserted it into the split end of the arrow and wrapped it tightly with leftover bow string. There began to be some muttering from the crowd as they recognized a new type of small spear. Last of all, I asked one of the women for a feather from her hair and quickly had offers from two. I cut it against a rock into small feather pieces, took some of the sap I had brought along, and affixed it to my arrow.

This first test had to be impressive. There was a worn-out leather sack for carrying firewood nearby. I stuffed it tightly with leaves and hung it from the nearest tree. The viewing audience had now grown quite large.

Twenty feet away was the most I dared. I set up and held up the bow for all to see, then held up the arrow, and with great exaggeration showed them how the arrow joined the bow. Their stone-faced silence worried me.

I drew and relaxed the bow several times to show how it functioned. Still silence. With a quick, silent prayer, I took a stance, drew the arrow full, made my best aim, and let it fly.

The arrow whistled through the air and missed the bag by six inches. It went slightly high and hit the trunk of the tree with a loud thump and twang. The arrow and tip held. The arrowhead embedded halfway, the shaft humming like a tuning fork from the impact.

Numerous excited discussions broke out. I had missed the bag but hit the target. There was not a Tusani there who did not understand what this meant, especially the Chief. Throwing rocks had suddenly become passé.

Ooda soon took over the war machine. These people had been sorely hurt by the attack. Suddenly they had a way to protect themselves. They had found hope. The manufacture of bows and arrows went on continuously. I drew three more types of spearheads in the sand and the flint knappers jumped on them. One tip was for a long spear, the second for a short

167

spear, and the third for a knife. The best of the flint knappers stayed at their craft. Others went into the assembly process. At one point, one of the women left went into the woods and came back with a black tar that she carefully heated near the fire and applied to the spear and arrowhead bindings while it was still hot. It hardened like cement, making the tips twice as strong. At the same time, it was like a form of napalm. If you put fire directly to it, it burned like fuel.

In the following days, archery and combat practice began. Archery became such a popular sport it became difficult to pull some away from it for other things. Four or five of the men were particularly gifted archers, almost born to it. Oddly enough, they were not the best of warriors, so their esteem within the tribe was suddenly greatly increased. A daily routine of manufacturing and hunting fell into place. Soon, the hunting became bow and spear, negating the terror of using each other to bait the prey.

In the middle of it all, I awoke one particular morning to an unexpected and worrisome Neanderthal social dilemma. An uninvited female had joined me during the night and was sleeping alongside. It was one of those who had lost her mate during the attack of the Scabas. I eased myself away, hoped I had not somehow unknowingly taken part in a Tusani wedding ceremony, and decided to ignore the incident completely. To my relief, no one seemed to act like any husbandly obligations were pending.

As the primitives settled into their new, artificial evolution, it became time for defensive strategy. No settlement walls could be built that ape-men couldn't climb, so other methods needed to be devised. The jungle was so dense there were a limited number of trails leading into the camp. Those trails became defensive points. The area above the cave entrance also had a few useful overlooks. Three fire rings were created on those overhangs to give archer snipers high ground for fire arrows. Boulders above the far side of the cave entrance were set and aimed. Levers were installed to release them toward the trails. Blinds were constructed high in the trees for additional archer sniper points. Each Tusani warrior carried three weapons, the long spear, a short spear over his right shoulder, and a flint knife in his waist tie. I was satisfied with their hand-to-hand training after only a week. They had lost enough ape-man battles that an instinct for the fight had already been developed.

As soon as a reasonable amount of confidence had been built, I went to Chief Dawna and Ooda with my plan. It was far too soon to test new Tusani warriors in real combat, but what I had in mind could not wait. I sat in the cave with them holding a handful of small rocks to make my point. Using a stick, I drew the Tusani encampment in the dirt and the neighboring hills and mountains around it. I pointed in the dirt to the encampment. "Tusani," I said, and I handed the Chief my pointing stick. "Scabas?" I asked.

The Chief understood. He handed Ooda the stick. Ooda drew two more sets of hills to the west and pointed in the dirt beyond them. "Scabas," he replied.

"One sun?"

"Two suns," he answered.

I laid out five small stones in the area he had designated for the Scabas. "Five taken," I said. I picked up the stones and moved them to the Tusani encampment. "Five taken back."

They both understood.

The Chief looked at Ooda. Ooda nodded.

We left nothing to chance. Five of the best archers, five of the strongest warriors, led by Ooda. We rehearsed the plan with hand signals and signal calls off-camp in a small clearing. Everyone understood their role. Everyone understood the plan. There was to be no harm done to young ape-men or females unless it was in self-defense. That concept took quite a while to convey. We packed up and headed out at the next day's first light.

I had to push myself to keep up. They could have out-walked me easily. Frequent stops so that Ooda could climb tall trees to get his bearings allowed just enough rest to stay with them. We camped without fires that night and resumed at daybreak. We crossed the last range of hills later that morning and spotted their encampment soon after.

The camp consisted of mounds of leaves, grass, and brush hollowed out to form tent-like structures. They did not have fire or just did not feel a need for it. We arrived at the perfect time. There were six of them milling around, frequently arguing with each other. All of the others, the main body of Scabas, were away hunting or accosting some other camp. On the opposite side of their clearing, we spotted what we had come for.

There were three Tusani women still alive. They were tied to trees by vines around their necks. They were pretty beaten up. One of the women was Ooda's mate. Not far from them were the mostly-eaten body parts of the others.

Without even a glance at me for approval, Ooda gave the hand signal to the archers to take positions. He motioned again for the warriors to circle the camp. Finally, he looked over at me with an expression that said, "There's no turning back now." I nodded in agreement.

With a single yelp of attack, the arrows flew. Surprisingly, it caught me off guard. Usually most men will hesitate a second before their first real kill. There was no such pause in the hearts of the Tusani archers. The arrows flew out from the forest and all but one hit their marks with deadly accuracy.

But the ape-men were hard to kill. They whooped and hollered and jumped around not understanding the rod sticking out of their bodies. They stumbled and fell and got back up. The only off-target arrow struck its victim high in the leg. He looked down at it and shook his fists angrily before noticing his mortally wounded comrades. Another ape-man, uninjured by an arrow strike, stood upright with a look of curiosity on his face, completely confused by the plight of his associates.

It seemed like less than a second and the next wave of arrows flew. This time all five hit their marks. The ape-man with the injured leg took one through the heart and fell immediately. The uninjured ape-man suddenly had an arrow through the throat. The others fell silent or rolled in pain.

Ooda's second battle cry turned loose the warriors. They charged in and finished the dirty work with long spears.

The enemy camp fell silent. The Tusani team gathered in a circle at the center of the camp, surprised by the speed of their victory. Ooda charged in, went directly to the women captives, and began sawing off their bindings. The women were in a state of shock, unable to speak, unsure of what was happening. No one had ever been rescued from the Scabas.

We did not wait around. All arrows were removed from the victims to keep the new weapon a secret. All traces of Tusani footprints were wiped over. The freed women were carried or half-dragged along the way we had come. We moved quickly enough to clear two mountain range trails before setting up camp for the night well off the beaten path. The next day we reached home just as the sun was beginning to set. Once again, wild celebration broke out. There was dancing and wrestling and chanting around victory fires. It was good for the tribe to celebrate. I sat with the Chief and Ooda, enjoying the new hope within the Tusani, our own expressions slightly less joyous because the three of us knew.

The Scabas would be coming.

Chapter 18

Fear is a volatile ally. It can command you to flee, or turn you into a mindless killing machine, or make you a hero when you don't deserve to be. Fear can clear your mind of all other trouble save the one that is coming. It can force you to take a stand with absolute resolve.

The Tusani were not immune. Once the facts of life had been explained to them, they chose the path of quiet resolve. They did not complain. They did not retreat. Beginning at sunrise, preparations began. Small stones were lifted to the tree blinds so that archers could keep small fires for fire arrows. New paths were cut through the forest surrounding the camp, paths so narrow Scaba attackers would only be able to move along them single file. Defensive positions were rehearsed so many times that even in fear everyone would automatically go to their assigned spot. A long barricade was set up in the cave, secure positions for a line of archers, backed by warriors. We rehearsed, rehearsed, and then rehearsed some more.

We had one big advantage. The Scabas always attacked in daylight. We knew they'd be coming from the west. In the distance, the last line of mountains provided only a single pass, a sharp fork bordered by high peaks. From a high platform above the forest canopy, a lookout could spot Scabas coming though. When he did, it would give us three or four hours of warning that war was on its way. We would be locked and loaded.

For two days, we continued to rehearse the defense, making little improvements here and there, adding new hand signals, creating better strategic visibility. We even set up a section within the cave to treat Tusani wounded after it was over. There was a solemn undercurrent to it all. The camp was quieter than it had ever been. It was difficult to sleep at night.

Midmorning on the third day, the call came. The remote lookout came running up the trail, out of breath, waving the stained-red leather flag that had been made for that express purpose. There was a moment of stark realization throughout the camp, and before any commands were even given, people

171

were racing to their assigned positions. Archers climbed to their posts, carrying fire to light their stone igniter beds. Warriors took their places, hiding within the jungle. In the cave, the assigned teams readied their weapons.

The lookout had seen movement coming through the pass. That meant at least three hours before the attack would begin. The Tusani were in position and ready in twenty minutes.

The wait began. The camp looked deserted except for six warriors out in the open, waiting to lead Scaba attackers down the blood-alley trails created just for them. The Chief, Ooda, and I took a position out of sight in a tree blind where we could see the entire encampment and into the cave. The Chief carried only my plastic knife in his belt. I had nothing at all. Ooda was heavily loaded down in case he needed to join in the battle rather than direct it.

When the first wave of Scabas finally made their charge, it was immediately a tragic comedy. They swarmed into the camp like eccentric shoppers at a half-off sale. They charged in pushing each other out of the way, hoping to get the best first kills. Others scattered toward the cave in search of the loot.

The brave Tusani warriors stationed out in the open acted surprised and afraid just as planned. They gave just enough time for groups of Scabas to form and charge after them. The Scabas roared death growls as they ran.

It was at that moment Ooda let out the attack howl, and the fire arrows flew.

I have never seen such a pitiful tragedy. The first wave of burning arrows came from every direction and every one struck a target. The Scabas were bunched together enough that it was impossible to miss. Those impaled by burning arrows roared in pain and yanked at the burning shafts as hair was set on fire. Several fell to the ground rolling. There was a deathly indignity among those wounded. Within seconds, the next wave of arrows came, striking the confused Scabas with equal accuracy. Those not preoccupied with flaming wounds began to scatter, still not understanding what was happening, and enraged that the Tusani would dare fight back.

The lines of Scabas that had taken off to run down the only Tusanis they could find dashed into the newly cut trails in pursuit of their prey. Along the trail they were cut down by the spears of the Tusani warriors hiding along the way.

Within the cave, fire arrows met the first wave of attackers. From there, the Tusani warriors charged over the barricades to meet those remaining. Two Tusani warriors for each Scaba, as hoped.

Most tragic of all was the Scabas' refusal to retreat. They had arrived so convinced of their superiority; they could not comprehend that they were losing. The archers' arrow

Shock Diamonds

strikes began to make for an even more gruesome battle. Now spread out, the remaining Scabas were not such an easy target. The archers were hitting arms and legs or missing entirely. Unfortunately for the Scabas, fewer targets meant more archers per Scaba. Some Scabas were still going, even with two or three charred arrows in them.

The massacre did not last long. It was over in twenty minutes. A strange deathly silence came over the camp, the ground covered with burning Scaba bodies. In the ominous silence, Ooda gave the reload-reset yell, expecting the next wave. It came a minute or two later.

We had expected the second wave to be worse than the first. Common battlefield technique, soften the enemy then send in the real regiment. But the Scabas were not that advanced. The second wave of attackers turned out to be stragglers, the ones who had not been able to keep up.

They charged into the camp, expecting the worst to be over, expecting to pick at the spoils of war, the scavengers of the tribe. The sight of their tribesmen's burning, dead bodies scattered everywhere stopped them in their tracks. As they stood staring in disbelief, Ooda's cry brought the next wave of arrows. Half a dozen were struck. The others ran away in the direction they had come. A second barrage of arrows finished off those remaining. Hand signals from the lookout towers signaled all clear. Ooda yelled "All-clear!" For the first time, I thought I heard emotion in his voice. The silence of death returned to the camp.

It was then that the Tusani people surprised me the most. This was the moment most warriors raise their weapons high and scream the victory screams, and dance the victory dances. The Scabas had raided, murdered, kidnapped, and tortured them for years and they had not been able to do a thing about it. Suddenly that threat was gone forever.

Warriors began walking among the dead with spears to be certain the enemy was finished. Others stationed in the forest began to emerge, unable to hide their astonishment at the sight of the massacre. A short time later, the women came from their hiding places looking just as aghast.

There was no celebrating. At first, I could not believe it. Some Tusani began hugging each other, making tiny grunting sounds as they looked over the battlefield. Somehow these primitive people, so harshly scarred by the Scabas, still understood the loss of life.

Chief Dawna emerged from the cave inspection with a small contingent of followers. He walked among the dead, waving the same crooked stick he had used to bless his own, chanting his guttural chant as he went. He glanced up at me once and I suddenly felt a frightening flush of guilt. All of this was my doing. How would the Tusani see me now? So many times in history, gunmen had been hired by townspeople to take on criminals exploiting a town. When the dirty deeds were done, and the town safe, often they had turned against the bounty hunter, blaming him for all that had happened, conveniently forgetting the role they played.

But the greatest guilt was indeed truly mine. The apemen had been the dominant species, the Tusani the submissive. My interference had changed that. I had greatly affected the balance of power in this place. What right did I have to do that?

The Scabas would have likely killed me on sight had they found me. The Tusani had taken me in, fed me, and healed me. There was a good chance I would not have survived this long without them. So this massacre had been in part a fight for my survival as much as for these people. The primitive Scabas had a natural right to attack whomever they chose. And whoever they attacked had a natural right to fight back.

The Tusani began gathering up Scaba bodies and carrying them off into the woods. Chief Dawna finished his offerings and approached me with Ooda close behind. We stood face-to-face and in his eye was the strange, contradictory look of a wise, yet primitive man. He seemed to sense my fear. He reached out a hand and grabbed my arm with his fat, worn fingers, and squeezed affectionately. He held up five fingers of his hand. "Five taken, three taken back," he said, and he nodded appreciatively.

Ooda whapped me a good one on my right shoulder and grunted his approval.

They carried the bodies to a wide, bottomless pit in the side of a nearby mountain. They dropped them in, no sound of impact to be heard. When all were interred, an ample pile of leaves, dirt, and branches were thrown in after, and more blessings invoked. I did not understand what was said. The tone of it seemed regretful. At the end, I heard the words, "Three taken back." That would be the legend of this battle. It would be called "Three Taken Back," and would be told through the spoken legends of the Tusani for centuries to come.

With that dark day behind them, the Tusani became a culture of self-discovery. The shadow of fear that had always been a part of their lives was lifted. The atmosphere in the camp had that too-good-to-be-true ingredient in it. People laughed more. They played jokes on each other. Newly discovered talents became games and contests. There was more painting and tattooing. Artistic talent had suddenly been allowed a place in everyday life.

Shock Diamonds

In the days that followed, a scavenging team showed me a forest of trees that were exactly like bamboo, incredibly strong, mostly hollow in the center. With the Chief's permission, we hauled a bunch of it back to camp, tapped into a mountain stream and brought running water down into the cave. A large stone cistern was constructed to provide drinking water and beyond it a second one for washing. The runoff was channeled through a small, stone-lined canal that led the water back to the mountain side. It happened to be a spot where terrace farming would have been perfect, but I did not have the knowledge to make that happen. I could hear R.J. scolding me somewhere a trillion miles away.

The girl who would regularly sneak away from camp went by the name of Avea. On two occasions, I was in the right place to follow her, but both times she lost me in a patch of forest and rock where paths led in too many directions. Finally, one bright afternoon, I managed to stay with her and watch undetected from on high. At first, she seemed only on the overhang to pick beautiful blue orchids that hung by the edge. After twenty minutes or so, I became troubled by guilt from spying and was about to sneak away when another figure appeared at the forest edge. It was a boy of similar age, but he was not from the Tusani clan. His tattoos were much more colorful, he wore leather cut clothes rather than fur, and his dark hair was carefully cut at the shoulder. He carried a spear with no Clovis point, nor was it fire-hardened.

They were lovers. I left at that point, lectured myself about being a snoop, and wondered where the boy had come from. In camp that night, sitting around the fire with the Chief and Ooda, I asked what lay beyond the north mountains as though it were a question of idle curiosity.

Ooda pointed at the north section of my dirt map and replied, "Oshoni."

I clutched my two hands together and shook them, and asked "Tusani and Oshoni?"

The Chief nodded, "Tusani, Oshoni trade good trade."

I repeated my handshake. "Tusani, Oshoni, no Scabas."

The Chief nodded once again. "Oshoni need Tusani."

I sat back and nodded my approval. It was yet another confirmation that the Tusani were basically a peaceful people, and had no intention of using their newfound power to subdue others. It gave me a reason to relax further from the fears of what I had done.

I spent most of the next three weeks exploring Tusani land. I found myself making regular trips to the smashed up escape pod, hoping it would help me to remember who I really

175

was. It was necessary to cut away vines and brush to see inside, but that became a pointless effort. The vegetation found too many ways to invade the pod. Eventually it would be completely hidden and too much work to uncover.

My flight suit was near the end of its useful life. The pant legs were shredded at the bottom. There were tar stains that could not be removed. Holes here and there in the arms and torso added to the annoying exposure it left. I lay in bed one night and mentally began working out a pattern for Daniel Boone wear. It was possible I would soon be a Tusani fashion designer and trendsetter. I went to sleep laughing at myself.

But that was an uncomfortable night. A bug, or creatures unknown, had chosen to bite my left forearm, leaving periods of itchiness that would not go away. It kept waking me up. I found myself wishing for a good stiff belt of bourbon and finally fell asleep wondering if alcohol could be manufactured here.

The next morning, I began searching for grapes, the first step in the fermenting process. There was a small clearing not far from the pod wreckage where something that looked like grapes hung in bundles from vines so heavy they dragged down tree limbs. As I stood appraising how best to recover the bright blue bulbs above me, the itching in my arm cropped up once again. I looked down at it with an angry stare and froze.

Beneath the skin of my forearm, a tiny green light was rapidly flashing. I yelped like a dog at the first sight of his master and fell to my knees in the dirt. I stared down in doubt at the little flashing green light and then snapped my head up to look at the pale orange sky.

I could not see her, but the Griffin was up there looking down. I had to stop and finger away pre-tears from my eyes, then quickly look for the flashing green light in my arm, still fearing it was imagined. It was not. The homing device in my arm had been activated. I looked skyward again. Beyond the sky orange, the crew of the Griffin was evaluating a response to their tracking query. They were trying to determine if it was a fluke or could really be me.

I turned and scanned the area. Eventually they would decide they could not discount the contact, and a landing would be needed. They might even be able to pick me out with the hi-res down-facing cameras, but my appearance made that a long shot.

Where would they land? When would they come? They would spend time evaluating all threats, decide how to protect against them, then pick the safest landing area that gave the fastest possible escape. That is what I would have done. All I had to do was wait and make sure they found me when they arrived.

The composite metals on the pod would show up in their scans. It would also suggest the transponder contact was genuine. They'd put down as close to it as possible. They would see the Tusani encampment and fear attack from them. They would also not wish to affect the culture by having a spacecraft land in their midst.

So they would probably land at night without lights, drop off a heavily armed Wilson, and wait for him to contact them after surveillance.

That is also what I would have done.

My first thought was to camp out at the edge of the forest near the pod to watch the open plain, but that was too dangerous at night. They would probably make the recon drop around early morning. Wilson was a jungle expert. He'd be carrying enough firepower to take down a T-Rex. He'd move in undercover and try to spot me or anything that would give off a false transponder signal.

I returned to camp and found I had the shakes. I had to hide them from the others. Pretending everything was normal was difficult. I held out until dark and pretended to sack out with the rest of the tribe. I did not sleep a wink. At the first crack of light, I crept silently out, a long spear in hand, and headed down the trail to the high-grass clearing. Except for the torn-up flight suit and boots, my uncut hair, beard, and overly tanned skin made me look like just another wild native. I hurried along toward the clearing, listening for the sound of a spacecraft.

I met them on the trail, headed for the camp. Wilson was dressed in green camouflage, green paint on his face, a heavy automatic weapon hanging from his chest, a larger one strapped on his back. R.J. was beside him, dressed in a standard green flight suit with only a belt and small stun gun stuck to it.

On sight, the three of us stopped in our tracks and stared in disbelief. R.J. let out an "Oh my god!" that sounded like a disapproving mother finding a lost child. All concern for manhood cast aside, I ran to them, drove my spear into the ground, and embraced them in a three-way bear hug.

"Oh my God!" repeated R.J. indignantly, as he pulled back to look me up and down.

"Adrian, what the hell...?" asked Wilson, but for some reason he was unable to finish.

"Man, you two misfits have never looked so good!" I clamped a hand on each of their shoulders and shook to be sure they were real.

"The beard is a nice touch," remarked R.J. "I like it."

"I don't," said Wilson. "Nice spear, though."

"You guys have no idea...."

"Looking at you, I'd say we do," replied R.J. He looked left and right. "Is it safe here?"

"How in god's name did you find me?"

R.J. nodded reluctantly. "It was Wilson, but it's a long story. I now owe him dishwashing and latrine duties for a week."

"Hey. Let me borrow your communicator for a second."

R.J. handed me his, as Wilson continued to guard the surroundings.

I keyed the mike. "Danica, maintain current orbit, stand by for further instructions."

There was a very long pause. Danica came back, "R.J., who was that? If you guys are screwing around, it's not funny."

"Danica, how do you clear a mountain range with dead engines when a thermal inversion has dragged you down too low?"

"Oh my god, Adrian! Thank God!"

"Give the others my warmest greetings and tell them I'll join you shortly."

She clicked off without answering, but as she did I could hear her calling them.

I shared a long look at my compatriots, and let out another great sigh of relief that bottomed out in my soul. "How long have I been gone?"

R.J. answered. "Almost three months."

"You returned to Earth and came back?"

"No, we couldn't do that," said R.J.

"What? Why not?"

"It's another long story. What do you need to do before you can leave?"

"How about you come with me and meet the people that saved my ass? There's quite a bit that needs to be done first."

"Do I need to cover you guys?" asked Wilson.

"No, they are friends. You come in with us, Wilson."

"If you say so."

We entered the camp as casually as possible. Most of the tribe was up. Those milling around the camp stopped to stare at the newcomers. Ooda was setting up with some archers near the target area. I waved him to follow. At the cave, there was much staring and silence. Chief Dawna was with his caregivers. They all stopped as we approached. I held R.J. and Wilson back and went to the Chief and explained members of my clan had finally found me and they would be honored to meet him. He nodded graciously, as a concerned Ooda came up alongside.

The Chief remained cordial. He maintained that slight standoffishness all veteran diplomats use. As best I could, I explained that other of my family were waiting nearby and would also like to meet the Chief and offer gifts of friendship. The unexpected intrusion was awkward for the Chief, Ooda, and the others, but the Chief's trust in me held. I promised we would leave and return after sunrise the next day. My leaving the camp seemed to increase the uneasiness.

We hiked to a clearing beyond the east mountains, where the Griffin's descent would not be seen. Danica zeroed in on our transponders, and for the first time in so many months, I saw the silhouette of the Griffin appear in the orange sky, descending toward me. I had to hide a choke. The damp green forest reflected its shimmering white skin as it whined down, kicking up dirt and grass as it jockeyed aground. The aft airlock door hissed open and the loading ramp deployed.

I stood at the base of the ramp and had chills from the experience. I could have fallen to my knees and kissed the ramp. In deference to male pride, I marched up the ramp, climbed into the airlock, then through the lab, gym, and sleeping quarters, and met the three astonished people waiting in the habitat area. Danica had left the pilot seat and was standing beside Patrick and Catherine. She shook her head as though she was about to scold me, then stepped forward and hugged me so hard it knocked the wind out of me. Catherine grabbed me tightly by one arm and whispered, "Adrian," then just stared while Patrick patted my shoulder.

I begged off from the barrage of questions, saying I just had to get a shower. Silent approval came immediately and was almost insulting. Afterward, I put on a clean blue flight suit, traded my beat-up boots for deck shoes, and decided not to shave. I did not want the Tusani to see me as someone else.

As I reentered the habitat area, R.J. stood up and cried, "Well, thank goodness, you didn't shave."

"Why do you say that?"

"Your entire tribe would try to imitate you, the Tarn-god."

"Maybe, but I made sure I wasn't a god to them, R.J. So, ladies and gentleman, shall we sit together and try to figure life out? I can't tell you how good it is to be here."

Danica stood in the airlock door. "Do you want to lift off so we're not seen?"

"It's okay, Danica. They saw the pod. There has already been that contamination. A few of them might sneak over here for a look but that's all. We can sit here overnight as long as the radar is scanning unless you know of some other danger."

E.R. Mason

Catherine spoke, "There's an active volcano in the southern hemisphere. That's why the sky is orange. And by the way, Adrian, I put it to you, we can't leave this place just yet."

"What do you have in mind, Doctor?"

"Your tribe. You've exposed them to pathogens a million years ahead of their time. Every one of them needs to be examined and inoculated as necessary. Otherwise, you could leave and months from now the entire group contracts something and is wiped out completely."

"To tell you the truth, in all the confusion to stay alive I hadn't thought of that."

Patrick asked, "Will they let us do that, Adrian?"

"Yes. They are a very peaceful people considering how badly they've been victimized."

R.J. said, "They can't be too peaceful. They've developed the Clovis point."

I shook my head. "Not until I arrived."

"Why would you do that?" he asked.

"To survive," I replied.

He looked at me and a variety of emotions crossed his face, ending in understanding. "How else have you changed them?"

"They have fire now. They were without it a very long time."

"Bow drill?" asked Wilson.

I nodded.

"Well, so much for worrying about contamination," said R.J. "But you know there are other species on this planet. You've probably changed its history forever."

"It was that or be eaten by the Scabas."

"I know what I would have done," said Wilson.

"These people were being regularly harvested by apemen. It wasn't a pretty sight. The Tusani took me in, healed my wounds, fed me and cared for me. It's a long story. But let's switch back to business. Since we're demanding explanations, why didn't you take this ship back to Earth, or at least report what happened and ask for orders?"

There was a long nervous pause. They all hemmed and hawed, waiting for someone else to answer.

"Well?"

"We couldn't report back to Earth," said R.J. in a half whine.

"Why not?"

Again a long pause in which everyone hoped someone else had a good response.

R.J. said, "Well, we all agreed that if we contacted Earth and told them you were taken, we'd then have to wait for the answer and they probably would have ordered us back to Earth. That's what Danica thought."

"We didn't want to go back," said Wilson.

"So you just went on your merry way, then?"

"We took a vote..." pleaded Wilson.

"Oh! A vote? How quaint. What was the tally?"

"Five not to contact Earth. Zero to contact Earth," said Danica, as though she thought it was adding legitimacy to their case.

"Unanimous then! You all agreed to violate standard agency rules? Is that what you're saying?"

"It was a private mission, Mr. Tarn," said Catherine.

"We were afraid when all was said and done they wouldn't send a search party for you, Adrian," said Patrick.

"For cripes sake, Adrian. We came out here to find a person, not lose another one," insisted R.J.

"It didn't seem like there was any harm in just looking around a bit," said Danica.

"And you. You and the big guy ended up in jail when I got knocked out, right? How'd you get out?"

Wilson looked at Danica. "How'd he know that? Who told?"

"Never mind that. How'd you get out of jail?"

R.J. spoke. "The blue stuff. The blue stuff you got on Enuro. It turns out that Marshall's deputies will kill for it. It only took six bottles. We're not even wanted any more. Not even a record, they said. Plus it was really lucky Dan and Wilson were in that jail. That's how we got a lead on you."

I gave an exaggerated, disapproving nod. "Oh good, very good. So, you busted yourself out of jail and went cruising around unknown space looking for me. I can't tell you the images that invokes in my mind. Did you get into any other trouble?"

Wilson piped up hopefully. "Nothing at all really, Adrian. Nothing. Except we did have to fire the ship's weapons system once."

"What! You had to shoot someone?"

Wilson looked over at R.J. "You know, he looks more authoritative with the beard. It makes me uneasy."

"Did you hit something when you fired? Did you kill anybody?"

"Certainly not!" insisted Patrick. "It was merely a warning shot."

Danica took over. "Oh, for Pete's sake. We were scanning an asteroid field for your pod. A ship not much bigger than us pulled up a few hundred meters starboard. They came over the com and demanded we prepare to be boarded. We said no.

They insisted. We turned into them, placed a high energy burst across their bow. Never saw any ship leave that fast. They must've thought we were serious and just missed. They never came back."

"I don't believe this! The four of you have become a bunch of pirates!"

Wilson cocked his head and laughed, "Aye, matey. We be overdue for a good plunder!"

"Wilson, this is no joke. What gave you guys the idea you had any chance at all of finding me?"

R.J. began, "Oh yeah, that's a pretty good one, Adrian."

"Of that, I have no doubt."

"While Danica and Wilson were in jail, it turns out the guy who jumped you just abandoned his guys and left them fuming in the next cell."

"He just left the guys he sent to round you up?"

"Yeah, they were in the cell next to Wilson and Dan. Anyway..."

Wilson interrupted. "Hey, you should'a seen Danica in that one, Adrian. I swear, she had them guys near tears. You would'a been proud."

"So I heard."

"You heard?"

"As I was saying," interrupted R.J. "They were really pissed off at the world, or should I say the moon.... Anyway, at first they just wanted to kill Danica for the gouged eye and stuff. But we were buying our guys out, and they were screwed. They started begging us to make a deal. We gave the Marshall enough extra bottles of the blue stuff and ended up partying with him and his deputies, while the other guys were begging us to help. We started cutting them in on the blue stuff, and the more they drank, the more they talked. The name of the guy with the cigar is Silas Killion. They were more pissed off at Killion than they were at us. They told us where he was headed; a planet called Enrika. We got the coordinates, and after promising to pay their fine so they could get out, we even got the longitude and latitude on Enrika where Killion was supposed to meet his contact. For a few extra bottles, we got the Marshall to agree to hold those guys for twenty-four hours to give us some distance between us and them, then we took off and headed for Enrika, but on the third day, the com station suddenly became overloaded with transmissions about some ship being destroyed. The moment he saw it, Wilson began insisting you had to be involved."

"Damn right. You still owe me the galley time," added Wilson.

R.J. scowled, "If you don't mind, Wilson? The rest of us wanted to continue on, but Wilson became a real pain in the ass."

"I was ...tenacious."

"Obstinate, pigheaded."

"Well, I was right, wasn't I?"

"Gentlemen, please..."

"Yeah, okay, so because of Wilson we stopped and began going through more of the communication streams. Finally, we came across one that said a rescue pod from the destroyed ship with two Sumani lizard-people females in it had been recovered, and the story was that the destruction of the ship was caused by an evil human. That immediately seemed like too much of a coincidence."

"Evil human made you think of me, then?"

"Well, it wasn't just that. From that point, we began plotting all the bodies in range of those escape pods and then started scanning each location. Problem was, there were so many places to search it was like a needle in a haystack. From there, you know the rest of the story."

"Wow."

"You wouldn't believe how much data we've gathered on this sector of space," added R.J.

I sat back and looked at each of them and sighed. "I'm sorry I screwed up and got taken in. It was stupid. I'm guessing you're all way past being sick of space and ready to get back."

There was a long heavy pause that surprised me. I had expected exclamations of relief.

Catherine spoke. "We have big leads on Patrick's daughter, Adrian. We think we know where she and some others might be being held."

"Ship's stores are still well-stocked, Adrian," added Danica.

"We have made a few allies here, too," said Wilson.

I looked again at each of them. "Are you kidding me? Are you guys saying you want to go on? I mean, I know how Patrick feels, but the rest of you want to go on, really?"

"Go," said Wilson.

R.J. nodded.

"Go," added Danica.

Catherine surprised me the most. She folded her arms and said, "I definitely want to go on."

I sat back and exhaled heavily. "I really must be dreaming."

Chapter 19

After sleeping late, followed by a massive conventional breakfast for the first time in months, then looking over flight deck standby lights, I rounded up Wilson and we led the two doctors with med kits up the trail toward the Tusani colony. There seemed to be something unusual between Catherine and Patrick. They lagged behind a bit and kept speaking in low tones.

Wilson was his usual jolly old self. "I was wondering, Adrian. You did blow up that ship, didn't you? Was I not right about that?"

"It's something I'm not proud of. Still coming to terms with it."

"Sure, I get that. But tell me, you had to have been on that thing when you destroyed it, didn't you?"

"Just between you and me, it was pretty close."

"So you set something off, and somehow got off the damn thing then?"

"Barely."

"So you must'a known where the escape pods were located and got there just in time."

"Nope."

"You're saying you didn't know where the escape pods were located when you blew it?"

"Nope."

"You didn't know?"

"Nope."

"So you blew the freakin' thing up and then went looking for a way off?"

"Yep."

"How the hell could you do that?"

"I hurried."

"Holy crap! You set that thing off not knowing you'd find a ride."

"I wasn't willing to go back to the cell."

"Roger that. How'd you get out of the damn cell then?"

"I committed suicide."

"You made it look like suicide so a guard would come in or something."

"Something like that."
"And he came in to look you over."
"It was the last thing he ever saw."
"No shit."
"Like I say, I'm still coming to terms with all of that. He wasn't the only one."
"Man, that was the last mistake those bastards will ever make."
"Were they bastards, Wilson? How do you know?"
"Oh, hell yes. You read some of that crap we intercepted on the B-station com panel. That ship was a regularly scheduled coffin for a whole lot of innocents. It had just made a dump of the latest victims and was on its way back for more. A bunch of the communications we intercepted were saying the destruction was way overdue, and how those lizard people needed killing, and I'm putting it nicely. You read some of them, Adrian. Some of the crap they were doing on that ship will make your hair curl. Don't take it from me, read it for yourself. It was so bad, the Docs and R.J. didn't want to believe you were on it. They thought you'd be dead or missing parts for sure if you were."
"I hate that surprised look they give you when you kill them. Can't get it out of my head."
"Yeah, something you'd only tell to another combat soldier. Only we can understand."
"What's the dues, Wilson? What happens when it's your turn and the bill comes due?"
"For killing somebody who's tryin' to kill you? What's the dues if you stand by and let them do it, instead of trying to save yourself? There's gotta be dues for that, too. Which kind'a dues you want to pay? All the civilians who were gonna be put down by that ship, I know what they'd say."
"I'm lucky to have a friend like you, Wilson. There aren't any others like you."
"God, I hope you're not turnin' sentimental on me. We're way overdue at tyin' one on, Adrian. We got plenty of blue stuff left."
"I'll put it on my to-do list."
"And I'll hold you to it."
As we entered the camp, the Tusani once again paused to watch the new strangers. Word had spread of the promise of friendship and gifts, so this time the atmosphere was silent but warm.
Chief Dawna greeted us at the cave, bowed to the doctors, and led them in where those injured in previous battles were still being cared for by the nurses with the green goop. After a few words to them from the Chief, Catherine and Patrick

went right to work. I had to hang around to help with translations. Wilson hung with me, not knowing what else to do.

As the doctor-patient relationships began to take hold, Wilson begged off and headed back to the ship. I sat by the cave entrance, watching the day's activities, and a short time later spied R.J. walking into the camp alone and unarmed. He passed through the Tusani, smiling, waving, and calling out, "Yei, yei." Tusani for hello. Aboard Griffin, I had recorded the Tusani dialect that I knew. R.J. had obviously already learned it. He came up alongside and looked out over the camp.

"This is so beautiful," he said.

"You should be carrying at least something, you know. There's some nasty prehistoric animals out there."

"Nothing bothered me."

"There are flightless birds three times the size of an ostrich, and they eat meat."

"Have you seen them?"

"Up close."

"Do they still have dorsal feathers on the wings or have they lost those?"

"I couldn't see, running as I was."

"Oh!"

"They do have spiked teeth."

"Oh! You were running from, as opposed to with, I take it."

"For my life."

"Perhaps I will begin carrying something."

"It would be prudent."

"These people are fabulous."

"I thought of you often as I was trying to teach them things."

"Yeah. I wanted to talk to you about that. How would you feel if I took that job over?"

"I would love it. Please do everything you possibly can to improve their lives and ensure their survival, as they ensured mine."

"I have to warn you; I'm thinking metallurgy."

"Wow. That would be one giant leap. Why so much so fast?"

"Because, to farm successfully, they need hardened tools. Have you seen any shiny deposits of any kind anywhere?"

"I'm not that dumb, R.J. There are iron deposits about a mile up the north trail. It's so plentiful some of it has collected as powder on the ledges. Can you really construct a furnace?"

"Leather and wood for the billows. Stone and mud for the oven. No problem."

"I can't wait to see the Professor at work."

"The other thing will be pottery. One must have jars to put one's harvest in."

"The women will love you. They may not let you leave."

"Don't tempt me. I can imagine staying here, forever."

"I'll let you in on a secret. So can I."

"You've got to be kidding. You?"

"You go from kidnapping and killing with bloodthirsty aliens to this, and it makes you think. The whole time I've been here I kept replaying your annoying lectures about technology versus nature in my head. At some point, you started to win."

"Have either of the doctors taken your temperature?"

"Sometimes disagreements here turn into fights, just like in the modern world, but you know what happens? The two that are fighting tire themselves out and end up laughing so hard they roll in the dirt holding their stomachs and pointing at each other. Then everyone around them breaks out laughing and it turns into a damn celebration. How did modern society lose that last part?"

"Did you hit your head or anything when you touched down?"

"There's not a Tusani here I wouldn't trust. All of these people just assume that's the way it should be. You know what? They're right. Why isn't our world like this? Everyone's life could be like euphoria."

"For gosh sakes, this isn't fair. I'm supposed to be the naturalist. You're supposed to be the rocket man. Now you're forcing me to give you the 5 percent lecture. It's not fair."

"Five percent what?"

"There are fifty-six people in this tribe. If 5 percent of them are troublemakers, that's 2.8 troublemakers and 54.2 people who are okay. Fifty-four people are a strong influence over two or three troublemakers. They can be kept in line and taught. On Earth, there are eight billion people. Five percent of eight billion people means four hundred million assholes. That's too many to control. You get just one real asshole in a restaurant and he disrupts the entire place. You get one asshole on a flight to somewhere and he makes the trip life-threatening. Even just the whiners will drive you insane. So, in our very large modern family, there have to be special people who prevent the five-percent idiots from blowing the place up. That's who Adrian Tarn turned out to be. We have police, but there has to be troubleshooters who know how to get around the rules and cheat a little to stop bad things from happening. You break the rules better than anybody I know. That's Adrian Tarn. Knight in tarnished armor. Breaker of rules. Rescuer of damsels in distress, which happens to be our current mission by the way. Occasional slayer of windmills, as Bernard Porre would put it. Player of all-night poker games. Drinker of whiskey often smuggled aboard. Scourge of Earth's premier space agency. Why do you think they always let you off? It's because they know they need you, that's why. Now, can I go back to being the naturalist and argue with you that technology is not the Holy Grail?"

"Whew. Was I whining?"

"A little bit. You were whining a little bit."

"That reminds me, I promised Wilson I'd tie one on with him. Care to join us?"

"Exactly what you need. And by the way, there's something I need to discuss with you privately."

"I'm not married here."

"Right... That's not it." R.J. stopped and looked around to see if he had attracted too much attention. "I've spent many an hour monitoring space communications, searching for clues about you."

"Yeah, apparently I'm infamous."

"Not important. During all the searching and cross-checking, I came across something unexpected, a reference to Danica's priceless diamond skull."

"God, I forgot all about that thing. You guys have been riding around the worst hoodlum sector of space known to man, with the most valuable diamond ever seen aboard. Tell me God doesn't have a sense of humor."

"Yes, this is another fine mess you've gotten us into. I agree."

"You were saying about the skull...?"

"As near as I can tell, there's a legend about a planet that no longer exists. It's carved in a strange sort of stone script called "The Legend of the Elohim." Someplace in this sector, a solar system died a million years ago in a supernova. As the story goes, and believe me this part is going to blow your mind, the skull was created with a set of companion crystals."

"Companion crystals like the ones..."

"Oh yes indeed, like THOSE crystals."

"The false radar emitter we removed from Griffin's tail section? That's a companion piece to the diamond skull?"

"Yep."

"Wow! But how? The fake transducer crystal was put in there at Enuro, during the gravity install. Are you saying they were in on this somehow?"

"We were wrong about that. I checked it out. The interference first began when we left Earth on our way to Enuro, not after we had been there. The trouble started when Danica showed up with the skull."

"When the skull came in close proximity to the fake transducer?"

"Yep."

"You know what? I got to admit that makes sense. Blackwell financed the building of the Griffin with money from human trafficking. He must have already had the crystals, but still did not have the skull. He hid the crystals in the tail of the ship during construction, while he continued to try to get his hands on the skull. But the Griffin was seized by the government and he was sent to prison. Danica said the skull was delivered to Blackwell's estate while he was still in prison. As soon as he got out, he needed access to the Griffin to get the crystals back. That would not be easy. He made Danica a test pilot offer he knew she couldn't refuse, hoping to use her. He was working on that when she flew the coop. So the skull is priceless but it's incomplete. He needed the crystals to complete the set. He was going to make a killing selling a complete, legendary skull set on the black market. What would they have offered him? A planet of his own? A solar system somewhere?"

"None of the above."

"What do you mean?"

"He wanted the skull and crystals for what they can do, not what they are worth."

"Okay, now you lost me. They really do something?"

"It's just a guess, but I'd bet money on it. The two crystal-halves we removed from the tail. One fits into the forehead of the skull. The other sticks to the forehead of the user. That's why it was sticking to my skin when we were messing around with it."

"You're starting to creep me out, R.J."

"Yeah? You think so? Well, listen to this. Putting the crystal on your forehead opens a link to the skull. At that point, the user only needs to think the name and location of anyone anywhere, and he can communicate with them telepathically."

"Oh, come on. You've gone too far now. Is that part of the legend, or something you made up?"

"Everything fits perfectly."

"You haven't been doing dangerous experiments with that thing while I've been gone, have you?"

"Of course the hell I haven't."

"So all of this is just wild conjecture?"

"Not really. There's ancient script supposedly associated with the thing that implies everything I've told you."

"Man, now that you mention it, Danica kept saying how Blackwell was trying to meditate to the thing thinking it would give him some kind of power or something. I think cigar man Killion mentioned something about Blackwell dreaming of world domination, too."

"See?"
"So he believed in it, but that doesn't mean anything."
"Only one way to find out..."

It took only one day for R.J. to rob me of my Tusani V.I.P. status. From that time on, Tusani men and women were constantly going to him for instruction. He was never in one place for more than a few minutes, overseeing a particular operation in each area, then moving on to the next. The Tusani women were neglecting their duties outright, gathered en masse around the pottery area, captivated completely by the modeling of river clay. Many of the men were enthralled by the construction of the smelting furnace. To my credit, the archery area remained very popular.

The doctors were no less in demand. While performing the necessary inoculations, they were curing a variety of problems that had plagued the Tusani for years. Traffic to their treatment section of the cave was continuous. To the Tusani women, injections were suddenly considered an absolute must. It was an irony that the tribe had gone from Tusani nurse-doctoring to two of the most advanced physicians in the modern world.

On the third day of the Griffin crew invasion, I watched R.J. break apart two stone molds he had shown the Tusani women how to carve. They separated to reveal the first Tusani iron ax head. The people stared in wonder as R.J. rubbed it against a sharpening rock, and when he made the motion of chopping on a nearby log with it, understanding came over them like tidal a wave.

By the end of that third day, the doctors were finished. It was finally time to leave. The doctors gathered up the considerable number of accessories they had ended up bringing to the camp, then said many goodbyes and were escorted back to the ship by Wilson. R.J.'s leaving was much more difficult. They had him by the arm, one after another, last-minute questions that were difficult to understand and even more difficult to answer in Tusani. A group followed him to the edge of the encampment, helping him to hoist his backpack on the way. When his chance came, he did not wait for Wilson's return but backed down the trail waving until he was out of sight.

I had no idea how to say goodbye. That difficulty was made worse by the fact I did not want to leave. The Chief and Ooda walked me to the forest edge. We said little but understood completely. When I turned to look back at the camp, I found all of the Tusani had gathered in a large group and stood silently staring. It made me choke and I had to catch a pre-tear with a forefinger. They noticed. It said more than I ever could have. I held my big bird tooth necklace high, and against all

Tusani custom hugged the Chief and even Ooda. With a last look, I turned to the trail and consciously had to force myself to put one foot in front of the other.

    Danica had Griffin idling. The airlock door swished shut behind me. The air conditioning kicked on and was too cold trying to catch up. In the habitat module, two seats were set up for departure for the doctors. They were already strapping in. Beyond the forward airlock, R.J. and Wilson were strapped into their respective engineering stations. On the flight deck, Danica had taken the right seat and left the command chair for me. I lowered myself in and felt the long absent Commander Adrian Tarn resurface. I tugged at the beard so unfamiliar to him.

    "Are you ready, Danica?"

    "Let's get into the sky, Adrian."

    "Checklists complete?"

    "Engineering and flight deck all green. Flight director loaded and standing by."

    "What'd you put in there?"

    "I programmed one orbit at 200. I thought you'd like to get a look at where you've been for the past few months."

    "You are an angel. You know that?"

    "I can't tell you how good it is to have you in that seat again."

    I tapped the intercom. "Launch in 3...2...1...mark." I hit the engage button and felt the ground-plane give us up. The forest below fell away as we dashed upward into the orange sky.

Chapter 20

We coasted on orbit around Tusania, a planet that until now had no Earth designation. I logged it in under that name, making it a keepsake forevermore for the Tusani people. It was an ovoid-shaped, green planet, spotted by frequent blue, no oceans, but many large lakes and rivers. I turned in the command seat and renewed my familiarity with the busy displays, panel lights, and clicking meters, as R.J. arrived forward.

"We're coming up on the break-orbit point, Adrian unless you want to alter the flight plan," said Danica.

"What have you guys put in there?"

"We're set up with the coordinates we got from Killian's henchmen. It's a system beyond the NGC 6188 nebula. It's another place that has not been mapped or visited by any Earth ships yet, another big blank spot on the charts."

"Where else would we want to go?" mused R.J. "Anybody can travel known space."

Danica cast a sarcastic look.

"How long a ride?" I asked.

"Only three days to reach the outer rim," she replied. "At max."

"How's the Griffin been?"

"Not one single no-go, not a single warning light since you've been gone. Just a dream to fly."

"Must be the engineers," said R.J.

Danica rolled her eyes. "God, he's been jovial since you returned."

"Hey, I don't have to come up front to be insulted. I can go back there with Wilson..." R.J. pushed himself away and retreated aft.

Danica looked at me with a more somber expression. "He's discovered something about the skull, but he won't tell me."

"Yeah, he thinks it's some kind of telepathy device. Those crystals that were in the tail go with it."

"Wow! That sounds ridiculous, but it makes sense. That could be what Blackwell was trying to do. Where'd R.J. get that?"

"He found some stuff in other people's data streams. He's been watching for something the whole time. I agree with you. It's bull crap."

"So what do the crystals have to do with it?"

"One-half crystal fits into the indentation on the skull's forehead; the other one sticks to the user's forehead. Theoretically, a connection is then made somehow."

"So, that's why Blackwell was spending so much time meditating to the thing. He thought he could get it to work without the crystals."

"If it's any consolation, I'll bet he's still meditating to the fake skull and doesn't know it."

"We can only hope. So are you guys going to try the thing, or what?"

"Undecided."

"I think I'd give it a shot. Maybe I could get into that bastard's head and screw him up good."

"Yeah, I heard you put a hurting on those guys in the bar."

"You should have seen the look of surprise on their faces."

"Unfortunately, I have seen that look recently."

"You have to kill somebody or something?"

"It's something you never get over. Keep that in mind the next time you're taking somebody's man-card."

"Yeah, it's better not to have to live with it if you don't have to."

"So let's keep the skull thing between the three of us. When we have a chance you and I can get together with R.J., and we'll decide what to do."

"Aye, aye, Captain. Ten minutes to break away. Better tell the kiddies."

"Tell me something, Dan. How many jumps to light is this for you?"

"You kidding? Lost count a long time ago."

"How many places did you have to search for me?"

"R.J. could probably answer that."

"Did you keep up the logs?"

"Oh, yes. Just the basic entries and a few of the more memorable sightings."

"Has there been contact with Earth, at all?"

"Just one message we managed to pick up. Don't know how long it took to get here. R.J. could tell you that."

"What was it?"

"It was a message to Wilson from Jeannie."

"Oh god, don't tell me."

"No, no. It wasn't a Dear John. It was a nice note saying the pre-marriage counseling camp sucked and would he please get his butt back there and marry her." Danica smiled and keyed the intercom. "Get in your high-chairs kiddies. We're going to jump!"

There was muted cheering from the habitat module.

Danica brought the ship to heading and engaged the flight director. I sank back in my seat and watched Tusania shrink to nothing in the aft cameras as we became light. My heart did another backflip. I had that sudden urge again; wait...hold on a second. Then it was a tiny star, then gone. All I had left was my big bird necklace and heart song.

But it did not take long to settle back to modern living. Shaving the beard was like a ticket back to the future. The Tusanis had no sugar or sweetener of any kind, so the first candy bar lit me up. I played R.J. a game of chess, and had he not underestimated the value of a pawn again, he would have beaten me. He sat for a half-hour after the game staring at the board.

There were unexpected soap opera undercurrents aboard. I noticed them the first day. Patrick and Catherine. Something had happened there in my absence. I spotted them in the med lab standing too close for too long. I was grateful they had not noticed. It was easy to understand. Chances had been good I would never be found. Three months in a tight space with enough luxury and just enough privacy. When two people have a connectivity they don't know about, they are bound to discover it.

Story of my life.

So all I had to do was make it easy for them. Say just the right things, be too busy to think about romance, use caution enough to avoid intruding on the secret meetings. The truth was, I was too concerned about our destination to think about anything else, anyway. Too much had gone wrong already, and we hadn't even gotten to first base.

Then there was the matter of Danica's godhead. If there was ever a good time to test it, this was not that time. The thing was a nemesis. Even if it did not possess the magic claimed by the legend, the thing was a diamond so valuable it could start wars. The only protection anyone who possessed it could ever possibly have would be that no one knew.

On day two, Wilson and I had the habitat module to ourselves for a time. We sat at the conference table with our feet up, drinking coffee. Wilson was bored until I asked him the keynote question.

"So pre-marriage counseling camp sucked, I hear."

His chin snapped up and he suddenly looked confounded. "What a surprise, eh?"

"She sure doesn't sound like she's undecided."
"You still gonna be best man, right?"
"You still going to be the groom, right?"
"Wow, that sounds funny."
"It's never gone this far, old friend."
"She's writing the vows for both of us. Is that customary?"
"I got a feeling you're going to promise to love, cherish, and obey."
"Now wait a minute..."
"Too late to back out now."
"Well, who knows how long we'll be out here..."
"Yeah. I know Patrick can take it. I don't know about Catherine."
"Tell me somethin', Adrian. What are we gonna do if we catch up to them?"
"We're going to be way smarter than we were before. We're going to be invisible thieves in the night. If Emma is still alive and we find her, I'd like to take her right from under their noses and be a trillion light years away before they realize she's gone. That's what I would like to happen."
"Okay, let's do that, then. But just one thing. Have you ever met Patrick's daughter in person?"
"Not just yet."
"So we're going someplace nobody's ever been, to find someone we've never met, and steal her back from people we don't know, is that about it?"
"I do believe you've got it."
"Okay then. No problem."

On the third day of travel, still six hours out from the heliosphere of the Enrika system, a nervous R.J. woke me early. He fidgeted around impatiently while I used the bathroom. I had to visit his engineering station before coffee could be served.
"This is weird space. We've entered weird space," was all he kept saying. Wilson appeared in the galley, still in pajamas, his hair sticking up in an Our Gang cowlick. He watched us with a sleepy, disconcerting stare.
"It's a flood of noise in the low-frequency spectrums. None of it makes sense. Never saw anything like this before. It bothers me."
"Is it affecting systems?"
"Well, no, but still..."
"What would you like to do?"
"Stop and investigate."

"But we're still in the interstellar medium. You said we're five-and-a-half hours from even the hemisphere of the place."

"The star is weird, too."

"Is the system what we expected?"

"Oh yeah, five planets, all on the ecliptic. We're twenty degrees above, so it's a straight-in just as the flight director and nav computer have programmed, but all of this space is strange."

Wilson came up next to me, sipping coffee. The smell was distracting. "He's right about the star, Adrian. I was looking at the emissions last night. It's not a normal solar wind."

"You want to stop out here, too?"

"Might not hurt. Take a close look at what we're flying into."

"Okay, R.J. You win. Tell Danica to stop and bring us to station-keeping. If she complains, tell her it was your idea."

I looked down at Wilson's coffee. "Are the doctors still asleep?"

Wilson leaned in and whispered, "In the same sleeper cell."

"I didn't need to know that."

"You want me to get you one of these coffees?"

"Only if you don't want a fight for yours."

"I better get you one."

Carefully balancing our coffees, we strapped in so that Danica could park us. When she was done, Danica called back. "Auto-pilot station-keeping, Adrian?"

"Sure, but make sure the CAS link to the flight director has the audible warning turned on, okay?"

"Well golly, that's a good idea."

"Sorry. Unnecessary reminder. But it's not old age kicking in."

She came back to the habitat module, passing Wilson on his way to the engineering station. She plunked down in the seat across from me and gave me an exaggerated smirk.

I shrugged. "Maybe I am getting senile or something."

Danica giggled. "I won't worry unless you start reminding me to take my space vitamins, Dad."

I shoved a cup of steaming coffee at her, made just the way she liked it. "I'm way not old enough to be your dad, girl."

I cooked her breakfast. We sat together eating while the two engineers hung over their stations, studying the oddity of the space around us. We were barely halfway through the eggs when the conversation between R.J. and Wilson began to heat up.

At first they refused to even look back at us. Finally R.J. straightened up, excitement in his voice. "We're behind the NGC

6188 Nebula, Adrian. We're looking at stuff nobody's ever seen before. Man, this is not normal space."
Wilson looked at R.J. and interrupted. "It is a neutron!"
R.J. argued, "Can't be."
"Is!"
"It's the NGC 6193 cluster. It's making everything look weird, that's all."
"No way, man. That is a blue star. A neutron SSS."
"A slow-burning star system? You're nuts. You're not an astrophysicist. You don't know what you're talking about."
"Neither are you. And I'll tell you, if there were any astrophysicists here right now, they'd be going crazy declaring it's blue light from a neutron star."
"It's the cluster effect, that's all."
"Okay, let's run it through the analytical programming. Let's see what that says."
"Okay. I'm inputting it."
They hung over R.J.'s station in silence for half a minute. Wilson erupted, "Theoretical neutron-based star! See!"
"I don't believe it. The computer is confused."
As I stood to join them, a squinty-eyed Patrick emerged from the sleeper section. He fumbled his way through the coffee stores, gave us a split-second guilty look, then began to mix his coffee.
I came up beside Wilson and stared down at their data screens. "Gentlemen, can we go in there or not?"
"Not as it stands right now," replied R.J.
Wilson raised his chin and gave an I-told-you-so look.
"What do we have to do?"
Patrick joined us, sipping his coffee, avoiding looking at me directly.
"We need to know this area of space is not harmful to biology before we get any closer," replied R.J.
"How do we do that, fellas?"
"I can do that," said Patrick.
"How?"
"Easy. Done it many times. We generate a few hundred stem cells of the most vulnerable tissue possible, expose them to the spectrum of radiations in this area for a certain amount of time, then simply watch for cellular aberration."
"How long?"
"Aboard the larger agency exploration vehicles the recommended minimum is six hours of exposure."
"Patrick, we don't want the trail to get any colder than it already is."
"I'll get Cather…. I'll get right on it."

197

E.R. Mason

I sat back down with Danica and stared out a portal at nothing.

"Everything okay with you these days?" she asked.

"Fine, just fine. You getting burned-out up front?"

"You know, I'm not. Something about the ship always talking to me. I almost never get lonely."

"It is a reliable relationship, at that."

"As opposed to some relationships which are not so."

"You're overdue for a sleep period."

"No way, Dad. From what I'm overhearing, we're heading into a slow-burning blue-star system. No one's ever seen one of those. You think I'll lie in my cell and be able to sleep?"

"No way I'm old enough to be your dad."

She eyed me in an unusual way. "I would be willing to relinquish the left seat to you."

"Smart. That way I'll be to blame if anything goes wrong."

"Never trust a woman."

"I thought I knew that."

We mulled around the habitat, waiting while Patrick and Catherine remained in the science lab. Six hours later, Patrick emerged. "You are good to go, Adrian. There's no sign of incompatibility at all."

"In that case, please tell Catherine to strap in."

I slipped back into the command seat. We wasted no time in resuming course to Enrika. Three hours later, the unexpected reared its ugly head once again. R.J. had remained at his engineer station. He abruptly came over the intercom with a tone of urgency. "Adrian, objects approaching on the long-range. They are quick."

"R.J. could you be a little more specific?"

"Three small conical-shaped spacecraft, approximately three feet in diameter, on an intercept course."

"Weapons energy signatures?"

"No, but we are being continuously scanned."

"How long before intercept?"

"Now!"

Before I could again ask for clarification, a shiny gray ball with probes sticking out of it appeared in front of us, matching our speed.

Danica wrenched her head to the right. "Another one to starboard, Adrian."

I twisted around and spotted the third out my port windshield. "Yep, over here, too."

R.J.'s voice came back over the com. "Our warp fields are being dampened, Adrian. We're slowing."

"Everybody strap in."

It was a thirty-minute slowdown which ended in capture by a three-point tractor field. For lack of anything else to do, we took the stellar drives off-line and waited. Just as I was about to ask R.J. to try transmitting greetings, he came over the intercom. "Something coming in, Adrian. Check out your main com screen."

TRANSIT THROUGH ADRIA PLANETARY SYSTEM PROHIBITED WITHOUT CELESTIAL CODEX.

SPACECRAFT—GRIFFIN—TERRAN SYSTEM—EARTH ORIGIN

NASEBIAN CODEX ALPHA-PI-THETA-UPSILON-XI-CHI-NU-NU

YOU ARE AUTHORIZED TO PROCEED

WARNING

EFFECT NO INTERFERENCE TO ENRIKA

The three small craft departed so quickly we did not see them leave. They simply disappeared.
"Wow!" said R.J.
I looked over at Danica. "Re-engage the stellar drives, please. Stay strapped in back there. We're going back to light."
We resumed course.
An hour later, after passing through the bow shock point, and entering the Enrika System's heliosphere, the conversation between R.J. and Wilson picked up. I could not clearly hear what they were saying, but I could tell many unusual things were popping up. As the blue neutron star began to take shape in our view screens, R.J. came forward and leaned between us. "Man, this is spooky, Adrian."
"Take it easy, R.J. I don't want you scaring Danica."
"Oh, funny," she replied.
"Yeah, you think I'm joking? The nav computer is having trouble plotting the movement of the planets and their moons."
"Why?"
"They're moving so slow. It's hard to project a future!"
"Huh?"

"Yeah, and it's the same thing with the rotations. We can see the terminator on Enrika from here, but the topography on it does not seem to be changing."

"We're still awful far out, R.J.," said Danica.

"Yeah, but everything here is crazy. You wait. I'll be back."

"He can also be trying at times, can't he," said Danica.

"Quite often actually. The problem is, he's usually right, especially when you don't want him to be."

Enrika's blue sun quickly grew large. Planets to port and starboard of us became bright, glistening diamonds.

Danica said, "Flight Director is displaying the countdown for braking."

I hit the intercom. "Time to strap back in again. Next stop, Enrika high orbit."

Danica pressed a key on her monitor and looked at me inquisitively. "Boy, some of what R.J. is talking about must be right. We asked for a geocentric orbit to study those surface coordinates, but the flight director is not calling for an orbital insertion. It's mapped a stop and station-keeping four hundred miles above the surface with a thruster firing schedule to maintain that distance. The planet's rotation is so slow we can hold geocentricity with nothing more than a drift. The CAS is showing no satellites or other man-made objects. It's a very clean thermosphere."

"Okay, some of that is strange."

The forty-five-minute slowdown put us exactly four hundred miles above the planet Enrika, at the coordinates Killian's henchmen had said were used for pay-off meetings. R.J. and Wilson wasted no time aiming the forward cameras at the surface. It took only a few minutes and we began hearing surprised laughter from them.

I looked over at Danica warily. "You have the spacecraft."

"I most certainly have the spacecraft," she replied. "You'd better go see what those rascals are up to now."

Behind the pilot seats, I stopped and looked down at R.J.'s station. "Okay, what?"

Wilson said, "Put it up on the main monitors so everyone can see it."

An image appeared on monitors all around the ship. It was a view similar to looking down from an aircraft at about one thousand feet. We were looking at a modern city that resembled the whitewashed buildings of Santini Island or parts of Greece. The architecture was built into steep hillsides, with sprawling communities in the valleys below, a large spread of very neatly organized and spacious buildings. There were small, light-colored vehicles on white roadways, a few citizens in mono-colored clothing here and there, among carefully placed light-green trees and foliage. And there was one very peculiar aspect to it all.

Not one thing was moving.

"What the...?" commented R.J.

"You gotta be kidding me," added Wilson.

"What is that?" called Catherine.

"I think it's a façade of a city," replied Wilson. "It's like a movie set. It's not real."

We stared at the monitors and tried to make sense of it, a paradoxical frozen alien city, full of the images of life, with no signs of life at all.

"R.J., show me the exact coordinates we want to see."

"Yeah, I've been looking at that, Adrian. It's behind this section of the structures at the base of the largest cliff side. There's a narrow slot in the cliff side that leads away from the city to a fairly large clearing with a waterfall and small lake, but it's not big enough for us to land there. We'd have to walk in."

"Okay then, find us a place to put down out of sight within walking distance."

"Just east of the township, behind this hill and that tree line," he replied, pointing at the monitor and looking up at me.

"Lower us down, Danica. R.J.'s sending you the coordinates. We need to get out and take a stroll."

Chapter 21

It was a long descent. I called out, "Wilson, what's the atmosphere?"

"A whopping 8 percent O2, no harmful gasses, gravity point-eight-six of Earth's."

"Adrian, the pressurization system will want to bring in outside air at eight thousand. You want to trust what's out there?" asked Danica.

"Tell you what. Put a hold on that. Let's stay isolated until we land and take a closer look."

"Agreed," she replied.

The ride down was the smoothest direct descent I had ever experienced. As trees came up in front of the viewports, the ship rocked unusually hard, settling down onto rock-hard ground. We kept the stellar drive and OMS engines at idle for a quick escape, if needed. The land outside the viewports seemed strangely quiet.

"So, does it still look breathable out there, you guys?"

"Particularly clean air, Adrian," replied R.J.

I unstrapped and pushed up from the left seat. "Stay ready, Dan. The boys and I will try to be quick about it."

"No problem."

Catherine and Patrick were glued to the port windows in the habitat module. I gave Patrick a slap on the shoulder. "Patrick, you're going to want to come along on this one in case we actually find something about Emma."

"Absolutely," he answered, and he fell in behind me.

Catherine glanced up with a half deprived, half guilty look, but she held her tongue.

With Wilson bearing arms as usual, and R.J. equipped with an equal complement of hand scanners, we popped open the rear airlock hatch and deployed the ramp. The strangeness of the place hit us again before we even had a chance to start down. There was no wind or sound. The smell of vegetation was strangely stagnant. Beams of sunlight seemed to be hanging from the sky-like curtains. It was the most deathly still environment I had ever experienced.

We tromped down the ramp and stepped off onto light-green grass. In keeping with the oddness of the place, the grass

Shock Diamonds

seemed not to give way to each step. It did not feel like real grass. We stopped and surveyed our surroundings.

"What the hell is this place?" said Wilson.

The trees were as unmoving and silent as everything else. Not a breeze, not a falling leaf, not the sound of a bird. We started up the hill that had been used to conceal our landing.

"This is too weird. Look, the ground is some type of sand, but we're not leaving any footprints," complained Wilson.

At the top of the hill, a portion of the township came into view. Wilson moaned, "No way!"

R.J. declared, "It can't be..."

From our hilltop vantage point, our view of the township was even more unmistakably bizarre. A well-manicured park separated us from a main thoroughfare. Beyond it lay the pristine white buildings we had seen from the air. People who looked nearly human in off-white, ankle-length robes were entering or leaving shops and other buildings. Their skin tone was pale, but their eyes brightly colored. Two small bubble-shaped cars with occupants were stopped at traffic lights to our right. Immediately to our left, some form of ball game was in progress. Nearby, people were walking small furry creatures that vaguely resembled shaggy dogs.

It would have been a friendly, familiar setting except for the one arcane fact. Not one vehicle, animal, or person was moving at all. Everyone and everything were frozen in place.

Wilson finally broke the stunned silence. "It's like I said, guys. It's a mock-up. None of this is real. But why would anyone do this? It goes on forever!"

"I believe you are mistaken, Bro," replied R.J.

"We all see it! There's no mistake. It's like a movie set or something. A really big, lifelike movie set. It's like the mock-ups we used to practice for combat missions."

"Nope," insisted R.J. "But I will say it is the most incredible thing I have ever seen."

"R.J., what the hell are you rambling about?" stammered Wilson.

R.J. pointed upward. We all looked up. There, hanging high in the air, was an aircraft shaped like a flying wing. It too was not moving at all.

"That's not all," said R.J. "Look at the guy throwing the ball over there. Can you see the ball?"

"Oh, now you're really blowing my mind," exclaimed Wilson.

We all stood looking at a softball-shaped object, also hanging in midair and not moving.

203

Patrick came up alongside R.J. "I am guessing you have some sort of explanation, R.J. I think we'd all like to hear it."

R.J. bent over and picked up a small stone in the sand. He straightened up, held it out, and let go. It hung in midair. He turned to Patrick, then looked at the rest of us. "Time. It's a different constant here."

"Oh for cripes sake, are you trying to say these people are real?" asked Wilson.

"Almost certainly," answered R.J. "Time is passing here at a rate so much slower than ours, it looks to us as though everything has stopped."

"Prove it," said Wilson.

"Look at that ball over there again," said R.J. "It has moved slightly. Just a tiny bit, but from my position I can see it has advanced. So has the aircraft."

We all studied the path of the ball and the flight path of the aircraft and were forced to admit to ourselves he was probably right.

"So if that's true, can they see us?" asked Wilson.

"I doubt it," said R.J. "We are ghosts here, not even leaving footprints in the sand, although I bet our footprints will probably appear sometime later as the sand eventually finishes forming the impression."

"So, Professor Smith, you're saying we brought our own time with us?" asked Patrick.

"There is an old saying that all matter is condensed starlight," answered R.J. "Everything here formed under that blue star. The best guess is that matter here is radically different than anything we're familiar with. This place is a physicist's dream."

I intervened. "Gentlemen, since we do not seem to be interfering with the population here, let's get going. Nobody touch anything and stay clear of these people. Let's get to those coordinates and make sure we leave this place just as we found it like we were warned to on the way in."

Entranced by the slow-motion world around us, we crossed the park, a field of dreams locked in time. The closer we looked, the more oddities came into view. Farther out in the game, there was a runner in mid-stride heading for a base. His right knee was raised, his left toe not quite touching the ground. The ball hung in the air, but it would beat him to the base. Another player, braced in the ball's path, had an expression of total concentration as he held up a round leather glove, anticipating a catch. Ahead of us, a woman in the same light-colored apparel they all seemed to enjoy was walking a large, shorthaired dog that looked like a greyhound carved out of marble. Three of its legs were off the ground, the fourth barely touching. The woman was also frozen in mid-step, her leash pulled tightly against her outstretched right arm. As we approached the white, sand-cement street, we realized the two vehicles were also underway. They looked like enclosed golf carts with bubble canopies. The drivers were both paying close attention to the road ahead. I glanced at my tablet map as I walked. There was an alley between two three-story adobe-like buildings that offered a shortcut. We emerged behind the buildings, where white cliff walls climbed steeply upward. On the right was the separation in the cliff, the narrow slot canyon we needed to transit. We had to turn sideways to enter, side-stepping our way along. Fortunately, the passage was smooth and unmarked. It did not seem to be well explored. The tight fit lasted for more than a mile before the walls gradually began to widen. Overhead, the divide was so steep the top was not clearly visible. It was an odd comfort that any falling rock would not be a threat.

Three miles into the hike, the tiny canyon trail opened up into a wide expanse of lake and waterfall, surrounded by more rugged, sloping rock walls.

"This is the strangest portrait of beauty I have ever seen," commented Patrick.

"Look at the waterfall," said R.J. "It's a snapshot in time. The water droplets glisten and the mist at the bottom doesn't change. It's unearthly."

"The shimmer on the water is the same way," said Patrick. "It's like tiny beads of light."

Wilson came up beside me. "Two kinds of landing craft have been here, Adrian. There are faint imprints in the sand." He pointed to the left. Marks from landing skids were plainly visible. "How can there be marks in the sand? We're still not leaving any footprints."

R.J. overheard him. "Because those imprints were made long enough ago that the sand has had time to catch up." R.J. pulled out a hand scanner and waved it across the area. "Definite engine signatures left behind. There's no doubt about it. Ships from our time constant landed here. There's a trail of footprints, too. But all this stuff is from weeks ago."

Patrick spoke nervously, "So are we too late? Is this a dead end?"

"I'm seeing a weak electronic emission coming from across this reservoir," said R.J. as he studied his hand scanner.

"Let's head that way," I said.

We skirted along the shore of the small lake, its surface so still it looked like ice you could walk on. The rock walls surrounding the lake led upward to a strange white haze, moisture from the falls that lingered with the same pause as everything else.

At the waterfall, there were clouds of moisture in the air, but the water did not cling to us. The spray reached out like transparent waves, making the air cooler in spots, but the falling water, like everything else, remained silent.

"The signal is coming from behind the waterfall," said R.J., and he looked at me wondering what next.

"Then there we should go. Anyone not comfortable with that?"

No one spoke.

I pushed through the curtain of water. Droplets decorated my flight suit, but they did not soak in and did not roll off. In any other place I would have been drenched, but here the moisture was almost like glitter. I found I could brush it off, leaving it suspended in the air around me.

Behind the falls, we found nothing but solid rock. We gathered and stood staring as R.J. worked his scanner.

"I'm definitely showing a chamber behind this rock," he said. "A big one!"

"There must be another way in," said Patrick.

"Can you map the space beyond?" I asked.

Wilson pulled a second scanner off of R.J.'s belt and joined in.

R.J. added, "High ceiling in there. Maybe with a passage beyond. Can't tell for sure. The radiations around this place are a jumbled mess."

"I am seeing something," said Wilson. "This huge slab of rock does not look natural. I mean it's been cut and fit. Oh, wow! It has a core! A composite metal shaft running down the middle, top to bottom. There are metals above and below, too. You know what? You know what this reminds me of? It can't be..." Wilson clipped the scanner to his belt, went up to the huge slab of stone, found just the right place, and with his hand, pushed.

The huge stone slab slowly rotated at its center and pushed open, revealing a ten-foot-wide passageway beyond.

Wilson looked at us with amazement. "You see that? The thing has got to be nine or ten ton. I pushed it open with one hand! Absolute perfect balance! It's just like the Coral Castle in Florida."

As we moved into the shadowy cavern, R.J. looked back at Wilson. "Okay, that's one atta-boy for you, Wilson. Why didn't I get that? I must be slipping."

"Yeah, but one aw-shit wipes out ten atta-boys, so it's no big deal," replied Wilson.

"Still, I salute you, sir. It was a wonderful example of perception and reasoning."

Wilson paused and turned back to R.J. "Why, thank you, brother. That's awfully decent of you."

"Gentlemen, if you're done swooning over each other, may we proceed?"

The passageway was dark. I pulled a chemical light stick from my flight suit leg pocket. The others followed suit. We cracked them on, giving the cave walls an eerie green glow. The entrance narrowed enough that we had to side-step through again, but soon it opened to the expansive cavern R.J. had described. The place was not empty and even in our chem light, it was stunning. It was a scene from an old Earth treasure hunter movie, complete with a grand Buddha-like idol on a throne at the far end, and alcoves filled with bowls of precious stones on either side. A time-frozen stream running through the place, crossed by a stone bridge, led to the magnificence of the central idol. There was a strange damp smell in the air unlike anything I had ever sensed before. There were faint sounds in the air, like the tail end of echoes dying slowly away.

"Place just keeps getting weirder," said Wilson.

"Why wouldn't the slave traders have looted this place, if they were already here?" asked Patrick.

"Easy," replied R.J. "We entered Enrika space legally. There's nothing legal or ethical about those people. They've got a back door into this system somehow. If they screwed with these artifacts, they'd probably be detected. So they don't dare mess with the guardians of this place, but it's a great spot to conduct illegal affairs. Nobody can see you come; nobody can see you go."

"You said you had a radiation signature, R.J. I don't see any electronics."

He raised his scanner. "Behind the idol. Do we dare cross that bridge?"

Wilson joined in. "Yeah, isn't this one of those places that spears pop out of the walls, or big rocks roll over you?"

I scoffed, "I'll go first, Indiana."

"You could probably walk right across that stream," said R.J. "The water won't part beneath your feet for hours."

"I'll take my chance with the stone bridge, thank you."

It looked safe enough. A simple matrix of stone slabs held above the water by other carefully spaced chunks of rock. There was no guardrail. I led with one foot, and went up the small incline a single step at a time, noticing that my chemical light did not reflect off the water. Nothing threatening happened. At the top, I paused and looked back at my companions. They stared in earnest as though certain death lay in wait. It did not make me feel any better about crossing. I shrugged, then hurriedly half-stepped all the way down to the other side and looked back with sarcasm. "Nothing to it, ladies."

207

They stared for a moment more, then fidgeted around like the Marx Brothers and finally scurried across, stopping next to me, still unwilling to proceed any farther.

The idol towered above us on a throne thirty feet high. The throne and image were both intricately carved. A healthy number of jewels enhanced their appearance. Carved into the walls on each side were armored warriors, complete with sword and spear. The floor was equally hand-crafted. We were standing on rectangular cuts of smooth stone; well fit. A spray of white sand partially covered them.

"Still nothing electronic anywhere, R.J."

"It's coming from behind the throne," he replied, and he walked behind the monument and searched. "Hidden doorway back here," he called.

We followed. An arched door cut into solid rock led to an antechamber of sorts. It looked like a large catacomb and had been a busy place at one time. Mummies suspended against both side walls had deteriorated to the point that some were no more than a pile of bone and cloth on the floor. Others still stood, barely. Between each, a display of ancient weaponry filled the hall. There was not an empty space on either wall or ceiling. Carvings covered every inch, some of them bearing particularly deep stonework, most of which was filled with faded stains of color.

Like the others, I surveyed the place, awestruck by the artistry, until something overhead captured my attention. Above each mummy position, there was an elaborate pedestal, and upon the pedestal, a life-size sculpted skull, six on the left side of the room, six on the right. Each skull was finely polished. One resembled marble, another topaz. The six pedestals led to the front of the room where the thirteenth pedestal sat in far greater decor than the others. The shelf was crystal and embellished with jewels. Beneath it was a stone plaque bearing a strange Greek-styled language. Upon this most cherished platform of them all, the skull that should have completed the collection was missing. My thoughts immediately flashed back to Danica's diamond skull, procured from Dorian Blackwell, merchant of human slaves, renowned dealer in this sector of space.

But the exotic beauty of the place was impaired by more than just the missing skull. Someone had been here searching relentlessly for something. They had chipped away sections of wall art, searched and desecrated the dead, and hammered holes into the polished floor. And there was the feeling from it that they had not found what they were looking for.

"There it is," said Wilson, interrupting the spell we were all under. He pointed to a cutout in the right corner of the far wall. There, sitting on a stone platform, was a communication station bearing a single com computer. It was still manned, in a

Shock Diamonds

manner of speaking. A dead body lay in a fetal position beside it, a stain of dried blood around the head. Wilson and I went for a closer look.

The body would have looked human except for the small pig nose and two large front teeth. There was that crumpled, hideous expression of death that made you want to look away. The thinning brown hair was very straight to the shoulders, splayed partly over the face. The skin had begun to mummify. There was a brown leather wrap-around jacket tied at the waist, the same leather used for the trousers. Brown leather boots were still snapped on.

Patrick came up and knelt over the body. "It was a blow to the head, of course. He's been here more than a month."

"How can you tell?" I asked.

"The mummification. It's a pretty universal constant."

"He doesn't look like a resident," said Wilson.

"You are correct. Too much decomposition, too fast," replied R.J.

Wilson stepped next to the Doctor and knelt. He began searching the man's clothing, moving the stiff body as necessary.

"I'm glad Catherine did not come along to see this," said Patrick.

"Doc, she's tougher than anyone here," I said.

"You're right, of course," he replied, with a look of embarrassment.

"There's no kind of wallet or anything, but there's a bunch of personal stuff here," declared Wilson. Without standing, he handed me some folded documents, then continued to search.

The very first item was a 3-D photo of a smiling, pig-nosed woman. She wore a diamond-studded crown across her forehead backed by thin, ivory blond hair. Her dress was equally diamond-studded, cut low across ample breasts that were accented by a lace pattern that may have been tattooed, but more likely natural. The back of the photo had an inscription in a language I did not recognize. The rest of the documents were scrawled with the same language.

"That's all of it, Adrian." Wilson stood and looked at me. "What do we do? Leave him like this, or should we bury the body?"

"I have a feeling the overseers of this place are not aware of this. We were told not to effect any changes here. R.J., those probes that intercepted us, can we send a message using the same basic binary they used?"

"Easy," replied R.J.

209

"I have no problem being a snitch here. We get back, we'll use that code to send out a message explaining what we found and that we believe a crime has been committed, and give these coordinates. We'll do that as we're leaving. I wouldn't want the overseers, whoever they are, thinking we had anything to do with this. In the meantime, let's scan this com console for everything we can get and head back. Maybe this guy's stuff has something helpful. Anyone else have any suggestions?"

There were none. When the scanners chirped complete, we carefully made our way back out to the waterfall and closed the nine-ton door. Back in town, it looked like the vehicles on the street had moved forward a few feet. As we passed the ball game, the ball was now just a few inches from the player's glove. The lady with the dog had changed positions, as had others in our line of sight. There were spots on the ground where we had walked earlier, our footprints just now beginning to form.

As we crossed the playing field, Patrick came up alongside me. He seemed to have something to say and kept looking back at the others. Finally, he could stand it no longer.

"Adrian, we need to talk."

"There's got to be some kind of clue to Emma's whereabouts. I'm sure we'll find something from that com station, or even in that guy's belongings, something that will give us a lead."

"That's not what I'm referring to, Adrian. I really don't know how to go about this. I don't have a leg to stand on. You take me in, help me, and agree to risk your life, and I end up having an… an…, that is, interfering with your relationship. I don't know how that happened. Honest to God. Never thought I'd ever do a thing like that."

"Interfering with my relationship? That's an eloquent way of putting it."

"Okay then, you come back from hell to find out the guy you're helping is screwing your woman!"

It made me chuckle. "Well, that's the way Wilson might put it."

"If I were you I'd just dump me out an airlock or something."

"Things aren't always what they seem, Patrick."

"I don't understand."

I stopped and looked back at the other two. They had fallen slightly behind. Wilson had stopped and kneeled to pick up something from the ground and it looked like R.J. was explaining it to him.

I turned back to Patrick. "Doc, I'm not sure if Catherine was treating me, beating me, or just trying to figure herself out. Did she tell you about the ejection?"

"A little."

"There are things you can only tell your best doctor. That's you, Patrick. It's like this, I try not to think about it, but I've come real close to the edge maybe too many times."

"Don't I know," he replied.

"But no matter how close I've cut it, I always believed I'd get out of it with my skin. To quote a character that has always inspired me, *I never believed in a no-win scenario.* When my Sabre Jet ate that bird, suddenly for the very first time I heard a little voice saying, you're not going to get out of this one, Tarn. A whole bunch of things went through my mind in those two seconds. I had to switch into the die-with-dignity mode if you know what I mean. I could not eject. The Sabre was inverted. It would have meant doing the lawn-dart trick into the ground. So that was it. The great finality. I had no chance. Then at the very last instant, for some reason that aircraft rolled upright just enough to let me pull the handles. Afterward, I had a tremor in my left hand I couldn't control. It was tiny enough to hide, but not from Catherine. I knew it was a ghost of the leftover fear. She knew it too. You don't shake that kind of thing too easy. She tricked me into staying with her for a couple weeks, and scared the hell out me enough times to open a little door inside and let that face of death escape. Cured me of the jitters. Since then, I think she's just been observing the patient to be sure. She's a damn smart woman. A genius, I'd guess. She knows I know. That's why she wasn't worried about taking you on. She knew I'd understand. The Tusani finished the job for her. Living with them was like whitewashing my soul. Now, to me, my life is divided into two parts. Me before the Tusani, and me after the Tusani. Adrian B.T., Adrian A.T. You and I are all clear, Patrick. But let me tell you, you may be in real trouble."

"How do you mean?"

"Is Catherine treating you, or involved with you? Figure that out while we try to find the person who means more than anything to you."

Wilson and R.J. came up alongside. "Adrian, nobody will care if I take just a rock, will they?" asked Wilson.

"I think only if it's a rock that might change the course of history," I replied with a smirk.

"Very funny," he replied, but he looked as though he was not sure.

R.J. took the grapefruit-sized chunk of sandstone from him, held it out at arm's length, waist-high, and let go. The rock hung in midair.

"Is that the damnedest thing!" said Wilson. "I can't get used to it!"

"It will do this exactly the same way on Earth," added R.J.

"Thanks for the demo, guys. We do need a sampling team to collect some simple specimens to take back and drive Earth's physicists mad."

"I can do that," said R.J.

"I think Danica and Catherine deserve a little surface time. You and I need to take a hard look at that com data, R.J."

"Yeah, you're right."

Wilson snatched his rock back from midair. "Well, this baby's mine. You guys get your own."

Back inside Griffin, Danica and Catherine scrambled around in joy at the prospect of seeing a time-shifted world. Wilson volunteered to keep an eye on them. Patrick begged to go along.

R.J. and I sat at the engineering stations, scanning everything we had found on the dead man, and downloading everything from the alien com computer. We sat back waiting, R.J. staring at the photo the man had been carrying.

"Funny how it's the same sentiment, even from species to species, isn't it?"

"You getting philosophical there, Professor?"

"Well, this has got to be a picture of a wife or lover. Something he could look at to remind him he was loved."

"The elusive dream..."

"By the way, while we're waiting, when we were in that hidden chamber, you saw what was going on in there, didn't you?" said R.J.

"Oh, boy."

"No, really, a chamber of skulls? The thirteenth skull missing? Danica's skull. That's where they found it."

"Yeah, I picked up on that."

"That skull was not originally from this system. It does not have the same time signature. That's probably why they were able to get away with taking it."

"Yep."

"But that's not all. The place was trashed by somebody looking for something else. Did you pick up on that, too?"

"Yep. Hard to miss the mess."

"They were searching for the crystals to go with the skull."

Shock Diamonds

"No doubt."

"So the crystals must have been hidden separately, but somehow Blackwell got his hands on them."

"I do believe you've outdone yourself, Sherlock."

"It's about time we tried that thing, don't you think?"

"The skull? You want to test it on yourself without even being sure of what it does?"

"It can't be bad."

"Why?"

"Because old Dorian Blackwell was just dying to try it."

"For all we know, it could fry your brain, amigo."

"Too late..."

"You have a point."

"First chance we get with just you, me, and Danica, let's try it just enough to see if we're right. You can be my bodyguard if things don't go well."

"Agreed. Here's comes the results on the dead man's documents."

We leaned in closer to the engineering station display, as the data scrolled down the screen.

"Bingo," said R.J. "He's from the CD-48 11069 system. I've seen that on a star chart we bartered from the Decrilians."

"The Decrilians? Have I heard about them?"

"Not yet. They're bipeds, but they have heads a little like insects. It's very discomforting to be around them."

"When the hell did that all happen?"

"About a month and a half into your disappearance. They were a big help. I was asking them about slavery. They said anyone wishing to purchase slaves might want to visit there. But that's a long story. If I remember correctly, the CD-48 11069 system is only a couple days away at P9. The locals call a certain planet there XiTau."

"Let us not waste time. Would you set it up and send it on to the flight director? I'll fill Danica in."

"Aye, Captain."

"You people need to stop calling me that."

"It's a childish need for parental authority."

"For Pete's sake."

The sampling party returned a short time later with a variety of Enrika leaves, soil, and rock. Each was carefully sealed in a clear rectangle of monolite, then proudly displayed on the conference table. Danica and Catherine could not stop talking about the still-frame world they had just witnessed. Their photos and videos gave little indication of the surrealism of the place.

E.R. Mason

When the nav computer finally alerted us with the newest flight plan, and a short time later the flight director concurred, we strapped in and rose up from our newly found shadow-box planet. At three hundred miles, we wasted no time in turning the spacecraft over to the flight director for the transition to light. At cruise, I begged off from Danica and went back for a drink of water. R.J. was waiting in ambush for me in the galley.

"There's one thing, Adrian. It's my job to mention it."

"What's that?"

"Both you and Danica have busted through the thirty-hour mark. Neither of you is supposed to act as pilot in command until you put in a full sleep shift."

"You want to stop and hang here in space while we sleep?"

"That's not what I had in mind, no. I can take the command chair."

"How's that?"

"Yeah. All those months that you were gone, flight instructor Danica gave me a crash course. It was the only way we could keep going with a single pilot."

"Wow! How many hours did you log while I was gone?"

"Counting hands-on instruction time, 750 hours as PIC."

"By gosh, I'm proud of you. You thinking about getting licensed when we get back to Earth or something?"

"Not really. Here in space, sitting in the command chair is like 98 percent mental. But to get licensed on Earth, as you know, you've got to fly atmospheric. I'm not so hot about the idea of being that close to the ground, where you must not make a mistake lest the ground rise up and smite thee, you know?"

"Hey, trust me, even when you're flying an ultralight, it's still 90 percent brain, 10 percent moving controls."

"I'll think about it, but I don't know..."

"So you're ordering the two of us to bed then? I knew you'd make captain someday."

"This is actually the second time, Kemosabi, if you recall the Nadir mission."

"I'm still trying to forget that three-hour tour. But okay, by your command I shall commit myself to my sleeper cell and will not come out until all criteria are met. You may take over from Danica and send her to her room as well."

"I knew I'd get the last word someday."

Chapter 22

It was slightly after midnight when an unexpected tapping woke me in my sleeper cell. Someone faintly knocking on my door. I opened it halfway to find Danica in rocket ship pajamas, standing there staring at me.

"Can I sleep with you?"

"What!?"

"Just sleep. No carnal knowledge, Dad."

"I'm way not old enough to be your dad."

"I had a bad dream and I just got lonely all of a sudden. It almost never happens."

"Well, okay. Just remember, I'm way not old enough to be your dad."

She looked left and right to be sure no one was watching, then climbed over me and nestled herself in alongside.

"Thanks. I won't be a bother. I don't thrash around or anything."

"What got to you?"

"I started thinking how life on Earth is passing me by while I spend all my time in space. It's where I want to be, but it's like there's another Danica who could be living on Earth doing all those things normal people do. Maybe I'm missing out."

"Oh, you mean like 2.5 kids, a white picket fence, a two-car garage, kitchen with island, TV in every room?"

"Keep going. I'm feeling better already."

I braced one hand behind my head. "Maybe what you need is a knockdown drag out love affair. That cured me."

"Really? You?"

"Yeah, it was a long time ago. The girl had me thinking it was all locked up, a done deal. One day she sort of won the lottery. Next day she was with mister tall and handsome. I was history. That's when I realized there's no such thing as the perfect marriage with two-point-five children, white picket fence, TV in every room, two floaters in the garage."

Danica muted her laugh, "Grandchildren on your knee, Vera, Chuck, and Dave?"

"Where have I heard that?"

"One of R.J.'s old music albums."

"So all fantasy lifestyles now ruined for you?"

"Lucky I had you to visit. I've always looked up to you like a father, you know."

"Hey, I keep telling you, I'm way not old enough to be your father."

"I know. I know. It's just that... What the hell is that?"

"I'm way not old enough to be your father."

"Is that all you? My god!"

"Hey!"

"You have nothing on under there? Oh my...! You don't!"

"Please, you're killing me."

Suddenly Danica Donoro became someone else. She pushed on top of me and stared down with a look I had never seen. "We both need therapy," she said in a hoarse whisper.

"But you said no...."

All chivalry immediately lost. The wrestling began. The rational human mind put aside. The reward-driven exchange instantly in complete control. Occasional suppressed sounds of passion driving the silent agreement further with each movement.

To my surprise, it did not end with a single merging. It began again immediately thereafter. A determination to reap all that was available from the impropriety. The awkwardness that might be waiting afterward, of no consequence at all. We slept finally, pasted together as one.

When I awoke the next morning, she had managed to slip away without waking me. I had not slept that well in a very long time. Then came a flush of embarrassment about the whole thing. Then the thought that Catherine and Patrick had been in the cell opposite us probably doing the same thing. Then came the absurd thought that maybe thrusters had been firing to stop the ship from rocking.

When I finally had the nerve to open my cell door, the ship was brightly lit and busy. I could hear someone working out in the gym, and voices coming from the galley. I kicked my way into flight coveralls and dared another look out. The coast was as clear as it would ever be. Slipping out, I spied Catherine and Patrick balancing cups and taking seats at the conference table. In a most nonchalant manner, I wandered out to the galley and fussed over a coffee of my own. The two at the table noticed and became slightly uncomfortable.

"Eight hours! That's a record for you, Adrian," said Patrick.

"Slept like a baby too. Did I miss anything?"

"Mr. Smith has the helm, Captain. He seems to be doing a sterling job," said Catherine coyly.

"I've got to get people to stop calling me that. You powder monkeys swab the deck when you're done, and make fast the mainsail. I'd better go check on the helmsman."

Catherine giggled. Patrick wondered if I was serious about the swabbing.

In the cramped flight deck, R.J. was slumped back in the right seat with one arm over the backrest. I pulled into the command chair, toasted him with my coffee, and glanced through a systems check.

"Green across the board, Captain," he said.

"Why is everyone suddenly calling me that? It's some kind of underground joke or something, right?"

"Well, at least you haven't been asked to marry any couples, but I wouldn't count on that never happening."

"Very funny. Has Danica been up yet?"

"Nope. It's a record for both of you. I've never seen her sleep for more than five. I guess I was right. You were both way overdue."

"So nothing up here but stars, then?"

"Actually a couple unexpected things did happen, but nothing to do with ship systems."

"Well?"

"Those samples we took from Enrika. As we passed from Enrika's heliosphere space into interstellar medium, Wilson watched them fade and disappear right in their monolite encasements. We have nothing at all from there except data."

"Wow! Spooky."

"The stuff apparently can't exist outside the radiance of that blue star."

"Although we're pretty sure that skull was taken from there."

"Yeah, it confirms the skull is not Enrika matter. And speaking of the skull...."

"Yeah?"

"I ran more searches while I sat up here. I finally found something from its origin, at least I think I did."

"Well, I can't wait to hear that."

"It's some records from that ancient culture that supposedly no longer exists. It refers to the Elohim again, supposedly the builders of the universe. The skull is called the Godhead. The crystals are referred to as keys. There is an ancient script that alludes to the use of the skull. It's only been partially translated."

R.J. pulled a tablet out from alongside his seat and handed it over.

E.R. Mason

> *Age and letter*
> *Seed lest _ _ _ _*
> *_ _ _ _ of sun*
> *Harvests begun*
> *man to man*
> *astride command*
> *woman to woman*
> *neither be sovereign*
> *Speak name and harbour*
> *be one the other*

"Well, that's about as informative as a rock carving," I said.

"I have some ideas."

"Like what?"

"As I mentioned before, we need to set up and try the thing."

"Like I've been saying, you don't know what it does, or even if it does anything at all. It could even cause brain damage or something."

"Nope."

"How can you be so sure?"

"Once again, because Danica's old boss there, Blackwell, was just dying to try it, and he knows more than we do. He's also one of those people who cares only about himself. He wouldn't dare chance hurting himself."

"Still..."

"We test it one little step at a time. If anything seems wrong, you're there to break the link."

"Let's think about it some more."

"Okay."

Danica suddenly appeared between us. I assumed my poker face. She looked down at R.J. and said, "I relieve you, sir."

R.J. looked up with a smirk. "I am relieved." He pushed up, squeezed by, and watched as she lowered into the seat.

"Don't forget the hand-off checklist, guys," he said mockingly.

"I do believe he's getting bossy," said Danica.

"It's his way," I replied.

"Off to the blue stuff and sleep," said R.J., and he disappeared aft.

There were a few uneasy moments. Danica finally said, "Wow. I slept like a log. I was asleep before my head hit the pillow. Don't remember a thing. How about you?"

Shock Diamonds

I paused and took the hint. "Same thing. Out like a light all night."

"I see the number four O2 is fluctuating, but it just switched over. Stellar Drives are right on the money, as usual."

"Yep."

"So we need to run through the hand-off checklist, then?"

"Already did it while I was talking to R.J. He didn't pick up on it."

"In that case, you are welcome to return to the habitat if you want to make me some eggs. I'm famished."

"Coffee or tea?"

"Tea and English muffins, please."

"A pleasure to serve you, ma'am."

"Make sure it's nice and hot or you'll blow your tip."

"So back to our regular shifts, then. I take it you want this first one. We're only two days from XiTau, so we should be able to make out its star tomorrow sometime."

"That always amazes me about this ship. You tell it where you want to go, ask it to please avoid any solid objects in the path, then sure enough, when you get near, there's the beautiful star you asked for dead center ahead in the view screen. It still knocks me out."

I nodded and smiled. "Me, too."

Without actually saying so, we had agreed to forget what had happened the night before. It was apparent she had sorted it all out, along with the soul-searching that had brought her into my sleeper cell in the first place. I doubted such an encounter would ever happen again, nor would it ever be spoken of, unless I broke the unwritten rule of indiscretions betrayed. Respecting her wish for solitude, I pushed out of the command chair and tucked in a loose seat belt. "I shall return with your service shortly."

"Okay. Thanks."

In the habitat area, Catherine and Patrick were glued to the port windows, a bit surprising since they had spent so much time in space already. I refilled my coffee and joined them, thinking I might defuse any social tension, but the view out those port windows was in such contrast to the forward screens it captured my attention completely.

NGC 6188 was far more a work of art than the best Earth telescopes had suggested. We were so deeply embedded in the cluster that even at light speeds we were getting phase-shift and a sense of velocity out the side windows. The closest of the stars passed by looking like streaks of ball lightning, changing color in a warped Doppler color stream. Behind those, the

219

universe was a dense tapestry of stars, clusters, and colorful clouds of astral phenomena, so much of it unrecognizable that it sparked a small amount of fear in me at how little we knew about where we were.

A little bit after midnight, R.J. emerged from his sleeper cell and joined me at the conference table where I was studying anything I could find about XiTau. He had his strange health concoction in a cup and was stirring it placidly, sprinkling in flakes of something as he went. "I'm ready, and the time is right," he said, and he sipped carefully from the steaming cup. There was a photo of Elvis Presley etched on it.

"You know what scares me about this place?" he said.

"A million things?" I responded.

"Exactly. There is so much stuff outside these windows; you could never learn it all, never study it all, not even a damn tiny bit of it."

"It must have felt that way to Lewis and Clark, don't you think?"

"Touché. Anyway, I'm ready."

"For which?"

"To quote one of my favorite trek episodes, 'to put upon my head the teacher.'"

"Lost me."

"There was an episode called Spock's brain. These uneducated women would put this electronic crown on their head and it would download knowledge to them. They'd become geniuses until it wore off."

"You still want to mess with the skull, to hell with the danger."

"It's time."

"You learned something more about it?"

"Not really. I've done some more com searching but so much of that stuff is like space graffiti. People out here ramble on to each other because they're so bored they don't have anything else to do. I need to give that thing a quick try to get more information on it, a foothold maybe."

"You think it's going to bestow knowledge upon you?"

"It's possible, but I'm more expecting some kind of communication link like I've been saying."

"Why do we need to do this at all? We could just bury the thing somewhere. As you've pointed out, it's so valuable it's dangerous to anyone who possesses it."

"Ignorance can hurt you."

"So can brain experiments."

"Dorian Blackwell was dying to try it."

"When and where would we do this?"

"Here and now. Catherine and Patrick are asleep. It's just you, Danica, and me."

"Maybe it wouldn't hurt to have a doctor on hand."

"They're just a sleeper cell away."

"Tell you what, let's get Danica's opinion, then decide."

"Fair enough."

We went forward with our cups and sat among the flight deck Christmas tree lights and star-filled forward view screens and took turns explaining the arcane story of the crystal skull to Danica. She did not seem surprised by any of it and mocked us with looks of skepticism each time R.J. suggested there could be metaphysical properties.

"It's late at night Earth time and you boys are trying to scare me with ghost stories. Sorry, I'm not that gullible. It looked dumb while Blackwell was trying to do it. The two of you will look just as silly."

"Then you have no objection?" asked R.J.

"No, and afterward we can break out the Ouija board and have cocoa."

R.J. ignored the sarcasm and looked at me. "I'll go get the crystal set. You get the skull."

"If you boys scare yourselves, just call and Mommy will come and protect you," joked Danica.

"You might want to set a few monitors up here to watch," I replied.

"I wouldn't miss it for the world."

With Danica setting up to watch from her seat, I pulled back the command chair and removed the fake pressure screws from the compartment below. Lifting the skull out of its hiding place seemed to cast an eerie ambiance about the flight deck. As I removed the wrappings, the strange glow from it reflected off the instruments. The effect jumped around as the skull was moved. Some of Danica's cynicism turned to curiosity. I shrugged at her and made my way back to the conference table. R.J. arrived a moment later, carrying the crystal set pedestal as though it were dangerous.

There was no question that when he set the crystals down on the table, the glow from both artifacts increased. It was possible I was hearing a supersonic tone in my ears, though more likely imagination.

"I'm seeing a definite interactive relationship here, don't you agree?" said R.J.

"I guess. How do you plan to go about this?"

"How about I insert the clear crystal half in the skull forehead, then we wait a few minutes, and if nothing bad happens I'll try the other crystal on my forehead for just a moment."

"Okay, but I feel like one of the Marx brothers for some reason."

"Here goes." R.J. removed the walnut crystal pair from the mount and separated them. He stood and bent over the table, and with the greatest of care positioned the clear half-crystal in front of the indentation in the skull. But before he could place it, the crystal jumped from his grasp and locked into the forehead of the skull. Instantly, different intensities of white light began to flow within the skull. R.J. straightened up, his eyebrows raised in wonder.

"Wow! Didn't expect that!" he said.

"Oh, brother."

"No, no. Let's just wait a minute and see."

We watched in silence the swirling glow within the artifact. R.J. continued to hold the other half of the crystal in his left hand. It was now glowing with equal agitation. R.J. had an expression that begged, *"Do I really want to try this?"* He looked over at me and bit his lower lip. "Do I really want to try this?" he asked.

"I do not think so."

"No. We've got to give it a shot. Just for a second. It's now or end up wondering forever."

"That could be okay."

"No. We need to know."

R.J. slowly sat, facing the skull at the table's center. I took a seat alongside. Ever so cautiously, he raised the companion crystal, as though worried it might jump from his hand like the other had. He lifted it to eye level and paused. "You be ready to pull this thing off, right?"

"Count on it."

Ever so gradually, he moved the crystal to his forehead and pressed it in place. For a moment there was nothing, but as I watched, a shadow came over his face, the kind you see on a late night Boris Karloff movie. His face became stolid and distant. His eyes dilated into wide dark lenses. He gradually stiffened in his seat.

"Aaahhhhh!" he yelled. He grabbed frantically at the crystal and scooped it away, slapping it to the table top. He sat back, wide-eyed, and shook his head, then began slapping his face as though trying to wake himself. I lurched from my seat and grabbed his shoulders and held on. He began to breathe in long, deep gasps, then looked around as though trying to reassure himself that he was alright.

"Oh my god!" he said with a blank look of astonishment. "Oh my god, oh my god!"

I eased up on his shoulders and jockeyed back into my seat without taking my eyes off him. "What? What the hell happened?"

He looked at me but continued to try to regain his focus. "Holy crap!"

"You're killing me here, R.J. What happened?"

He took a deep breath, sat back, and rubbed his face. Slowly, he lowered his hands into his lap. "How the hell do I describe that?" he said. "It was like my head went up through a bubble to a whole different world. It was like looking around in another dimension or something. It scared the crap out of me because I was afraid I couldn't get back."

"You were in a bubble of some kind?"

He thought for a moment. "You know what? It was like we are in a bubble and I was able to stick my head outside it. It felt like I had access to every living thing in the universe."

"You got to be kidding."

"Man, oh man."

"Well, that's that for that."

"No, no. I just need time to sort it out and collect myself. It did not hurt and it wasn't unpleasant. It just scared me. I understood something while it was happening, but I need to digest it. Let me back away from this for a while and then try it again after I work it out. I don't feel injured in any way. It was not harmful, just unbelievably intense."

"I don't know, man. You're scaring me. I'll tell you that."

"This thing is no fraud. It's real. We've proven that, at least. They told you Blackwell had visions of world domination, right? This thing was going to give him that. Who we going to trust this thing to? Give me a little time for reflection. You can watch me and see if I'm going crazy in the meantime."

"How will I tell?"

"Tomorrow night, same time, same channel. I'll keep it hidden in my sleeper cell until then. Trust me."

"Don't even think about screwing with it unless I'm with you, okay?"

"Are you kidding? I wouldn't dream of it."

The next morning brought even more stellar phenomena outside the portals. I wanted to put in some workout time in the gym, but the reclusive Catherine and Patrick were spending most of their time in the lab, and the workout equipment was uncomfortably close by. I bided my time, finishing up studying the CD-48 11069 system, yet another place of alien mystery and intrigue. And the closer we came to XiTau, the more infor-

mation there was to be gleaned from the myriad of transmissions that originated there.
    It seemed to be a planet designed to support the privileged, even though they only accounted for about 10 percent of the population. All others seemed only to contribute to the needs of the few. The com interceptions were wrought with petitions for service positions that promised an opportunity to eventually become one of the glorious elite. I kept trying to fit a philosophy of ethical fairness to the social image of XiTau but kept coming up short.
    Oddly compatible with the doctrine of the privileged was the diverse society that enjoyed it. There were no restrictions on which species were allowed to obtain the large estates offered to aristocrats. The wide variety of languages intercepted in XiTau's communications pieced together to show that the Sumani lizard people were just as influential as Tagons and Kantarians. In fact, there were no majority groups of aristocratic species, at all. That level of wealth was held by so many different bloodlines; it was like a United Nations of the rich.
    So the bill being sold by all the official language coming from XiTau was that it was a planet comprised entirely of satisfied middle class, topped by gifted social architects who maintained the eminently successful economic structure. But if you looked closely at the less official communiqués, there seemed to be a very macabre undercurrent to it all. The more I read between the lines, the more it left me with a sick feeling in my stomach.
    Late that evening, the XiTau star came into view in the front view screens. Wilson came forward to the flight deck where Danica and I were contemplating what lay ahead, and asked, "You need anything before I dial out, Adrian?"
    "Just one thing. It affects all three of you. I won't be screwing up the way I did last time. We need to reprogram our transponders and our com stations. We do not want to identify ourselves as the Griffin or as an Earth-based ship. Everything we emit needs to indicate we are from somewhere else. We'll become the Starship Exxeter for the time being. We're registered on Sirenia."
    R.J. suddenly appeared beside Wilson. "Blue people? You're kidding. Are you going to disguise yourself as a bald-headed blue person?"
    "Probably, and Danica better hope I don't decide I need a female companion."
    Danica frowned.
    "The story will be that I'm an extravagantly rich bastard and am visiting XiTau because I'm interested in purchasing an estate there."

"Do we need to set up a phony financial assets path somewhere?" asked Wilson.

"No. We do not keep our money in any institution. It has not always been acquired legally."

"When do you need this by?"

"Tomorrow morning. We haven't been scanned by anything since leaving Enrika, but tomorrow we'll be close enough to XiTau that we need to be ready."

"So you got some big plan for XiTau, then?" asked R.J.

"Pieces of one. Still working on it. We'll drop into high orbit and hang there a while collecting more data. If and when they contact us, I will be a presumptuous, self-indulgent individual on a never-ending party cruise who is too aloof to speak directly with them."

"My kind of role," joked Wilson.

"We'll need real hi-res surface imaging, maybe some Denard IRIA infrared interior views if we think we can get away with it."

"I'll start setting that up in the morning, too," said Wilson.

"That's it for now. Expect more later."

"Sayonara, you guys." Wilson backed out and disappeared aft.

R.J. leaned against Danica's seat and folded his arms. She looked up and gave him a sarcastic stare.

"You ready?" he asked me.

"Really? You're not going to back out?"

"Did some more research, thought it all over, can't wait."

"There's probably more risk that he'll be made sane than anything else," said Danica. "I mean, he can't get any crazier."

"So, what have you figured out from all of it?" I asked.

"I believe I will be able to communicate with anyone anywhere once I get the hang of it."

"You mean telepathically?"

"Exactly."

"Oh, brother. It's the great Houdini show in space again," said Danica.

"How do you go about that, exactly?" I asked.

R.J. cast a sideward warning glance at Danica and said, "Well, at the risk of inviting yet more derogatory remarks from you-know-who, I've been studying those poem fragments for a while. They reminded me of a famous psychic named Cayce who could go into a trance and tele-physically find people anywhere, examine their physical bodies, and prescribe cures for them. All he needed to know was their name and location to do it. That ancient poem implies something like that. It says, 'Speak name and harbor,' which to me would suggest a name and location."

"Kinda reaching a bit, aren't you?" I said sympathetically.

"Cuckoo," scoffed Danica, and she drew circles alongside her head.

"I was in there. I felt it. You don't know," argued R.J.

"So you're going to try to contact someone? Who will you choose?"

"I hadn't thought about it, but now that you mention it, how about Ms. Donoro, my greatest skeptic?"

Danica let out a coughing laugh. "Oh, that's perfect. Go right ahead. I'll be here."

R.J. appeared unruffled. "I'll set up." He turned and headed back.

"You have the spacecraft," I said and pushed up.

"I have the spacecraft," answered Danica. "Standing by for incoming communications," she added, and she laughed.

R.J. came forward with the skull wrapped in a terry cloth sack with a string. He opened it with the greatest of care and placed it in front of his seat at the table. He drew the crystal pedestal from inside the front of his flight suit and set it down with equal respect. Once seated, he rubbed his hands together and looked at me with excitement. I sat slowly with new misgivings.

"Are we sure the others are asleep?" he asked.

"You know Wilson. I can't speak for the other two."

Danica was watching us on monitors and listening over the intercom. She clicked on and said, "Really, is there anything I'm supposed to do up here? Splash holy water? Hang up some garlic?"

"You could listen within yourself," replied R.J. sarcastically.

"Listening..." she said with equal disdain. "Nothing yet." We heard her laugh before the com squelched off.

R.J. scoffed and shook his head. He separated the crystals and held the clear one out to the skull. As before, it jumped from his fingertips and snapped into place on the forehead. After a deep breath and a moment of consideration, he lifted the companion crystal to his forehead, gave a short wince, and fastened it in place. Immediately the shadow fell over him as before. His eyes blurred and closed. His head tipped back slightly. There was a sudden jerking of his body.

He spoke in a very low tone, sounding like a man on a tightrope. "My God, my head's outside the bubble again. It's like a world a trillion times larger than ours. There's a faint golden light surrounded by darkness. I see galaxies a zillion miles away in every direction."

He paused. I began to worry. Before I could say anything, he began a chant in that same low, slow voice. "Danica Donoro, barycenter Ara, 423/112/51 P9, Danica Donoro, barycenter Ara, 423-112-51 at P9, Danica Donoro, barycenter Ara, 423-112-51, P9, Danica Don….."

To my dismay, he suddenly jerked upright and stopped chanting. He sat suspended, in captured silence, not moving, not speaking. It was even difficult to tell if he was breathing. This time my concern overcame my patience. I began to stand. After a minute more of nothing, I carefully reached out, intending to snatch the crystal from his forehead.

Danica's voice interrupted. "Adrian, you need to get up here right now!"

"Are you crazy, can't you see what's going on back here?"

"He's alright. Just get up here right now!"

"How do you know he's alright?"

"Trust me. Get up here now!"

Reluctantly, I backed away, refusing to take my eyes off of R.J.'s frozen form. Through the airlock, I was forced to lose sight of him. I hurried forward to the flight deck and found Danica still in the right seat. All systems looked normal.

"Why the hell did you call me up here?"

Danica turned her head in a manner so slow and spooky it rivaled The Exorcist. Her eyes blinked several times in rapid succession. She looked at me, eyes dilated, and said, "Adrian, it's me."

"What?"

"It's me, R.J. I'm here up front."

"No damn way!"

"Hurry. We need to confirm this. Give me a keyword to take back. Anything."

"How about The Exorcist?"

"Go aft now. I'm withdrawing and removing the crystal from my forehead."

I raced back to the habitat module as fast as humanly possible. I arrived to see R.J. lowering the crystal from his forehead. He placed it carefully into its half of the pedestal and sat pale-faced and silent.

I slowly took my seat without taking my eyes off him. "Are you…alright?"

He wiped his face with both hands, turned and looked at me, and said, "The Exorcist."

"What?"

"The Exorcist. It's the key phrase you gave me up on the flight deck."

"No shit!"

"Is Danica alright?"

I straightened up, jumped from my seat, and flew back to the flight deck. Danica was sitting in her seat, adjusting one of the flight displays. She looked over at me cheerfully. "Nope. Sorry to disappoint you two. No psychic contact at all. Is the test over? Are you silly men satisfied?"

"You don't remember I was just up here?"

"Yeah, you were, before we began this idiotic ghost story thing."

"No, I meant just a couple minutes ago. I was up here."

"Were not."

"The Exorcist, that doesn't mean anything to you?"

"It was a very scary movie. A lot scarier than you guys, at least most of the time... Why? Should it mean something?"

"I guess not. Hold that thought. I'll be back."

"Yeah, you will," she called after me. "My shift ends in a little bit, you know."

I returned to R.J. and took my seat staring at him in disbelief. "She's okay. Now...what just happened?"

Chapter 23

"I'm telling you, I took control of Danica's body."

"Come on! This can't be happening."

"Oh, it's happening alright."

"You said you were going to communicate with her telepathically."

"I was wrong. It's way more than that."

"If you took control of her body, where was she?"

"Asleep...I think."

"Asleep where?"

"In there with me... I think."

"You mean you could move her body like remote control?"

"Nope. I was in there. I could feel everything she would normally feel."

"You felt what it was like to be a woman?"

"It was quite a new experience, I'll tell you."

"You're sure about this?"

"I could have taken control of this ship and flown it into a sun if I had wanted to."

"I'm having just a bit of trouble buying into this. There must be some other explanation."

"I turned her head and looked right at you. I told you to give me a keyword. You chose 'The Exorcist.'"

"Damn!"

"Do you realize how dangerous this thing is?"

"I have an idea."

"What did Danica say?"

"She doesn't know anything happened at all."

"Oh, my God!"

"What have we gotten into here?"

"Dorian Blackwell maybe really could have ruled the world with this thing. Tap into any president, dictator, or military leader any time you need to. Make them do whatever you want. They won't remember a thing. How convenient is that?"

Danica's voice cut in over the intercom. "I'm listening in, you guys, but I'm not understanding what you're saying." Her voice had a touch of fear in it.

"I guess we'd better go forward and try to explain," I said.

"Okay," replied R.J. "You first."

It was not an easy task. Records were possibly set for the greatest number of facial expressions in the shortest amount of time. She was adamant in her dubiety. That eventually gave way to indignation at the suggestion her private domain had been violated. From there, anger kept popping up in between layers of denial. She knew we would not lie to her, and the evidence was irrefutable. The argument gradually diminished down to long periods of silence, interrupted by occasional, aborted expressions of contradictory reasoning.

As the debate gradually settled down to surrender, the three of us huddled on the flight deck, finally willing to discuss our options, "just in case," as Danica insisted on putting it, what we were claiming was true.

"Well, let's just take a time-out and give ourselves a chance to consider all of this before total insanity sets in," I suggested.

"The crystal set should still be kept separated from the skull," suggested R.J.

"For security, you mean, of course," I said.

"The least we can do," he replied. "If somehow someone got their hands on the skull, we would not want them to have the crystal set."

"Better find a more secure hiding place in the lab," I said.

"I have one in mind."

"Only the three of us know about this. Let's keep it that way," I added. "Wilson knows about the skull, but not any of this. We should keep it that way, for now."

R.J. nodded his head vigorously. "Absolutely. The thing is dangerous enough, even to anyone who just knows about it."

Danica sat speechless, a look of bewilderment still on her face. I suspected she was finally getting past the feeling of violation and beginning to wonder about the greater implications.

When the skull had been carefully tucked into its bogus pressurized compartment, and the crystals hid securely away in the science lab, I returned forward and slipped into the left seat. CD-48 11069 was no longer a twinkling speck in the blackness. It had become dime-sized, dominating all other stars. The larger of its ecliptic family members were now diamonds in the space around it. The scene looked like any typical solar system, but I was already certain that what we would find there would be anything but typical. Danica climbed from her seat and put a hand on my shoulder as she headed back to her sleeping compartment. Neither she nor I spoke, all necessary sentiments understood. I spent the quiet time of my shift learning and practicing enough Sirenian language that I could get by impersonating one with help from the translators in my ears.

Our arrival at XiTau high orbit was mercifully unheralded. There were only two or three orbital corridors containing artificial satellites. There were enough to give complete global coverage but too few to support the planet's population. Apparently, satellite support was only available to the aristocracy. Wilson used engineering station B exclusively to study the planetary defenses. R.J. used station A to evaluate everything else. We were careful not to scan sensitive areas. No police vehicles intercepted us. No warning transmissions were received.

At shift change, the six of us huddled around the flight deck and engineering section for an informal discussion of what we were finding.

"No orbital defense at all that I can see," said Wilson. "They have ground-based laser and pulse cannon at various places on the surface that can take out any spacecraft or armament headed their way. They have a few spacecraft down there that look like police–style cruisers. I guess they're only used as needed. Their surface-based police installations are substantial, though. Small armies located strategically around the planet. They seem to be set up more to chase down violators on the surface than to wage war in space."

"You notice any weaknesses there?" I asked.

"One big one. The system itself. As long as no alarm bells are set off, it seems like you could go anywhere and do almost anything."

"But not on the major estates," countered R.J.

Wilson agreed. "Yeah, the whole place is a network of large estates serviced by many servant-class individuals. Those estates are usually sectioned off by high walls, with heavy intrusion detection. You do not enter or leave them unless you are allowed to."

"You have a breakdown of the perimeter intrusion systems they use?"

Wilson answered, "Can't get that without a detailed scan of one of the estates. You said not to do that. I did find an industrial complex which was manufacturing security stuff, so I have some information on the types of devices they are using, but not an actual estate layout."

"How about an unoccupied estate? Could we find one of those and do a detailed scan?"

E.R. Mason

"Thought of that," replied Wilson. "I'm working on it."

R.J. summarized. "The place is beginning to look like what we expected, Adrian. The army of servants who maintain the estates do not seem to be free individuals. We haven't done interior scanning, as Wilson said, but I have a feeling most of the servants live in barracks-styled quarters. The only ones that come and go outside the estate walls seem to be the ones who service the estate. The others never leave. It gives me the creeps, I'll tell you. I would not want to break the law down there, or show up illegally."

"Or be kidnapped and taken there?" I suggested.

Everyone looked solemnly at each other.

"They know we're up here," said Wilson. "We've been pulse-scanned several times. They're probably trying to verify our registry. But there's been no attempt to contact us. What you gonna do about that?"

"It takes a long time to make inquiries to Sirenia from here. Even if they can't verify us, I have a feeling many ships that visit here are illegal. That shouldn't bother them at all. They may be hoping we have a fresh supply of slave labor to bargain with," I replied.

"Aren't you afraid of the Griffin being recognized if you put down here, Adrian?" asked Patrick.

"The Griffin made no trips to deep space before she came into my possession, Doc. The scum at the Tolkien Minor moon recognized her because she had been built for illegal trafficking and some of them worked for Danica's dear boss, Dorian Blackwell. But out here, there's no chance she's ever been seen. We'd have to run into someone who knew her. That's a chance we'll have to take."

"So you're going down there?" asked Catherine.

"I shall shop for an exotic estate and will need a great deal of servitude to support it. I possess a great deal of wealth. I might even be interested in contributing to the XiTau cause, to enhance my standing in the community."

"I want to accompany you," said Patrick. "This is about my daughter."

"You are already on the list, but you may not like it all that much."

"You just name it. I'm ready."

"There is a long-shot chance your daughter is down there somewhere. If we were to run across her in a one-in-a-million coincidence, she'd likely start screaming bloody murder to get your attention. Then we'd all be really screwed, wouldn't we? You will need to be unrecognizable. You will be my chief accountant. In fact, all of you are my bought and paid-for servants. You will all need to be something other than human, except for my Earth slave Catherine."

Catherine interrupted. "I should have known."

"We can't give them any idea we're from Earth. Catherine will be the only human slave. My executive consort. She's the only one of us that speaks English. She'll do most of my talking for me because interacting with others is below me. Catherine will need something that looks like restraint bracelets. Everyone else here will need to be convincingly alien, and I'll need you doctor types to make me blue. Do I need to paint myself or is there another way?"

Patrick shook his head. "No, no. That's easy. The Sirenian sweat glands turn outsiders who get too close blue anyway. I can replicate that in the lab. You'll be a genuine Sirenian blue for about forty-eight hours."

I glanced at R.J. He returned a don't-you-dare look. "Danica will need to stay on the flight deck. The rest of you will also need to accompany me off the ship to enhance my authority."

"So I'm to be your slave? That'll be a switch," said Catherine.

Wilson blurted out laughter but stopped abruptly when he noticed no one else was laughing.

"You'll need a temporary tattoo of ownership somewhere on your face, too, Catherine," I added.

"What? A big phallic symbol on my cheek or something?" she replied disparagingly.

Wilson began another short burst but again thought better of it.

"Catherine and Patrick will be my main entourage. Financial questions will be referred to Patrick. You'll need to learn a few lines of whatever species we choose for you, Patrick." I looked directly at the two of them. "Can you both do it? Either of you care to bow out? Nobody's saying it will be safe."

"So, what exactly is the objective?" asked Patrick.

"To weasel as much information out of them as possible without making them suspicious. For example, I'm very fussy about my slave servants. I prefer Earth women when they can be obtained. They're expensive, but I can afford them. I would like my estate to reflect wealth as much as possible. Can I personally screen my Earth women slaves before purchasing them? How is that done? Can I begin reviewing the profiles of human females currently available?"

"It's still like looking for a needle in a haystack," said Patrick.

"Maybe not so much. We know approximately when Emma was taken. We have a time frame. We know her age. The stuff we found in that cave on Enrika suggests this place is one

233

of the primary distribution points for human slaves. Somewhere down there are records of all that. Even if she's not here, if we can get into the right records library, there's a good chance we can get a facial recognition match and find out where she is. We don't want to set off any bells by scanning confidential libraries, but there's nothing to stop us from tapping into satellite transmissions being made to the surface. The biggest data centers will be the busiest. We'll hang up here for a while longer and see if we can get any more leads, then try to set up an appointment to talk about property. If that works, we'll make a gauche landing in the most public area we can find. Once again, anybody want to opt out?"

They looked at each other with misgiving. No one spoke until Wilson. "You sure you want to leave me behind on this one, Adrian?"

"You're the Cavalry, Wilson. If it all goes to hell our best chance is to have you locked and loaded."

"What's to stop them from just commandeering this vessel and imprisoning us when we land?"

"Greed, Wilson. The belief that they stand to gain much more by dealing with us, and I'm sure they're already aware of the Griffin's weapons capability. Even if they tried to take us and won, they'd lose a lot. We'll have Danica lift off and resume orbit as soon as she drops us, though. Just for safety's sake."

The group looked at each other with deepening concern, but no one objected. We disbanded to our appropriate tasks. The doctors went to the lab to concoct a bluing for me and to tattoo Catherine into slavery. R.J. and Wilson hit their engineering stations to search for the control centers on XiTau. Danica remained up front, monitoring status, shields energized to automatic, weapons always available.

After intense soul searching, I decided shaving oneself bald would be best done alone. With my tablet of Sirenian phraseology in hand, I retreated to a shower and began the discomforting process. The showers give you adjustable mirrors all around. The vision of the bare back of your head makes you feel like you're looking at someone else. The laser razor did a fine job of removing any last traces of hair. I looked down at my pubic area, argued with myself, and finally decided that the dead Sumanian lizard people on that slave ship would be the last to see me naked against my will.

Back in ship's stores, the boxes of spare apparel allowed me an adequately garish suit of rainbow-colored Nehru clothing, intended for a woman, but just extravagant enough for a self-absorbed Sirenian lord. Dressed in my new-found Halloween garb, I went to the med lab for my bluing.

Catherine took me by surprise. She turned when I entered to reveal a tattoo of the Sirenian sun with a crest inside its corona emblazoned on her right cheek. She appraised my bald head and outlandish outfit put one hand over her mouth and blurted out a muffled laugh.

Patrick turned, raised an eyebrow, and gave a forced half-smile.

"It's a pill," he said, and he held out a small tablet in his left hand. "Six to eight hours to take effect, probably forty-eight to wear off, though you'll have a blue tint for a while after that."

"Nice tattoo job," I replied.

Catherine said, "It's the Sirenian sun with your family crest in the center. We pulled it off a data page we found. If they research it, it will hold up. The family is too large to trace all the way through. Your name is Lord Descarius Mandarin."

"By the way, your pale gray eyes happened to be perfect for the larger-sized Sirenian male," added Patrick.

I reached out and accepted the little blue tablet from him and looked down at it with trepidation.

"Best taken with food and drink," said Patrick.

"Bourbon and pretzels?"

"Hardly," replied Catherine.

I turned and left the lab, staring down at the tablet. In the galley, I drew a large glass of water, said a short prayer, swallowed the thing and shuddered, then decided to change back into a flight suit.

Forward, at their engineering stations, R.J. and Wilson were painting each other's face and neck with a lacework of fractal-like patterns. They stopped to gawk at my bald head but resisted any attempts at humor.

"Nice 'toos. What's the latest?"

"It's good," replied Wilson. "We've isolated four government centers, a dozen police installations, and three major communications centers. We have the com scanners set up on auto to look for several hundred keywords. This orbit happens to be perfect for global coverage. We also have four links to what you would call real estate centers. The representatives are referred to as Chancellors of Domestic Affairs. We can contact the best choice whenever you're ready."

"It's the end of Danica's shift. I'll relieve her, let her sleep, then get some myself. In the morning, if everything still looks okay, we'll all get our stories straight and give it our best shot."

I went forward to turn Danica loose. After she was gone, R.J. came forward and took her empty seat. He sat, silently staring out the forward view screen at the big ball of CD-48 11069. Without looking away he said, "This plan feels fraught with peril."

"What's your point?"

"I've been thinking. The skull could possibly come in handy if it all went to crap."

"I hate to admit it. The thought has crossed my mind, too."

"All I'd need was the name and location of anyone that you wanted to become suddenly helpful."

"We've only tried the thing once. You haven't noticed any harmful effects, have you?"

"No. None. And you know something? I have the strangest feeling that over time I could eventually learn to do the same thing without the skull."

"God forbid."

"Apparently He does not."

"Well, having experienced slavery recently, I do not plan on accepting anything resembling it again. If it comes to that, I'll call on you."

"We need a hidden communication setup between just you and me, something the bad guys would not notice. That way, in a pinch you can give me the name and locale I would need."

"I've got translators in my ears and a homing beacon under the skin of one arm. What else do you suggest?"

"A transducer behind one ear, one that transmits and receives. You tap once behind your ear to transmit. Then I can always open a channel to warn you as needed."

"We have those?"

"Wilson does. I've already discussed it with him. He likes the idea."

"Okay. I'm sold. Tomorrow morning you can stick me behind the ear. It's way better than being hosed down naked in front of lizard people."

"What?"

"That's another story. I'll tell you about it someday."

I awoke with a start in my sleeper cell and stared up at the adjustable overhead lamp as consciousness slowly seeped back in. Immediately I jerked one arm up to look.

Blue.

My palm was a light blue. My nails were light blue. The rest of me an evenly blended dark blue. I reached up and felt my head to confirm that the baldness had not been a dream. It was shiny smooth up there. I was hesitant to look in a mirror. A cream hair remover would be needed to erase the beard shadow completely enough. It felt like morning had arrived ahead of schedule.

In the habitat module, everyone was already there. The most eye-catching of the bunch was Catherine. She had used what looked like a long one-foot-wide piece of silk to wrap around herself, beginning at the neck and descending to the knee. Wide gaps had been left in the wrap, exposing her neck and upper chest, stomach and hips, and thighs. It was quite an ample amount of skin. Others in the group were stealing glances when they could. She had two wide silver bracelets with lighted jewels on each wrist, giving the impression of restraining devices. Everyone else bore intricate facial and neck tattoos, except Patrick. He wore a tanned leather jacket and pants that made him look like a trader. He had inserted dark tinted contact lenses that covered all of his eyes. It was a great disguise.

For a moment I wondered why they were staring more at me than anyone else, then I caught a glimpse of my blue reflection in a nearby panel. "I see we are all suited up for war. Anybody having any second thoughts yet?"

"I ought to be going, Adrian," said Wilson.

"Careful what you wish for."

Wilson added, "We've got a good lock on things. When you start asking questions, we think we know what to monitor to watch for their communications about it. Also, photo analysis shows one particular estate that seems to have an unusually large contingent of service people with no indications that it's actually a residence. The walls have razor wire facing in."

R.J. said, "We're set up to contact the Chancellor of Domestic Affairs office that seems to lead the rest. Anytime you're ready."

"Well, gentlemen, in that case put on some reggae music for background. This is a party ship after all. Let's see what they have to say."

We gathered around the A engineering station. I gently pulled Catherine forward. "You're my executive consort. Your name's Areana. You get to do the talking."

She looked at me with skepticism. "Wow. We're really going through with this?"

"Send a typed message to R.J.'s link. Your master respectfully requests an audience with the Chancellor to discuss matters of significant commerce."

Catherine slid into the station control seat and typed the message. R.J. leaned over and transmitted it. We stood around, staring with anticipation, the annoying reggae music playing in the background.

Our wait was surprisingly brief. An incoming audio message indicator began flashing on the console. A moment later, a voice came through speaking a language none of us recognized, though the voice translators quickly converted it.

"Greetings and warmest welcome, Exxetor. I am Chancellor Akai. I may be of some humble assistance. May I inquire as to the nature of the commerce to which you refer?"

Catherine spoke without being prompted. "I am Areana, Chancellor. Chief Executor for Master Mandarin. My master has heard such wonderful things about XiTau. He wishes to explore the possibility of residence here. Would there be any estates of considerable breadth available now or in the near future?"

Chancellor Akai did not hesitate. "Indeed there would possibly be something that could be made available for the right individual. XiTau holdings require a substantial investment however, Areana. There are so many interested, you understand."

"My master is not concerned with matters of compensation, Chancellor, although he is quite discriminating about staff availability. May we visit you to discuss arrangements that might be conducive to us both?"

"We would be most anxious to greet you, dear friends. However, a substantial deposit is required as a show of good faith."

Catherine looked up at me. I turned to R.J. "Can I use your new diamond set?"

"My diamond set?"

"For god's sake, the one they gave you on Enuro."

"How did I get that again?"

I whispered into Catherine's ear. She nodded and keyed her transmit button. "Chancellor, our gold deliveries are made by special courier. Would diamonds be an acceptable medium?"

The Chancellor's voice abruptly became friendlier. "Most acceptable, Areana. Please give your master my warmest regards. We will transmit landing coordinates to you immediately. I so look forward to showing you the beauty XiTau has to offer those in a position to appreciate it."

The receiver light went dark. Everyone gasped and relaxed as though the operation had been announced a success.

Wilson spoke from the B engineering station. "Well, that sure set off a flurry of communications." He looked at me through the crowd. "Take a while to break them all down, but the ones that I suspect we caused are all going to the security centers, the main government center, and to the other office complexes. I'm betting they think they have a live one on their hands."

"Let's hope greed overcomes caution," I said.

Danica called back from the flight deck. "I already have the landing coordinates. It's up ahead."

"Ladies and gentleman, let's strap in for landing. It's not every day you purchase a huge estate complete with slaves."

Shock Diamonds

Wilson said, "I just hope we're not buying the farm."

Chapter 24

The landing area was a bed of roses, literally. There were no service facilities, nor were there any service personnel. We set down gently on Griffin's wheels within a huge flower garden, low walls of colorful blooms around the ship, large beds of flower color scattered in every direction across well-trimmed, green grass lawn. The only pad of hardened surface was the one we had touched down on. A few workers of varying species in bright white overalls were maintaining the gardens. Directly ahead of us was an oval-shaped glass building protected by a moat of glistening blue water with many running fountains. A wide white bridge with no railing offered a way across. In every direction, the place looked like Shangri-la.

The aft airlock door hissed open to reveal Chancellor Akai and two of his handmaidens. The Chancellor was one of the most oddly-proportioned men I had ever seen. His head was slightly mushroom-shaped. There was no forehead. His wide-spread eyes were fixed just below the flat top of his baldness. His nose was too low, leaving an empty spot in the face. Immediately beneath it, his small mouth was set slightly to one side. His skin was an unpleasantly grainy, milky white. His arms were too low on his torso, and both his arms and legs were not jointed midway. He wore fancy, ruffled clothing, a red jacket embellished with gold buttons, fit for an audience with the queen. His black slacks were tapered to match the queer knee joints. His dark shoes were heavily engraved and flat-topped.

The females standing alongside Akai were not only nicely formed; they were exotically beautiful in an alien way. I did not recognize their species, but their hair was a sparkling white and tied to fall across one shoulder. They wore colorful, one-piece, see-through robes that touched the ground but did not conceal crystal-covered slippers. They were green-skinned and emanated sensuality. The features of their faces were small and beautifully sculpted. They wore silver, metallic neck collars that looked like restraining devices.

We had worked out the details of our charade very carefully. As planned, Wilson and R.J., blatantly tattooed and in matching flight suits, marched down the ramp and stood at attention at the bottom. Black-eyed Patrick, carrying a satchel with financial tablets, went next and stood in abeyance between them. Lastly, my human slave Catherine went gracefully down and did it well enough that I caught just a glimmer of appreciation in the Chancellor's narrow stare. At the ramp's bottom, she turned to survey the area, introduced Patrick and herself, then signaled me that it was an acceptable setting for my presence. I paused at the top of the ramp, inspected my entourage, and walked belligerently down to meet the Chancellor.

When emulating a selfish, self-important person, one must be careful to show recognition and admiration for others of his kind. I stood in front of Akai and bowed at the waist, holding my two hands in prayer form. I held the pose slightly longer than was perhaps proper, to emphasize the man's importance. He responded with a quick duck of his head and fashioned a very weird smile from his offset purple lips.

"Lord Mandarin, what a wonderful means of transportation. Large enough for comfort, yet perfect for timely travel," he said.

I looked to Catherine.

"Yes, Chancellor. My Master uses it when he is anxious to see a potential purchase."

"Then I am glad," replied Akai. "Let us leave the garden's beauty for the comfort of the reception area."

I bowed again. The Chancellor bowed politely in return. The six of us headed for the bridge, leaving Wilson and R.J. standing at attention. It looked like Wilson squinted, trying to ward off laughter.

The reception area was as lavish as the garden. There were flowers in exotic vases everywhere. There was a globe the size of a beach ball in the center of the room, intricately detailed with the topography of XiTau. Walls, floor, and ceiling were all tinted glass that was a collage of display screens showing very slow-moving, swirling color. Plush seating formed meeting areas in various spots around the room. Although the place looked pristine, I had the feeling the room had been closed and covered until our arrival, as though real estate on XiTau was not a fast-moving commodity. There were adjoining offices that looked seldom used, but also exotically decorated. Akai led us to a circle of seats and motioned us to sit. He took a position next to a control panel built into a glass center table. His female companions headed elsewhere.

"They'll return with appropriate food and drink. If there's anything in particular you'd like, simply ask. It's our pleasure."

I leaned over and gave instructions to Catherine in Sirenian. She nodded and spoke. "Perhaps we should take care of the incidental matters, Chancellor." She looked at Patrick. He understood without being asked. He drew out the small cloth bag we had transferred the diamonds to and held it out for Catherine. She took them, stood, and bowed to Akai, handing him the bundle, smiling with practiced sincerity. "May this be a wonderful symbol of the benefits we may provide each other in the coming days, Chancellor."

Akai's eyes lit up. He looked up at Catherine and accepted the bag. He opened it briefly, seemed unable to conceal his joy, and tucked the bag inside his stiff dress jacket. "Of that I have no doubt, Areana." He sat back and made himself comfortable. "You indicated a larger category of holding would most interest you."

Catherine answered. "My master is hopeful it will make the selection process somewhat more expeditious, Chancellor."

"Indeed it will, Areana. There are three large villas available, any one of which may suit your needs nicely. The largest of them just happened to become available very recently. Regretfully, its owner was lost in a tragic explosion aboard a spacecraft. The property is still technically in probate status, but that process can be hurried along as necessary. I believe you will find any of the three quite extraordinary, in any case."

"Let us start with the largest of the three then, Chancellor if you don't mind," suggested Catherine.

With that, a transparent screen rose from the table. Images of the requested estate began to appear, one after the other. A very smooth discourse of the property's advantages was dispensed by Akai. When he had finished, he rose from his seat and went to the large globe. He pointed out the location and acclaimed its wonderfully stable climate and very desirable topography. He returned and sat.

"Of course, a personal tour is a must for this type of residence," he said. "It will take most of the day, but you will find it a very comfortable experience."

Through the glass wall near the entrance, we heard a faint whine and looked to see the Griffin lift off and disappear overhead.

The Chancellor seemed surprised. "Your majesty, you may use the landing pad as much as you deem necessary."

Catherine answered, "Chancellor, after each leg of a trip, the crew is required to check and align each spacecraft system for the safety of our Lord. Those must be done on orbit. We greatly appreciate your hospitality and look forward to employing it."

"Our tour vehicle is located just outside. We can depart for the site if you are ready. Is there anything you need in the interim?"

There was not. Our tour vehicle was a light-blue, eight-seat golf cart floater with a tinted one-way domed canopy that hinged open wide. The body sagged slightly as we stepped up and in. In a wonderfully rare instance of role reversal, Catherine climbed up, stood, and helped me in. I sat alone in my most dignified posture.

The Chancellor typed in a few keys on a keyboard. The canopy swished closed and we were off at a brisk pace. The carriage floated close to the ground. The trip was a carefully laid out path showing the best parts of XiTau luxury. Flower gardens, glistening streams, and large sculptures lined the route. It was an exotically beautiful landscape, the best wealth and slavery could provide.

The estate was even more lavish. We cruised the grounds around the main mansion and were told of the many other buildings and facilities that were also a part of the spread. The main doors of the residence opened automatically as the carriage approached. Inside, it was not necessary to dismount. The halls were wide enough to accommodate two such vehicles, the rooms so expansive they too could be toured that way. The main elevators were no less accommodating. To our surprise, after a brisk tour of the upper floors and towers, we were taken to the subterranean facilities, equally lavishly decorated. The next surprise was the chamber of wide tunnels that led to other buildings. At each point of the tour, there were servants in militaristic uniforms tending to the estate. Akai explained it was only a skeleton crew. Catherine asked all the appropriate questions. Patrick also performed his character well, saying little, but constantly typing information and observations into his tablets.

Back at the reception building by late afternoon, we were whisked away to an adjoining chamber laid out with enough food for ten people. We sat and ate, exchanging our enthusiasm about the tour. As the servants began to pour after-dinner drinks, I leaned over and spoke in Sirenian to Catherine.

Catherine nodded and turned to the Chancellor. "Chancellor Akai, when could a contract for the sale be made ready?"

For a moment, I thought the Chancellor would choke on his food. He caught himself nicely, dabbed a napkin at his sideways mouth, and nodded as he spoke. "My friends, we have yet to discuss the realities of such a purchase."

Catherine smiled, "My master expects that should the amounts indicated seem exceptionally extravagant, negotiations can be conducted to find mutual agreement. He does not expect a problem, however. In fact, would it be possible to evaluate staff support at this time, and perhaps have those contracts drawn up, as well?"

The Chancellor seemed to have forgotten his dessert completely. "My friend, Lord Mandarin, what would be involved for you to provide the necessary level of compensation indicated by an agreement of this magnitude?"

Catherine had become even more comfortable in her role. "Chancellor, in these cases, generally three separate shipments of gold are delivered by special courier from three different depositories. Our couriers are available on a continuous basis. Our financial institutions are equally at your disposal. Given XiTau's location, we would expect the first of the deliveries in three days time, the last in five days or less."

Akai swallowed. "Then perhaps staff evaluations would be a prudent measure at this time. Would you like to retire for the evening and begin in the morning, or continue?"

"Chancellor, my master wishes to assist us in beginning the selection process right away. We can then complete it in the morning. Would that be acceptable?"

"Most acceptable, Areana. We have a personnel resources center set up in the next room for the express purpose of reviewing potential staff selections. We do not allow scanners or other electronic transmission devices there due to the personal nature of the information that is provided. A security tablet is provided for your records and selections, which you return when you are finished listing your choices. If you have any disallowed electronic devices, they will be safe here on this table. We can then proceed to the personnel resources center and begin."

Leaving our electronics on the table was disconcerting. But when showing someone the dossiers of kidnapped people, one cannot allow recording devices to be present. Of some comfort, I still had a sub-dermal transmitter behind my ear.

The resource library in the adjacent room was a large, circular station surrounded by transparent display screens, clear tables, and well-cushioned black office chairs. There were small black tablets, on the table for slave-shoppers to use. Akai waved to someone in a nearby office, then brought us within the circle where we took seats and waited. An attractive red-haired female of some species I did not recognize joined us and took a seat at the controls. Her floor-length rainbow gown parted at the hip, revealing matching rainbow leggings. She turned and looked at us in search of the person who would operate the computer controls. In response, Catherine stood and bowed slightly. She called up a main menu as Akai stood over her, watching. From the main menu, she made a selection I could not make out. A few moments later, all of the screens around us displayed four female faces with details alongside.

I should have been prepared for the shock of it. I was not. They were human faces, carefully made-up to be sterile-clean and attractive. Their appearance was very well arranged by some talented cosmetic artist, but even that could not hide

Shock Diamonds

the shadow of despair behind the eyes. It made my stomach turn and I had to fight the urge to appear aghast.

The operator turned back to Catherine. "For additional information simply select any face you like. This button advances to the next screen. This button brings up the previous screens. This button will allow you to select any language you wish. There are twelve pages of language choices. If you do not see a subject you'd prefer, remember to advance to the next page."

Akai butted in. "We have selected humans and human-like species. Often, variations from the fundamental human form can be very desirable. You may find potential staff that is even more to your liking in that group."

Rainbow girl picked up a tablet from the counter. "You may record your selections on any of these. When you have finished, simply turn them over to us for creation of the contracts."

Akai spoke once more. "You will find some of these candidates are listed as 'employed.' Those are cases where that individual is currently serving at an estate or government office, but they are available for transfer."

Catherine asked, "Chancellor, how long does it take to assemble our staff after execution of the contract?"

"All of these candidates reside on XiTau. Therefore, procurement of these individuals can be performed immediately. If you do not find everything you need, we are able to procure other off-planet individuals, which generally takes a few days."

"How wonderful," said Catherine, with a smile. "What a perfectly exceptional example of a well-designed organization."

"We have been very successful for quite some time," replied Akai. "If there is nothing else, we know you would prefer privacy in these matters. I will be in the next office if you need me. Xana will wait in the lounge area over there if you need further assistance with the display."

Akai waited for any questions, then bowed slightly and departed. Xana, our keypad instructor, followed along. We were left to scroll through the devastation of kidnapped souls forced into slavery. We had to look as though we were enjoying ourselves. We exchanged a quick look of disbelief and Catherine began the search with Patrick dutifully holding up a tablet, periodically entering names as though we approved of certain selections.

One hour later, a new realization set in and I once more began to feel sick to my stomach. I was certain the others felt the same way. Only fifty percent of the candidates were human, but in that hour we had perused seventy-eight faces. As Catherine called for the next page of the lost, I sat back and wiped my

245

blue face with one hand. I tilted my head down and rubbed my bald crown, and when I looked back up Patrick's face was locked in a cold, silent, sheer terror.

There, at the top of the screen, was Emma.

Chapter 25

Catherine recognized the danger immediately. Patrick was set to explode. We were just out of sight of Akai in his office, but our female computer guide across the room was occasionally glancing our way.

As Patrick's dead stare began to change into one of fury, Catherine spun in her seat and placed a hand on his leg, shaking her head with a pleading expression. As he opened his mouth to scream in protest, I had no choice but to lurch up and clamp one hand over it, using my body to block the attendant's view. I tilted his head back and gave the I'll-kill-you-if-you-yell stare. He sat captured and wide-eyed, his eyes bloodshot from anger. Finally, there was the fluttering of the eyelids as composure began to return. He nodded that he understood. As I withdrew and sat, the silent tears began to escape.

Computer girl looked up, possibly having caught some of the movement out of the corner of her alien eye. Patrick's back was to her. Catherine was already smiling and twisting back and forth in her seat. I sat and resumed my improvised aloofness. Patrick remained still, staring at the two of us, the tears rolling down his face. There was a whole lot of telepathic communication. After a few deep breaths, he wiped away the tear lines as inconspicuously as possible. Composure finally regained, he stared down at a tablet and pretended to make entries, wiping new tears away with cautious, casual gestures. Computer girl went back to her display screen.

"It says she's employed," said Catherine in a low tone.

"Does it say where?" I asked.

"The Bureau of Labor Relations and Receiving, the Department of Bio-Refuse Management."

"What the hell is that?"

"I don't know, but I sure don't like the sound of it."

"Is she expensive?"

"Unfortunately, no. It would make our fussiness about servants suspect. Apparently she has not done well here. She has a low-performance rating."

"I will kill these bastards," said Patrick in a low but controlled tone.

"You get your act together, Patrick, or we'll all be on this list. You hear me?"

"Patrick dear, we have found her. A needle in a cosmic haystack. Be happy. We have a chance," added Catherine.

Patrick bit his tongue.

"Remember this page number. We'll go on a few pages and then ask to return in the morning to finish," I said.

"But we know where she is," complained Patrick in a barely controlled whisper. "Why come back here? Let's go get her."

"It won't be that easy, Patrick. Trust me. We have at least another day before our identities may begin to be questioned. The more intel we have, the better our chances. Besides, I want everything from this computer."

Patrick looked confused. "Why?"

"Because there's a lot of other sons and daughters here, Patrick. Not just yours. Earth needs to know about this place. People need to know why their loved ones disappeared."

Catherine joined in. "I agree, Adrian. But how will you get any data out of here? It's like Fort Knox."

"I have an idea. Step to the next page, Cath. We don't want to linger on Emma's too long. Patrick, do not list her on our tablet."

When the time was right, we withdrew from our research station and met Akai at his office door. Out of the corner of my eye, I watched computer girl take our station, clear the info, and shut it down. Then another timely break befell us. She left the station and went to a metallic door next to Akai's office and placed her hand on a palm reader on the wall. The door slid open just long enough for her to enter, and just long enough for us to catch a glimpse of two mainframe computer stacks in the center of the room.

Chancellor Akai was most gracious. He still had our diamonds. Yes, of course we could return in the morning to complete staff selection. Were we certain we did not need to visit any of the other prospective properties? Yes, he would transmit an approximate total amount for property, service, and staff so that we could begin having the necessary gold currency shipped to XiTau. Yes, he could provide a list of government services on XiTau and would transmit that up to us, as needed. Yes, he had enjoyed our visit, as well.

With our com units and scanners returned, we called for the Griffin and thirty minutes later were back on orbit, the spacecraft abuzz with excitement. R.J. and Wilson managed to isolate the Bio-Waste Management Building in less than an hour. They intercepted several communications streams from it. The most interesting, air conditioning had to be cut off to the building's servant quarters in the basement until the system could be recharged. Overall, the facility itself was a moderate risk target near higher risk buildings. It looked like a late-night job for Wilson and me.

The best way is to remain invisible. Loot the bank, never be seen, leave no evidence except counterfeit money to replace what you've taken so that the misdeed will not be uncovered until long after you are gone. Leave them wondering how it could have been done.

That's the best way. In our case: make off with the hostage, leave clues that the hostage had run away somewhere, or was just AWOL having a good time, then be a trillion light years away before they even suspect the truth. With detailed planning and a flow chart for alternatives, it can almost always be done.

If everything goes as planned.

We needed an interior scan of the building so that Wilson and I could lie in our beds and mentally learn every floor, every office, every closet, and every elevator and stairwell. It sounded like a bureaucratic kind of office building, one less likely to have scan detectors built into its security system. A single three-second sweep would give us a detailed 3-D interior view. Even if there were detectors, a healthy, momentary solar flare could set off the same radiation footprint. We would launch a probe, wait until we were on the opposite side of the planet, remotely pulse-scan the building, then immediately drive the probe out into space and have an orbital alibi that left nothing to be found overhead. It wasn't absolutely foolproof, but it was very, very good.

The drop would be more difficult. We could absorb, delay, and then reflect back their radars, essentially giving us an electronic cloak, but this planet had advanced systems, not so easily fooled. But there was one very big irony. The Griffin had been designed so that it could fly in the atmosphere with wings. Blackwell had planned to shut down the ship's drive systems and glide in to pick up abducted slaves, leaving no descent engine signatures to be tracked by authorities. In a complete reversal of that scheme, we would glide down to XiTau, recover a kidnapped individual, and escape to Earth. They might eventually find our momentary ascent engine signatures, but those would be so brief that was unlikely.

The plan was still risky. The quicker the drop the better, and there was no one in the galaxy better at that than Danica. She would have to power down the OMS and Stellar drive engines along with the gravity repulse system, then glide down to one thousand feet, power up the gravity repulse system for a vertical descent to the drop-off point, then blast out of there. The ride up would be quick. Catherine and Patrick would be learning what nine Gs felt like.

The most disconcerting part would be the weapons Wilson and I would need to carry. I did not cherish the thought of shooting anyone else. I'd had my fill of violence. We could only program two settings on the big guns; heavy stun and kill, and when someone is trying to burn holes in you, you cannot take the time to search for the right setting. Wilson had brought along one wonderful addition to the armory. Chameleon camouflage. Combat clothing that automatically changed color and design to match the surroundings. Comes with a hood that can be pulled over the face and is see-through one way. Clear armament belts support the illusion. You could stand with your back against the wall and become the wall, then leap behind brush and be part of the foliage.

Wilson never goes anywhere without the good stuff.

Although we still had our slave selection meeting in the morning, it did not appear we would get much sleep. People began to retire to their quarters around 1:00 A.M. That finally allowed R.J. and me to meet on the flight deck with Danica.

"So you understand what I'm thinking then? What I have in mind?" I asked.

"My gut feeling is that it will work," replied R.J.

"So his full name is Akai Naktu. You have the coordinates down there."

"I'll keep the skull in my sleeper cell with the crystals. When you signal, I'll shut myself in and try to link sitting upright on the bed. No one except the three of us should be aware that anything is happening."

"If it looks like anything has gone wrong, I'll send Wilson into your cell to pull you out of it."

"There is a possibility they may detect the signal from your hidden transmitter when you call up here," said R.J.

"Yeah. Let's keep it as short as possible. I'll tap the transmitter and say the word 'proceed,' then tap it off immediately."

"Maybe a one-second transmission. I'd be surprised if they pick that up."

"If you do get control of Akai's body, give me a wink so I know, okay?"

"This is going to be a trip."

Danica said, "I still don't believe in that thing, but if anything goes wrong I can leave the flight deck long enough to help."

"Yes, we'll use you, but only as a last resort," I answered. "Now that we've scanned the interior of Emma's building, we need to keep an especially close eye on the long-range and orbital radar. If they figure out we're not who we say we are, the first sign will probably be another ship showing up. If that happens, you should break orbit immediately and hide the Griffin any way you can. Then contact us whenever possible."

Danica twisted in her seat. "That's an ugly little scenario. You'd better go over it again for me. What happens after tomorrow morning's visit to the surface?"

"If it all goes well, we finish our personnel selections, sign the contracts for the estate, and tell the Chancellor we will maintain orbit waiting for our payments of gold to arrive. Then, if everything looks okay, you will drop Wilson and me on the surface in the early morning darkness, and we will quietly attempt to find and extract Patrick's daughter. We will then depart this place in great haste."

"My favorite part," said R.J.

"Danica, you're a little overdue for your six. I'll take over here and use my shift to finish memorizing the floor plans of the building."

"You know, this all better go well because beginning tomorrow night you're going to start losing your blue, Adrian," said R.J.

"All the more reason to make this plan work. I do not want another pill."

The next morning, Danica, R.J., and I carefully went over the plan to steal slave data. Afterward, I gave custom-programmed scanners to Patrick and Catherine and told them only that it was in case a special need arose.

On the planet's surface, the Chancellor was his magnanimous self, promising to deliver some of the completed contract documents in short order. Inside the Personnel Resource Center, we were again required to leave our scanners and com units on the lobby table. Our computer operator, Xana, the most volatile element in my plan, was waiting with the personnel selection station already up and running. She had even called up the last page from the day before. As we took our seats, she left us and went to her station.

With Catherine slowly scrolling through the faces of slaves, and Patrick dutifully recording one now and then, I tapped the back of my ear and made the call to R.J. "Proceed."

In keeping with the plan, he did not acknowledge.

Chancellor Akai had gone to his office and left the door open, exactly as he had the day before. From my position, I could see his hands on his desk, tapping at a display terminal. Three or four minutes passed and nothing changed. I began to have doubts.

All at once, a curious thing made me pause and stare. The Chancellor's hands had stopped moving in mid air. They were frozen there, the left hand about to point to something, the right ready to punch a key. After an excruciating thirty seconds of motionlessness, the hands withdrew from my field of vision. Seconds later, the Chancellor appeared at the door. His expression was the very same one I had grown accustomed to seeing on R.J. when he was confused or perplexed. He looked around the room, spotted us, and winked. Keeping Xana in the corner of my eye, I gave a slight nod.

The Chancellor nodded back.

With a slight awkwardness, he went to the lobby door and exited. He was gone no more than two or three minutes and returned. He went to the mainframe computer door, paused for a moment, then placed his hand on the wall palm reader. Yellow lights flashed, turned green, and the door slid open.

Xana looked up and stared, but remained in her seat.

It took all of ten minutes. At last, the Chancellor appeared again and went directly back to the lobby. He returned moments later to his office, took his seat, and placed his hands back in the position they originally had been. There was another long pause of motionlessness, and abruptly the hands resumed the work they had been doing before the trip to the lobby.

We continued our charade for another forty-five minutes and were finally interrupted by the Chancellor holding several sheets of clear paper with engraved gold print on each.

"Ready for your signature, at your convenience, sir," he said, looking directly at me.

I gave a gracious bow of my head, accepted the queer-looking pen from him as an added gesture of respect, and signed in gold on seven sheets. There was a great sigh of relief from the Chancellor and he scurried away back to his office.

Our commitment to buy fully formalized and staff selection complete, we were escorted to the waiting Griffin where we conveyed our profound appreciation, paused for a few moments to give the impression we did not wish to leave, then boarded and lifted off for orbit. In our pockets, Patrick and I carried the fully loaded scanners R.J. had used to upload the data from the Personnel Resource Center mainframe computers. There was no doubt the deed had been done. The scanners read empty during descent and were now flashing "memory full." I could only hope there were no ill effects from R.J.'s secret possession of the Chancellor's body.

Once on orbit, we gathered around the engineering stations as Wilson and R.J. transferred the stolen data to ship's computers.

"I still don't get how you got this stuff," said Wilson.

"Sleight of hand, you might say," I replied.

"Okay, but someday you got to explain the trick to me," he replied.

R.J. cut in. "As expected, it's encrypted. It will take a very long time to decipher it."

"Maybe not. We memorized Emma's page, so we have a Rosetta stone, so to speak."

"That may work if we can find the right data block," answered R.J. "But their password system might still hang us up."

"You want to begin transmitting this stuff back to Earth?" asked Wilson.

"Not yet. Don't want to accidentally attract any unwanted attention. Let's sit on it for now."

Patrick began to whine. "I should be going with you, Adrian."

"No, Patrick. You're a doctor, not a soldier. You want the best chance for your daughter? Stay here."

He grimaced and stormed off.

After a quick raid of the galley, Wilson and I left the others and took refuge in the aft airlock to begin staging for the morning's extraction. We sat for a while and drank a beer, an extravagance that would require the taking of an anti-tox tablet afterward to nullify the effects. We watched all the scan data on the small airlock monitors and took note of each individual within the target building and on the grounds around it. The place was heavily manned during the day. We expected very few in the early morning hours when we would visit.

The down-facing camera views showed the area to be yet another garden of beauty. The building was pristine and colorfully decorated. The lawns around it were equally well maintained and elaborate.

Closer analysis of the interior scans combined with monitoring of the building's communications suggested the place was a house of horrors. It appeared that the Labor Relations and Receiving section was there for the purpose of bringing in and processing new slaves. The bio-waste management section of the building was much smaller. Whatever kind of bio-waste they were handling was processed on the west end of the first floor. The waste products were shoveled into chutes that took them to the basement. From there, large horizontal underground tunnels carried the stuff away to destinations unknown. The basement collection area took up most of that floor. A narrow strip was sectioned off for housing of the building's workers. Those living there had private rooms, barely the size of a walk-in closet. It was impossible to tell if the rooms were actually cells.

We would not achieve invisibility on this mission. There just was not enough time to learn the locks and checkpoints. We would carry plastic explosive, laser cutters, and no-nonsense weaponry. The mission would need speed to take the place of invisibility. Wilson and I suited up and practiced mimicking the imaginary route we would take, stopping to pretend to burn locks or set charges, rehearsing our lucky find of the captive, then bringing her out to the pickup point. From there we went on to contingency planning until we knew for certain what each would do under any of the many possible circumstances that might arise.

As drop time approached, everyone on board tried too hard to appear confident and casual. I kept to business. Wilson, as always, was confident and casual. While the rest of the crew strapped in, he and I met in the aft airlock to load up.

"This ship is something else," said Wilson. "I love the way the engineering stations are set up. R.J. and I mapped every radiation source. R.J. wrote a program that will make us a vacuum cleaner for radar. We'll suck it up and feed it back as though nothing has been reflected off of anything. By the way, Danica will glide us down in as tight a circle as possible so there will be minimum ground coverage. The only thing anyone could pick up would be a silhouette or a little bit of wind sound. I went around and warned everyone no communications unless it's an emergency. By God, Adrian, I love this ship. It's a special ops dream."

"With you on that. Now if we can just get back to her."

As we dropped out of orbit, the Griffin became alarmingly silent in its death dive. In the aft airlock, the two of us became weightless, leading me to worry about the artificial gravity's ability to adjust, and the ship's pressurization system to react, but knowing Danica, I had to believe she had already taken those into consideration.

Holding on to anything available, we rode out the steepness until our falling bodies were able to catch up to the falling ship. Nearing the surface, we suddenly went from zero weight to heavy, and as Danica put on the brakes, we became even too heavy to stand, crumpling to our knees against the side wall panels. I had planned to pop the airlock door open early. My timing was off. Before I could tap the big red button, the door slid open from a flight-deck command issued by Danica. The woman is scary smart.

We pulled ourselves to the open door and stared out into the night as we continued down. It was 04:00 A.M. XiTau time, but there were lights everywhere. On the well-lit roadways, no traffic at all was visible, nor did we see any signs of life in this section of the government facilities.

She stopped the Griffin so abruptly it almost felt like we had hit the ground. Wilson and I rubbed shoulders jumping the eight feet to the dark ground. We fell and rolled, and lay on our backs for a moment watching the Griffin shoot back up into darkness, wondering how Danica could have cut it so close. Wilson signaled me toward the nearest cover, well-trimmed hedges a few feet away.

The drop seemed to have been perfect. We were near the rear of the target building. When wearing blackface and carrying weapons, rear doors are generally more desirable. I looked down at my suit. It was not only dark green; it had the same design as the hedge. I glanced at Wilson. He also looked like an untrimmed section of it.

Our plan was to decode the door lock. As luck would have it, we did not have to. An elderly female in a gray janitorial outfit came galumphing out the door pulling a small cart with an overflowing collapsible waste container. She was not human but she was humanoid. There were so many contour lines in her face; it would have been impossible to guess her age except for the familiar hunched-over, labored movements she made. Her dark eyes were slightly large and slanted upward. The crown of her head was pointed, with additional pronounced crowns on either side of her skull. Her earlobes were profoundly wide with the same type of contour lines. She had a flat mouth, heart-shaped upper lip, and a contoured nose that ended in a point. Her four long fingers were webbed.

She labored to dump trash into a large tube sticking out of the ground by the door, then paused to catch her breath. She lumbered back to the door, entered a key code, then braced the door open with one oversized foot, jockeying around to get the cart back inside. As it swung closed behind her, Wilson sprinted the ten yards across the lawn, caught it, and held it so that it looked closed. He scanned side to side, then motioned me all clear.

I crossed over and joined him, and just as we were about to make entry, the sound of the com squelching on gave cause for a momentary spike of fear. It was not to be used except in emergency.

There was panic in Danica's voice. "Adrian, large spacecraft approaching on long-range radar. Too late to jump. Gonna hide on the other side of the planet. Danica out."

I exhaled in exasperation and shook my head. Wilson nodded in agreement and motioned to the door. We slipped inside.

There was a foul-smelling hallway, tiled from floor to ceiling with dirty brown matchbook-sized tiles. The sound of janitor lady's rickety cart creaking along somewhere ahead. The smell was so rancid it made you want to spit. The gritty, shady hallway was a perfect contrast to the beauty of the building and grounds outside.

Wilson motioned us forward. We took a left at the first intersection, entering another hallway so far-reaching you could not see its end for the shadows. There were occasional dull echoes from forward and behind.

As expected, we came to a wide four-way intersection. A left would take us to the elevators and staircase. Wilson edged cautiously to the corner, his back against the wall. He slowly leaned forward to take a look but jerked back at the sound of janitor lady's cart suddenly starting up and heading our way. The nearest door was next to me. Wilson joined in and we pushed through just in time to avoid being seen.

We found ourselves in an alien restroom. On one side, a long counter with running water. Opposite it, four open toilets in a row, no booths. The first may have been for humanoids. It was a narrow rectangular seat. Beside it, four feet away, the next was a bowl attached directly to the floor with a chrome shaft rising out of its center, ending in a queer-looking bulb shape. Beyond that, the next one was a flexible hose sticking up out of the floor with a suction cup on it, and finally, a barrel-shaped thing suspended above the floor with a door in its side.

Wilson stood by the door listening. He stared at me with his head cocked and his ears tuned to the hallway. He had a look that said, "She can't be coming in here."

But she was.

We heard the cart bang against the door. I was the lucky one. I made it to a corner at the back of the room and in final desperation pulled my hood over my face and swung my weapon behind me. I became the dirty tiles on the wall. Wilson tried but only made it as far as the first toilet. He stepped behind it, stiffened against the wall, and pulled down his hood. From my vantage point, he made quite a good imitation of tiles, but he was no more than four feet behind the humanoid toilet.

In she came, drearily pulling her cart along. She did not bother to look up, stopped at the waste bin in the wall by the door, and emptied it into hers. Then, to both our horrors, she left her cart, went to the toilet in front of Wilson, and began removing clothes. To Wilson's great dismay, she adjusted herself on the toilet and stared straight ahead with the thousand-mile gaze. A series of loud booms began that sounded like a car backfiring. I could not see Wilson's face, but I could tell it was turned away, probably with an expression of utter indignation.

Janitor lady finished up, dressed, and slowly ambled out of the restroom, banging her cart as she went, never bothering to look up at all. From my position, the room's bouquet had been significantly degraded. I was surprised Wilson was still standing.

We departed the bathroom with haste, pulling our weapons forward as we went, preferring a firefight to remaining in that room a moment longer. The hallway was again empty, except for the distant clanking of janitor lady's cart heading away.

Back at the main intersection, we managed to get a look around the corner and spotted the service elevator and a heavy metal door nearby. In all four directions, the place was desolate and eerie, an endless blanket of tiled walls. We crouched and hurried to the door nearest the elevator, but by the time we reached it, it felt like we were hiding from nothing. There was not a sound to be heard or a creature to be seen. The rancid smell in the air persisted.

The black, iron-wrought stairs beyond the heavy door were unusual. Instead of a standard stairwell, these wound down into darkness. They rang like a giant tuning fork when you stepped the wrong way. Like everywhere else, the stairwell was devoid of the feeling of life. At the bottom, we met our first resident, something very much like a rat, dirty dark fur, no visible legs, long oily tail, pointed face with spiked teeth. It was a large rat, and it did not like us. It scurried away into the shadows. We pushed through the dark gray metal door at the bottom and into a new maze of dirty tiled corridors.

Here were the small rooms that were designated for the workers. They lined the long, morbid hallway. Big heavy metal doors with small, barred windows and waist-high locked access hatches for food or water to be passed in. There was an individual in the very first one we looked into. She was asleep on the floor. No blanket, no sleeping pad. Orange hair splayed over the face. Sunburned-red hands and arms, a filthy gray work uniform, a fresh new one hanging on the wall. We began our search, one door at a time. Wilson took the right. I took the left.

By the time we reached the end of the first corridor, we were both soul-sick. We had not spotted Emma, though every single cell was occupied. A few had blankets or rags, but that was it. A few of them had looked up but regarded our blackened faces as just more of the enemy. We did not have to sneak here. No one was coming. Hand scanners showed no cameras or other monitoring devices. If you became ill in your cell here, you were on your own.

Wilson looked at me with an expression of desperation I had never seen from him. He spoke in a half whisper. "My god, Adrian. What are we going to do?"

"Yeah, I know what you're going to say."

"More than half of them are human, probably from Earth. We can't just leave them."

"The Griffin's designed for eight, Wilson. POM says the air handler can take up to sixteen. There's six of us already. There's just no way, even if we could get all these people aboard. There's just no way."

"What the hell can we do?"

"Come back with bigger guns."

"My god, my god."

"Yeah."

"Are we in deep shit anyway? She can't pick us up."

"I don't think so. She'll hide on the opposite side of the planet. As soon as that arriving spacecraft gets settled into orbit, she'll match it and stay out of sight. In a standard orbit, she should come around in about forty-five minutes."

"We'll never finish searching the rest of these shit cells in forty-five."

"Yeah, if we haven't gotten lucky and located her, we'll take a chance and let the Griffin make another spin so we can keep searching."

"We'll be cutting the pickup time close to sunrise."

"Should still be dark enough. We'll jump straight to light as soon as we leave the atmosphere. Be a trillion miles away before they know we were here."

"Place makes me sick," he said.

"Goes without saying," I replied.

Thirty minutes later we had still not found Emma. Our com units suddenly came alive and vibrated with a signal from Danica.

I keyed in. "Go ahead. It's clear."

"Adrian, you're not going to believe this."

"Is everything alright with the ship?"

"Yes. It's not that. They're keeping a 240. We can stay out of phase with that no problem. It's you guys that may be in trouble."

"What's the problem?"

"They dispatched a small shuttle from their ship and it put down right where you are. We thought maybe you had been discovered, but a short time later two large transports came up to rendezvous with their ship. We think they are transporting cargo or something down to your location."

"No shit." said Wilson.

"It wouldn't be cargo, Danica. It would be new slaves."

There was a long pause. "Oh..."

"Dan, we're going to need at least another orbit to complete the search. Can you handle it?"

"Sure. We won't be picking you up while all that's going on, anyway."

"It's okay. Wilson and I can hold up for a day if we have to. Can you guys stay safe?"

"No problem. We have mini-probes set out keeping track of them. Worst case scenario, we can jump at any time and come back later."

"Be careful, Danica."

"That's what I was going to tell you."

I signed off. Wilson looked at me with a wrinkled brow. "Is it just me, or is it getting deeper?"

"It's not you."

Chapter 26

    We spent more than an hour searching the remaining maze of lost souls. No luck. There was no choice but to explore the upper levels. At least we knew the place well. We returned to the winding stairwell and ascended to the first floor. It was still just as deserted. It was a place of formal, cold emptiness. The rear section was yet another network of cells. Only a few were occupied by the vanquished. The front section was quite different. The lights were off. Shadowy street light from outside seeped through the doors and windows. There was a reception area that surrounded the entrance, a pristine and colorful sitting area with an oval desk. To the right of the entrance, a double-wide elevator trimmed in gold waited. To the left, ominous steel double doors were brightened by a mural of various happy individuals of many different species.
    In an adjacent front room, we found another winding stairway that led to the second floor. We climbed it, expecting the upper area to be just as abandoned. We emerged into a wide open area with dozens of cubicle desk stations with computers. Some of the computer stations were on, periodically refreshing their data. There was an electronics hum in the air and the smell of air conditioning. We scanned a few of the stations, being careful to avoid affecting them.
    Hope for Emma was fading fast. It was beginning to look as though we would make the scheduled pickup time, empty-handed. But as Wilson and I turned the last cubicle corner, we abruptly ran headlong into janitor lady again, and this time there was no hiding from her. All three of us jerked to attention and stood appraising one another. To our surprise, it was not the layered face of the janitor lady.
    It was Emma.
    She stared wide-eyed at our blackened faces for a frozen moment, then hurriedly stepped aside, folding her hands at her waist, looking down at the floor as though she expected to be admonished for being in the way.
    As the shock wore off, I spoke, "Emma?"
    She started to look up, thought better of it, and returned to her withdrawal.

"Emma, I'm Adrian Tarn. This is Wilson Mirtos. We're here to take you back to your father."

Her head snapped up. Hesitantly, she reevaluated both of us. She had trouble allowing herself to speak. "My father?"

"He's aboard my ship. It's orbiting XiTau. We're taking you back to Earth."

She stared in disbelief, still afraid to speak out loud. "My father has come for me?"

Very slowly, I reached out one hand and touched her arm. "Yes. He's been worried sick since you've been gone. We're here to take you back."

She looked at the weapons hanging from our shoulders and the paint on our faces, and as believing set in, the tears began to flow. She staggered, forcing me to catch her. She was terribly underweight, a feather in my arms.

Wilson became nervous. "Adrian, we're too out in the open. Let's get out of here."

Suddenly, a bright glow from the windows began to cast shadows everywhere. Quickly it became intense white light, as bright as day. We ducked down and took refuge behind the stairwell wall, stealing glances at the sudden daylight. As we watched, a shuttle dropped down and landed on the lawn in front of the building.

Emma wiped away her tears and spoke. "It's today. The new arrivals. They're right on schedule. I'm supposed to be finished by now. If they find me or my cart up here, I'll be punished severely."

I held her in front of me. "No, Emma. It's over. You're never coming back here. No one is ever going to punish you again. Now, what are you talking about, new arrivals?"

She looked up at me, eyes streaked. "The new slaves. They'll be indoctrinated on the first floor. Then the other ship will arrive."

"Other ship?"

"The one that picks up the mine workers. The ones who can't be used here or the ones who flunked out. If you flunk out here, they send you to work the mines."

Just as she finished saying it, my com unit vibrated. "Go ahead, Danica. We're clear."

"Adrian, a second ship has arrived. It's docked with the first. They're both heavy drafts."

"We just had a shuttle land here, Danica. We won't be able to make the scheduled pickup. Stand by for further instructions. Break silence only if there's an emergency."

Danica cut in. "Expect a second shuttle shortly, Adrian. One has just separated from the ship that just arrived and it's departing down."

"Roger that, and Danica tell Patrick we have Emma. Assign R.J. to keep him settled down."

R.J.'s voice cut in. "I heard that, Adrian. Unbelievable. I'll do my best."

"We've got to move. Tarn out."

We dared a look out a nearby window. Below, people were beginning to emerge from the shuttle. They were gathering around a ramp deployed from an open forward hatch. They were well armed and wearing combat apparel. As we watched, a line of beat-up individuals with their hands tied behind their backs and a line of rope around their necks emerged and headed down the ramp. They were ushered along by men with prods. They were a diverse collection of species. I did not see any humans until the very end of the line. He was tall and muscular, head bowed, unshaven, wearing a dirty brown dress shirt, torn black slacks, wingtips. It looked like he had put up a pretty good fight. He had a bright star-shaped emblem tattooed on his left cheek. The parade was marched across the lawn and into the front entrance.

I turned to Emma. "What was that tattoo on the human guy's face?"

"It's not a tattoo. It peels right off. It's an identity chip and it was red. That means he's designated for the mines unless somebody here wants him, but nobody will. They don't like human males here. Too hard to control. But they love human females. They are considered the most beautiful. I kept running away. That's why I got sent here. One more infraction and I'll be sent to the refuse section. That's where they turn you into pet food."

"What will happen to those new prisoners now?"

"They will be assigned cells on the first floor, evaluated, and then scheduled for training or designated for mine work. The ones being sent to the mines will be taken up to the lizard ship as soon as they're ready. We can't stay here. People will be coming to begin entering the computer records."

"Lizard ship, you said?"

"Yes, the next shuttle will take the mine workers up to the lizard ship and it will go on to the mines. We need to go. They'll be coming soon."

"Where is the best place to hide, Emma?"

She looked at me with a regretful stare. "There's no choice. I have to get back to my cell in the basement, otherwise when the maitre d' comes in and checks us, they'll think I've run away again and all hell will break loose."

Shock Diamonds

Wilson said, "That sounds like a great place to hide, Adrian. Who'd look for us in jail?"

Emma shook her head. "But you can't get out until midnight. You'll both be locked in."

Wilson smiled. "No, we'll fix the locks so they think you're locked in, but you won't be." He looked at me. "We'd better use the back stairwell."

Emma said, "I have to take my cart down to the basement. I need to use the elevator. We need to hurry."

We started to leave when something happening down by the shuttle caught my eye. The prisoners were all gone. Three people who looked like VIPs emerged through the hatch. The last of them caused a flush of anger in me. There was no mistaking him.

Cigar man Silas Killian.

He wore a long black trench coat that fanned out behind as he walked. Black gloves with no fingers. Black boots up to the knee. Hair shaved down to a bristle. Beard shadow. He and his two compatriots were giddy. They slapped each other on the back as they entered the building.

"Please, we must go, now," begged Emma.

I quickly regained my composure. "Go ahead. We'll meet you downstairs at the elevator."

The trip to the stairwell and down was uneventful, but the sighting of Silas Killion plagued me. It wasn't so much what he had done to me as it was his absolute resolve to do it to so many.

We blended in with the corner walls and watched the elevator descend and the doors open. Emma hurried her cart out and motioned us to follow quickly. She turned down the first hallway, stopped at a utility closet and shoved the cart in, then trotted a short distance to a cell on the left. Wilson already had his pen torch ready.

We found the laser diode sensor in one of the bolt holes in the cell doorjamb. I held the door steady as Wilson cut slots in the locking bolts so that they were only holding by a thread. We could kick the door open at any time and the locking bolts would break off and stay in place, making the electronic monitoring system think the door was still bolted. We closed ourselves in and heard the ominous click of the latches, a daily reminder to the occupant that he or she was a prisoner forever without hope.

"What happens now?" asked Wilson of Emma.

"The maitre d' will walk the halls and release the day workers and make a visual check that the night workers are in like they're supposed to be. The day workers will tend to the

263

gardens and lawns and other facilities and then be brought back here before dark."

"What about the slave delivery? How does that go?" I asked.

"The lizard ship will be here until 6:00 P.M. or so. That's to give the accountants time to advertise the ones that are scheduled for the mines. If no one is interested, they'll be loaded on the lizard ship tonight and it will leave for the mines. The other ship, the one that brought the new slaves, they hang out here until the lizard ship leaves and the accountants have finished their work so they can get paid. Then tonight a three-day party begins to celebrate the new deal. The slaver VIPs all head out to a big estate somewhere with the XiTau higher-ups and they live it up."

"When do you eat?" asked Wilson.

"At dinner, we get the food that's left over from the high-rise kitchens."

Wilson looked at me with even more disdain. "I really hate this place, Adrian." He dug in an upper leg pocket of his suit and pulled out a candy bar wrapped in bright red foil. "Any rule about you having dessert early, Emma?"

Her eyes went wide and she dove at him, snatching the candy from his hand. She peeled it away and chomped on it, moaning with each bite. After a few moments, she realized her savagery and straightened up, trying to look more like a proper slave. "Sorry," she said, and after a moment's hesitation, she licked her fingers.

Wilson spoke in a low tone, "Don't worry, girl. I feel the same way about 'em."

"Emma, you have no tracking collar or anything else I see. How do they keep tabs on you?"

"In my leg. An implant. The same type like they use in dogs."

Wilson looked at me. "Not a problem. Right now it shows her here where she should be, and when we leave we'll be so quick about it we'll be out of range before it's any use to them."

I checked through the bars of the door window. There was no one around. My mind kept back-flipping to the cigar man. Without my consent, a devious little plan kept piecing itself together in my mind, a plan completely unnecessary, yet irresistible. "Emma, that human prisoner with the red star chip on his face, would there be any way to find where they're holding him without having to search every cell on the first floor?"

"Oh, yeah. No problem. He's scheduled for the mines so they'll put him in one of the cells closest to the front entrance 'cause they know he's going right back out."

"Tell me something else. They hold a lot of angry prisoners in this place. Is there an office where they keep drugs to help subdue them?"

"Sure. In the front section there's a kitchen area right near the temporary suites where the slaver VIPs wait. In the kitchen area, there's a separate room for special refrigerators. There's two glass units with keypads that hold all the drugs. The drugs are set up to be used quick, too. But you got to have the keypad code."

Wilson looked at me and wrinkled his brow. "Adrian, you're not thinking of..."

"I might take a short stroll later."

"Adrian, we've achieved the mission objective. You gonna risk blowing everything to try for one more?"

"With Emma we've got a crew of seven right now. Ship is designed for eight. Hate to fly with an empty seat."

"This ain't the airlines, Adrian."

"That man is going to the mines, Wilson. Even if some kind of rescue mission is set up, he won't be alive when it gets here."

"Well, I didn't say I wouldn't join you."

"No. Your job is to get Emma to the pickup point on time. I'll take care of the other."

Wilson carefully crossed over in front of the cell door and pulled a scanner off his belt. He pointed it at me and began a scan.

"What are you doing?"

"You still have the homing device in your arm. I'm setting up a continuous link. This scanner has the building floor plan. I'll be able to tell where you are every second."

We watched and waited. A short time later, echoes of activity began to carry down the halls. Harsh voices roused the beaten souls behind the dirty steel doors. There was a clanging and clanking of lock bolts snapping, and the sandpaper shuffle of tired feet dragging on the coarse cement floors. The sound of it was so medieval it made Wilson and me sink deeper into our corners on each side of the door, our hands resting lovingly on our comfort weapons.

They all went away. The place again became a hollow shell. Like good lifers, we used our hand-held mirrors to periodically check the corridors through the bars. On her next fly-over, Danica called in, and we set the pickup time for 8:00 P.M., XiTau time. The lizard shuttle and ship would be gone by then. Enough darkness would offer a fair visual cloak. Even if we were seen by someone, we would depart and be at light before anyone could do anything about it.

Then another long wait. Around 5:00 P.M. the walking dead began to return. I had to wait for their influx and the yelling of the guard to end before taking my stroll. It was after 6:00 P.M. before I was able to slam a shoulder into the cell door and pop the bolts. The three of us agreed we would meet at the Griffin's pickup point.

I was cutting it too close, especially since Wilson's guess about my plans had not been entirely correct. Extra time would be required as it was my intention to pay Mr. Silas Killian a visit. They say revenge will always get you in trouble, but they don't mention the part about living without having served some up.

Using an excess of caution, I worked my way up to the main floor. The journey was so uneventful it seemed like an empty bad dream. Apparently the aristocracy that worked here favored abandoning the place like a sinking ship the moment they could. With each turn in the corridor, I braced for an encounter, only to find a vacuum left by the earnest haste of the staff. At the first-floor holding cells, I took a moment to glance into the nearest cells and found the one holding my prisoner. His hands were still tied behind his back, rope still on the ankles, white tape across his mouth. He was sitting on a wooden bench attached to the wall, staring down at the floor. No use to stir him up yet.

Pushing carefully into the VIP section, the air suddenly became cool and smelled like perfume. I knew there were people here about but found no one in the kitchen area. The locked door to the medical room nearby had a narrow safety-glass window. The glass medicine case was just inside, exactly as Emma had described. The keypad lock program on my scanner took an excruciating thirty seconds to come up with the number, leaving me standing exposed in the hallway, constantly looking left and right. Inside, access to the glass door of the case was quicker, and to my relief, the scanner was much better at reading the labels on the chemical vials. The XiTau elite had provided every chemical known to man and then some for the purpose of subduing an uncooperative prisoner. There were also pen-sized pneumatic injectors made to order. I took two of the longest-lasting sedative-hypnotics I could recognize, tucked one in my lower leg compartment and the other inside a breast pocket. As I quietly closed the dispensary door, voices came from somewhere nearby. They were speaking English. I hurried back through the double doors to the holding cell area and watched through the windows.

"They're still all pissed off at you, Silas. I'd keep clear of them if I were you."

"They'll come around. They got no choice."

"I don't know. They still blame you for that fiasco with the Arkenau. They say it was the human you sold them that destroyed their ship."

"What a crock a' shit. One man couldn't have done all that. In any case, I don't give a crap what they think."

"I'm telling you, don't turn your back on any of them, lest you want to get a dagger in it."

The two men had pushed through a lounge door into the hallway. The first man was shaggy-haired with too many lines in his face. He wore a brown, wrinkled, V-neck shirt and gray pants with pockets in the legs, and laced-up combat boots. He had a side arm in a holster. The second man was none other than Silas Killion himself, in an expensive-looking brown leather jacket, well-tailored brown leather pants, and black boots that came up to the knee. They paused as the door closed behind them.

"Yeah, yeah, yeah, the Sumani lizard faces are bad. I get it. If any of them gives me any trouble I'll kick their asses."

"Silas, you don't want to fuck up the good deal we got goin' here, do you? You got to hang low. They'll be gone in an hour. Just keep out of their way, that's all I'm saying."

"Careful how much advice you go givin' me, Diggs. Don't forget who's in charge here."

"Sorry, Silas. Just watching your back, that's all. You heading to the Governor's mansion after the Sumanis bug out?"

"I guess. They've got some new imports I'm supposed to check out. I'll see you there."

"No, you won't. I got a thing set up in a high-rise. I probably won't come up for air for two days."

Cigar man gave a guttural laugh. "So it's not all bad, is it, Diggs?"

Diggs headed for the front entrance, stopped, turned, and gave a quick salute. "Not bad at all, Captain. Let's keep riding the wave for as long as it lasts, eh?"

Killion watched him disappear out the front doors, then turned and came up the hall toward me. Vending machines along the way stopped him. He put his thumb up against a payment screen, hit a few buttons, and took something out of the dispensing compartment. It was a band of a half-dozen cigars. He pulled one out, stuck it in his mouth, and tucked the rest inside his jacket. He started to head back the way he had come, stopped and eyed a door by the machines. It looked like a lavatory. He pushed inside.

I slipped back into the hall and went to the door. With it opened a crack I could see my guess was right. A line of sinks and a huge mirror were visible. I quietly entered.

E.R. Mason

This restroom was lavish. There were booths to the left, and sinks with gold-plated faucets on the right. Killion was in a booth. I went to the wall near the sink counter, leaned against it, and casually crossed my legs. With one hand concealing a small stun weapon and the other draped across the butt of my slung rifle, I waited. Killion hummed a happy tune.

He emerged buttoning his pants. He looked up but gave the blue tinted man with the stubbly skull only a passing glance. He went to the sink farthest from me, placed his unlit cigar carefully on the edge of the counter, and began washing his hands, still humming. He began taking occasional sideward glances my way.

He pulled a very fancy-looking towel from a dispenser and turned to face me as he dried. "What you looking at? What the hell are you, anyway? You sure aren't a Sirenian and you ain't part of the royal guard. You just security for somebody? What are you?"

"I'm your worst nightmare, Killion."

It took him aback. He stiffened and stopped drying. "How do you know my name?"

"Got a cigar?"

For a moment, he thought he recognized me. Logic assured him it could not be. Doubt reappeared. His face went through a dozen different expressions. He stepped back in a ready stance. "You can't be..."

"They never did find all the bodies from that ship, did they, Killion?"

"You got to be kidding."

"Would I kid you?"

"So, painted yourself blue and came looking for me, is that it?"

He was stalling for time.

"Not really. Just luck."

"You weren't so tough on Tolkien Minor. Maybe you're not so tough now." He eyed my rifle still hanging by the strap, estimating if he could get to me before I raised it, sizing up his chances if he did.

"You're wasting your time, Killion. I'm not going to give you any more chance than you gave me back then."

"You'll never make it out of here."

"I'm as good as gone."

He made his move. He was a quick bastard, faster than I had expected. With two lightning-fast steps, he had one hand on my suit as I brought the stun gun to bear. I popped him a good one and he slumped over onto the sink, knocking the valve to the on position, water flowing beneath him.

No time to waste. I had already spent enough languishing in the moment. A quick glance out the door showed the hall still deserted. The body was slightly too heavy, but adrenaline made up the difference.

One arm over each of my shoulders held together like carrying straps. Dragged him out into the hall and plastered him against the wall to get a better grip. Dragged him through the heavy double doors to the holding cell area, but had to stop again, the dead weight too uncooperative. Holding him against the wall, I looked to my left and saw someone in a security-type uniform passing by an intersection. The man stopped and stared. I hooked cigar man under the shoulders and dragged him along like a drunk. The security guy watched for a moment, then waved and continued on.

The closeness of the cell was a blessing. I plopped Killian down in a sitting position on the hallway floor. These cell doors had locking bars. I lifted it out and opened up. The prisoner inside looked up, saw me, and stood. Behind the white tape on his mouth and the star identity chip on his cheek, he had the expression of someone expecting another beating. I did not bother to introduce myself. I dragged cigar man in and set his body prone on the floor. The prisoner's expression turned to one of confusion.

A quick glance out the door showed the hallway still clear. I closed us in and went to the prisoner. He glanced at the body on the floor, took a step back, then stopped and held his ground defiantly. I reached out and tore the tape off his face. He continued to stare but did not speak.

"What's your name?" I asked.

He did not answer.

"I'll call you pathetic if you like, but you and I are leaving."

"Who are you and where am I being taken?"

"You were being taken to the radiation mines. Instead, we're returning to Earth. Now, what's your name, Pat?"

"I'm Christopher Demoray. CEO for Space Services Incorporated."

"Get your clothes off, Chris. We don't have much time."'

He hesitated and looked again at Killian sprawled out on the floor. "Is he...?"

"Dead? Hell no. I wouldn't want anything to happen to him….just yet."

Demoray held his hands out for me to untie. They were held by oily rope. His ankles had the same. Why waste expensive restraints on someone headed to the mines?

When Demoray was finally free, he began hurriedly unbuttoning his filthy shirt.

"Give me a hand with him. We need to put him up on the bench."

Together we hoisted the unconscious Killian up onto the wooden surface. As we did, he began to move his head from side to side, trying to shake off the stun. I reached into my lower leg pocket and drew out the injector. I popped the top, held Killian's chin, and gave him the full dose in the neck.

"What is that?" asked Demoray.

"He'll be a bad drunk for a good forty-eight hours or so. Hurry up with the clothes."

Together we fussed and fumbled and got Killian into Demoray's clothing and Demoray into his. We rolled him over and tied his hands and feet, then repositioned him on his back.

I straightened up and turned to Demoray. "Last but not least, I need your chip."

He stepped back. "No way. They said if I tried to remove it, it would explode."

Without warning, I reached out and tore it off. "Guess not."

As precisely as possible, I stuck it to Killian's face. My scanner only needed a single pass to read and translate the thing. It came up with Demoray's photo, fingerprints, palm print, DNA code, full name, and home planet. I updated the info with Killian's finger and palm prints, a hastily taken photo, and his DNA signature, all provided by the scanner. We stood back and looked at the new Christopher Demoray. He looked just as he should except he was a bit too clean. I wiped some of the black off my face and smeared it on his. It did the trick.

Time to leave. We stepped outside, closed the cell, and dropped the locking bar in place but before we could take a single step, voices came from the hall intersection.

There was a single cell door a few feet away that had been left ajar. I did not need to explain to Demoray. We hurried to it and ducked inside.

The sounds of grunting lizard voices echoed outside our cell. With great care, I dared a look in time to see the backs of three lizard men dragging Killion out. As soon as they rounded the first corner, we crept along behind and checked. Through the windows in the dividing doors, we could just see Killion being dragged up a ramp and into the lizard ship. Its hatches slid closed. Dust kicked up around, and a second later it jumped upward and out of sight.

I looked at Demoray and spoke in a low tone. "We cut that a little close, I think."

He whispered back, "You must have really hated that guy."

"He's probably the one who brought you here."

"Yeah, he is."

"So he's taking your place where he was sending you."

Demoray gave me a solemn stare and did not know what to say.

I looked at my watch. 7:10 P.M. Out the window, the front entrance area was dark now that the lizard shuttle and its lights were gone. "We've got twenty minutes to make the pickup point or we may be here forever."

Demoray needed no further coaxing. We began a cautious trot on a path that would lead to the rear entrance. We did not get far. Voices were approaching from somewhere ahead. We ducked through the nearest door and held it open to hear. There were four different voices. The conversation was troubling.

"You are certain you saw them enter from the front gallery?"

"Yes, Captain. One had blue-tinted skin and was dragging the prisoner along to the cells. It seemed perfectly normal to me. I thought it was a late inductee."

"There were no late inductees admitted. All were safely in their cells being documented. And there were no Sirenians aboard the delivery ship. There is something very wrong with what you saw. How could you not have known that?"

The four men were in police-styled uniforms. Civil War gray with silver trim. They wore helmets that looked like German World War 2 issue, black with a plasma pulse emblem on the front. We silently closed the door as they passed by.

We were in some large, very fancy meeting room. Glass meeting tables. Glass podium. Prints on the walls of famous slaveholders. As I turned, I realized Demoray was not with me. I spotted him climbing on a chair behind the podium, reaching for something mounted on the wall. It was a pair of crossed swords that looked like Japanese Samurai weapons. Demoray managed to get his hands on one and pulled it down to inspect it. He saw me watching and hurried back with his prize.

He leaned close and spoke in a whisper. "It's real! Do you believe it?"

"Better than nothing, I guess."

"One hell of a lot better."

"You know how to use it?"

"Oh, hell yes."

"We may find out."

I knew the foursome would soon break up and spread out in their search. The real question was, were reinforcements on the way?

Chapter 27

The game had suddenly become much more difficult. The hallways had been deserted and easy. Suddenly, they were now confined space with no cover, corridors that could be cut off at both ends. Every stretch would be a life-and-death gamble.

Demoray surprised me. He was no slouch. He carried his sword with the blade up behind one arm, keeping the other hand and arm free. We pushed out of the meeting room and moved quickly along two big throw-of-the-dice hallways until reaching a four-way intersection. We were down to fifteen minutes, and I knew Danica would not keep that ship on the ground. I checked my weapon to be sure it was set to heavy stun.

Then Demoray surprised me again. He asked which way, and when I pointed, broke out in a dead run to the next corner. I dashed along to catch up with him and grabbed him by the collar.

"What the hell are you doing?"

"Easy. I go first, you don't get killed. I'm the decoy. They see me that gives you a second to react. I drop to the floor; you take them out, get it?"

"Standard special ops. They call it 'Turkey Shoot,' and that makes you the turkey."

"Hey, I'm not really here. I'm actually on my way to the...what'd you call it? The radiation mines. I owe you. This is a good way to start payback."

"You've done this before?"

"Paintball?"

"You got to be kidding. Well, just make sure you drop down fast. I don't want to be dragging your stunned ass all the way home."

"I'm sure you'll have my ass's full attention. Which way?"

We made two more sections of corridor before Demoray's antics flushed the enemy out. Halfway down the third stretch, two security types rounded the corner without checking and met him head-on. As promised, he went down hard, and four pulses from my very ready weapon dropped both of them

Shock Diamonds

where they stood. We sprinted over the bodies and held at the next corner.

"Nice shots," whispered Demoray.

"Nice drop."

We made the rear entrance with just five minutes left. Even through the dim light, beyond some trees and hedges, I could make out the forward upper end of the Griffin, already on the ground. It was a thirty-yard sprint. There was no decision to be made. Thirty yards in the open. Thirty yards to reach freedom. But the internal warning systems were on full alert. The prickly feeling on the forearms. The hair standing slightly on the back of the neck. Those thirty yards looked like a killing field.

Demoray now had one of the guards' weapons, though he insisted on bringing the sword along, as well. I grabbed and turned his rifle to be sure it was fire-ready and on heavy stun. Although the markings were in alien, I was pretty sure it was set right. He looked me in the eye and noticed a change there. It tightened him up. I braced and gave him the hand signal to move out. Whether or not he knew special ops signals, it was one he understood.

We made our break. For the first ten yards there was nothing. We got as far as the point where your mind starts thinking you're going to make it when the first rapid-fire cracking of plasma rifles sounded behind us. Flashes of plasma tubes began zipping by. Either of those can cause you to stoop automatically as you run, but the barrage was so heavy we could not continue at all. We hit the ground, spun, and returned fire with no cover.

A column of security personnel were flowing in from around the corner of the building. Too many to count. Some kneeled to shoot at us; others continued pursuit. We had to take out the ones closing in for fear of being overrun, but that only made others stop to take better aim.

There were at least thirty. Plasma beams began to come so close they were ruffling our clothing. There was no way we'd escape. Demoray ditched his sword. It spun once in the air and stuck in the ground behind us. He was doing a fair job with the rifle, but in my peripheral vision I saw a shot catch him square in the shoulder and flip him over. There was nothing I could do. I had to give my attention to the enemy out of sheer desperation. Surprisingly, a moment later, rifle fire rang out alongside me, meaning Demoray was back up and shooting. It was then I took a direct hit in my left arm.

The shot skidded me back on the ground. Stars and lightning flashes appeared. I kept firing blindly and tried to pull back up to where I had been, but discovered my left arm was

273

now completely off duty. I had to drag and shoot with the rifle hand. Demoray had rolled once to change his position. It looked like together we had dropped at least a dozen of them, but there were plenty more. We had slowed them quite admirably. They had given up on their charge, spread out, and were piling on the automatic weapons fire.

Demoray was the first to go. He tried to roll once more but a beam caught him square in the chest. His rifle went flying in the air and landed beside the sword. I knew I was now firing my last rounds.

Three or four very long seconds later, I was hit in my left hip. Not so many lightning flashes this time, but for a few moments all of me was paralyzed. A few of the enemy resumed their charge, and a moment later they were upon us. I was disarmed and held with a knee in my back. I still had some use of the right arm, but my left and my legs were no longer a part of me. Suddenly, I was on my side and watching them check Demoray for other weapons. They turned him onto his back and dragged him away by the collar. As his boots passed by, someone suddenly had me by the collar, and I was dragged alongside him. It had been a good firefight. It was over. The future looked bleak.

But then came Wilson.

The world was still slightly blurry. There was smoke and trash in the air from the firefight. Through the haze he emerged, a heavy automatic weapon in each hand, firing continuously, wearing upper body armor and a face shield that looked like Batman. He did not stop, just kept tromping forward like a monster from hell. The few plasma shots that hit him were poorly aimed and glanced off the armor, knocking him back slightly each time, but not stopping him. Through the ringing in my ears, I could hear the moans and cries behind me of many enemies falling.

Whoever had been dragging me had stopped. Beside me, Demoray's feet were no longer moving. My right arm was tingling but beginning to work again. I managed to push up at the waist and glance behind. The continuing plasma fire from Wilson sizzled and crackled as it passed overhead. The enemy was a scattered, wounded bunch. They had been well organized, but totally unprepared for Wilson. They staggered and fell among the two dozen or so already down, trying to find cover or fire back at the strange monster that refused to die. Wilson finally took a hit dead center to the stock of one rifle. It flew out of his grasp and snapped the harness off his shoulder. He wiped the stun from his hand but kept firing with his other.

Some hasty retreating began by the security force. Only three of the attackers that remained had true grit. They continued to advance awkwardly. They'd fall, fire, and then scramble ahead. As I watched, one of them took a hit and dropped his rifle. Dazed, he held one arm but still kept moving forward. His partner took notice, tripped on a fallen comrade, and fell, burying the muzzle of his rifle deep in the dirt. He reached down and drew a Bowie-type knife from a sheath on his ankle.

A split second later, Wilson was on them. He was still squeezing at the numbness in his stunned hand as he drew a bead on the two and fired, only to find his weapon fully discharged and recharging.

It was suddenly an unarmed Wilson facing off with two unarmed security soldiers. I wanted in badly. I pushed up and tried to get to my feet only to find I was still shut off from the waist down. I clawed around trying to spot a weapon within reach. Demoray remained out cold. For a moment, it looked like hand-to-hand combat, two against Wilson. Those were good odds for Wilson, even with a bad arm.

But the security man nearest him spotted the sword sticking up out of the ground, and the automatic weapon beside it. He did not hesitate. He dove for the rifle.

It was the worst choice he could have made. It left Wilson with a sword. As the guard rolled upright with the rifle, Wilson's good hand already had the grip. He sliced the blade upward in time to catch the rifle just in front of the trigger guard. The barrel of the gun was knocked upward, striking the attacker squarely in the forehead, knocking him out instantly. He fell in a heap. In one continuous motion, Wilson made a quick, tight circle with the sword tip so that it cut down across the chest of the second guard wielding the Bowie knife. It opened a new seam in the man's uniform top, left a shallow red line down his bare chest, and came back around to end up a few inches from his face. He looked at Wilson, the ragged opening in his uniform, let out a squeak, and ran.

Suddenly, there was silence, interrupted by occasional moans or cries. Wilson disappeared from my field of vision for a few moments, then returned with his guns. Once again, I tried to regain my feet, but the lower extremities were still not working. The next thing I knew, I was again being dragged on my back by my collar, the unconscious Demoray dragging alongside me. But this time we were headed for the ship. I craned my head back and managed an upside-down view of Wilson pulling us both along like sacks of wheat. Behind us was the carnage of sleeping or whimpering security force men wondering what the hell had happened.

At the base of the Griffin's loading ramp there was suddenly a great deal of fussing and dashing about with choruses of cursing and woeful commentary. In the background, I could make out Danica's voice on the intercom adding her own version of foul-language motivational speaking.

Then we were inside with the hatch sealed, on the floor going up at a blistering 9 Gs. Except for the whine of the OMS engines there was not a sound. Those of us flattened out on the floor could not take enough air into our lungs to express any sentiments of discomfort.

Finally, a commanding female voice came over the intercom and yelled, "Stay down!" and we were left there for the jump to light. We slid across the floor into a heap against the back wall like the unsecured cargo that we were. No one minded. Wilson was sitting against the wall with his knees raised, smiling down at me like a kid who had just visited Disney World, now on his way home. Demoray was lying next to me, his head rolling from side to side as he mumbled incoherently and tried to come to consciousness to get back in the fight.

With one good hand and one hand still tingling, I managed to push myself up against the wall next to Wilson. To my surprise, the right knee was willing to bend and came up to help hold the position. I pointed to it and shook my head proudly.

"You better hope everything else still comes up too, partner," he said with a smirk.

"Wilson, did we just kill a bunch of people?"

"My guns were on wide-beam heavy stun. What were yours on?"

"Heavy stun. So you're saying we didn't kill anybody?"

"I don't know. If any of them had pacemakers I wouldn't bet my life on it."

"So they were in stun, too. Wanted us alive."

"Some were, some weren't. Got some burns in my armor."

"Was I hallucinating or did you take out two dozen guys?"

"Ah, but I've done better, days past."

"De Bergerac! You're trying to quote de Bergerac at a time like this?"

"Your other knee is twitching. There's still hope for the more important parts."

"You cut that guy with the sword."

"Barely scratched him."

"It was a long one, though."

"It had to be convincing."

"Apparently, it was."

"It will be a trophy he will brag about for years to come. He'll probably get promotions because of it. Eventually, after the tale has been told a hundred times, he will finally win the battle and save the fair maiden. Look, your extra-points prisoner is about to join us. We deserve ale."

Demoray jerked his head up, raised a hand to fight, looked around and realized he was on a spacecraft, then plunked his head back down with a sigh of relief.

Wilson continued, "You know, he wasn't too bad out there. I don't believe a single shot hit anything, but he sure was game."

"He had an affection for the sword. Too bad we had to leave it."

Wilson leaned over. "You mean this sword?" He pulled Demoray's blade out from behind him.

"Wow! You have truly outdone yourself, sir."

My other knee finally came all the way up. Wilson smirked and gave me a knowing nod.

Demoray looked left and right and spoke. "What happened? If it's bad, don't tell me."

I tilted my chin forward to get a better look at him. "We're on a ship headed for Earth. We're about to drink a bunch of beers."

Still flat on his back, he looked over at me. "That's the best news I've had in a week. What kind of beer is it?"

Wilson blurted out a laugh. "My god, he's even got a sense of humor. He may be worthy of we Musketeers after all."

I made an effort and managed to push and pull myself to my feet.

"You're not leaving?" said Wilson. "I was just beginning to enjoy our little after-the-battle blog."

"I'm going to get the beers."

"Oh, well, carry on then. We'll meet you in the med lab."

"A quick visit to the flight deck is necessary."

I staggered off and passed through the sleeper compartments section to find the atmosphere that awaited me in the habitat module was unlike any I had ever experienced. Patrick, Catherine, and Emma were standing there together by the conference table having the most intense conversation any family could have. At least, that was my first impression. They were a family now, and as I entered, they stopped and stared with a reverence I knew I would never deserve.

Patrick spoke. "Adrian, my god, you did it!" He held his daughter by the arm as though he feared she would be taken again.

"We did it, you guys. But we're not home yet."

I tried to duck past, but Emma caught me with her free hand. "You don't know..." She choked off.

"Believe me; I have a good idea."

She began again. "I would have died."

"Nothing here now but family and friends, Emma. You were worth it."

"And I need to thank the other man who brought me here. His name is Wilson?"

"It's okay, Emma. I'll pass it along."

"But he risked his life, too."

"You'll have plenty of time to catch up with him on the way home. He's a special guy, but don't tell him I said that. And let me give you a tip. If you ever hear him say, 'Now I don't want any trouble,' it's already too late. Hit the deck or take cover. All hell is about to break loose."

She let me go and hugged her father. Catherine gave me a knowing smile. I escaped to the forward airlock and into the engineering section. R.J. was sitting at his station.

I slapped him on the shoulder. "How's it going?"

"Oh, you know, just passing time."

"Radar's clear?"

"Nothing to see here. Your face is still black, by the way."

"I really am black and blue, believe me." I smiled and went forward. On the flight deck, I stooped over to get a look at the instruments.

Danica looked up. "Thank God."

"No one in pursuit, I hear."

"No, but the ship took a dozen or so hits while we were on the ground. You may want to go outside for a look."

"Pressurization?"

"No problems, but no idea how the skin is out there."

"No stopping and no excursions. We don't want to give anyone any chance to catch up. What's your course?"

"It's not direct. It's set up so we can tack home. Nobody will be able to plot our flight path to show them where we're going."

"Very impressive, Ms. Donoro. I salute you."

"Is everyone alive in the back?"

"Everyone and then some."

"Is anyone hurt?"

"Just knocked around some. I'm heading back there to have a medicinal beer or two if it's okay with you. Then I'll come and relieve you, poor dear."

"Watch who you're calling 'poor dear,' dirty-face."

"That was a hell of a launch off that ball, Dan."

"Wilson wouldn't let us leave."

"The man is a terminator."

"You do owe him that beer."

I squeezed Danica's shoulder and headed back. R.J. stopped me.

"Adrian, we need to talk. Where you going?"

"Back to drink beers with Wilson. It's medicinal, you understand. You stay here and keep an eye out, okay?"

"I'd say you guys deserve a beer, at the least."

"If you see any ships on long-range, scream out? And go ahead and transmit that stolen XiTau data to Earth, in case we don't make it."

"Wilco. Is everybody okay back there?"

"I think so. I'll bring you back one of those beers."

I managed to get by the new family with only a wave, and continued back to the battle-weary. I found them in the med lab in not quite as good shape as they had pretended to be. Wilson was applying salve to plasma burns on both forearms. Demoray was wrapping them as he went. Demoray's eyes were beginning to blacken, and there was a burned hole in one pant leg I had not noticed before.

"Did that reach the skin?" I asked, staring down at it.

"Just a touch. I'll get to it in a minute," said Demoray.

I looked at Wilson's arms. "How deep are they?"

"Not too bad I think. Didn't feel them at all while it was going on."

Demoray paused and looked at me. "What'a you got? You got some. I know it."

"Nothing that'll give me bragging rights. But I do have pain killer." I reached down and pulled up a floor plate that covered the refrigerated storage. Inside, I drew out half a dozen Red Moon beers, left there previously by another medical doctor.

With the floor plate replaced, we pulled out the counter stools and found the best places to slouch or put feet up. Wilson made the toast.

"To the successful rescue of a fair maiden and the newest member of our 'Mission Impossible' team."

We held up our bottles, clinked them, and sat back, smiling at each other for no particular reason.

Demoray asked, "I don't get it. Why'd they come after us with most of their weapons on stun?"

Wilson swallowed his gulp and answered. "There was so many of 'em, they didn't think we had a chance. They're so used to rounding slaves up it was probably the standard routine. They wouldn't want to kill any valuable property, after all. They were very well organized, but not very experienced, not at all-out warfare anyway. There were two or three that were pretty game. One or two of them did fire kill shots. That's how I got the burns through my sleeve armor."

The three of us shared a somber moment and drank.

Finally I couldn't resist. "So Wilson, about that alien janitor lady in the restroom..."

"That should never ever be spoken of again, Adrian." He quickly changed the subject. "Christopher, how'd you wind up going from CEO to slave?"

"I owe it all to a bastard back on Earth, one I'm looking forward to tracking down when I get home."

Wilson raised his bottle again. "Hear, hear." He took a long drink.

Demoray continued, "One of my companies handles the technicians who do spacecraft processing at the space center. This high-powered jerk wanted to highjack somebody's spacecraft. There was no way he could pull it off without my techs, so he kept trying to convince me it was in my best interest to look the other way. I refused." Demoray paused, took a drink, and stared off in thought for a moment. "His people began bumping into me out in public with intimidating comments, or I'd get calls on phone lines that he shouldn't have known about. Of course, I turned it over to the law. They were very interested but didn't seem anxious to do much about it. Then the messages became too threatening. I was going to demand police protection. Long story short, I went to bed and woke up on one of Blackwell's buddies' spacecraft on my way to XiTau."

I almost choked on my drink. "Who did that to you?"

"A guy named Blackwell. He was after a ship that was in the news a while back, the Griffin, and he didn't care what he had to do to get it."

Wilson jerked forward and spit his drink back into his bottle. "What the hell?"

I gave a muted laugh. "Christopher, by the way, welcome aboard the Griffin."

We stared at each other in disbelief. Demoray waited to see if it was a joke. "How can it be?" he asked. "It's impossible."

Wilson kicked back. "It's a message from God, it is."

Demoray looked at me.

"Oh no, don't look at me. I'm not touching that with a ten-foot pole."

Wilson persisted. "Plain as day. Don't you guys get it? Chris, my man, the ship you refused to sell out came and rescued you back home."

"I think I need another beer," said Demoray.

I held my celebration to one beer, and let the other two polish off the rest. We assigned the last sleeper cell to Demoray and broke up. They headed for the horizontal. I took a moment to clean up and change, then went forward to relieve Danica. R.J. was waiting at the conference table.

"Where's my beer?" he asked.

"I was thinking a little bit later. I just popped a detox. I got to give Danica a break."

"Who's the new guy?"

"He was scheduled for the same radiation mines that I was. Seems like a damn nice fellow, too."

"How'd you get him out?"

"Long story, an interesting one you'll appreciate. By the way, I just thought of it, sorry about your diamonds."

"You mean the ones in my sleeper cell?"

"What?"

"They were in that Akai guy's bottom desk drawer with a bunch of other gems. I stuffed other stones from the drawer in the bag and tucked the diamonds into the accessory pocket on one of the scanner jackets. You didn't know it, but you brought them back with you."

"Well, I'll be."

"And by the way, we need to get together with Danica and have a real serious think tank about the skull."

"Is it well stowed?"

"Very well stowed."

"Okay, but I'd better get up there. She deserves some unwind time."

"I'll bring you some coffee in a little bit."

"You are a gentleman and a scholar, sir."

On the flight deck, I slipped into the right seat and took a moment to watch the fading haze of the NGC 6188 emission nebula on a monitor.

"You clean up nicely, even after war, and you're hardly blue at all," said Danica.

"Nothing at all on the long-range, I guess?"

"All clear. We must have caught them off guard."

"They're probably still hoping the gold shipments will arrive. Greed is a wonder for self-delusion."

"Who's the new guy?"

"Christopher Demoray. Oh yeah, he was headed for the mines. He and I could have ended up working together there. But that's not the interesting part. Guess who had him abducted?"

"How would I know?"

"It was Mr. Dorian Blackwell. Demoray refused to help him get his hands on the Griffin. The mines were the ultimatum. Either do as we ask, or you will end up there."

"You're shitting me!"

"My, my! Such foul language. I'm shocked."

"That bastard is a curse on society."

E.R. Mason

"When we get back to Earth terra firma, we'll need to see exactly what's what, and then decide how to handle Mr. Blackwell. Personally, I'm pretty tired of him. With Demoray's story, we should be able to get him locked back up."

"Where he belongs," said Danica with venom in her voice.

R.J. appeared between us. "We should have a clean ride back. Radars are clear and we're far enough along now that it would be hard for any ships to catch us."

"Everybody all tucked in back there?"

"All sleepers shut up for the night. It will be the best sleep Patrick's daughter has had in a long time. She practically ate everything in ship's stores."

I looked over at Danica. "About your diamond skull, ma'am..."

"Oh, yeah. You still want me to believe that thing is a mind-control device?"

I sat back as much as possible in a pilot's seat. "The real question is, what are we going to do with it?"

R.J. sounded adamant. "We can't do anything with it. It's probably the most dangerous artifact in the universe. Who we going to give it to? Who is above temptation?"

I looked up at him. "The Nasebians have crossed my mind. They're more advanced than even the skull's technology. But, for some reason, I have a feeling they would be annoyed if I asked them to take it."

"Well, the answer is easy," said R.J. "If there's no one to safely hand it over to, then we must keep it and hide it."

"So we are the incorruptible, then?" asked Danica.

"She has a point," I added.

"The three of us will have to guard each other. There's no other choice," insisted R.J.

"And you guys have already used it once," said Danica.

"I sure don't regret that," I replied.

"Me neither," said R.J.

"So when is it okay to screw with someone, and when isn't it?" continued Danica.

"The three of us will have to agree," said R.J.

I squirmed in my seat. "For the time being, let's hide it and keep it to ourselves. No one but us knows what it does. Very few people even know it exists. R.J., make a better hiding place in the lab for the crystals. We'll keep the skull under this seat. We can talk more about this when the time is right."

R.J. seemed satisfied. Danica said nothing. We all stared out the forward view screen at the blanket of star haze. Secretly, I was trying to spot Earth's star even though we were a trillion miles too far away.

Chapter 28

Two-and-a-half weeks later we watched the Terran sun grow large in our forward view screens. Earth became a twinkling blue diamond in its light.

We called in to OTC early just to let them know we were coming. It seemed a little odd that at first the controllers did not respond. Eventually, we got a "Griffin, OTC, stand by," which was even more curious.

When finally within the approach envelope, we called in again and asked for standard orbit at our usual 235-mile parking. Once again, we received a message back saying, "Griffin, OTC, stand by for further instructions."

I knew then something was up.

As we slowed to sublight and began to worry about our insertion clearance, there finally came an answer. "Griffin, OTC, you are cleared for orbital insertion at the 211. Orbit profile being transmitted to you now."

I sat in the left seat and looked over at Danica. She crinkled her brow in a confused stare. "What the hell is this about?"

"Maybe we should ask."

She clicked her com button. "OTC, Griffin, any reason for the unusual orbit?"

There was too long a pause. "Griffin, OTC, expect further instructions in five minutes."

She looked at me again in wonder. "Wow!"

I finished entering the orbit parameters and sat back. "Guess we'll find out."

It got worse after we settled in on orbit. After completing the checklists, it was time to go down. Danica looked at me with a quizzical stare. "Well, here goes. OTC, Griffin, ready for de-orbit burn as filed."

Once again there was too long a pause, then finally an answer. "Griffin, OTC, you are not cleared for landing. Please maintain 211 and expect further instructions in five minutes."

Danica was beside herself. "What the hell? Further instructions? What are they going to do, ask us to leave?"

"It could be a temporary flight restriction in effect. I've had them open TFRs even when I was on final approach and cleared to land. Maybe there's some VIP down there using our airspace or something."

"Well, sure, okay. We'll just hang here in space while some politician finishes his latte!"

It was another full orbit before we heard from them again. "Griffin, OTC."

"Griffin, go ahead."

"Expect rendezvous with the security cruiser Glenn in 45 minutes."

Danica looked at me with total confusion and clicked in. "Copy USS Glenn rendezvous in 45." She clicked off the com and stared. "What the hell?"

"Yeah, I'm just a bit concerned now, as well."

R.J. unstrapped and came forward between us. "Well, fellow 'Lost In Space' fans, this is a fine mess you've gotten us into."

Danica raised her hands in frustration. "What'd we do?"

R.J. said, "Yeah, I been goin' over this in my head. Let's see, Adrian, you blew up an alien ship, altered the evolution of a primitive planet and a resident species there, found a dead body on a planet with slow time, bought a luxury estate on a slave planet, stole two of their slaves, and before leaving started a small war with their security force. Gee, I can't for the life of me think of any reason security might want to speak with us."

I looked at him with amusement. "Well, now that you put it that way..."

"We have 45 minutes. Anyone want a latte?" he added.

"Oh yeah, I'll take one, sure," said Danica.

"Just a regular for me, please sir," I said.

"I may put vinegar in yours," replied R.J., and off he went.

Still sipping refills, we watched the ship on radar as it rose up from the surface to catch us. The Glenn is a respectably large draft cruiser, more than twice the size of Griffin. They came quickly alongside and deployed their accordion transfer tube against our forward airlock hatch. They matched our pressurization in less than five minutes. It bumped us around a bit, an unsettling experience in space.

R.J. was asked to open the outer doors, but in his comedic mentality, he insisted on waiting for a knock. Then he called out, "There's someone at the door. I'll get it."

I fully expected him to ask, "Who's there?" but at least he managed to forego that.

With Danica at the controls, I took a position just outside the airlock and watched the hatch opening. To my surprise, three men in dark suits floated down into our gravity. Even

Shock Diamonds

more surprising, the third man was Stan Lee, my allegiant friend from the Agency's security bureau. It was unusual that the three of them had not taken the time to change into flight suits. They greeted R.J. without exchanging names, looked around to get their bearings, and when they spotted me, Stan Lee took the lead. Acclimating to the gravity very quickly, he walked up and held out a hand. "Fancy meeting you here."

"This is quite a surprise, Stan. Couldn't it have waited until we were on the tarmac?"

"Nope. Where you want to talk?"

I led them into the habitat module to the conference table. Patrick, Catherine, Emma, and Demoray were gathered in a group like an audience for visiting dignitaries. Looks of curiosity were exchanged. There were a few light hellos until Stan Lee spotted Wilson.

"Mirtos," he said with a nod.

"Lee," replied Wilson.

The men sat around the table and quickly became comfortable with their position, never a good sign.

I tried to take charge of the unexpected inquest by asking the first question. "Did you get that big block of data we transmitted?"

Stan Lee answered. "Yes, we did, thank you, Adrian. It got management's attention quite quickly."

"Were you able to get past the encryption?"

"Why don't we put that aside for the moment. Can you confirm there were more than one hundred Earth humans on that planet being held against their will?"

"Then you did break the encryption."

He looked at me and shook his head. "I'll never learn." He pinched his lips for a moment, then stood. He went to Patrick and held out his hand. Patrick shook it with a wary glance.

"Dr. Pacell, may I call you Patrick? This must be Emma. I'm so glad you are safe. Your father reported your disappearance to us." Stan Lee turned to Demoray. "Dr. Demoray, we had the report on your sudden absence, also. Glad to see you're okay." Once again Stan Lee held out his hand. Demoray shook it apprehensively.

"I don't believe you and I have met," said Lee, as a handshake was extended to Catherine. "Stan Lee, Executive Administrator for the agency's security division."

"Dr. Catherine Adara, M.D."

"Yes, of course I know that." Lee turned to me. "Adrian, we need to transfer Dr. Demoray, Dr. Pacell, and Emma to our ship for a special debriefing. We need to do that right away. If there are belongings you folks need to gather up, please do that now, would you?"

"I'm coming along," demanded Catherine.

Stan Lee looked at her for a moment, then nodded. "Very well. You may wish to collect your personal effects also, then. We will not be returning to the Griffin."

I stood. "Stan, if I did not know you..."

"Please bear with us, Adrian. I'll explain everything in a minute."

I had to stand and watch as the foursome gathered their belongings from their sleeper cells and paraded by into the weightlessness of the transfer tube. When the exodus was complete, only Stan Lee remained. We returned to the conference table and sat. R.J. and Wilson stood in the galley silently looking on.

"Was that necessary?" I asked.

"For a number of reasons," he replied. "Under the circumstances, we need every bit of accurate information we can get. If they do their depositions together, they will affect each other's memory of what happened. If we depose them separately, we'll get different versions; then we can reconstruct exactly what occurred."

"Then what?"

"They will be taken to intelligence headquarters to assist in our investigation. They can refuse if they choose, but they won't."

"So you are investigating the abduction of the humans on XiTau?"

"We have been for some time. That's why I couldn't say more when you called. We've had a ship in the Mu Arae sector working on this, but we weren't getting anywhere. When you called, we suddenly realized we might have another card to play. I gave you the best intel we had, hoping you'd do better. We tried to stay out of sight and tail you, but our cruiser had a coolant leak from being pushed too hard to keep up. We're going to need depositions from you and your crew, and your ship's logs, of course."

"We'll help you in any way we can. What are your plans for those people on XiTau?"

"Tell me something, why did it take you this long? We expected you'd either give up or be back with some intel after a few weeks, not months."

"There were stops along the way."

"A large Sumani transport ship exploded some time ago in that sector. You didn't have anything to do with that, did you?"

"Let me think..."

Lee waited, then turned in his seat. "Did he, Wilson?"

Wilson stiffened up and tried to look innocent. "Don't look at me. I didn't have anything to do with it."

"You know we'll piece this together from your location logs and time entries."

"They weren't going my way."

"You're kidding me? You were on that ship?"

"It was still intact when I left."

"My god, Adrian. More fodder for Bernard Porre. I guess there's no use in talking to you. I'll have to go through the logs and then let you squirm out of things during your deposition afterward." Lee stood and looked around at the others.

"But what are you going to do for our people on XiTau?" I persisted.

Lee went to the airlock and turned back to look at us. "That's classified, Mr. Tarn, and so is everything else concerning your visit to the Mu Arae sector. You are not to speak of any of it to anyone except ATS people from the agency. That goes for all of you. Ms. Donoro, I know you're up there listening."

"Seems like this happens to me every time," I said.

"Yeah, every time you go somewhere, Adrian. Did you know your record shows you are involved in 82.5 percent more controversies than the average space agency officer?"

"I have heard that."

"We'd all like to know how you always come out smelling like a rose," he added.

"Stan, before you fly on out of here, there is one thing."

"Yes?"

"Danica. I mentioned to you about that guy Dorian Blackwell."

Lee laughed an evil laugh. "Yeah, the only reason Blackwell was let out of prison was in the hope he would give us a thread to follow on the slave trade. His name is plastered all over that encrypted data you sent us. He's back in prison on probation violations, just as we had planned. We've frozen all his assets, and put out APBs on most of his associates. I don't think anyone will bother her again. Blackwell doesn't have the money to pay them, and they know we're already looking for them, anyway."

"That's very good news. You hear that, Danica?"

The intercom keyed on. "Loud and clear. Tell the man I owe him a drink."

"Careful what you wish for, Ms. Donoro. By the way, Blackwell seems to have gone a bit berserk, if you will forgive the term. He tried to bargain his release by telling us he had a crystal skull which could control the world. He was neurotic about it. We recovered the thing from the safe in his place. It's

287

standard formed Earth crystal, nothing more than a decoration. He still carries on about it during every interrogation. We'll be setting up psychological evaluations for him."

"I'm glad to hear he's where he belongs, Stan."

"There's one other key culprit we'd like to get our hands on. The guy's name is Silas Killion. Supposedly he runs the delivery to various pickup points and then on to the slave distribution points. Any leads on him in your logs, Adrian?"

"I believe I heard he was out of action indefinitely."

"You got any more than that?"

"Let me think about it."

Lee paused and gave me a threatening stare. He began to leave, then stopped again and looked back. "Oh yeah, you guys are cleared to deorbit to the space center. A special ground handling crew is waiting to scrub the Griffin's memory banks. We'll be in touch. Have a nice day."

We put down on the apron by the VAB and were towed inside before we even had a chance to open the spacecraft. In the hangar, unfamiliar technicians secured the Griffin. Others, with special recording equipment, asked for permission to come aboard, which I granted with great misgiving.

At the bottom of the ramp, a man in a black suit with an ID card that announced his name loudly as Cummings seemed to be in charge. He promised the techs would only need half a day to amass their required information. We were mercifully allowed to leave after promising near-future debriefings.

Over the next two weeks there were periodic visits and phone calls from a wide variety of Space Agency higher-ups who invariably asked for clarifications on things they already seemed to know. But they were always respectful, and they always broke off seeming to want more. I could never get answers about the humans still held on XiTau.

By the end of the month, it began to taper off. We finally found the time to attend ourselves to a very important occasion that had seemed unlikely to ever happen. I was best man. R.J. gave the bride away. Danica was head bridesmaid. A variety of other folks we did not know played a part, and there were some sudden tense moments when one of the Norsicans Wilson had befriended on Enuro showed up unexpectedly in full battle gear, as is their custom. A few of the wedding party women ran off, only to be overtaken and passed by their husbands. Another group hid behind the bar but continued to make drinks. Wilson's fighting friends grouped together in a ready formation and tried to act casual.

But peace was soon restored, and with at least some sobriety regained, the ceremony went off without a hitch.

We gathered at the reception, drinking with all caution set aside, toasting the occasion as many times as we could come up with something to say.

Finally, Jeannie in her blazing white wedding dress made Wilson stand, held up her glass, and said, "I now have my very own warrior. You better be ready, Mister. I'm coming at you."

Wilson swayed just a touch, looked down at her, and answered, "Now, I don't want any trouble."

"Too late again," she replied, and she kissed him on the cheek.

There was an eruption of great applause and cheering, though it was all but drowned out by the stomping and chanting of the Norsican.

Printed in Great Britain
by Amazon